FLOYD STEWART

GIVEN TO ME BY JEFF ♡

CHRISTMAS 1984

Fourth And Long Gone

Pepper Rodgers

PEACHTREE PUBLISHERS LIMITED
Atlanta, Georgia

Published by
PEACHTREE PUBLISHERS, LTD.
494 Armour Circle, N.E.
Atlanta, Georgia 30324

Manufactured in the United States of America

Second printing

Library of Congress Catalog Number 84-60919

ISBN:0-931948-61-4

For Janet,
a.k.a. Livingston

Fourth And Long Gone

Prologue

IT WAS NINE O'CLOCK on one of those brilliant, cobalt-blue, December mornings when Charles Forrest "Buck" Lee entered the football department in the bowels of the West Alabama State University Coliseum for the last time. Buck was dressed in his macho outfit, designed to intimidate — gold cowboy boots, tight-fitting khaki Sansabelt trousers, obscene T-shirt featuring a hawk scavenging at the crotch of a pair of willing thighs, gold Mickey Gilley cowboy hat, and black nylon jacket emblazoned with the Golden Hawks' logo. He chuckled as he caught the reflection of the logo in the swinging glass doors: What a delightful irony that the acronym of West Alabama State was, well, *WAS*.

"Morning, Coach Lee," said Adelle Muncie, the football department secretary who had been at WAS since shortly after *the* Flood.

"Morning, Miz Muncie," said Buck.

"How you doing this morning, Coach Lee?"

"Fair to partly cloudy, Miz Muncie. Fair to partly cloudy."

"I swear, Coach Lee, if you don't have an answer for everything." She cocked her head and smiled.

"Miz Muncie?"

"Yes, sir, Coach Lee?"

"Can't you just once call me Buck? I mean, after all these years?"

"Well," Adelle Muncie said, toying with the silver stickpin in the bun of her dyed black hair, then demurely checking for dandruff on her black blazer, "I think it's *respectful* to call a coach 'Coach'. Coach Shavers feels the same way. You want some coffee?"

"No, thanks. I'm coffeed out."

"What can I do for you, then, Coach Lee?"

"Buck."

"All right. Buck."

"That's good, Miz Muncie, that's good."

"Well, what can I do for you?"

Buck glared directly into her eyes, smiled, and said, "You can tell that crimp-eared sumbitch I want to talk to him. Right now! Old Buck wants to say something to old Buddy, and if he don't open the door, I'll do it for him."

"Why, I *never*," said Adelle Muncie, thoroughly rattled, her tidy world coming unglued so early in the day. She punched a button on the phone atop her fake walnut desk, cluttered with pink WHILE YOU WERE OUT memorandum slips, and whispered to Head Coach Buddy Shavers (his given name was Reginald Benbow Shavers, but he certainly wouldn't let his sports information director put something like *that* in the football brochure) that Coach Lee would like to see him. Tight-lipped, Adelle Muncie said, "He'll see you in a few minutes. Sit down and read a magazine if you'd like. The new *Sports Illustrated* just came in, and Coach Shavers is on the cover, you know."

Great timing, Buck thought, slumping into one of the Naugahyde sofas in the foyer of the football office. Give me two years and I'll blow him right off the cover of *SI*. Instead of leafing through the magazines on the chrome and glass coffee table, Buck whipped out a ballpoint and a wrinkled envelope from the pocket of his Golden Hawks jacket and began doodling. They were random scribblings about the new life he was about to begin: "Eaarnel . . . Snapper Riding Mower for Gail . . . Stanleyville . . . EAU Rattlers . . . Get Shavers . . . Eaarnel right, Eaarnel left . . . Rattler Power . . . Blockers for Eaarnel." He scrawled a couple of plays, X's and O's, scratched his congenital jock itch, stuck out his tongue at Adelle Muncie when he caught her staring, glanced at the clock, and made a note about a prospect in Newark named Ivie Buchanan. Adelle's phone buzzed; without answering she said, "Coach Shavers can see you now, Coach Lee."

Buddy Shavers sat behind his huge, oak desk positioned on a foot-high platform. The platform ensured that he could always lord over his visitors, whether they be high school prospects or the very president of the university. Shavers was a dog-eared old horse who had seen the elephant and heard the owl and found a way, through various chicaneries, to beat each at his own game. Say what you would about Buddy Shavers, but he was a force. And today, on this December morning, Buck Lee intended to confront that force.

"What can I do for you, Buck?" said Shavers, whomping smoke from a dark Havana cigar, diamond-studded Sugar Bowl rings flashing as he hovered over the desk without looking up.

Buck stood directly in front of him. "Wish me luck, for starters," he said.

"How's that?" asked Shavers, finally looking at Buck.

"Well, you know how much I hate planes."

"Going somewhere, are you?"

"Stanleyville."

"We got prospects in Stanleyville?"

"It's not *we* anymore, you crimp-eared old fart. I, Buck Lee, it's old Buck Lee who's got prospects in Stanleyville. Maybe if you'd take that frigging cigar out of your mouth, stand up, and come down off that goddamn pedestal, you'd have a chance to shake hands with the new head coach of the East Alabama University Rattlers. How's that old saying go? 'Be nice to those you meet on the way to the top, 'cause you may meet them on your way back down.'"

Shavers did, indeed, stand up. He *roared* up from his swivel chair, threw his cigar into the trash can, crashed his fist on the desk, and began frothing at the mouth. Buck stood below him, smiling like little David while Goliath bellowed in pain. Shavers threw his Cross pen, one of hundreds given to him by his favorite bookie, against the walnut-paneled wall hung with autographed portraits of Bear Bryant, Ara Parseghian, Frank Broyles, and all the other great college football coaches of his era. His crimped ear, the one bitten in half by a dog when he was a kid, turned purple as it always did when he was furious. Then he slammed his meaty hand into the desk again.

"You gon' hurt that desk, Buddy," said Buck.

"Why, you rotten little goddamn pissant! You goddamn little traitor!" Shavers screamed. "The very goddamn idea! Leaving West Alabama for the fucking *enemy*. After all I've done for you."

"Yeah, that was a hell of a recommendation you gave me for the Ole Miss job."

"Christ, I ain't gonna recommend you to somebody we gotta *play*."

"And the Air Force job. You said I was lazy and screwed cheerleaders."

"Well, that's different, Buck . . ."

"Don't call me Buck, you asshole."

". . . that's different. You see, when somebody's been as loyal to me as you have and they're as good a coach as you've been, hell, I'd be crazy to go around recommending 'em. You understand that, don't you?"

They were both standing, both tilting forward in anticipation, only the oak desk separating them — this young coach on the way up and this old coach in fear that he might be on the way down. Buck wondered, even in the heat of the moment, when he would be the one on the other side of the desk.

"You mind if I sit down?" Buck asked.

"Damned right, I do!" shouted Shavers. "It's *my* goddamn sofa."

"Bullshit!" Buck shouted back, matching Shavers oath for oath so as not to give any ground. "It's the WAS Alumni Association's sofa. It's Jackie Summerville's sofa. You remember Jackie Summerville, don't you? He's the kid who threw twenty-eight touchdown passes for us and put us in the Cotton Bowl this year. That sofa don't belong to you. It belongs to the 300,000 people who came here this year to cheer Jackie Summerville and the Golden Hawks." I'm on a roll here, thought Buck. Got him where he lives. "That sofa ain't yours, old buddy. That sofa belongs to all those mamas who raised all those boys who bought all your bullshit about education."

Buddy Shavers flinched. But so did Buck Lee. Shavers took a gold, silk handkerchief from the breast pocket of his black blazer and wiped his face with it. Lee reached into his hip pocket and pulled out a red bandanna to rake across his mouth. Only the drone of the heating unit in the West Alabama Coliseum broke the silence. Each knew the truth, however momentarily — that they were two grown men ready to strangle each other over the pursuit, development, and exploitation of teen-age boys.

"Buck. . . ."

"You can't call me that any more."

"All right. Coach Lee."

"Got a nice ring to it. Coach Lee, East Alabama Rattler."

"Rattle the Rattlers," Shavers said sarcastically.

"Whatever your alumni want to say, Coach Shavers."

"Lee," he said, "I'll race you to Eaarnel Simpson. But I'll tell you one goddamn thing right now: He's *mine*."

"We'll see about that," said Buck Lee.

There was no hypocritical handshake since there were no alumni watching. Each man knew exactly how the other felt about him. This was war and they were wearing different colors. Shavers bent over his trash can in search of his wasted cigar. Buck Lee spun around and slopped through the plush, gold carpet, slamming the door behind him. Buck was emptying his billfold of his last credentials as an assistant football coach at West Alabama — credit cards, office keys, keys to the locker room, the laminated Golden Hawk ID card for parking, business cards (BUCK LEE, ASSISTANT COACH, WEST ALABAMA STATE, COTTON BOWL, SUGAR BOWL, ORANGE BOWL) — throwing them onto Adelle Muncie's desk, when he heard the intercom connecting her to Buddy Shavers.

"Miss Muncie?"

"Yes, Coach Shavers?"

"Get The Raven on the phone. Right now."

"Yes, Coach Shavers."

1

THE SLEEK BABY JET backed away from the gate and taxied toward the runway under a bright, cloudless sky. Sporadic breezes of crisp, December air swept back the grass between the long strips of pavement. Air traffic was typically light for midmorning. In fact, air traffic was *always* light, any time of day or night, at the modest airport in Evergreen, Alabama. It had taken an act of the state legislature in Montgomery to force Trans-Dixie Airlines to provide Evergreen with even a modicum of jet service. When the control tower issued clearance for immediate takeoff, Buck Lee — terrified by the mere sight or sound of an airplane ("It ain't *flying* that scares me, it's *not landing*") — interpreted it as an omen that the odds were at least fifty-fifty the plane would make it to Stanleyville.

Safely airborne, sitting on the aisle so he wouldn't have to look out the window and see how far it was to the rolling farmland of west Alabama, Buck lay back, tightened his seat belt, closed his eyes, and temporarily buried his fear with other thoughts. Gail had gone on ahead in order to check into the motel and look over their new town, Stanleyville, and to get used to the idea of being an East Alabama Rattler's wife. The EAU athletic director and university president were probably already driving to the airport to meet his plane. A press conference was scheduled for tomorrow. He was grinning and trying not to break out laughing, wondering how bad a case of diarrhea Buddy Shavers had this morning, when suddenly he was jolted from his reverie.

Blap! Buck was sure a wing had snapped. He bolted upright in his seat, eyes filled with terror, certain the plane was in an earnest spiral headed for some Alabama farmer's SEE ROCK CITY barn. He felt blood rush to his head. In his dizzy state, he imagined banner headlines in the *Birmingham News* saying COACH LEE DIES IN FIERY CRASH. But as his head cleared, he realized that what he felt was a welt in the middle of his forehead, and what he saw was all of the passengers pointing at him and laughing deliriously.

"What the hell's going on?" Buck said defensively.

"Sorry, mister," answered a tow-headed, eight-year-old boy. "I was trying to throw it to Daddy."

"Throw? Throw?"

"Could I have it back, mister?"

Buck dared to lean over toward the window, across the lap of the man sitting beside him, so he could pick up a reflection and see the damage to his forehead. There was a bump the size of a walnut encircled in red. Then he squatted back into his seat and saw in his lap an egg-shaped, plastic football. Printed on it was the logo of West Alabama State, WAS's mean-looking Golden Hawk, staring him in the face. For a moment Buck and the boy glared quizzically at each other, like two street urchins in an alleyway showdown, switchblades flashing, waiting to see who would make the next move.

"I hope you can catch better than you can throw, kid," Buck said, flipping the ball in a perfect spiral to the boy. He caught it and gave Buck a thumbs-up. Buck grinned. The irony that this was the last pass he would throw with a WAS football was not lost on Buck Lee.

"Nice pass," said the man sitting next to the window. He had silvery hair and wore a dark, pin-striped, three-piece suit.

"Practice," Buck said. "God knows. Practice."

"I *figured* you was an ex-player."

"Yessir. Got a great future behind me."

"Bazemore, Duncan Bazemore," the man said, extending his hand.

"Lee, here."

When they shook hands, Buck winced. He knew what was coming. As an assistant football coach at West Alabama State, Buck had flown hundreds of hours across the country in search of big-necked, fleet-footed boys and had spent a great deal of those hours sitting white-knuckled next to the Duncan Bazemores: well-dressed businessmen who loved talking about their athletic accomplishments. They all had that same reminiscent look in their eyes.

"Yessir, I flung a few balls down the field in my day," Bazemore said, lighting up a cigar that looked like a dildo. "Had a pretty good completion percentage going at East Alabama before I wrecked my knee." Bazemore stroked his bad leg and glanced out the window at the checkerboard of farmland. "By the time I got it back in shape, good old Noble Rockwell had recruited Trip O'Hern."

The name didn't ring any bells, but Buck resisted the temptation to say anything clever. After all, he had already gotten the job as head coach at East Alabama and he didn't want to stir up any wealthy alums before he had a chance to win a few games. Besides, when East Alabama Athletic Director J. A. Symington had called Buck at home and told him he had the job and asked if he could fly down to Stanleyville to meet the athletic board members, he had said they wouldn't announce his appointment as head coach until the press conference the next day. So the Duncan Bazemores of EAU didn't even know about him yet. Buck was lying low.

"Ol' Trip was a good'un. He could punt, run, throw from any position," said Bazemore. "Little on the wild side for my taste. We never could get him to go to church or come to any FCA meetings."

Buck stared blanky ahead, nodding politely every now and then. He wasn't interested in Bazemore's exploits on the gridiron. He figured the man *might* have been on the specialty teams in high school and maybe later played some hellacious fraternity football games for Alpha Sigma Omicron or something, but that was it. Buck could always spot a former football player — they all had great faces — but Bazemore, with his sharp nose and receding jaw, looked more like a former water boy.

"Yeah," Bazemore continued as Buck checked out the honey-blonde Trans-Dixie stewardess making her way down the aisle with an armload of magazines, "we had a lot of guys who came to school without any kind of moral guidance, but I always believed that Coach Rockwell could take any *good* player and make him *great* by just providing the right moral guidance." He added, lowering his voice, "Any *white* player, that is. You know what I mean?" Bazemore chuckled and quickly surveyed the immediate area with a mischievous look on his face. "Hey, Mister, ah — what did you say your name was?"

"Lee."

"Mr. Lee," Bazemore said conspiratorially, "you know how to

stop a nigger from drowning?"

"How's that?" Buck asked as though he hadn't already heard the despicable joke a hundred times.

"You take your foot off his head."

Bazemore howled. Buck continued to pick at a hangnail, being careful not to do anything to encourage Bazemore. But even without encouragement, he reeled off a few more from his sordid repertoire.

"Hey, honey," Bazemore finally said as the blonde stewardess approached again, "you got a martini for me?"

"We'll serve drinks in just a minute, but would you like a magazine?"

"Not unless it's got an olive in it." Bazemore cackled again.

"Sir," the stewardess said to Buck, while ignoring Bazemore, "you can loosen your seat belt now."

"That's OK," Buck replied. "I feel safer if I leave it tight."

"But, sir," she said, "this plane has one of the safest flying records of any passenger jet. You shouldn't be afraid."

"Oh, it's not the plane I'm afraid of," Buck said. "I'm just afraid of *flying* in it."

Bazemore punched Buck on the shoulder. "That's funny as hell. What did you say your name was?"

"Lee."

"Did you hear about the West Alabama offense last year?"

Buck's eyes followed the stewardess's fanny down the aisle and back into the galley, where she bent over to help with the food. He was doing his best to ignore his seatmate's jokes.

"I said did you hear about the West Alabama offense last year?"

"Some," Buck said.

"They called it Nigger Right and Nigger Left," Bazemore said, completely ignoring Buck's answer. "Are you really afraid to fly?" he asked, changing the subject.

"Sure am." Buck thumbed through an old *Sports Illustrated* the stewardess had left behind.

"That why you sit at the back of the plane?"

"You ever hear of a plane crashing *backwards*?"

"Guess not." Bazemore howled. "Well, Lee, you've got a damned good sense of humor — you'll appreciate this one." Buck rolled his eyes and gave his itching crotch a long scratch under the cover of his magazine.

"You ever hear about Coach Cameron, our former coach — you know, the one we fired this year — calling up Coach Booker Jones? You know, coach at that nigger school in Tennessee." Bazemore waited for Buck to answer.

"I do remember Coach Cameron," Buck said as he continued to check out the galley crowded with stewardesses. T and A. T and A.

"Well, anyway, he called up Coach Jones and said, 'Coach Jones, I've got to ask you a question. How in the world do you handle those two white boys on your team?'" Bazemore roared again, coughing smoke all over the upholstery and Buck. "You see," Bazemore began to explain when he noticed Buck hadn't joined in the laughing, "that school only had a couple of white players on the team and. . . ."

Before Bazemore could explain his joke, the stewardess brought him his martini. Buck excused himself and made his way to the bathroom with his briefcase. He needed to look over the material he was going to discuss with the board and Dr. Clarke Lowe when he got there, and the toilet apparently was his only escape from Bazemore. He also desperately needed to douse his crotch with the soothing powder which he always carried with him on flights. Buck was sweating heavily, and the salt from the sweat was not only stinging his rash, but it also was beginning to soak through his lucky khaki pants. Three years earlier he had signed more than his share of top prospects while wearing these khakis, and he had been on a roll ever since. Three of the players Buck had signed had made all-American for the Hawks, and they had been the nucleus of one of the winningest teams in the country for the last two years. So, like any other athlete on a hot streak, he intended to keep wearing the particular article of clothing that seemed to bring him luck. That's why he always wore the khakis when he flew.

Buck edged his way down the galley back-to-back with the stews, who were preparing snacks. He snitched a feel of several butts as he passed, but the girls, so accustomed to butts meeting butts in the small galley, didn't even look up. He was disappointed but not surprised.

Buck stepped into the tiny, stainless-steel bathroom, closed the door, snapped the lock, and dropped his pants. He let out a long sigh as the Desenex soothed the rash. Standing there, wedged in the toilet with white powder covering everything from his chest to his scarred knees, Buck hunched his six-foot frame down to mirror level and took stock of his looks. Not bad for forty-two, he thought.

Although Buck never jogged like a lot of coaches (he always said jogging was like masturbating; if you couldn't get someone to play tennis or racquetball with you, then you jogged), he was in very good shape. By playing tennis and racquetball at least three times a week, he had kept his weight around 185 pounds for the past six years. He also had sex with his wife about three times a week, which he told her helped to keep his weight down. His dark hair was full, except for the thinning around the forehead, and cut to cover the tops of his ears. His quick, honest smile was disarming and made him seem younger than he was. Like most of his coaching cohorts, he maintained a suntan from his collar up and his elbows down. The jock itch and his trick knees were his only physical complaints. Cartilage was removed from the left knee during his senior year of college, and the right knee went under the knife after he was hit on the sideline during a game five years ago. The rash had been around since he was a kid. It was a constant reminder that God has a peculiar sense of humor. Buck believed that the Almighty, just to break the monotony of creating life after life, had awarded him the sweat glands of a Clydesdale just to see what would happen.

His thoughts were interrupted by a knock on the door.

"Just a minute," Buck said, jerking up his pants.

"Please hurry, sir," said a pleading female voice. "My little boy has to go."

Buck opened the door and there was the tow-headed kid of the plastic football.

"That's him, Mama," he said, wide-eyed, pointing up at Buck. "That's the man who threw me the touchdown."

The boy's mother looked confused for an instant, but then her eyes were drawn down to Buck's waist, and her look changed to horror. Buck glanced down to see Desenex powder covering the fly and crotch of his lucky khaki pants. He quickly brushed himself off and made his way back to his seat. He would have enjoyed giving the kid a good belt, but he knew he might grow up one day to be 6′ 4″ and play quarterback. Losing a prospect was worse than a lump on the head.

Buck reached his seat just as Duncan Bazemore was finishing his fourth martini. Buck hoped the stewardesses would keep 'em coming until the plane landed or until Bazemore passed out, whichever came first. Duncan Bazemore could swim in his memories, for all he cared, as long as Buck Lee could be left alone long enough to fly with his dreams.

* * *

J. A. Symington stood in the gift shop of Stanleyville Municipal Airport puffing slowly on his pipe and thumbing through the January issue of *Penthouse* magazine. The eagle-eyed clerk snatched her bifocals from the bridge of her bulbous nose, let them drop to her chest at the end of their safety cord, and stared angrily at the balding, gray-haired man at the magazine rack.

"Please read the sign, sir," she snapped. "Either pay or move on."

"Yes'm," said Symington, blushing slightly. He placed the magazine back on the rack behind the *Mechanix Illustrated*, picked up Sunday's paper, and breezed out the door into the terminal. He glanced back to see the big-boned woman tidying up the magazine rack. Grown man, athletic director at a state university, and still can't read a dirty magazine without some old biddy looking over my shoulder like I was a kid, thought J. A.

J. A. checked his watch and ambled over to the coffee shop. He bought a styrofoam cup full of weak coffee, took a table by the window, and waited for Buck's plane. Sunday mornings were always quiet in Stanleyville, and the airport was even more so. The good folks of Stanleyville were in church, the student population was still in bed in an attempt to sleep off the weekend, and the local businessmen wouldn't be leaving on their assignments until Sunday night. It was exactly how J. A. had planned the arrival of his new football coach: no fanfare, no press, no nothing. Just him and Buck and Dr. Clarke Lowe, the school president. There had been plenty of speculation about whom the new coach would be, but no one would know for sure until J. A. made the announcement at the press conference on Monday morning.

The actual hiring had been done ten days earlier in the privacy of J. A.'s room at the coaches' convention. J. A. then made sure the press was kept in suspense by interviewing almost a dozen other coaches before the end of the convention. He had laid a heavy smoke screen, and now he hoped that some reporter or the wife of a local businessman didn't see him at the airport, waiting around for Dr. Lowe and Buck to arrive, put two and two together, and spoil the whole show. His show. J. A. had been a one-man selection committee. Sure, he had called back to the school and told the athletic board members of his decision, but what did they know? A potbellied dean of mathematics, two ass-kissing faculty board members, two students who would be on the board for only one year, and the alumni members. They, the alumni, were the worst of the lot, in J. A.'s mind. They all were ex-jocks who remembered the score of the 1959 Iowa State game and had no idea about what transpired behind the scenes of a successful athletic program. Not one of them had ever recruited a player; they owed their limitless strategical know-how to the YMCA League, where they established dynasties with eleven- and twelve-year-olds. J. A. considered the whole concept of an athletic board to be a perfect example of a bureaucratic double standard. After all, he didn't tell Lowe whom to hire for the geology department, and he sure as hell didn't make recommendations to the alumni about whom they should hire in their businesses. So, J. A. figured, they sure as hell weren't going to tell him whom to hire as his football coach.

J. A. rapped his pipe against the ashtray and scraped the charred contents from the bowl. He repacked it with a pinch of fresh tobacco and checked his watch. 10:35. Ten minutes before Buck's plane arrived. The pipe bowl glowed to life, and J. A. began to emit great clouds of smoke. The clouds hovered for a moment, then drifted slowly over to engulf a feeble old man sitting alone three tables away. J. A. was so engrossed by the man's wheezing and coughing that he didn't even notice when Dr. Clarke Lowe walked into the coffee shop. But that wasn't unusual. J. A. had always found it surprisingly easy not to notice Lowe, who seemed to have a way of blending into any crowd. It wasn't until Lowe sat beside him that J. A. realized the president of East Alabama University had joined him as planned.

J. A. admired Lowe's Harvard Business School grooming and good looks, but his small, darting eyes betrayed the lack of confidence concealed beneath the dark suit and perfectly knotted purple tie, dotted with dozens of white rattlesnakes. Lowe sat with his hand shielding his face from the coffee shop entrance and hunched over the center of the table, waiting for J. A. to speak. J. A. had told him to keep a low profile, and that was exactly what he was going to do. He had never met Buck Lee, but he trusted J. A. when he said that Buck was the man for the job. J. A. knew so much more than he did about sports, and because J. A. had been his track coach in college, it seemed to Lowe that for most of his life he had looked to J. A. for guidance. Lowe came from a wealthy, Southern aristocratic family. He grew up in Montgomery, Alabama, and was virtually raised by their maid. His father traveled extensively for business and pleasure and never took much interest in his only son. J. A. had filled that void.

"Clarke . . . Dr. Lowe," J. A. said as he folded the newspaper and flashed Dr. Lowe a quick smile. "It looks like Buck's plane will be here in a few minutes. I just want to tell you how much I appreciate your being here with me to meet my new coach." There was a slight emphasis on the word *my*.

"J. A.," Lowe replied while straightening his tie, "you know how much I want to have a good football program. If you say Buck Lee's the man, then he's the man. I'm all for him." Lowe searched J. A.'s face for some sign of approval. J. A. took a slow drag from his pipe, exhaled, and for a moment both men were shrouded in smoke. When the air cleared, J. A. was searching the skies for Buck's plane.

"Clarke," he said, not looking away from the window, "there's one thing I forgot to mention yesterday. I told Buck that we have a committee of faculty members which evaluates the transcripts of the potential student athletes we're going to be recruiting. Now, I also assured him that you and I are on that committee and that we have final say-so."

Lowe cracked a broad grin and reached over the table to grab J. A.'s hand. "That's great. Really great. That's what I'd hoped we would do. Yes, sir, put the transcripts in the hands of the faculty. I'm sure we'll be just as conscientious about letting athletes in as we are about our regular students. Yes, J. A., I think that's wonderful."

"Clarke, you don't understand. I realize you've been president for only a few months but, well, there is no committee, *per se*. I am the committee."

Lowe's shoulders drooped and his face looked like a beagle who had just lost his favorite hambone. "Don't you think we should have some faculty members to monitor the transcripts?" he asked. "I mean, what if they ask me about some player with terrible high school grades? What if they ask me how he got in school? What will I say?"

J. A. winced at Lowe's whining and waited until he had relit his pipe to reply. "Dr. Lowe," he began, looking Lowe in the eye for the first time. "Do you remember when you ran track for me here at Eastern?" Lowe nodded. "Of course, you do. Well, do you remember all the great athletes we had running with you on the mile relay team? Surely you haven't forgotten Fisher, Arzonetti, and Breedlove — those three great quarter-milers who ran the first three legs so you could run the anchor leg and bust through the tape and get all the glory. Do you think you would have won the Big Six Medal if we hadn't let those idiots in school? And don't you remember all those cheers from all those rich alums up in the stands? Well, goddammit, Clarke . . . Dr. Lowe. I do. And we need the same kind of help today. We need the same help from you that we used to get from President O'Brien."

Lowe took a deep breath and decided to stand his ground. "J. A., I'm president of this school, and I think it would be of long-range benefit to the students and to the school if we had a real committee. I want Meecham, head of the mathematics department. I want Walker, head of physical education. And the two of us. Now, I think that is fair as well as wise."

J. A.'s eyes narrowed. He took his pipe from his mouth and leaned across the table until his nose was inches from Lowe's. "Clarke," he said, "I remember the time that we had a meet against Ole Miss in Memphis. I was checking rooms at the Peabody Hotel, and when I walked into your room for bed check, you weren't alone. There was someone else in your bed that night." J. A. paused to relight his pipe and continued to speak slowly and distinctly as sweat collected on Lowe's forehead and ran down the length of his nose. "Clarke, that someone in your bed, I mean in your room that night, was not a female. Now, a female after hours the night before a big meet is bad enough, but. . . ."

Lowe's face contorted in pain; he looked near death. He stared red-faced at the bottle of ketchup on the table and began to tremble. J. A. had always felt sorry for Clarke, and it hurt him to have to bring up the incident. He had never told anyone, even though the person in bed with Lowe had been the team trainer, now a successful veterinarian and part-time youth minister in the Stanleyville Baptist Church. He probably wouldn't tell anyone now, but he wanted Lowe to think he would. J. A. leaned back in his chair and continued in a more friendly tone of voice. "Now, as you know, Clarke, that has been our secret for a long time. I fully intend to keep it that way, so don't you worry about that. In some ways, you're like a son to me, and I feel obligated to protect you. But I also have an obligation as your athletic director to assure the existence and perpetuation of a winning football team. I know my priorities, and that's the reason I recommended you as president to Briggs Webster, the chairman of the search committee. Now, are we straight on all of this? Dr. Lowe? Just you and me on the committee, right?"

Lowe blotted his damp cheek with the sleeve of his suit and tried to pull himself together. He had almost forgotten about the night that he and the trainer had gotten drunk in the parking lot and decided it was a good time to massage his sore hamstring. It was part of his past that he wanted to forget, and he knew that J. A. meant what he said. J. A. had been around for a long time, and his power and influence were far-reaching.

"Fine, J. A., just fine," Lowe said, shaking J. A.'s hand. "We'll do the best job possible on those transcripts. We really don't need any help, do we? Do we, J. A.?"

J. A. nodded and removed the sports section from the Stanleyville *Courier Times*. The lead story was about the fantastic senior season for a running back named Eaarnel Simpson. J. A. scanned the article and found it gorged with the same rushing and scoring statistics that had been discussed and recited by every farmer, lawyer, student, and coach in every bar, office, street corner, and locker room in the state: 2,650 yards rushing in ten games; 8.8 yards per carry; and twenty-two touchdowns. He ran the 100-yard dash in 9.4 seconds, weighed 225, and loved his mama. It was also well known that Eaarnel never played a down his junior year, because his mother had broken her hip and he had worked after school to support his family. The press took weekly delight in perpetuating the Eaarnel legend and never failed to mention his humble nature and his desire to be one of the world's great architects. He was an alumnus's wet dream and lived in a small, white-frame house only ninety miles from Stanleyville and the East Alabama campus. But the general opinion was that Eaarnel would be scooped up by USC, Notre Dame, or the West Alabama Hawks. The Hawks had won the conference title five out of the last six years, and their recruiting was getting even stronger.

"Dr. Lowe, if we get this boy," J. A. said, sliding the newspaper across the table, "we are on our way. With him and four or five like him up front, we'll be in high cotton. But Lord knows, it'll take some doing. A recruiting miracle. And Buck Lee's been known to work miracles."

* * *

As Duncan Bazemore continued to fondle his cigar, Buck realized that for the first time in his life he wasn't thinking of crashing and burning. He was considering the pros and cons of stomping the pompous bastard sitting beside him and inserting his remaining cigars into several of his smaller orifices. Buck finally felt the plane surge forward as it touched down. Bazemore continued to ramble.

"What do you do for a living, sir?" Buck asked as the plane taxied in. Maybe there was some way he could use this little man.

"Furniture bidness, Mr. Lee," Bazemore said, popping a mint and trying to sober up. "But in all honesty, I devote a great deal of my time to the church, my family, and my alma mater. I made a lot of money early in my career distributing Naugahyde sofas and La-Z-Boy chairs, and since that time I've been able to relax, bidness-wise."

"That's great, Mr. Bazemore," Buck replied in a slightly sarcastic tone. "I may be moving to Stanleyville pretty soon and may be in the market for some furniture."

"Do dat," Bazemore slurred. "The store's called Bazemore's Furniture Barn. Out on Highway 7. Right north of the Red Lobster."

The plane rolled to a stop and Buck unfastened his seat belt. He breathed fully for the first time since leaving Shavers' office. He and Bazemore were the last passengers up the aisle. He said good-bye to the honey-blonde stewardess who had been so helpful in taking his mind off plane crashes and midair collisions. Then he gave a sincere "thank you" to the pilot, even shook his hand, and made his way down the steps behind Bazemore.

It was slightly overcast but warmer than in Evergreen, and many passengers were shedding jackets and sweaters as they entered the gate. Buck wanted to make a good impression on J. A. and the school president, so he stopped at the foot of the steps and gave his khaki pants a good dusting. Small puffs of white smoke shot out from the material as he slapped at the front of his pants. With the jock-itch powder removed, Buck walked briskly toward the gate behind Bazemore.

"Over here, Buck," J. A. said in a stage whisper as Buck and Bazemore entered the terminal and rounded the corner. Buck turned to see J. A. standing beside a Maidenform bra ad with pipe ablaze and a grave expression on his weathered face. Beside him stood a slightly shorter, clean-cut man wearing what Buck guessed to be a $500 suit. Buck thought it went well with his $50 smile. Bazemore almost dropped his cigar as he watched J. A. greet his seatmate and introduce him to Dr. Lowe.

"Why, J. A.," Bazemore said. His eyes darted between Buck and J. A. "You two know each other?"

J. A. reached over and grabbed Bazemore by the arm and led him aside, leaving Buck to make small talk with Dr. Lowe in front of the brassiere ad.

"Duncan," J. A. said as he walked Bazemore around the corner, "I would appreciate it, as your athletic director, if you wouldn't mention that you saw us here at the airport with Buck Lee."

"Is that his first name? Buck?"

"You don't know who he is?" asked J. A.

"Is *he* the new football coach at Eastern, J. A.?"

"Look, Bazemore, I don't know nothing. Just remember what I said — keep it quiet."

"Well, sure, J. A., I won't say nothing."

"Good man. I'll talk to you later."

Bazemore waved goodbye to Buck and Dr. Lowe as he left the terminal, feeling somewhat confused and a little embarrassed, but there was no way he'd betray his school by mentioning Buck Lee's arrival.

"Well, Buck," J. A. said as he butted in on Dr. Lowe's conversation, "let's go to my office and discuss the future. My car is waiting right outside the door." Dr. Lowe walked to his car alone while J. A. and Buck climbed into the back seat of the Cadillac waiting at the curb.

"So, Buck," said J. A., "how'd Shavers take the news?"

"Like you'd expect. Complete asshole."

"You're right there. He's never been the most gracious loser in the world."

"You know what they say, J. A.," Buck said. "Show me a good loser and I'll show you a loser."

"And show me a school that gets Eaarnel Simpson," J. A. said, handing Buck the sports page, "and I'll show you a school with a conference championship and an ath-uh-letic di-rec-tor who can retire a happy man. Get that stud, Buck."

Buck stared at the file picture of Eaarnel stiff-arming a linebacker and recalled the game in which Eaarnel ran for long touchdowns on two consecutive carries. Buck had most of Eaarnel's high school game films in his briefcase. He had stayed up past two o'clock in the morning on more than one occasion sitting behind the projector, watching Eaarnel demolish two-hundred-pound linebackers and outrun quick little defensive backs. Buck thought he knew more about Eaarnel than anybody else, but he suddenly was aware that J. A. knew a lot about him, too.

"Buck," J. A. continued, "I'm telling you that without this boy and a few others, we ain't got a chance next year. Matter of fact, I don't give a shit what kind of field general or gridiron strategist you are. I just care about you as a recruiter." Symington paused. "Just so you'll understand what we're doing, I'd like to clear up one point about academics. Everybody with questionable grades has to go through the committee before they can be accepted."

"But how many people are on the committee, and how do they feel about football? That's the important stuff."

"The committee, you say?"

"Yeah," said Buck. "Who's on the committee?"

"Buck," said J. A. Symington, "you're talking to the committee."

Buck sank back into the leather upholstery and began to feel much better about uprooting his wife and family. It was hard for Gail to leave the close friends she had made in the small town of 30,000 people where they had lived, but she really did understand Buck's ambitions. She also understood how progressively worse things had gotten between Buck and Shavers. She knew it was time to leave. And, besides, Gail was looking forward to being a head coach's wife.

The Cadillac rolled silently past the stadium, and Buck tried to visualize himself standing on the sidelines watching his team stomp the Hawks and Buddy Shavers.

* * *

R. Buddy Shavers loved looking at himself in the mirror. No one in the coaching profession, as it was called, dressed as well as he did. The only thing about him that wasn't just right was his ear. It really wasn't that bad, he felt, but he always did everything he could to make sure that no one got a good look at it.

Walking back to his desk, he picked up his pen and began to write a note to Dr. Clarke Lowe, President, East Alabama University.

> Dear Dr. Lowe:
>
> As an alumnus of this school, I want to tell you about something that has been bothering me. I really didn't like it when you hired Buck Lee, but since you did, I have tried to get behind the program. However, several things have been bothering me. A friend of mine who has a son at Eastern told me that some of the assistant coaches have been letting the players at the school use their phone. Is this legal? I'm not sure, but I think he said that the player got the coaches' telephone credit card, took it over to the fraternity house, and they all used it. He also told me there were some irregularities on the transcripts they

> were sending in from high school. I love my school, but I want the new coach to play by the rules.

Shavers picked up a copy of the 1975 alumni book and thumbed through it until he found the name he wanted to use. J. Jonathan Higgins, Class of 1945. That name ought to get some reaction out of Lowe, thought Shavers. Those presidents jump like dogs through a hoop when they see a name like that from the Class of '45. They presume they're all wealthy.

Shavers signed the letter, placed it in an envelope, and put it in his OUT box along with instructions to mail it the next week. This will keep that asshole busy for awhile, he thought.

2

BUCK AND GAIL LEE. That was the marriage that set even Herb Caen of the *San Francisco Chronicle* to cackling when the two married while Buck was an assistant coach at Stanford and Gail LeBlanc was a fashion photographer in Carmel. They weren't exactly made for each other — he a lanky jock, groveling in the dirt with teen-age boys, she a lissome intellectual, hanging out with millionaires at Big Sur and in Pacific Heights. But then again, maybe they *were* made for each other. Both were radicals in their own ways. Gail had graduated from Smith, knew the wine list, read Proust, understood Liszt, could rig a yacht, spoke fluent Spanish, sent Coretta King a yellow rose on Martin's birthday every year, and refused to eat any vegetable that didn't crunch when she bit into it. Buck, on the other hand, was considered an animal in the world of Gail LeBlanc: crotch-scratching, foulmouthed son of an Atlanta mechanic, loved blue jeans and George Jones, hated airplanes and dogs, never voted in his life, slept in the buff, and drank Pabst Blue Ribbon beer. When Herb Caen attended their wedding in the backyard of friends in Burlingame, California, and asked Buck how the hell he wound up marrying a woman of such quality as Gail LeBlanc, Buck answered, "I reckon I was the best available at the time."

They were propped up in bed at the Holiday Inn in Stanleyville, Gail in her sexiest purple gown and Buck in his best forty-two-year-old skin, the Panasonic blinking from the dresser. Tomorrow morning would bring the press conference announcing Buck as the head football coach at EAU — it had been his dream since he was a snot-nosed, second stringer in junior high school to be head football coach at a major university — but tonight meant waiting for the eleven o'clock news and dealing with his erection.

As Gail nibbled away at a bag of Cheetos and sipped from her canned Coke, Buck reached over and prodded at her crotch.

"That hurts," Gail snapped.

"Aw, Honey, I thought . . . ."

"People who don't register to vote never think. Get away from me, boy. Later."

"But, Honey, I need it."

"Me, too, Ace."

"Well, *when?*"

"In due time, in due time."

So they lay there in the Holiday Inn of Stanleyville, Alabama, Buck and Gail Lee of America, she popping Cheetos and he trying to quell his libido by thinking about who won the national championship in 1969. The wandering French Jew and the mobile redneck, blinking back at a television set. ". . . and it was South Alabama 82, UAB 69," said the fuzzy-faced sportscaster for WSFA in Montgomery. Suddenly, then, an unflattering black-and-white picture of Buck Lee appeared on the screen.

> "Hello, sports fans, this is Rusty Dillon with the college football scoop of the year. Hold on to your Rattler-shakers, 'cause a reliable source reports that Buck Lee, former assistant coach for the legendary Buddy Shavers, will be the new football coach at East Alabama. J. A. Symington will announce Buck Lee tomorrow at a press conference. Our sources tell us that Buck Lee was fired by Shavers prior to getting the job at Eastern. Now, we can't substantiate this story, but, as we said, it comes from a most reliable source. Either way, it looks like the Eastern people have gotten themselves a proven winner. And the Hawks will finally have some in-state competition. This is Rusty Dillon, yours in sports."

Gail sat straight up in bed with her eyes as big as baseballs, and Buck felt her long fingernails dig little half-mooned ditches into his right arm. She always loved seeing Buck on television, but this was a little too much even for her. Buck pried loose from her death grip and reached for the phone. Before he could lift the receiver, the phone rang. It was J. A.

"Buck. Now don't worry. They called about an hour ago and tried to get me to confirm a rumor that you were the new head coach. I wouldn't do it, but I knew it was out anyway. So I've called all the other stations and leaked the same rumor. Anonymously, of course. It's on every channel right now, and it'll be in the papers in the morning. So don't worry. Just get ready for the press conference tomorrow. I'll take care of everything."

Buck hung up and turned to another channel, where another young sportscaster with bad skin and nice hair was reading.

> "One of the major jobs facing the new coach will be to hire a staff and get out on the road recruiting. The No. 1 prospect in the state and maybe the country is Eaarnel Simpson. How the Rattlers and their new coach do recruiting him could determine their success for the next four years. Channel Seven would like to wish Coach Buck Lee and his staff the best of luck. You'll need it, Buck!"

Buck mumbled back to the TV, "Thanks a lot." Hiring a staff was his first priority, all right, and after doing a little homework on the previous staff, he knew that there wasn't one member he wanted to keep. But he'd have to keep someone. Must be the same at the White House every four years, Buck figured. They keep somebody around from the previous administration because they know where the skeletons and slush funds are buried.

When the newscast was about over, Gail leaned over and kissed him on the cheek. Buck knew she always got affectionate when he made speeches, and evidently the same thing happened when she saw him on TV. To certain women, there must be something undeniably sexy about men in front of an audience — controlling them, making them laugh, cheer, agree, right on cue. It was for Gail, anyway, and she had that familiar lusty gleam in her eye (the same one she flashed at Johnny Carson every night).

"Pussy Cat," Gail whispered as she slithered under the sheets, pressing her thighs against Buck's, "what time's the press conference tomorrow?"

"Nine o'clock," Buck said, reaching for Gail. Just as he kissed the most sensitive spot behind her ear, Ed McMahon's voice boomed from the small speaker of the Panasonic saying, "And now . . . heeeere's Johnny!" The orchestra struck the familiar "da da dadada," and instantly Gail's eyes were riveted on the tube and away from Buck's.

Buck leaped out of bed and headed for the bathroom.

"Where you going, darlin'?"

"To take a cold shower."

"Take your time; Johnny won't be through for at least an hour."

3

THE PRESS CONFERENCE WAS quick and painless. J. A. had done most of the talking, and Buck's only quotable remark came after one reporter asked him to elaborate on his relationship with Buddy Shavers. Pens were poised as Buck began his short but diplomatic account of the Buck-and-Buddy Show. "Basically," he said as he smiled and looked into the camera without blinking, "our relationship was not unlike a lot of others. It's called, 'When you get to be the head coach, you can do it your way.' But now that I'm the head coach, I intend to do things *my* way. We just had two different personalities, that's all, and sometimes that creates problems. Let's forget the negative and accentuate the positive. I'm happy as hell, and so is my wife, Gail, to be part of the Rattler athletic program led by the one and only J. A. Symington."

The reporter continued probing, but J. A. took over and shoved the reporters out of his office. Then he guided Buck and Gail out the door and toward a blue Continental. Duncan Bazemore, the obnoxious man from the plane the day before, sat behind the wheel.

"J. A.," Buck said as they got into the car, "thanks for your help in there. That wasn't bad."

"What the hell did you expect your ath-uh-letic di-rec-tor to do in his own office?" J. A. slammed the door and added, "You just handle the Rattleshakers like you did the press and you'll be OK." He waved good-bye as they drove away.

Bazemore drove the big car through traffic expertly as they headed for the airport. It was Buck's first official duty as head coach to address the Rattleshakers in the north end of the state. The Rattleshakers were the $25 contributors and, unlike the big donors, they all wanted a piece of the action for their money. They rode buses to every game, and if you lost, they all got together on the bus coming back and figured out what you did wrong. They were a dangerous group, but they were necessary and could be helpful if controlled.

"Mr. Bazemore," Buck said, ignoring Gail as she tried to point out areas of town where they might want to live, "J. A. said you could fill me in on the Rattleshakers. So tell me, what do they want to hear? What can I say that will get 'em on my side?"

Bazemore turned onto a dirt road behind the new shopping plaza, which didn't set well with Gail because it meant that she would miss her tour through town. "Ah, well, Coach Lee, they're a good group, but winning is the only thing they care about. They want to hear how you're going to beat the shit out of . . . excuse me, Mrs. Lee." Without waiting for her reply, he went on. "They're starving for conference titles and national rankings. They only give $25 apiece, but there are a lot of 'em. Now, next week we'll talk to the Sidewinders, they're the big-bucks people, a thousand dollars or better. They'll want to hear you talk about integrity, academics, things that make them proud of their degrees. They say things like, 'I don't want my degree diluted by lowering academic requirements.'"

Buck turned and patted Gail on the shoulder as he saw her neck stiffen and a vein in her forehead pop out. She was really irked that Bazemore had turned off the main road and was taking a shortcut to the airport.

"But remember," he continued, not noticing Gail pouting in the back seat, "the Sidewinders, unlike the Rattleshakers, bet big bucks, and they sometimes care more about the point spread than they do about who wins. So just a word of advice, Coach Lee: Always know the point spread."

Buck stared straight at Bazemore and asked, as casually as he could, "What group do you belong to, Mr. Bazemore?"

"This Lincoln ain't rented, Coach Lee. I belong to the Sidewinders, and I do like to bet on a game once in awhile. Always bet on the Rattlers, and, just between you and me, old Coach Cameron didn't do very well on the spread." Bazemore made a sharp turn just as Buck was getting ready to change the subject. The sudden turn threw him up against a still-steaming Gail, who shoved him back across the car and yelled, "What kind of crap is this?"

Buck just laughed at Gail — he knew her temper had the lifespan of a comet — and she laughed and suddenly was herself again.

Bazemore, though, was mystified. He didn't quite know what to make of Buck and Gail. They were different. Buck dressed a little sharper, weighed a bit less, and was infinitely better looking than the other coaches he had seen. Gail was beautiful like a fashion model and obviously had not lived all her life in, say, Iowa. As Bazemore glanced in his rear-view mirror, Gail and Buck started hugging, kissing, and laughing in the back seat. They looked like a couple of teen-agers on their first date.

Bazemore pulled up beside a graying hangar, turned to Buck again, completely ignoring Gail, and said, "Coach Lee, remember one other thing about the Rattleshakers: Every time you lose, it's like you've castrated every man in the club."

"I'll remember that, Mr. Bazemore," Buck said, as they climbed out of the car.

The school plane, an aging twin-engine Beechcraft, had been rolled out of the hangar and was waiting for them. Buck eyed the old plane with the purple rattlesnake decals on the sides and looked at Bazemore with a quizzical look in his eyes.

"You *are* kidding, right?" Buck said.

"Oh, I forgot," Bazemore said. "You don't like to fly, do you?"

"It's just crashing and dying that pisses me off, remember?"

"Don't worry about a thing, Coach. Our pilot has been flying for thirty-seven years — ten years in the Air Force and twenty-seven for the Alumni Association. He hasn't killed a coach yet, although he's scared quite a few." Bazemore laughed as he stepped into the plane.

Buck and Gail sat down in two torn, nasty seats, and Buck immediately strapped himself in extra tight, making a face as he did.

"What's the matter?" Gail whispered sarcastically.

"This tin can smells like the inside of a '61 Valiant," he whispered back.

"Oh, it's not that bad. Besides, you've got nothing to worry about; you're wearing your khaki pants."

Bazemore came out of the cockpit with the pilot. "Coach and Mrs. Lee, I'd like you to meet Mr. Cornwell. You can just call him Ollie. He's our ace pilot." Ollie looked at Buck with a big grin that revealed most of his twelve teeth and all of his darkened gums. He looked well over seventy, and Buck stared in horror at his round glasses that looked like glass paperweights.

"How you, Coach? You a pretty thing, honey," he said to Gail. "Now y'all strap in real good there. Might shake a little bit at first, but she'll be all right."

"You're a dirty old man, aren't you, Ollie?" Gail said.

"Sweetheart, I was a dirty *young* man." More gums.

* * *

Ollie adjusted the controls, checked the ailerons, threw a few switches, checked the rudders, hit the starter switch for the left engine, and then choked the sputtering engine until it was roaring. Ready on the left. Ready on the right. Ollie taxied out to the runway.

"Y'all ready back there?" he shouted.

"Ready as I hope to be," said Buck.

Ollie revved up the throttles while standing on the brakes. The sound of the two engines racing was like the roar of a freight train bearing down on you. He released the brakes and lurched forward, thundering down the runway, using his rudders to steer the plane. Ollie looked like a barnstorming World War I pilot, decked out in a small leather hat with goggles and a leather jacket with a big Rattler on the back. The Beechcraft finally gathered enough speed to lift itself and the four of them off the ground. Buck gritted his teeth and thought about the bright side: It could have been a helicopter. He often had nightmares about those wingless insects and woke up more than once sweating and breathing heavily. Gail would rub his chest and calm him down by reassuring him that it was just a dream, and that he'd never have to climb aboard one of those awful machines.

When the plane leveled off to cruising altitude, Bazemore, who was sitting in the co-pilot's seat, loosened his seat belt and turned to face Buck. "Is there anything I can do to make your job easier?"

"Yes sir, there *is* something you can do," Buck said, feeling Gail's head slump over onto his shoulder. "We need informants who'll keep us posted on everything our opponents are doing. I want to know when Shavers visits a prospect, where the prospect drinks his beer, where his daddy works, and for whom. In other words, the Rattleshakers can help us with information."

"What can the Sidewinders do? You know most of them are too busy to be looking for things like you just mentioned, but they do have money." Bazemore was twisting his purple tie.

"Tell 'em we need some money, and make sure they know it's not tax deductible," Buck answered. He reached over and repositioned Gail's head. By now she was so deeply asleep that if the plane were to go down in flames, she would miss the show.

"I'll take care of that, Coach, and I *do* understand how you play the game." Bazemore plucked a pen from the front of Ollie's shirt. Ollie didn't take his eyes off the sky; his hands seemed frozen to the controls. Buck was afraid rigor mortis had already set in. Bazemore began scribbling on a pad he had taken from his jacket pocket.

Ollie emerged from his trance briefly and told the passengers to buckle up. They were beginning the approach, which meant Buck was beginning a new series of prayers. The plane came in too fast, then too slow, then too high, and then it dropped almost straight down. It hit the ground, bounced twice, and then without warning, Ollie ground-looped the plane. They did a 360 right in the middle of the runway. Buck was rigid in his seat. Gail bolted awake and shouted, "What the hell was *that?*"

Ollie answered, "Like I always say, any landing you can walk away from is a good one."

The "Rattler Express" taxied to a halt outside the small terminal of the Culver City Airport, and Buck took a deep breath. It was the first move he'd made since the landing. Even Bazemore appeared shaken.

As they staggered from the plane, Buck looked up to see a swarming crowd of press and Rattleshakers moving toward them. It was a greeting party, twenty or thirty strong, and most of them were shaking plastic rattles above their heads. "My God," Buck said to Bazemore, who was waving to a couple he recognized, "they look like a bunch of Hare Krishnas."

When the mob was about twenty yards away, the small, round-faced man Bazemore had waved to broke free of the crowd with his wife in tow. She was chanting something about Rattlers "kickin' ass" and shaking her purple rattler frantically over her freshly sprayed hairdo.

Buck talked briefly with reporters before being ushered into a station wagon. Gail was steered into the back seat along with Bazemore, while the wife of the round-faced man shoved Buck into the front and crawled in right beside him.

"This is terrific," Gail said of the reception, waving out the window.

"Coach Lee," Bazemore said as they made their getaway, "I'd like you to meet Mr. Dwayne Perkins and his lovely wife, Penny Catherine."

"My friends call me Cannonball, Coach Lee," Dwayne said, offering his hand and swelling with pride.

"Coach Lee, I've heard so much about you," his wife chimed in a nasal tone, completely ignoring Gail. "You look so much better in person than you do on television."

"Thank you, Mrs. Perkins," Buck said, wincing at her flirtatious eyes.

"You can just call me Cathy," she said.

Buck was uncomfortable with her flirting, and not just because her husband was next to him and his wife was in the back seat; it was because she was downright ugly. She was probably about forty-two, but fifteen years of tailgate parties and drinking Bloody Marys out of sixteen-ounce purple Rattler cups had taken its toll. Her gaunt face, bloodshot eyes, and spidery limbs made her look much older.

Buck knew it was best to direct his attention to Mr. Perkins, who was busy waving at people in hopes that they would see the new head coach in the front seat with him.

"When did you play football, Mr. Perkins?" Buck asked, knowing full well that he was probably, with his face and body, an ex-oboe player in the marching band.

"Oh, I didn't play football, Coach Lee," he replied. "I would have, but I hurt my knee, so I became a manager."

"That makes sense, Mr. Perkins. If you can't play, then you can contribute in other ways." Perkins was typical of team trainers and managers. He had a soft, round face, narrow shoulders, and wide hips. He looked like an avocado with legs.

"Buck, please just call me Cannonball. All my friends do."

Buck looked at Perkins and in his most veracious tone said, "That's all right; Cannonball it is. To win, you've got to have some *cannon balls*."

Ah, the magic word: Win. "Damn right," yelped Perkins. "That's the name of the game." He turned the station wagon sharply to the left and headed down the main street of town.

"How about you, Mrs. Perkins?" Gail asked from the back seat. "Where did you go to school?"

She looked at Buck to answer Gail's question. "Oh, I didn't go to college, but I just *luuve* those Rattlers." She shook her plastic, bean-filled Rattleshaker over her head and squealed, "Yah-hooo!"

"Nobody hates to lose more than Penny Catherine," Perkins said. "When the Rattlers lose, she won't talk to anybody for three days. Beats anything I've ever seen."

"Well, we won't have to worry about that next year, will we Buck?" She brushed her hand ever so slightly across his leg.

"We're going to do our best to keep you from being unhappy next year, Mrs. Perkins, you can bet on that." Buck felt Gail's eyes burning a hole in his neck.

"Yah-hooo!" she screamed again as they pulled into the parking lot of the Ramada Inn.

Bazemore spoke up for the first time as he helped Gail out of the back seat. "We're here, Buck. This is where we meet the Rattleshakers."

"I'm ready for 'em," Buck said. Then he looked up and saw the motel marquee that read, "Fuck Lee and the Rattleshakers welcome."

"Goddammit!" Perkins screamed, slamming his fist on top of the station wagon. "I'll bet you anything that little Jimmy Badock did that! He went to Western last year. I'll get his ass fired for this."

Gail walked over to Buck and squeezed his hand. She leaned over as if to straighten his tie and said quietly, "She's a star-fucker, so you stay away from her."

Buck patted her butt. "Sugar, I'm not going to fool around with anybody unless she's prettier than you, and I haven't met that one yet."

Buck and Gail followed the Perkinses and Bazemore into a lobby jammed with Rattleshakers and their spouses. Buck quickly excused himself and headed for the bathroom. It had been a long trip. He was walking down the corridor to the men's room, thinking about his new audience, when a grinning, young face leaped in front of him.

"Hi, Coach!"

Buck fell back against the wall and clutched at his heart. It was almost vibrating, it was beating so fast. He had always been easily startled, and the face had appeared out of nowhere suddenly enough to almost cause cardiac arrest.

"Sorry, Coach, I didn't mean to scare you. My name is Richard Culpepper, and I just wanted to tell you that I'm a good coach and I want to work for you. Here's my number." He handed Buck a small piece of paper with his name, address, and phone number handwritten on the front. Buck eyed the youngish, all-American-looking guy in his mid-to-late twenties and put the paper in his pocket.

"I'll call *you,* Richard, don't call me," Buck said. He then squeezed by him in the hallway and entered the bathroom. He should have brought his powder, he thought.

Buck emerged from the bathroom to chat with the Rattleshakers and to have his drink refilled every five minutes by Mr. Perkins. Gail smiled blandly but was nice to everyone. She was complimented regularly and seemed to enjoy the attention, even though she knew the members were only being polite and waiting their turn to talk with their new coach.

In time, they adjourned to the banquet room for a buffet dinner of salad, roast beef, fried chicken, sliced tomatoes, cornbread, biscuits and gravy, spare ribs, turnip greens, okra, mashed potatoes, string beans, and lots of sweetened iced tea. The banquet rooms — "The Bonanza," "The Ponderosa," and the "Little Joe" — had been combined by drawing back the collapsible partitions between the rooms to accommodate the overflow crowd. The carpet, permanently stained from years of similar affairs, was maroon, and the wallpaper was gold with tiny wagons and horses all over it. Tablecloths covered the round tables in the expanded room, and on the wall over the head table hung a purple and white, hand-painted banner that read in bold letters, "Welcome Buck, Good Luck."

Buck felt at ease at the head table, even though it was his first experience as a head coach. He had been to a thousand banquet rooms at Ramada Inns as an assistant and made his speech, but never had he been where what he said was the chosen word.

He buttered his cornbread and looked out over the audience of Rattleshakers. There was a sameness about them that he had never noticed before. Suddenly he realized for the first time why most coaches dress the way they do: They're in constant contact with representatives of Middle America, and they've got to fit in. Mr. Averageman loves his football and couldn't care less if his tie and coat match. He is unconcerned if sideburns are out of style, if long hair is in and short hair is out. He doesn't even care if his white socks shine like beacons of light between his double-knit black pants and brown half-boot, zip-up shoes. The group's obvious aversion to natural fabrics and tapered shirts left Buck feeling a little self-conscious about wearing his light wool, tailored sport coat, cotton Oxford shirt, and pleated pants. He wondered what they would have thought about his urban cowboy outfit.

The crowd ate quickly and noisily. Most of the men shoveled in the food like there was no tomorrow. Within minutes, without lifting their heads six inches above their plates, they were through and headed back for seconds. They exchanged bawdy jokes through mouths full of potatoes and washed them down with big glasses of sweetened iced tea. The women laughed loudly and often as they nibbled away at the food in front of them. Every so often, they reached over and picked a piece of meat off their husbands' plates. Some of the wives were dressed fashionably, but they were the ones working on their fourth bourbon, and they seemed not to eat anything.

As the food was eaten and the plates taken up by sweet young girls, the crowd became restless. They hadn't driven this far for Ramada Inn food. They wanted to hear their new coach get up and tell them how the Rattlers were going to win.

Sensing that it was time to begin the meeting, Cannonball Perkins stood at the podium and addressed the eager Rattleshakers with potatoes on his chin and grease on his wide, purple tie. Perkins made several announcements concerning dues and the club functions. Then he drew the winning drink ticket stub from a baseball cap and awarded the centerpiece at the head table to a man named Ralph. Ralph waddled up to accept the plastic flower arrangement and then, to the cheers of the crowd, presented it to his wife. She surprised seventy-five-year-old Ralph by kissing him smack dab on the mouth.

Perkins took his spoon and rapped on his iced tea glass. When the crowd quieted down, he started his introduction of Buck. "It's my humble privilege as president of the Rattleshakers to introduce to you all our new head coach, Buck Lee . . ." As the applause died down, Perkins continued. " . . . and his pretty wife, Gail." There was a smattering of applause.

Then Buck stepped to the microphone and went to work. "Rattleshakers," he said, "it's really fantastic to be a part of your program. You've got a great president, Dwayne 'Cannonball' Perkins." Several people applauded but were immediately *shooshed* by several others. "You know Dwayne used to be a football manager for the Rattlers, and managers are really indispensable. They'll do *anything* for the head coach. There's nothing too big for a manager to handle. Why, I remember several years ago when East Alabama went to play LSU, and their cheerleaders had that big Bengal tiger in a cage, pushing him around the stadium. They finally pushed him in front of the Rattler dressing room and left him there to roar into a microphone they'd placed inside the cage. Cannonball and a couple of the other managers were standing outside the locker room when one manager said, 'I wonder what the coach would do if this tiger got out of the cage and went into the locker room?' 'I know what he'd do,' said Cannonball. 'He'd say, "Manager, get that tiger out of here!"'"

The room exploded in laughter. Some of the older Rattlers, and most of them were old, wheezed and coughed as Perkins doubled over. He held his bouncing belly and wailed. The crowd had responded to the old story better than Buck had hoped. He figured it was harmless fun as long as the jokes were not personal. He continued on by plugging in the name of a man he'd met an hour earlier at the cash bar.

"A little while ago, I was introduced to Hoss Hannah, one of the greatest linemen in Rattler history. You know, different people get to different schools in different ways, and this is how Hoss got to East Alabama." Hoss Hannah was a mass of sweating flesh sitting near the front of the room. Most of his neck dropped over the sides of his collar. Hoss was 260 pounds of cholesterol and probably had grunted out his last wind sprint in November of 1950. "You see, Hoss was a country boy and never had played football. They used to hook him up to a tractor when it got stuck. Well, one day he rode his horse up on the football field at Eastern to let him graze a little. Coach Noble Rockwell saw him, walked over and said, 'Son, you look like a mighty healthy youngster. How would you like to play football?' Hoss replied, 'I don't know anything about playing football, but I'll try anything once. How do you play?' Coach Rockwell replied, 'Here's how you play. You take this football and run through all eleven of those men. That's how you play.'" Buck paused and looked at Hoss, who was wondering what would come next. "Well, I want to tell you folks one thing about Hoss. He not only ran through all those men down to one end of the field, but then he turned around and came back. He wasn't even breathing hard when he went up to the coach and pitched him the ball. 'How's that, Coach?' Hoss said to Rockwell. 'Pretty good, son,' answered Rockwell. 'Now get down off that horse and try it again.'"

As the crowd laughed and slapped their legs, Buck realized that one of the best things about changing jobs was that the new crowd hadn't heard your stories or seen your wife's old clothes. Everything was brand-new to this group. Buck winked at Hoss, who was blushing but loving every minute of it. The young people in the crowd, the few there were, whistled and yelled and stomped their feet. As the crowd got quieter, Buck thought now was the time to poke some fun at the people this crowd couldn't stand.

"I know you'll appreciate the problem this one youngster had," Buck began. "He went to Notre Dame and asked the coach if he could try out for football. The coach said yes and gave him the ball, and he whipped right through the defense for seventy-five yards. 'That's terrific,' said the coach. 'You *are* a Catholic, aren't you?' 'No, I'm not,' replied the youngster. 'Well, you can't play here,' the coach said. 'Why don't you try out for Baylor's football team?' Well, he did. He went to Baylor and did the same thing — seventy-five yards for a touchdown. The Baylor coach said, 'That's fantastic! You *are* a Baptist, aren't you?' 'No sir, I'm not,' he replied. 'I'm sorry, but you can't play here. Why don't you try Southern Methodist University?' So he did and again he zipped seventy-five yards untouched. The coach said, 'That's great, son. You *are* a Methodist, aren't you?' 'No,' he replied, 'I'm not.' The SMU coach said, 'I'm sorry, but you can't play here.' The frustrated youngster finally blurted out, 'Well, I'll be a son of a bitch!' 'Oh, in that case,' said the coach, 'why don't you go play for Western and Buddy Shavers?' "

The Rattleshakers loved it. The crew cuts, the starched hair, the bad ties, the leisure suits, the polyester blazers, and the three-piece suits were all there for one purpose: to find out something about their new coach. They liked what they'd seen so far.

"Before I go any further, I'd like to apologize to you for not introducing Brad Roberts to you," Buck said. "Stand up, Brad, and let 'em see you." Brad stood up shyly, pushing his tight pants legs down. He was pretty to look at: 6′ 3″, blond hair, blue eyes. The kind of player that you want to represent *your* school, not *theirs*. Brad's only problem, Buck had found out after watching hours of game films, was that he was chicken-shit and wouldn't hit anybody. Of course, he wouldn't bother to mention that now. "Folks, Brad plays tight end for us, but more important, he is a 3.6 student in chemical engineering. He is a potential Rhodes scholar and won the award for the football player with the highest grade-point average."

As the crowd clapped and showed their approval of Brad, who stood there with his "aw-shucks" grin on his face, Buck planned his final words to the group. When the noise quieted down, he said, "It's been a great evening for Gail and me. You're a wonderful group, and I know that with your support, we can put this program into great shape. The name of the game is recruiting, and if we don't get our share, we don't have a chance. Now, I've told Duncan Bazemore here how you can help, and I'm sure he will tell you and your president, the honorable Dwayne Perkins, what I said. The only other thing I have to say is, GO RATTLERS!"

Buck stepped away from the podium as the women in the audience with the shakers began to wave them in the air. The crowd began to sing the alma mater, and everyone had to stop and put their hands over their hearts. As soon as the singing was over, Buck grabbed Gail's hand and headed out the door with Bazemore and Perkins.

"Gail," Buck whispered as they walked toward the door for a nightcap, "just one time, mind you, I'd like to bring some big, black super stud who weighed about 260 and had a giant Afro to one of these all-white parties and say, 'Roy's dumber than hell, but he'll knock your cock off.' I'd love to see their faces."

"You're awful. How do you think of those things?" Gail smiled as she teased Buck, but her attention was diverted by two women who had her cornered. They smiled and laughed and seemed to be captivated by Gail's hair and its lack of spray. Buck shook more hands and worked his way towards the door. Finally he broke free of the Rattleshakers surrounding him, only to find one last supporter blocking the door.

The man stood there with his hand stuck out. His round, handsome face had a big grin on it. His stocky build and strong arms made Buck think he could probably hit a golf ball a mile. But it was that face that Buck liked most. He could be a beer salesman, a priest, or an ex-football player, but he had the good face.

"Coach Lee, I'd like to introduce myself. My name is Patrick Flanagan. My friends call me Pat."

"My friends call me Buck."

Flanagan said, "I don't know one thing about football, but I do know something about selling. Without thinking I'm bragging, I've been one of the most successful real estate salesmen in the state. Now, what can I do to help you?"

Buck felt an immediate closeness to this man. "What do you say we get a beer," he said.

"The only thing I like better than beer isn't here, so I'll take you up on that offer," answered Flanagan.

Buck walked over to Gail, who seemed to be surviving the women who had her surrounded, and said, "Honey, I'm going to the bar for a nightcap. Tell Perkins and Bazemore I won't be long."

"Gotcha, Ace."

As the two men entered the dim room, they looked for a table that would give them as much privacy as possible. They found a booth over in the corner, away from the front and also away from the jukebox, so that Waylon's wailing wouldn't interfere with their conversation.

"What you boys gonna have?" asked the middle-aged blonde in a brown, low-cut blouse.

"Couple of beers, honey," answered Pat. "And don't you look lovely tonight."

"We got Pabst, Bud, Miller Lite, Schlitz, and Michelob," she whipped off in a nasal voice, ignoring Pat's remark.

"Make it a Pabst, sweetheart, preferably in a long-neck bottle." He reached over and patted her on the butt.

"Make that two," said Buck. Flo, according to her name tag, walked away shaking her behind at Pat.

"So," Buck said, "you want to help us win, but you really don't know anything about football. Why are you so all fired up?"

"Buck, I really *don't* know anything about the game, but I do love my school, and last year when Shavers had our team down fifty-five points, he didn't take out a single one of his starters. I felt real sorry for Coach Cameron, who was a decent sort of fellow. When the game was over and he went out to shake hands with Shavers, Shavers ignored him. I said right then that if there was anything I could do for the next coach to help beat that turd, I would." Pat reached down for the beer Flo had just placed on the table. He took a big, long swallow of cold Pabst, and said, "Damn, that's good."

"Patrick, I've got an idea about what you could do to help."

"Shoot."

"You wouldn't happen to have fifty grand on you, would you?"

"There are limits on my hate for Buddy Shavers."

"A pity," said Buck, "a pity. No, but look. One of the problems in recruiting is that you have to pretend that you're director of an insane asylum."

"Huh?" Pat said.

"What I mean is, if one of the inmates walks up to you and says, 'I'm Napoleon,' you don't say, 'You're not Napoleon.' You say, 'How was Waterloo?' The same thing applies to a recruit. If he says, 'I want to be an archaeologist because I like to dig ditches,' you don't say, 'Hey, stupid, you can't even *spell* archaeology, much less pass it.' You say, 'Certainly you can take archaeology. We have one of the finest schools of archaeology in the country.'" Buck stopped to pick up his beer and take several swallows.

"I understand what you're saying so far. But you still haven't told me how I can help."

The two men looked at one another as they finished up their beers. An instant friendship was developing between the men, like Butch

Cassidy and the Sundance Kid. Something special. Buck held up two fingers for Flo. She pretended she didn't see him, but she headed straight for the bar.

"Here's the basic problem as I see it," said Buck. "If I take a blue-chip prospect up to the dean of the School of Archaeology, who first of all is boring as hell and couldn't sell an ice pick to an Eskimo, he'd tell my prospect that he can't get into school. Now even if he *could* get into school, more than likely our man would do such a poor job of selling him that he'd go to another school where they had a better salesman."

The beers arrived and both men took big swallows. Pat looked across the table at Buck, who was nervously peeling the Pabst label off his first empty bottle.

"Buck, I'm sure of one thing. If we don't get some horses in here this year, these people are gonna melt down their rattleshakers or beat up your wife. So, whatcha want me to do?"

"You ever wanted to be an actor?"

"Are you kidding? I've been acting all my life, except I never got to work in a movie. Are you going to put me in the movies?"

"Here's what I have in mind for you," Buck continued. "When we have a prospect come over to the campus for a visit and he wants to be an engineer, instead of sending him up to see the dean, *you* play the part of the head of the School of Engineering. If Notre Dame is our big competition, you play the part of a priest. Whatever we need, you do. What do you think?"

"Won't I have to know something about the part I'm gonna play?" Pat asked. He watched as Buck began to scratch himself. "You got the itch or something?"

"It's my goddamn jock itch. When I get nervous or excited, I start sweating, and it inflames my itch. But back to your question. You'll have to know something about what you're doing, but I'd rather have a salesman who didn't know shit selling the School of Engineering than a dean who knew everything but couldn't make out in a whorehouse with a hundred-dollar bill."

"You're on, Coach. What's my first assignment?"

"We've got a kid coming in this weekend who wants to become a doctor. Now, first of all, we don't even have a School of Medicine, but we have a School of *Veterinary* Medicine. Your job, if you want it, is to convince Ed 'The Hammer' Sledge that he doesn't want to see the medical school."

" 'The Hammer,' is that what he likes to be called?" Pat asked. He held up two more fingers to Flo.

"Yeah, he said his daddy gave it to him when he first saw him run with the football in junior high." Flo arrived with two more beers. As she left, Pat stared at her behind. Then he raised his full beer bottle and waited for Buck to follow suit. Their bottles touched one another and the contents were inhaled. The two men knew they had just become a team. Buck started to slide out of the booth, but Pat sat still.

"Tell you what, Buck, I think I'm just gonna stay awhile and see if I can't drink that little ol' Flo pretty," said Patrick Flanagan.

The two men said their goodbyes. As Buck left the darkness of the bar, there was a mischievous grin on his face and a special jauntiness to his gait. Gonna have me a regular goddamn football factory before this is over, he thought. Buck spotted Gail in the lobby still talking to a gaggle of Rattleshaker women. He kissed her full on the mouth, leaving the women stunned, and whisked her out of the Ramada so they could hotfoot it to the airport for the flight with Ollie back to Stanleyville. He told her all about Patrick Flanagan.

"So what's this fellow going to do for you?" said Gail.

"Win an Academy Award," Buck told her.

4

BUCK AND GAIL FOUND a four-bedroom, three-bath, two-garage, split-level home in a good neighborhood close to the best school in Stanleyville. The house had a big, fenced-in backyard, just in case they ever got a dog for twelve-year-old Bucky, which was highly unlikely. Buck had hated dogs since he was a youngster delivering the *Gazette*. There was an old chow dog that would wait for him every morning in the bushes next to the old Martin house. As the paper left Buck's hand, the dog would attack his legs. Buck would drop his papers and run for the nearest tree, where he would stay until the dog got tired of chewing up paper and went home. Buck lost money delivering papers, and he never cared much for dogs after that.

While Gail took care of the move, Buck tackled his biggest problem — hiring a new staff. He was flabbergasted by the number of calls he got from college and high school coaches, ex-pros, and even some who had never played or coached but thought it would be fun to start a new career.

Buck also discovered in his interviews that coaches change jobs for a lot of different reasons: It's easier to get players in at your school than at the one where they've been, or you pay them more money, or they might get a new title like offensive or defensive coordinator, or they can get to be a head coach faster at your school, or they were having an affair with a dean's wife and had to get out of town.

After exhaustive interviews and hundreds of recommendations, Buck finally settled on his staff. He didn't want to offend anyone, so he covered all bases. He hired a black, a Catholic, two ex-players, an ex-pro, a yankee, a member of the previous staff, a coach who could imitate him on the phone, and three WASPs.

Everything was going smoothly except for the recruiting of Eaarnel Simpson. Buck had committed a big faux pas on the phone when he pronounced it ER-nell. He was told in no uncertain terms that it was not ER-nell, but *EAR*-nell. Buck quickly apologized, but since then it had been uphill. They were still in the hunt, but bagging this trophy would be tough. "*Ear*-nell." It reminded him of Shavers every time he said the name. Wonder how Shavers feels saying "*EAR*-nell?"

* * *

The empty stadium echoed with an occasional whoop and holler as the coaching staff trotted out onto the artificial turf. They looked terrific to below-average in their purple double-knit coaching shorts and their white, short-sleeved, coaching shirts with the coiled rattlesnake on the left breast. It was coaches' picture day, and they couldn't wait to get hold of the footballs so they could run for underthrown passes and play grab-ass touch football. They loved running on the artificial turf. It made them all feel quick and fast again. Like they hadn't lost a step.

"OK, I'll be captain of one team," said Billy Tom Harris, who looked like a J. C. Penney model from the sporting goods section. He was the most stunning of the group with his tailored shorts, perfect-fitting shirt (which he'd had tailored at the local men's shop), and white socks taped to his hairless legs.

"If you're *one* captain," said Harry Ignarski, "I'm captain of the other side." Looking like he had just stepped from the pages of *MAD* magazine's best-dressed coaching list, Ignarski's shorts hung loosely over his hairy, varicose legs. His shirt was already hanging out, and his socks were down over the tops of his black, high-top football shoes. His shoes looked totally out of place compared to the low-cut, white, ripple-soled shoes worn by all the other coaches.

"Fine. Ugly goes first," said Dave Barton, pointing to Ignarski. A sarcastic grin seemed to stretch the entire width of Barton's bulldog face, which sat atop massive shoulders. Barton emptied the bag of footballs onto the turf, and all the coaches scrambled around his pencil-thin legs scooping up balls like starving mongrels.

"OK, I'll take Chuck," growled Ignarski, pointing toward Chuck Driscoll, who was bouncing the football against the turf and back into his right hand without looking.

"I'll take Perry," said Billy Tom, drilling a pass into the gut of Perry Jackson, who then turned it upfield and stiff-armed a frightened photographer. "Nice catch, Perry," yelled Billy Tom.

Perry lofted the ball to Billy Tom and trotted back. They were the best athletes on the staff, and everyone knew the game was in the bag with them on the same team. They always hung around together and looked like two peas in a pod — except that Perry was black.

"I'll take Kyle," said Ignarski, pointing his hairy finger at Kyle Moore, who moved his hard, compact body beside Ignarski. His long torso and short legs were in perfect shape, and his swagger said, *I'm the best player out here*. His swagger lied.

"I'll take Bullet-Head Battle," continued Billy Tom, spinning the ball up in the air, catching it, and tucking it repeatedly under his right arm. Kirk Battle smiled and trotted over to join his growing team. His young face and whippet body gave no clue to his kamikaze playing style. He had played for Coach Cameron three years earlier, the stud on a team of nags, and was now a pre-med student helping out as a graduate assistant. Kirk had been hired as EAU's "skunk." His primary function was spying on the other team.

"Hyspick, I would choose you, but they wouldn't have any chance then, so I'm going to take lard-ass Barton," said Billy Tom, noticing the hurt look on Johnny Hyspick's face. Dave Barton, whom all the players loved because of his enthusiasm and sense of humor, did a forward roll, jumped up, worked his feet in place, and yelled, "Old lard-ass reporting for duty."

Ignarski looked around and saw that only Hyspick, Jack Stone, and Charlie Smith were left. He was really enjoying the situation. No one likes to be picked last in any game. "OK, I'll take you, Johnny." Hyspick, who was so intense that he hyperventilated when he had sex, rushed over to Ignarski and started pounding everyone on his team.

"I'll take Stone," said Billy Tom. That left only Charlie Smith, who went by default to Ignarski's team. He immediately tried to figure out a way to switch sides so he could play with a winner. If J. A. happened to come by, Charlie certainly wanted to be seen in the best possible light. You never know when you might need a recommendation for a head coaching job, he thought.

"Hey, Ignarski, you don't want me, man. I've got a pulled muscle and can barely walk fast." When he got Ignarski's attention, Charlie Smith turned and limped pitifully down the field.

"OK, Smitty," said Ignarski, setting the ball on the tee. "You go play with Mr. Wonderful. I'll take Stone."

Jack Stone drop-kicked his football to the sidelines and joined his four new teammates. Charlie Smith sprinted to Billy Tom's team and took a couple of quick passes from Kirk Battle to warm up.

"Ignarski, let me kick off," said Hyspick in between pushups. "I'll bust it over their fucking heads!"

"Cool off," said Ignarski, pacing off his path to the ball. "I'm the captain. I kick off."

Billy Tom and Perry Jackson hung back behind their line to receive. Ignarski raked the sweat off his flattop, raced toward the ball on the tee, and kicked a line drive that never got more than waist high. It slammed into Dave Barton's groin with a great thump. He dropped to the ground in a curled-up heap, trying to breathe.

Hyspick never slowed down. He sprinted full speed across the field, uttering bloodcurdling screams to frighten the enemy. Five yards from Barton, Hyspick stopped in his tracks and worked his feet so fast they looked like pistons.

"What the hell are you doing, Hyspick?" Perry Jackson asked in disbelief. "Can't you see this man is in pain here?"

"It could be a trick," Hyspick said with a mad look in his eyes. "This could all be a plan." His feet were still stuttering.

"Sorry about that, Dave," said Ignarski. "But you should never try to catch the ball with your dick."

Finally Dave Barton made it to his feet, and the blue tint started to leave his face. Minutes later, the ball was kicked off again, and the ten young to middle-aged coaches began to play a bone-crushing game of touch football.

* * *

Buck looked out the window of his office where he was dressing and saw his coaches, most of whom were too slow, too little, or just not good enough to play pro football, trying to relive their days as college players. The cheers of the crowds echoed in their memories.

Buck thought he'd better hustle out there before they got too bloodied. After all, this was picture day for the calendar they were going to make. It would go out to every high school in the state, and hopefully it would hang in a place where every athlete in school could see it.

Buck finished dressing, looked at himself in the mirror, patted his stomach, sucked it in, and decided he didn't look too bad in purple and white.

* * *

"All right, coaches, let's line up for the picture," said Ned Peacock, the leathery little publicity man for the Rattlesnakes.

"We can't line up yet," Dave Barton yelled as he tried to snag a long pass from Jack Stone, who had already thrown his arm out of socket by trying to heave fifty-yard passes when his range was only thirty yards.

"Tell me why you can't line up for the pictures, Raymond Berry," said Doc Langley, who was waiting in his coaching gear to get his picture taken as team doctor. "I've got to get out of here and deliver a baby."

"Because Coach Lee isn't here yet, and I don't think he'd want us to have our picture taken without him," Hyspick gasped as he tried to cover Perry Jackson on a fly pattern down the field.

"Well, Coach Lee told me to get you all lined up before he got here so we could expedite the picture. Said he wanted to get right into the recruiting meeting," Ned said, not wanting to take on the wrath of the assistants. Invoking the head coach's name worked; they all began milling around the middle of the field where the camera was set up.

"Hey, Ignarski, you're the hairiest mother I ever saw. Is that a hair shirt you're wearing?" said Barton.

"If I had legs like yours, I wouldn't wear short pants. When did you have polio?" asked Ignarski.

"I think Perry is real cute, don't you?" Billy Tom said to no one in particular. "He doesn't have any hair on his body at all. He could probably get a job as the African Queen if we don't win around here. He wouldn't have to do anything except put on a wig and a dress, with that pretty body and face." Billy Tom was trying to poke fun at his friend, but it came out a little too sarcastically.

"Well, if it isn't Mr. Three-Piece Suit trying to be funny," countered Perry. "I'll bet you even screw with that three-piecer on. In fact, that old gal in the laundry room told me you did. You better hope the wind doesn't come up and blow one hair out of place. I hear you give the best hair in town." Billy Tom blushed. He wasn't ready for Perry to jump on him like that in front of the others.

"What about Hyspick?" said Dave Barton, playfully punching his victim on the shoulder. "This is his first big assignment, being strength and off-season coach for a big-time school. Y'all know Johnny went to such a small school that they could only get ten men out for football. His girl was the biggest one in the school, so they got her to come out. You guessed it — she played center and Hyspick played quarterback. They used to practice after school until he got the *feel* of it."

"I don't think that's funny at all," said Hyspick, who tried to look inconspicuous but didn't quite make it.

Stone looked around at all the other coaches and said, "Hey, have you noticed how we're all about the same height? All about 5′ 9″. Is that unusual?"

"You all might be 5′ 9″, but I'm at least 5′ 11″," said Charlie Smith.

"Oh, bullshit, Charlie, you're not 5′ 11″. You're just saying that because you think that it'll help you get a head coaching job," said Dave Barton. "We've seen you close your door and make all those phone calls every time there's a head job coming open."

"Well, I could eat peanuts off your head, Curley," Smith fired back nonsensically; it was he all he could think of.

"A rat's ass you could, let's see who's the tallest," said Barton, fluffing up his perm.

"I think this has gotten a little out of line here, fellows, but if you'll all line up back to back, we'll see who's the tallest," said Chuck Driscoll, who was again bouncing the football on the ground and making it pop back up into his hand every time.

Trying to change the subject and avoid a confrontation, Kyle said, "Chuck, don't you ever do anything badly? I've never seen you miss that ball even once."

"I schedule myself so that I have time to do the things that one must do to make himself better in all areas," Driscoll answered with an affected British accent.

"Wait'll you hear this," said Ignarski. "I saw this yellow pad in his office, and he even scheduled the time he was gonna take a crap. No kidding, he'd written down first cup of coffee 9:00 A.M., take newspaper and go to toilet 9:15." Driscoll blushed but just kept bouncing the ball.

"Hey, troops, here comes old Double-Walk-Away-Straight," yelped Kirk Battle. "It looks like he's already had about one too many of those double vodkas at the race track." All eyes turned toward coach Larry Hildebrand, the leftover from the previous administration. He was weaving like a broken-field runner. His little pot gut was hanging over his white coach's belt, "lovehandles" were sticking out on the sides like wads of dough, and his nipples were showing through his shirt. As Hildebrand waddled over toward the troupe, he spotted Buck coming out of the locker room. He immediately broke into a trot; he didn't want to be late the first time they were all together.

"I'll guarantee you the only thing he's been recruiting is drinking buddies," said Stone.

"What say we have some fun," said Dave Barton, his big bulldog face lighting up like a Christmas tree. All eyes and ears turned to hear what Barton had to say. "Here's what we do. In the meeting after we finish with the picture, I'm going to mention the name of a great fictitious prospect to Hildebrand. Coach Lee's ears will perk up, and Larry will make out like he's seen him. Then we can really have some fun. Every time we have a staff meeting, he'll have to talk about this great player who doesn't even exist."

"That's great, but how will we keep him convinced?" asked Chuck, who really resented the fact that they all worked their asses off while Hildebrand never even visited a high school.

Barton looked at all the coaches and smiled. "We'll tell him there's a great alum in the northern Alabama region who'll keep him informed about the prospect. Each week he'll get a phone call telling him how many yards this stud gained and how many schools are after him. Of course, the person who'll be doing the calling will be one of ours."

"Sensational," said Kirk, who loved practical jokes. They all laughed as Hildebrand and Buck arrived at the same time.

* * *

"Picture time, coaches," said Ned Peacock, nervously surveying the crew of purple and white. "Line up with offensive coaches on the left and defensive coaches on the right of Coach Lee. All the rest of you line up so it balances out," he continued. Buck slipped into his spot in the middle of his coaches and staff.

"Come on, Ned, we're all set. Let's get this done so we can get back to the office," said Buck. As Ned and his photographer started to take the picture, however, Buck yelled, "Hold it!"

"What's the matter, Coach, something wrong?" Ned asked in a voice that matched his weaselly looks and wimpy personality.

"No, Ned, you didn't do anything wrong," replied Buck. "It's just that if Kirk is going to skunk the other teams, he can't have his picture taken."

Kirk Battle frowned and moaned. "Aw, Coach, I don't think anyone will recognize me. You know how many disguises I wear."

"I'm real sorry, Kirk, but if you're captured, we'll have to pretend we never heard of you," Buck said. Kirk kicked at the artificial turf and walked over to sit on the ground next to the bag of footballs.

The photographer began snapping photos of the dozen men smiling uncomfortably. Buck stood proudly in the middle, sporting the biggest and most honest smile. He felt good about being where he was, and he felt particularly proud to be several inches taller than any of his stunted assistants.

5

ALL RIGHT, BEFORE WE get this meeting started, which one of you guys put out that awful pink chalk?" Buck asked. When nobody answered, he went over to the board, picked up all the chalk, and tossed it into a wastepaper basket that hadn't been emptied in at least a week. "I'll tell you about pink chalk. If you wear a white dress shirt and go to the board to diagram a play or talk about a prospect, and you get pink chalk on your shirt, do you know what it looks like? If I'm going home with something on my shirt that looks like lipstick, it's gonna be lipstick, not chalk." They all squirmed lightly in their seats.

Buck already loved being a head coach. It was one of the most powerful positions left in the so-called corporate power structure. It was also fun because he could wear coaching togs adorned with school insignias to work; not only was that comfortable, but it also saved wear and tear on his own clothes. The real fun, though, was the power. Buck stood up in his chair, stepped over onto the table, and yelled, "Position take!" Eleven grown men jumped out of their chairs and assumed a bent-knee position.

"Do we have the best coaching staff in America?" Buck screamed.

"Hell, yes!" yelled back eleven coaches.

"Do we have the prettiest girls on our campus?" screamed Buck.

"Hell, yes!"

"Do we have the best engineering school?" Buck yelled even louder.

"Hell, yes!"

"Then why aren't we signing more prospects?" he asked in a much calmer voice. Before anyone could say anything, Buck, still standing on the desk, said, "I want to tell you all a story." Everyone looked up at him. It gave him a great advantage, much like Shavers sitting behind his desk on the platform.

"It seems as though this sales manager called his dog food salesmen together and asked them, 'Do we have the best dog food in America?' 'Hell, yes,' replied all the dog food salesmen. 'Do we have the best salesmen in America?' 'Hell, yes,' was the answer from all the salesmen. 'Then why aren't we selling more dog food?' the sales manager asked. 'I'll tell you why,' some little voice from the back of the room replied. 'It's the damn dogs. They don't like it.' So remember: No matter what we have, if the prospects don't like it, we can't sell it." Buck stepped down from the table and the others sat down.

"Coach," said Kyle Moore, obviously enthused by Buck's speech, "let's get started. I need to get back out on the road. I've got a lot of work to do."

"OK, Kyle, you start it off. I want to know what you guys have been doing for the past month while I've been speaking to any group who'd listen. I want to know who your prospects are and how we stand with them."

As Buck watched Kyle Moore go to the board, he liked what he saw. Kyle was good-looking, neatly dressed, really liked recruiting, and was damned good at it. Chased women a little too much, but he practiced discretion. Kyle never drank in town and was a perfect family man, but when he got on the road, he downed vodka like RC Colas and had a waitress under each arm.

"OK, the No. 1 prospect I have is a kid from New Jersey. His name is Ivie Buchanan. He's about 6′ 3″, 220, and he's got a real nose for the football. He plays linebacker and I think we can get him," Kyle said as he started writing down all the pertinent information on the prospect board.

"What kind of student is he, Coach," asked Buck, making notes.

"I'd say average," answered Kyle.

"Let me put it another way. Is he smart?"

"I'll tell you this. After one play, the man in front of him won't be any smarter."

Kyle listed about ten more prospects, all of whom sounded great. Not as great as Ivie, but almost as great. His chances of signing them were good, he thought. Finally, he sat down and wiped the sweat off his brow.

"Kyle, you remind me of the coach who said he never went to bed with an ugly woman, but he sure woke up with a lot of 'em," Buck said, scratching his crotch. "It's called results, gentlemen. They all look good when you sign 'em, but they had better look good when they walk out on the field. Now, how about you going to the board, Coach Jackson, and telling us who your prospects are, and give us a little more information on the best one."

Perry stood up and walked over to the board. Even though he was the only black in the room, he had never felt the least bit uncomfortable with these guys. He liked country music, drank Pabst Blue Ribbon, was the only Catholic on the staff, and his English was better than anyone else's. Perry also listed about ten prospects on the board. He was a good detail man and gave out sheets on every prospect to all the coaches.

"We all know that the No. 1 prospect in the state, and maybe the country, is Eaarnel Simpson," said Jackson. "If we get him, we have a chance to have a great season this year. I'm going to do my best to get him for us, and. . . ."

Buck cut in. "Coach Jackson, you've got about nine other good ones on your list to recruit. You've got plenty to do. Shavers is going to do everything he can to get Eaarnel. I worked for him for seven years, and I think I know most of his tricks, so I'm going to take over the recruiting of Eaarnel. I'll be personally responsible for getting or losing him. Now, I want you and everybody else to help, but he will be *my* responsibility."

Perry was stunned. He looked like he'd just been slapped in the face. "But Buck, I thought Eaarnel and I had established a great relationship."

"Sorry, Coach, but you've got other prospects on your list that are damn important, so get 'em and you'll have done a great job." Perry looked obviously dejected as he walked back to his seat.

Buck turned to Ignarski and said, "Harry, your turn. And look, Coach, I don't want you to list all those 190-pound defensive linemen who come from small towns, wear crew cuts like you, and run five-flat forties. Bring us some *studs*." Ignarski stood up and waddled over to the board. His Popeye arms and stubby fingers began to write:

> Warner Frick, 6′ 6″, 275 lbs., white, offensive tackle.
> C average in school. State wrestling champ, Class A.

"Coach Lee, this is my best man. You go down there with me to visit him and his mother, we'll sign him. I guarantee it," Ignarski said.

"First of all, Coach," Buck said, "you don't have to put down that he's white. We really don't give a shit what color he is if he can play. Now if he *can't* play, that's what we care about. But you set up the trip, and I'll go with you." Buck looked around the room and nodded to Chuck Driscoll.

Driscoll picked up his purple and white notebook and walked over to the board. His ring-bound notebook was indexed perfectly. His propensity for detail was the reason Buck had hired him. The staples he put in a paper were lined up like soldiers. He began to write on the board:

> Rick Manos — football player.
> He'll knock your cock off.
> Breaks two headgears a game.
> Greek family, and do they like to eat.
> Barroom fighter. He won't take no shit off anybody.

Driscoll turned to the coaches and said, "This boy is not just another swinging dick. He's a real stud."

"Well, Coach, your report wasn't the most comprehensive I've ever heard, but I'm sure everyone understood what you meant," Buck said. "Anything you want to add?"

Driscoll grinned and looked around the room to see if everyone were listening. He wanted to make sure they all heard what he had to say. "Well, there is one other thing. I checked out Rick's pubic hair in the locker room, and he rates A-1. I didn't want to write that down, but I think it's real important."

"What are you, a freako faggot or something?" yelled Ignarski.

Chuck ignored him and turned to Buck. "I firmly believe that you can tell something about a kid's masculinity by looking at his pubic hair."

"Jesus," said Buck, shaking his head in disbelief. "Pubic hair. All right, Coach Barton, you're on."

Dave walked over to the board carrying his paper cup full of spit from his chewing tobacco. His right jaw was packed to the brim with Red Man. Before he picked up the chalk, he put the cup up to his mouth and spit out a thin, yellow, watery glob of tobacco juice. Now he was ready. With his cup in his left hand and the chalk in his right hand, he began to write:

> Grant Johnson, 5′ 11″, 176, QB
> 4.6 forty
> 28 inches — squat jump test
> 3.4 GPA in all the important courses
> Baptist Church
> Father sells insurance
> Mother, housewife
> Has two sisters, 11 and 13

Dave looked at Buck and handed him a piece of paper. "Coach, this is the information in detail that I've just given on Grant. He's one of the finest prospects in the South, and we need him. We're a little behind to Western, but we can make up for lost ground if we get in there and pitch."

"Thank you, Coach. What else do you have for us?"

"There's another real good one down in Selma. His name is Peter Abernathy and he's a real ball-buster. He won't stop until he hears glass break."

"I've seen that coon-ass play," interrupted Ignarski. "He's a real pussy."

Dave put down his cup full of tobacco spit and his chalk, looked at Ignarski, and snarled, "I'm tired of all your bullshit, you hairy asshole."

Ignarski instantly lunged across the table for Barton's throat. He knocked everything in his path right off the table. Before Ignarski could get up, Barton pounced on top of him and pinned him to the table. Every coach in the room was yelling, "Hit him! Knock him on his ass!" As Ignarski and Barton were struggling on the table, Buck continued working on his prospect list. He'd seen too many of these to get excited. He'd let 'em fight for awhile, then he would break it up. After they had rolled around for a minute, Buck stood up and said, "Let's go back to work. You been at it long enough." Eight pairs of hands reached in and pulled Ignarski and Barton apart. They glared at one another for a moment and then started laughing. After they sat down, Buck started laughing, too. Soon everybody was lighting up cigars.

"Can you believe that?" Buck said to no one in particular. "Fighting over a prospect. Who'd believe it?"

Jack Stone said, "One time I saw two IBM salesmen fighting, but they weren't fighting over a business deal. They were fighting over a woman. Same thing, I guess. We don't fight over a game. We fight when somebody talks about our prospects or tries to steal them from us."

"I love that little homespun story, Jack, but let me hear about your top man first," said Buck, resuming control of the meeting.

"My top man is Butch Martin." Jack didn't bother to go to the board to write anything down. He reminded Buck of a young Shavers, except for his clothes. His purple, plaid coat didn't exactly match his green pants, but it *did* catch your attention. He was the only coach who had changed clothes after the photo session.

"Why don't you go to the board and write down the information on your prospect?" Buck said.

"I'd rather just talk about them right now and then give each one of you an information sheet later. OK?"

"OK. Talk."

Jack continued with his prospect list, but Buck couldn't take his eyes off his clothes. His belt was white, his socks were green, and his tie and shoes were white. He could have been running a used car lot or the sideshow at the state fair. He was a hustler and you wanted him on the staff, but you had to watch him. He'd get you in trouble.

Jack sat down and Billy Tom Harris went to the board. "Before I list my prospects, Coach, I'd like to ask a question."

"Go ahead, Billy Tom," said Buck, "the floor is yours."

"As you know, Coach Lee, I played football here and I'm very proud of that." Billy Tom pulled himself up to his maximum height.

He reached up and threw his big mop of hair back out of his eyes and grinned to show the most beautiful teeth Buck had ever seen. Even though he wasn't wearing the three-piece suit which was his trademark, his coaching gear fit his body like a wet T-shirt fits Bo Derek. "I received a great education here, and I want to make sure that it's not diluted by letting anybody in school who doesn't meet a certain criterion. One of the reasons I took this job, being an ex-player and all, is that my wife wanted to go back to school here, and this was the best way I knew to get back. Now, I like my job, but are we going to just let anybody in school?"

Buck bolted from his chair and shook his finger at Harris. "Listen to me very carefully, Billy Tom. You might have been a hotshot player and an academic all-American when you went to school here, but times have changed. When you played for Coach Rockwell, it was strictly a white-meat league. Don't tell me all those players you played with were academic geniuses. That's bullshit and you know it. I'll tell you who we're going to get in school: any hard-hitting son of a bitch that the registrar will let in. And if you want to work at your alma mater, you'll get on the ball and tell us who your prospects are." Buck thought he might have gone a little too far with Billy Tom, who wasn't a bad guy, but he already had a gut full of the old alums. There were just too many old farts out there who wanted it to be 1951, the streetcars running downtown, no blacks in school, and Noble Rockwell planning to ride in through the south end zone on a white horse and save the football program from the Black Menace.

Billy Tom stuck his finger in his mouth, pulled it out, and held it in the air. He looked at Buck and said, "Now that I know which way the wind's blowing, Coach, I'm all set. I want to work hard and do a good job for my alma mater."

"Great, Billy Tom, now give us your list of prospects."

Billy Tom took the chalk in his left hand and began to write:

Jimmy Johnson, Def. Back
Member of the Fellowship of Christian Athletes
Eagle Scout
Teaches Sunday School

Dave Barton spoke up. "Billy Tom, I like Eagle Scouts as much as you do, but one question: Will this pissant hit anybody?"

"Before I told you about his athletic ability, Coach, I wanted to tell you about his character," Billy Tom said.

"My wife has character, too," said Barton, "but she don't weigh 220 and run a 4.7." Everybody laughed and Billy Tom sat down.

"All right, Coach Smith, your turn to tell us about all those fabulous prospects you've seen."

"As you know, I've told you everything I've been doing in regard to Ed Sledge," Charlie began. "I consider him a good prospect, but certainly not a blue-chip football player. Let me list for you all of Ed's credentials." Smith went to the board, opened his briefcase, and began looking through the contents for his information sheet on Ed. As he fumbled for the sheet, Buck looked him over. Charlie was nice-looking, neat, and had a pleasant way about him. On the down side, he was a little too ambitious, cut the other school up a little too much, and agreed with everything Buck said. He wanted to be a head coach by playing the role instead of working hard. Buck would have to watch him closely.

"OK, the poop on Ed Sledge," Charlie said as he began to write:

Ed "The Hammer" Sledge — Running Back
5′ 11″, 200 lbs.
4.8 40-yard dash

As Smith rattled on about The Hammer, Buck thought, I don't need anybody to tell me about Ed. I don't want him, but I'll have to take him because he's local and white. Several other schools were after him partly for the same reason, but mostly because his statistics were outstanding. He'd broken enough tackles, gained enough yards, and scored enough touchdowns to be heavily recruited, but he just wasn't that good. Buck knew that Smith was at a real disadvantage in the recruiting war because The Hammer wanted to be a real "honest to God practicing physician." Problem was, Ed could hardly get into any school, much less medical school. His SATs and grades would barely get him out of high school, but he'd heard there was a shortage of doctors, and he thought he would help out. Buck figured that

Patrick Flanagan might be able to change his mind.

Before Smith could finish, Buck said, "Haven't we been recruiting Ed forever? I thought he was the No. 2 recruit in the state."

"That's true, but you wanted the top prospect I had, and he's it," Charlie said. He continued without giving anybody else a chance. "Coach, Ed isn't outstanding, but because of the circumstances, we have to go after him hard, if you know what I mean."

"I know what you mean, and we'll talk about it later. Now, go on with the rest of your boys." Charlie finished and sat down.

"All right, Coach Hildebrand, it's your time." Buck got up and changed chairs, seeking some relief for his raw crotch.

Larry Hildebrand, former member of the last staff, supposedly knew where all the skeletons were hidden. He was the man who knew which alumni to call when you needed donations that weren't tax deductible. Buck had been forced to keep Hildebrand by a strong group of alumni, led by Duncan Bazemore. He drank too much, didn't do any work in recruiting, and was too close to Noble Rockwell, but there he was at the board, writing down names with no information on any of them.

As he was on his twenty-fifth name, Dave Barton asked, "Coach Hildebrand, have you seen that fabulous prospect, Tnassip? He's supposed to be one of the best in the country."

"*Certainly*, I have. How do you spell his last name?"

"T-n-a-s-s-i-p," said Dave. "In case you don't have all the information on Tnassip, here's the name of the alum you can call and get some help."

Buck, who didn't want to miss out on any great prospect, admonished Larry to do a good follow-up job on Tnassip. He noticed a lot of smiling faces, but he thought he must have missed the joke. Before they could continue with the meeting, Buck's secretary called to remind him that he had a meeting with Coach Noble Rockwell.

"Y'all go ahead and discuss recruiting while I go meet with Coach Rockwell," Buck told the coaches as he started out the door. "Coach Barton, why don't you come with me and go by and get Hyspick and Trousdale. They need to be in the next part of our meeting."

Leaving the staff meeting for any length of time was OK with Dave, so he gladly accompanied Buck. As they walked along the picture-lined hall, Buck said to Dave, whom he considered his confidant on the staff, "Perry's a little pissed off at me for telling him I'm going to be responsible for recruiting Eaarnel, so I need your help to smooth that over. What bothers me about recruiting is that if you ever suggest to someone that somebody else might do a better job on a certain athlete than they could, it's like you wanted another man to make love to their woman because they're not doing a very good job."

Dave looked around to make sure no one was listening. When he was sure they were alone, he said, "I'll tell you one thing, Coach. If you don't get involved with Eaarnel, we'll never get him. In my experience with black mamas, they react negatively to young, hip, black men. They've dealt with older white men all their lives, and that makes them a lot more confident that they'll be taken care of."

Buck said, "Dave, I really don't give a damn what Perry or any other coach thinks. *I'm* either going to get Eaarnel or *I'm* going to lose him. I'll be totally responsible. You try to explain that to Perry." Dave turned off at the bottom of the stairs to fetch Hyspick and Dr. Trousdale. Buck continued up the stairs two at a time, not because he was that anxious to see Coach Rockwell, but because his pants rubbing against his jock itch felt better than scratching.

* * *

Peggy felt a little sorry for Coach Rockwell as he waited for Buck. He'd been sitting there for more than an hour, since before three o'clock, even though his appointment wasn't until four. She couldn't take her eyes off him, this wilted man in baggy tennis shorts that accentuated the skinniness of his legs. His varicose veins were grotesque, to say the least, but he covered most of them by taping his white socks to just below the kneecap. The coach's shirt he was wearing said "Noble Rockwell" beneath the pocket. Since it looked brand-new, he must have had someone in the equipment room monogram it for him.

"What time did you say he would be here?" Rockwell asked.

"He said he'd be here at four o'clock. It's only 3:45."

"Do you mind if I use the phone?"

"Go ahead, Coach, you can use mine."

"I'd rather use his," said Rockwell. He entered Buck's office and sat down in the big high-back chair behind the desk. He dialed the equipment room and waited for someone to answer.

"Hello, equipment room, Sally speaking."

"This is Coach Rockwell. Can I speak to Sarge?"

"Sarge isn't here. He's in a meeting, and I'm in charge while he's gone. Who did you say this is?"

Peggy watched from her office as Rockwell's face got blood red, and the big vein in the middle of his forehead looked like it was going to burst. Whatever someone had said to him had really made him angry.

"This is Coach Noble Rockwell. I don't know who you are, but I was the coach of this team for twenty-five years, and without me it wouldn't be anything," he sputtered.

"When was your last year of coaching here?"

"Nineteen hundred and sixty-five, and we won eight games and lost only three."

"That's why I don't remember you. I was two years old then. Now, what can I do for you?"

"Did they leave a girl in charge of the equipment room? I never had a female around football players. It was just not the thing to do."

"They do now, so what can I do for you?"

"I need some tennis shoes, size eight and a half C."

"Forget it, Coach, we don't give out stuff to anyone unless Sarge OKs it. He'll be back in maybe an hour."

"Why, all I want is a little pair of tennis shoes to wear. Sarge told me any time I called and he wasn't there to talk to the sweet little gal in the equipment room."

Peggy stared at Coach Rockwell as he made the complete cycle — vindictive old man to a sweet, charming one. He was amazing. Thought he could get anything he wanted because he'd coached once.

"I'm sorry, Coach Rockhead, but I still can't give you any shoes without Sarge's permission."

"It's Rock*well*," he yelled into the phone in that twangy, nasally voice of his. "Not Rock*head*, you. . . ." He slammed down the phone and stormed back into Peggy's office just as she was calling Buck.

Rockwell collapsed onto the couch. His old, wrinkled face folded over itself like an old hound dog, and he began to bite his lower lip. He'd get something out of Lee when he got here. They owed him.

* * *

"Hi, Peggy, has the old coach been waiting long?"

"He's been waiting about thirty minutes, and he sounds a little angry. He's in your office now," Peggy said from behind a big wooden desk with at least four empty coffee cups on it. She drank too much coffee and smoked far too many cigarettes, as the full ashtrays indicated.

"Old coaches never die. They just hang around and criticize," Buck said.

"How could you say that, Coach? He's a nice old man."

"So was Adolf Hitler." Buck laughed as he opened the door to his office and went in to greet Noble Rockwell.

"How are you, Coach Rockwell? You look great. Have you been playing a lot of golf?"

"Well, I feel OK, I guess, but my arthritis has been acting up and it's been bothering my golf swing."

"So how's Ethelyn, Coach?"

"Fine, but a little under the weather. We've been bird hunting down in Georgia the past two weeks. Had a great time. We flew down in the Cornwell's plane. They haven't forgotten what I did for the school like a lot of people have. They're great friends."

While Rockwell continued to ramble on about how no one was giving him any money now and how all he did for the school had been forgotten, Buck was making a few notes:

Get some pictures for the office.

Put purple carpet on the floor with a big rattler in the middle.

Get a stereo. Soul music for the black prospects, country for the whites.

After Rockwell got into his football career and how half of the big-time coaches were still using his playbook, Buck finally got a little bored. He stepped on the emergency button underneath the desk, which alerted Peggy: *Save me, I'm trapped*. His phone rang. It was

Peggy. "You've got an appointment in five minutes. You better hustle."

"Thanks, Peggy. Coach, I have to go now. My secretary just reminded me that I have an appointment in five minutes."

In the most pitiful voice Buck had ever heard, Rockwell said, "Before you go, could you ask Sarge if he has any old socks left over I could have?"

"You know we're always glad to help out one of our great coaches. I'll have Peggy call Sarge as soon as he returns. He's in a meeting right now."

Buck watched the skinny body with bony legs leave the office. "Can you believe that man?" he asked Peggy. "In all the years he was the head coach here, he never once put on a dirty pair or even a used pair of socks. Everything he wore was brand-new." Peggy looked mildly impressed. "Anyway, call down to the equipment room and leave word for Sarge to give him his new socks."

Buck started to leave when he remembered the cute little blonde he had met at one of his speeches. She had offered to help with recruiting, and Buck wasn't turning down any help — especially beautiful help. "Peggy, get a hold of Cathy what's-her-name and tell her that I'd like for her to come by the office next week. You set up the time around my schedule."

"Coach, I don't know who you're talking about. What does she do?" Peggy's question was in that female tone of voice which says, *She better not be intruding on my territory*.

"She's the one who's putting together the forty-five beautiful gals for us to help with recruiting. I sent you a note about her. Take care of it, Peg, I'm back to the salt mines."

* * *

When Buck returned to the meeting room, he saw Hyspick wearing his coaching gear and a gigantic, brown leather, weight-lifter's belt. His windbreaker was soaked with sweat, and his face was pinkish from lifting. He must have just arrived. Dr. Trousdale sat beside him. Even though he hated the idea of being in the same room with all the coaches, he did so because he loved being academic counselor to all that meat. Buck always knew when Trousdale was in the meeting room because he could smell him.

"What's going on?" asked Buck. "Talking recruiting?"

"I was just showing the pass-blocking technique I used at CSU," said Dave Barton. "I was just lining up the coaches so we could have a little half-speed blocking to demonstrate my point."

"You know what half-speed blocking is to coaches. It's like saying, 'I'm only going to put it in half-way.' So, let's get on back to our recruiting and forget the blocking."

"That's my point," said Barton. "This *does* have to do with recruiting. I was telling Ignarski that the way we teach line blocking, the little guys he's recruiting wouldn't have a chance."

"I'll tell you what you do, Barton. You put down that can you're spitting tobacco into and we'll have us another little one-on-one," Ignarski growled.

Everyone looked at Buck. He didn't want this rivalry to get out of hand, but a little competition was good for the soul. "All right, we'll do it, but let's just *demonstrate*. Nothing full speed."

The room became a madhouse. Tables were pushed out of the way, chairs were set up on top of the tables, and all the coaches got themselves into positions to watch — except Trousdale. He was trying to sneak out the door. Physicality made him uneasy.

"Hyspick, don't let Dr. Trousdale leave. I want to talk to him when we get through," said Buck. Hyspick grabbed Trousdale and gleefully pushed him right out front so he wouldn't miss a lick.

"The first thing is the type of pass block I'm talking about," said Barton. "It's called the Rooster Block. What you do is drop back like this." He jumped backwards and started flapping his arms and hands like a rooster would its wings.

"Before you go any further with your Rooster technique, Coach Barton, somebody call up Sarge and tell him to bring over two headgears. I don't want anybody to get hurt," said Buck. "This Rooster Block looks dangerous to me. Go ahead, Coach."

"OK. After you assume the fighting rooster position, you then retreat and absorb the rusher with your body." Dave demonstrated what he meant by sticking out his chest and gut with his arms still flapping.

Before Ignarski could respond, Sarge appeared in the doorway with the headgears. He handed one each to Barton and Ignarski and backed up against the wall.

As the two coaches pulled the helmets over their ears, Chuck Driscoll volunteered to give the snap count. "The snap is on two. I'll call out hut-one, hut-two. Let me know when you're ready."

"I'm ready," Dave said as he buckled his chin strap and got into a three-point stance.

"I can't get this goddamn thing over my ears," said Ignarski, struggling with the headgear. Finally, he got the helmet down to where it covered his ears. Buck had to refrain from laughing at Ignarski: headgear too small, sweatpits under his arms, his shirttail hanging out, his white socks down over his shoes, and hair growing from every square inch of skin.

Driscoll called out, "Are we ready?"

"I've *been* ready," said Barton.

"Bet your ass I'm ready," said Ignarski as he put both of his hairy hands down on the floor in a four-point stance.

"On the second hut."

"Hut-one, hut-*two*."

Barton came out of his stance and assumed the rooster position. His arms were flapping in the breeze, and his feet were going crazy. Ignarski was off on the snapcount like a cat. His headgear hit Dave right on the chin. Ignarski's force, plus the headgear striking Dave where he had no protection, straightened Barton up. He stumbled backward and fell over the table, where he landed upside down with his feet sticking up in the air like a dead bug. The room roared with laughter.

As Kyle and Driscoll helped their fallen comrade to his feet, Ignarski strutted around the room. "You can take that Rooster Block or whatever you call it and stick it up your ass."

Dave pulled off the headgear, fluffed up his curly hair, and wiped the blood off his chin where the top of Ignarski's headgear had hit him. He glared at Ignarski and didn't say a word. Buck knew that this battle wasn't really over.

"Let's continue on with the meeting, now that we've had our fun," Buck said, clapping his hands together in a loud pop.

"Anything you want to say, Sarge? I know you've got to get back."

"Coach, there are couple of problems in the equipment room."

"Go ahead, Sarge."

"The first thing, Coach, is the players. Instead of putting their wet jocks in the laundry bags I assign them, they throw them at me as I walk down the corridor." The coaches resisted the urge to make any smart-ass comments. Sarge had power. If he didn't like you, he would hand you the worst socks, jocks, or shoes.

"I'll talk with them about that, Sarge. Anything else?"

"Yes, sir, Coach. You know that cute little girl, the assistant manager? She's causing some morale problems."

"What's she doing, screwing the wrong guy or something?"

"Nothing like that, Coach. You know I assigned her to give out the clean socks and jocks to all the players. Every time a player asks for a clean jock, she asks, 'What size?'" There were a few snickers in the room.

"Seems like a fair question to me," Buck said.

"But when they say extra-large or large, she says, 'You look more like a small or petite to me.' The players don't think that's funny."

"I think that's pretty funny, Sarge, but then she hasn't handed me a small jock. I'll talk to her. Thanks, Sarge. Dr. Trousdale, do you have anything to add to our recruiting meeting?" asked Buck.

"Coach Lee, being the academic counselor here at Eastern is probably the most important job in the athletic department. Since I became the academics counselor twelve years ago, we have done extremely well in graduating our athletes. Our students have always done well in the classroom." Trousdale loved what he had just said. He pushed his glasses down a notch on his imperialistic Roman nose and fingered his graying mustache. When no one spoke, he continued. "We must bring in the best students we can. I can work with only so many nincompoops," he lisped. Still, no one said anything. Trousdale had a captive audience and he wasn't about to stop. "Our job here at the university is to educate the student-athlete. Dr. Clarke Lowe has made that very clear at the faculty meetings I have attended. That, according to Dr. Lowe, should be the first and uppermost thing on our mind in the athletic department."

"*Doc*-tor Trousdale," Buck said with a touch of sarcasm, "we all want our students to graduate. That includes jocks, non-jocks, everybody who attends this *greaaat* institution. But they do not hire football coaches to graduate student-athletes. Coaches are hired to win football games." Buck decided to pause for a minute to see if Trousdale had any rebuttal. The bookworm looked as uneasy as a man playing a $100 Nassau in golf when he had only $20 in his pocket. His big Adam's apple was going up and down.

Buck continued. "I can just see them calling me up before the athletic board next year and Dr. Clarke Lowe saying, 'Coach Lee, we know that you won only one game and lost ten last year, but you did graduate ninety-nine percent of your players. Since your job is to graduate the student-athlete, we're going to give you a new five-year contract.'" Buck let that settle in before he went on. "Now, I can just hear Dr. Lucious Richardson, the president at Western, say 'Coach Shavers, we know you won eleven games last year, but we cannot renew your contract because you graduated only forty percent of your student-athletes.' Anybody who believes that horseshit believes the Fairy Godfather put the money under your pillow when you left your first tooth there." Buck could see the academic counselor starting to squirm. He wasn't accustomed to the earthy language that coaches used.

By now all the coaches were smiling, and the academic man was trying to find a way to get out. He stood up and pulled his stained, sweaty trousers away from his buttocks. His glasses had fallen almost off his nose, due to the sweat pouring down his face.

"One last thing, Dr. Trousdale, and then you're excused. We cannot field a team if they're ineligible. We cannot win if the great and good players are not eligible. The thing I want you to remember is this: If I get it, so do you. The coach who replaces me will know from me that you were the reason I got it."

Trousdale thanked everyone for allowing him the time, and he promised that he was going to work with them in any way he could. He stepped out the door and sprinted down to his office. He needed a Valium. All the coaches smiled.

"Coach Hyspick," Buck said, "when can we get our off-season program started?" Hyspick stood there with his feet spread apart, hands on his hips, and a toothpick in his mouth. He felt good. He was going to run the toughest program in America. "Coach, I plan on running the off-season program just like I would run boot camp. I believe that I became a born-again Christian so I would have the strength to drive these players beyond their limits. This commitment to Christ will not only make me strong on the field, but off the field as well." Hyspick moved his hands away from his hips and started waving them in front of himself like a preacher. "I want nothing but good Christian boys playing for me. Before they can really go out on the field and knock the shit out of somebody, they have to have faith in the Lord." Hyspick was slobbering out of both sides of his mouth. The pupils of his eyes were dilating, and his breath was getting shorter.

"Excuse me for interrupting," Buck said, "but can't a Jew, a Muslim, or maybe even an atheist play if he, as you say, will knock the shit out of some cocksucker wearing the other team's colors? I mean, the Muslim might not go to your same heaven, but we ain't playing football to find out who goes to heaven. We're playing to send the other team to hell."

"Well, I know what I believe, and we're going to get after some candy-asses if they don't shape up."

"Sit down, Coach. We're all looking forward to your off-season program." Buck's jock itch was beginning to burn again. He needed a break.

* * *

Jack Stone thumbed through the twenty-five pages of computer printouts that each coach had in front of him. Buck had turned the meeting over to him with the responsibility of teaching the other members of the staff how to pick up the phone and find out personal information about a prospect.

"I've picked out one of your prospects, Ignarski: Clarence 'Chopper' Ursey. Now listen to what I do so each one of you can switch off with another. You have to let someone else call your prospects for you. *Never* call your own unless you're using your own name."

Jack dialed 407-653-7850 direct. While waiting for someone to answer, he switched on the call box so everyone could hear. Finally, after five or six rings, a woman answered the phone.

"Is this Mrs. Ursey?"

The voice came back loud and clear, and obviously irritated. "Yes, what can I do for you?"

"Mrs. Ursey, this is Robert Walsh, sports editor of *Tops Magazine*. We want to talk to Clarence and get his reaction to being picked on our all-America team."

The tone of her voice changed immediately. "I'm sorry I sounded so irritable, Mr. Walsh, but these coaches have been calling here day and night, and I'm just tired of it. I know Clarence will be glad to talk to you. I'll go get him."

While Jack waited for Chopper to come to the phone, he looked over the information sheet to see what kind of questions he wanted to ask.

"Hello, this is Chopper."

"Chopper, you've been selected as an offensive tackle on the *Tops Magazine* all-America team. We'd like to ask you a few personal questions for the article that'll come out this fall."

"Go ahead. I'm ready."

"First of all, have you made up your mind as to which school you're going to attend?"

"I haven't made up my mind yet, but I do have it narrowed down to three schools — USC, Boston University, and East Alabama."

"Chopper, what will be the biggest factor in your decision — education, summer job, location of the school, the head coach, or the opportunity to play?"

"All those things are important, especially the education, but I've been told I can get an education any place. So I'd say the most important thing in my decision will be the helmets."

"Why the helmets, Chopper?"

"I've just always had a thing for them. When I used to watch games on television, I loved the Air Force Academy helmets. They were great. If I had the grades, I'd go there."

"That's interesting. Now, who will be most important in helping you make your decision?"

"I have all the respect in the world for my parents, and I'll certainly sit down and talk with them before I do anything, but Willie Bean, who runs the pool hall, has been my inspiration, and he and I'll sit down and discuss my decision before I accept the final offer."

"Chopper, I know this is a little personal, but our readers would like to know. Do you have a girlfriend?"

"No, sir. I just lift weights and play football. I don't have time for no girl."

"Thanks a lot, Chopper. Our readers will be happy to get an inside look at a future star of the NFL. Oh, by the way, we got your name and recommendation from the East Alabama Rattlers. Coach Buck Lee said you were one of the top players in America."

"Thanks a lot, Mr. Walsh, I'm real happy to be on the *Tops* all-American team."

Jack hung up, looked at the coaches and said, "Three schools, his pool hall chum is important, he loves headgears, and he's got no girl. But the big thing is that I told him Coach Lee recommended him. He'll love that. Now do you lamebrains see how it's done?"

6

REMEMBER, GALS, OUR JOB is to help the Rattlers in recruiting," Cathy said to the forty-five beautiful young ladies who had been selected as Rattlerettes. Cathy was what every college football program needed: an effervescent, well-endowed cheerleader who dropped by each week to see what new prospects were coming in. Her father, grandfather, and all her relatives on both sides of the family had attended Eastern, and she absolutely hated every other school in the country.

Cathy's recruiting contribution was to keep a working list of equally gifted, dedicated, bubbly coeds who could be called on when a prospect was in town and needed a date for a home game. Every sixteen- or seventeen-year-old wanted a date with one of these self-sacrificing young ladies. The prospect, whether he was a narrow-hipped, Greek god or a three-hundred-pound hog molly, went home with a hangover, a hard-on, and hopefully a favorable emotional experience.

"You all know the reason that you've been selected," Cathy told them. "There are no A-cups in this group. Our criterion for selection was what we thought would help most in recruiting, and T and A came out No. 1. Ladies, pay attention and quit giggling. I know y'all are excited, but there's a game plan for everything we do, so let's go over ours."

She reached into her pocketbook and pulled out a list of questions. Putting on her glasses, she began to read.

"One: How close should you dance with a prospect? The answer is, close enough for him to feel your tits and just a touch of your belly. But whatever you do, don't do any belly-rubbing.

"Two: Should you ever sleep with a prospect? Answer, no. Promise him you will when he comes to school.

"Three: Should you ever place your hand on a prospect's leg?"

Cathy looked around at her gals and then went back to her sheet. "Yes, but don't leave it there for more than ten seconds. Anything longer creates anxiety, but anything less creates interest."

"Cathy," came a voice from the back, "I've got a question. What if he takes my hand and tries to put it on his you-know-what?" The whole room hooted and whistled.

"Here's what the book says. Let him do it like you're not paying attention. Then when you feel it, jerk your hand away. Then before he can say anything, whisper in his ear, 'I'm not ready yet, Steve. But where did you get that elephant trunk?' They'll eat it up."

More whistling. "Right on, Cathy, right on!"

"Ladies, that was just a sample of what you have to learn. You'll receive a copy of this book that answers all your questions, and you'll be quizzed at our next meeting."

Cathy stopped pacing and stood in front of her gals. She folded her arms across her size-forty chest and gave her closing statement.

"Rattlerettes, there is one thing about football that never changes: Everybody recruits — alumni, students, wives, faculty, they all pitch in to help, or try to help you do your job. It's probably the only profession in the world that has complete strangers trying to help you sell your product. Vacuum cleaner salesmen sure as hell don't have total strangers calling their sales prospects long distance just to tell them that your model was terrific and Hoover's sucks. So don't overlook a single resource. And remember, we take orders but we don't deliver."

Cathy held her index finger up in the air, and the Rattlerettes chanted with her, "We're number one! We're number one!" Forty-five of Eastern Alabama University's finest, tits and asses flying into the fray, prepared to give almost their all for their beloved Rattlers.

7

DON'T FORGET, COACH LEE," Peggy said as Buck was about to leave the office, "you and Mrs. Lee are supposed to go with Coach Ignarski to Prattville tonight. It's the Frick boy. Coach Ignarski says he's a good one."

"I've never seen a coach with a bad one at this time of the year."

"Well, anyway, Coach Ignarski said he'd pick you up in his truck about six o'clock."

"I wish we had something to go in besides a pickup truck. This kid can't be that country."

Peggy flipped through her notes, found the right page, and read: "Warner Frick, nickname, 'Bush Hog'. Lives on a forty-acre farm. Wants to study veterinarian medicine. Hates big cities."

"That settles it," Buck said. "It's gonna be an hour and a half of dodging the rifle rack and breathing Ignarski's cigar smoke. I'll see you tomorrow. Have a nice evening."

Buck walked down the front steps of the athletic building, tossing his keys up in the air. He was in a good mood and felt confident that East Alabama would have its best recruiting year ever. As he opened his car door and slid under the wheel, he found himself humming the school fight song. *Go, go, fight; The Rattler's going to strike*. Buck had made up a second verse and sang the words out loud as he put the key in the ignition. *Go, go Buck; Those Hawks they really suck*. Just as he was about to start the engine, a hand reached through the window and tapped him on the shoulder. Buck gasped and jumped halfway to the passenger's seat.

"Coach Lee! It's me, Richard Culpepper! I'll be glad to drive you to Prattville tonight."

"Jeessuuss Christ, Richard! Do you really want to kill me?" Buck was breathing hard and had one hand clutching his thumping heart.

"Sorry, Coach. I didn't mean to. . . ."

"Holy shit, man!" Buck shouted. "No, you *can't* drive me anywhere, but if you do this one more time, one of us is going to be driving the other to the hospital. Now go home, if you have one."

The big Ford screeched away from the curb, leaving Richard Culpepper standing in the street with a confused look on his face. As Buck sped down beautiful tree-lined Hanson Avenue, he imagined he heard Rod Serling's voice narrating his life. "Submitted for your approval: Buck Lee, ordinary football coach at an ordinary college, walks to his car and. . . ." He felt just like a character in an old episode of "The Twilight Zone," where the same mysterious character is standing on every street corner watching him drive by. In this case, the enthusiastic face of Richard Culpepper was popping up routinely, begging for a job.

Pulling into the driveway of their new home, Buck noticed the large garbage can sitting by the garage door. He'd forgotten to take it to the curb so the garbage men would pick it up. He got out, grabbed the can, and rolled it to the corner. Opening the side door to the house, Buck entered the kitchen where Gail was fixing dinner.

"I can't believe Bear Bryant had to take out the garbage," he told her.

Leaning forward and kissing Buck on the head, she said, "You won't have to take out the garbage, either, if you win all your games."

"You can help me, my pet, by putting on your best country, Southern drawl tonight. We're going down into the boonies to see if we can't get a commitment out of a big hog-molly tackle. Name's Warner Frick."

"Damn it, Buck, you know how hard it is for me to talk country. I've done pretty well for a girl from California, learning to talk Southern, but country is hard."

"You'll be OK. Just go get some clothes on that won't show too much skin," Buck said, patting Gail's bottom. "How 'bout that high-neck sweater, the one that's a size too big, frumpy, drab colored, but dignified? Tonight you're a hook, not a hooker. Don't wear anything that'll get the kid excited. Save that for the star quarterback. And remember to smile benignly while I'm giving my dissertation on how much an education will benefit this poor little underdeveloped hog molly."

"Hey," said Gail, "I've played this part before. I know how to knit brows and purse lips to show how deadly earnest we are about his education. I've listened to your bullshit so long, I know all the cues. When you say he can get the best education at Eastern, I nod constantly while looking at mother. When you say we have the best School of Veterinary Medicine, I look at the boy and start nodding."

"You wrote the book. Now go get dressed."

"One question before I do that. Is this school *really* the one with the best education? You said that at the last three schools we worked at. Tell me," she cooed, "which school *really* is the best?"

"Oh, shut up, and get those cookies you made. I want to show how domestic you are. And tell our sweet sixteen-year-old daughter to call you about 8:30."

"But we don't have a sixteen-year-old daughter, Buck. We don't even have a daughter."

"Big deal. Just get Harriet Ignarski to call. I want Mrs. Frick to know you're a mother and you're making a great sacrifice to visit them."

* * *

Ignarski was proud of his family and his home. For someone who had been brought up in poverty and made it in football to the rank of assistant coach in college, life was good. He carefully put on his purple and white checked pants that the school had given him to wear to the games and on recruiting trips. He slipped into his white, button-down shirt and carefully tied the purple tie with the white rattler on it with a big Windsor knot. His penny loafers were the last piece of clothing that he normally put on, because he always had a hard time deciding on socks. He liked the white socks, but everybody made fun of them, so he settled on robin's-egg blue.

"Harry, you'd better hurry!" Harriet Ignarski yelled from the kitchen. "It's almost six o'clock."

"I'm coming," he yelled from the bathroom. "Soon as I put some wax on my hair."

Harriet put down her *National Enquirer*, opened another beer, and walked back to the bathroom to watch her husband put the finishing touches on his flattop. Her favorite thing, though, was watching Harry shave. It made her feel all warm inside to see him remove his heavy beard with a safety razor and splash on half a bottle of Old Spice. It was about a thirty-minute operation, since Ignarski had to shave his entire neck and change blades once. Harriet smiled and helped Harry on with the purple blazer.

"Where you got to go tonight, and why can't I go with you? I'm tired of being cooped up in here all day with five little Polacks."

"Kid down in Prattville. Gail Lee is going, and you know you can't go when the head coach's wife goes. Anyway, honey, one woman is enough."

Harry put his arm around his wife, and they walked out the front door of their mobile home. "This boy is a real stud, and I've been recruiting him all year," Ignarski told her. "I mean, he's really got some humongous pecks on him. And his dang legs are fantastic. Great wheels. We've got to sign him."

"Harry, I wish you wouldn't talk like that around the house."

"Like what? What do you mean?"

"Oh, you know, stuff like, 'He's a stud,' or 'He's got a great butt.' Things like that. Your son's friends all kid him about his dad talking about men the way other men talk about women. They called you a fag."

Ignarski didn't say anything for a moment. He opened the door of his muddy GMC, climbed inside, and kissed Harriet on the mouth. Then he made a fist and rammed it into the roof of the cab. "You tell Rocky that his old man didn't have five kids being no faggot." Ignarski pumped the gas, started the big motor in the jacked-up, four-wheel-drive truck, and roared down the dirt driveway. Harriet waved good-bye and killed the last swallow of warm beer.

* * *

When Buck heard the horn, he looked out the living-room window and saw Ignarski's truck idling in the driveway. Right on the money. Six o'clock sharp. "Let's go, Honey!" Buck yelled. In seconds, Gail was bounding down the steps, ready to go. She grabbed her purse, gave her hair one last check in the hall mirror, and they left for Prattville.

"Harry, tell me some more about Warner," Buck said, turning down the volume on the truck radio. Merle Haggard was blasting out of the tiny speaker, and for the first five minutes of the trip, Gail sat with her hands cupped over her ears. Buck liked country music and loved Merle Haggard, but it was time to get down to business. "I know what you said in the coaches' meeting," Buck said, "but I need to know all I can."

"Coach, he's a great kid. He's a little *pus*-ey at this time, but he'll grow into his skin. I've seen him take a man on the wrestling mat and almost maim him. He's been the state wrestling champion for the last two years. His father passed away, he has no brothers or sisters, and his mother works in the mill."

Gail spoke up. "Before I take a nap and leave you two gentlemen to your discussion, would you please tell me what the word '*pus*-ey' means?"

"*Pus*-ey, like what comes out of a boil," said Buck. "Soft and mushy. Better yet, he looks like an overweight toad."

"Thank you. Now I can rest. Wake me when we get there."

As the truck whizzed by the last Pack'n'Shop and out past Alabama farm houses, Ignarski asked about the progress with Eaarnel.

"I don't know how we're doing," said Buck, "because the whole world's recruiting him. I'd guess it's down to us and the Hawks. I don't know who'll get him, but you can bet on one thing — he's like a gorgeous woman; whoever gets her might be old and ugly or young and handsome, but he *won't* be poor."

Ignarski whipped out a big cigar, smoked up the cab of the truck, nodded knowingly, and in fifty-five minutes they were nearing the city limits of Prattville.

"Harry," said Buck, "I need to know the big answer on Warner before we get there. How do we stand on him? What are our chances? Can we sign him tonight?"

"Coach, if you put the hat on his head tonight, I believe we can sign him. He's a big boy who doesn't want to go too far from his mama."

"I'll romance him for awhile, but then I'm going to put the question to him. If he says no, I'll give him a day or two to make up his mind."

With the game plan settled, Ignarski turned the truck down a country road and headed for the Frick farm. Gail woke up, fixed her face, and got ready for the recruiting game.

As they turned into the long drive leading to a slightly dilapidated, two-story Victorian house, Buck remembered one of his most important questions.

"They don't have dogs, do they?"

"Oh, big baby," said Gail, winking at Ignarski. "We won't let the dog bite you. We promise, don't we Coach Ignarski?"

"Yeah, we'll choke him or something. Or blast away with my sixteen-gauge."

"Now look, Ignarski, I'm serious."

"Just kidding, just kidding," he said. "I've been here at least four times and ain't seen a dog yet."

"Ignarski, the last time you told me that, I spent half the night trying to get out of the car, while a boxer the size of a Toyota clawed all the paint off the doors."

They pulled up in front of the house, and Buck stepped cautiously out of the truck. As they approached the front steps, a Pekingese came charging across the yard yapping and slobbering all over itself. Buck jumped behind Gail and used her as a shield against the attacker. Gail pulled away, and Buck sprinted toward a station wagon propped up on blocks under a big oak tree. He leaped onto the hood of the car only a half-step ahead of the snapping jaws of the little dog. Ignarski couldn't believe his eyes and turned away to laugh. Gail walked over and petted the yapping Pekingese on the head.

The screen door of the house swung open, and Mrs. Frick and Warner, her hulking son, stood in the doorway with their mouths open. Buck threw up his hand toward the Fricks and said, "How are y'all, Mrs. Frick? Warner? I'm Buck Lee and that's my wife Gail, and of course y'all know Coach Ignarski already."

"Nice to meet you, Coach Lee," said Mrs. Frick as she dried her hands on her apron and stared at the famous coach seated on the hood of their Country Squire. "You having some problems?"

"Come here, Tammy, come here right now," Warner sang in his falsetto voice. "Bad dog, bad dog."

Tammy ran to Warner at the bottom of the steps, leaped into his leg-sized arms, and licked him all over his pimply face. "You can come on down now, Coach Lee," said Warner, wiping the dog slobber from his nose and mouth. Buck thought the kid looked like Baby Huey with his sleeves ripped off. "Well, I don't think she likes me, Warner. I'd feel better if you just locked her up somewhere." Ignarski took Tammy from Warner and dropped her over the fence. Buck climbed down from the hood of the car and walked over to formally meet the Fricks.

Mrs. Frick was about 5′ 2″, weighed at least 170 pounds, and was wearing a floral muumuu under her apron. Omar the Tent-Maker must be her dress designer, Buck figured. The big flip-flop sandals she wore looked comfortable on her swollen feet. She was so excited to have company that her bear hug almost crushed Gail's chest.

Gail presented Mrs. Frick with the cookies she had bought at Nina's, the best bakery in Stanleyville. "I made these just for you and Warner, Mrs. Frick. I hope you enjoy them."

"Thank you so much," gushed Mrs. Frick. "But I'm on a diet. I'll just save them for Warner."

"Let's, ah, go in the house," said Warner, wiping the sweat off his nose. "Hot out here, ain't it?"

They all shuffled into the living room of the big farmhouse, where all the furniture had been covered in plastic slipcovers. As Buck took his seat beside Gail on the sofa, he began to smell something that resembled the zoo. He looked at Gail to see if she was reacting to the smell, but she was too busy into motherhood with Mrs. Frick to see Buck's face squinch up.

"Coach Lee," said Warner as he sat on the floor, "if you don't like dogs, how about cats? Mama collects stray cats. We've got about eight."

Buck instantly recognized the odor. Two of the big alleys jumped up on the back of the sofa, and two more appeared right behind his head. The odor grew stronger. Buck had to do something to take his mind off the smell. "So, ah, Warner, ah, what did you enjoy most about your high school career?" he asked.

"Coach, I really enjoyed my wrestling career. I didn't lose one single match in high school. I beat everyone . . . except at the Tri-State, but that don't count. I lost to the champion from Georgia."

Buck looked over at Ignarski, whose face was the color of milk of magnesia. The smell obviously was getting to him, too. Gail was still carrying on with Mrs. Frick about how if her boy came to Eastern, she would have a home away from home.

"Let me see your favorite hold, the one you used to win all those matches," Buck said. Just as Buck started to get down on the floor with Warner, Ignarski made a beeline for the front door, saying he had left something in the truck. Buck felt the same urge. "Before you show me that hold, I guess you better show me the men's room. It's been a long trip."

"All the way to the back, Coach," said Warner. "Hang a left when you get to the deer on the wall."

Buck quickly surveyed the living room as he made his exit, looking for telltale signs like calendars, pictures, or programs from other schools. He walked slowly down the hallway, inspecting as much of the house as he could. It was a well-kept house, except for the cat smell, with plenty of antique furniture. In the hallway were several framed photographs of Warner as a baby. He was the ugliest baby Buck had ever seen. Little Warner's head was shaped like a watermelon and approximately the same size. Buck faked a left at the deer, walked into the adjacent bedroom instead, and took the phone off the hook. He didn't want any other schools calling while he was there. After cracking a window and breathing a little fresh air, Buck joined the others in the living room. Warner was passing around fried chicken livers and potato chips. Buck diplomatically took a handful of each.

"Now offer Mrs. Lee and Coach Ignarski some, Warner," said Mrs. Frick in her kind, soft voice. Warner obliged, but Ignarski remembered something else he'd left in the truck.

Gail pulled out the picture of their son, Buck, Jr., and passed it to Mrs. Frick, who raved about his dimples and then handed it to Warner. But Warner already had Buck in his famous hold, the "Bush Hog Strangle." Warner finally released him, and Buck returned to his seat on the sofa beside Gail, who was putting Bucky's picture back in her purse. Then Buck was up again. "Excuse me one more time, but I've got to go to the men's room to fix my tie. After being pinned by the state champion, I need to clean up."

Buck went into the bathroom and splashed cold water on his face.

Maybe that will help kill the smell, he thought. He wiped himself off with a Holiday Inn towel and tiptoed across to the phone in the bedroom. He looked at his notebook and turned to the dog-eared page with Eaarnel's number at the top. He sat down on the four poster bed and dialed the number on his credit card.

"How are you, Mrs. Simpson? This is Coach Buck Lee. Coach Buck Lee from Eastern. Coach B-U-C-K L-E-E. Yes'm, that's right. Is Eaarnel there? Oh? Well, you just tell him I called. Yes, ma'am." Buck left the phone off the hook and went back into the living room. Ignarski had returned, but instead of a milky color, he was now ashen.

"Coach Lee," Mrs. Frick asked as Buck took his place on the sofa, "Mrs. Lee couldn't answer this question, so will you?"

"I'll try, Mrs. Frick. Shoot."

"You don't use the scramble block, do you? I don't want Warner to get his hand stepped on, scrambling around on the ground. You know it would hurt his wrestling. But in case you didn't know, he's also a great shot-putter."

"Watch out, Coach!" yelled Warner. "That big yellow cat is right behind you, and he almost tore my arm off the other night."

Buck froze. He just sat there while Warner slowly walked over and knocked the big yellow cat off the sofa. Buck's crotch started itching; his nerves were just about shot.

"Mrs. Frick," he said, looking for the cat, "I can assure you that we do not use the scramble block. Anyone as big as your son should not block low. He should block high. That's why we have Coach Smith as our line coach. He knows all the pro techniques, and he'll help your son make the pros."

"That's a relief. Oh, would y'all like a cup of coffee or a Coke?"

"No, thank you, ma'am. I'm fine. What we need to talk about is whether or not Warner is ready to become a Rattler and wear the Purple," Buck said, turning his eyes from Mrs. Frick to her son. "Warner, you can help make us champions. We need you, so make Coach Ignarski happy, my wife happy, our kids and me happy by saying you're going to be one of us."

Ignarski didn't look happy, but it wasn't from Warner's impending decision. "I need a little more time," mumbled Warner.

"Warner, we've offered more scholarships than we have available.

So, you think about it. I'm going to leave Coach Ignarski down here until you sign. He'll stay here if it takes forever. We want you."

Ignarski looked faint. Warner swelled up like a big toad as he and his mother led Buck and Gail to the door. Ignarski told the Fricks that he'd be back as soon as he dropped off the Lees at the car rental place.

* * *

"Goddammit, operator, I've been calling this number for two hours. Somebody must have taken the fucking phone off the hook . . . Well, go ahead and report my ass for bad language. I'm going to report you for *incompetence* . . . Who *am* I? I'm Coach Buddy Shavers, and I've been trying to get a hold of this number in Prattville. It's been busy and all you say is the phone is off the hook . . . Oh, it's the supervisor now, is it? Well, you listen to me. You get a hold of somebody in Prattville and tell them the phone is off the hook at 964 Springdale Road. I want 'em to get over there right now and put the receiver back on . . . What do you mean, you can't do that, you asshole. I'll have your job for that . . . Well so is *your* mother."

Shavers slammed down the phone in his office. So, he thinks he can beat the master. We'll see about that, Shavers thought. He dialed Prattville again.

"Hello, is this the sheriff's office? I want to report a robbery at 964 Springdale Road . . . That's it, Sheriff, a robbery, and they've taken the phone off the hook . . . Just a concerned citizen. Bye."

* * *

As Ignarski headed back to the Fricks', he spotted the blinking red lights behind him. He couldn't believe he was being pulled over by some policeman from the City of Prattville. He wasn't even driving fast, and all the lights on his pickup truck were working. What could they want? He wished Coach Lee were with him, but he'd dropped him and Gail off at the U-Drive-It, and they were probably on their way home by now.

"Where you been, boy?" said the brawny, red-faced cop with a big chew of tobacco in his mouth. "Down robbing the Fricks' house?"

"I just came from there, Sheriff," Ignarski explained as he leaned against the truck. "Why? They have some trouble? I was just driving back over there."

"Hey, Frank," the deputy said, holding up an empty Pabst can. "There's about three cases of empties in this truck. You'd better give this boy a breath test and make him walk the line."

"Hey, wait now, fellas. . . ."

"OK, come on back to the patrol car and let's just see how many cold beers you've sucked down today."

"What do you mean?" shouted Ignarski. "Those cans have been in there for six months, you stupid son of a. . . ."

Before Ignarski could finish, the sheriff slipped out his handcuffs and ordered Ignarski to put his hands behind his back.

"What the hell's going on here?" Ignarski yelled as they snapped the cuffs around his furry wrists. "I'm a football coach, and I'm on my way to the Fricks' house. He's a boy we're after, and we want his ass to play football for us at East Alabama."

"Well, ain't that interesting," said the deputy. "I played *my* football at Western for the Hawks."

Ignarski tried to calm himself as the two lawmen pulled him into the car. "Boy, we just got a call that somebody was in the Frick house, and we got to check you out, so just you be quiet unless you want this stick up 'side yo' head."

Ignarski settled into the back seat as the patrol car headed down the dirt road toward the Frick house. Mrs. Frick isn't going to like this, he thought. No, not at all. Think fast, Harry, ol' buddy. Think fast. Yo' ass is mud.

8

PAT, THIS IS DAVE BARTON, assistant coach for the Rattlers. Coach Lee told me that you were going to do some work for us, and if I had anything I needed, you'd try to help."

Patrick Flanagan changed the phone from his right hand to his left in order to take notes. "Dave, I told him anything I could do that was in the spirit of fun and games, I'd do. What's up?"

"I don't even want you to tell Buck about this. We've got a coach on our staff who doesn't do crap in recruiting. He just lists names and positions but never goes by to check 'em out to see if they are bona fide players or not."

"Keep going."

"In the staff meeting, we gave him the name of a prospect who really doesn't exist. We told him that Tnassip was the finest running back in the country. Naturally, he acted like he knew all about him in front of Coach Lee. Now, here's what we want you to do. Pick up the phone and call Coach Larry Hildebrand and tell him you're an alumnus and you're going to help him with Tnassip. Tell him you'll call him every week and give him a scouting report. Fill him full of shit, but don't tell Buck. We want to surprise him."

"You're on," Pat said. He was having fun already. "When do we start?"

"We start today."

* * *

"Coach Shavers, this is The Raven."

"What the hell do you mean calling my house at eleven o'clock at night?"

"I've got some vital information. Tnassip is from somewhere in California. In one game last season, he not only rushed for over 200 yards, he also passed for another 150 when they put him in at quarterback."

"California boy, huh? Not a faggot, is he?"

"I'll call back next week with more information. Please send my check. I need the money. This is The Raven, signing off."

9

ON THE MORNING AFTER the visit with Warner Frick and his mother, Buck was sitting behind a desk piled high with WHILE-YOU-WERE-OUT messages, unopened mail, and eight-by-ten glossy photographs of himself to be signed. Hell, you're gone for half a day and it takes five days to catch up, he thought. He opened some of the mail — requests for tickets, half-legible, handwritten notes from well-meaning Rattler fans putting him onto hotshot prospects his coaches had never heard of, a scented note or two from women who'd been in the audience at Rattler banquets. After fifteen minutes, he couldn't take it anymore, so instead he started making notes for an afternoon staff meeting where he would discuss the off-season conditioning program. "Quit in the spring, not on the one-foot line against WAS . . . Character . . . Quitters never win. . . ." After Buck's meeting, the staff then would go to the players and explain exactly what was expected of them. Buck shuddered as he remembered how much he hated the off-season conditioning program when he was a player. All work, no glory. The phone buzzed and summoned him to the present.

"Yes, Peggy?"

"It's Coach Ignarski."

"Put him on."

"He's not on the phone. He's right here."

"What? Shit, he's supp. . . ."

Harry Ignarski cracked open the door. He was disheveled, wearing the clothes of the night before, unshaven, and he had the sheepish look of a little boy who'd been caught gaping at a *Playboy*. "Look, Buck, now look, Coach, I can explain everything."

"Harry, what in the hell are you doing here? You're supposed to be in Prattville."

"Wait, now," Ignarski said, "I can explain everything."

"Baby-sitting Frick. Hell, Harry. It better be good."

Ignarski, his baseball cap in his hands, slowly entered the office. He timidly took a chair against the wall, as far from Buck as he could get. With his head down, Harry told the whole story about the Prattville cops. The one who'd played at Western had found ways to detain him until midnight. His one phone call had been to his wife, who promised not to tell anybody, least of all Buck. The cops had made him sing the WAS fight song and chant "Buck Sucks" fifty times before they'd let him go. Then when he finally got back to his pickup, somebody had tied twenty Pabst cans to the bumper. As Ignarski finished his story, he raised his head to confront Buck's eyes for the first time. Buck was about to fall out of his chair laughing. Before he could catch his breath, in came Peggy and about half the coaching staff, who had heard Harry's tale when Buck slyly flipped on the intercom. Soon Buck Lee's office sounded like the laugh track from a television sit-com.

"Well, Harry, what . . ." Buck couldn't control his laughter. "Well, Harry, just exactly what'd they charge you with?"

"Aw, it wasn't nothing."

"But, surely, Harry, they had to charge you with *something*."

"Wasn't worth the paper he wrote it on."

"But what'd he write, Harry?" Buck's side was hurting.

"Where?"

"On the piece of paper. What's the citation for?"

Ignarski looked back down at the floor. "Being ugly."

* * *

As Buck entered the coaches' offices that afternoon, he stumbled into another stormy, name-calling meeting. Maybe it's healthy like this, he thought, remembering how hard each coach had fought for his favorite prospects. At least they give a damn. Every coach in the room was involved in the argument about whether the off-season program was important.

"Builds character, pure and simple."

"Bullshit, just gets rid of the ones who ain't got it."

"Mamas and papas build character. We *use* it."

"It can break the great ones. Damned near killed Namath."

"Yeah, it's the marginals it helps."

"If we're gonna have the program, then, why don't we just sign pissants?"

"All right, all right, that's enough," Buck shouted. The coaches plopped down in metal folding chairs and listened while Buck had his say. The way he saw it, he told them, the off-season program was as much a recruiting ploy as anything else. "It's the macho trip. In a way, we're using the players we already have for two purposes: One, they'll be staying in shape, sure, and maybe we find out some things about their guts that we don't know. Two, we'll have a lot of prospects watching every day. Every one of the little pissants wants to think he's the toughest man on the hill. So he can watch all the blood and guts he wants to, thinking it's a snap, and he'll love every minute of it. They'll love it while they're watching it. They won't love it so much next year."

"Well, hell, Coach," said Charlie Smith. "We got seventy-five of our own right here. I say screw the sideshow."

"Yeah," somebody else said, "looks like we're running another Parris Island."

"Blood," said Hyspick, who would run the program. "I want blood."

"OK, OK, let's cool it," said Buck. "I know where you're all coming from. I remember hearing Bear Bryant say at a coaches' convention one time, 'If a boy's gonna quit on me, I want him to quit in April; I don't want him quittin' me when it's fourth down and a foot with ten seconds to go against Auburn.' I'll buy that. I've got nothing against a good old ass-kicking spring conditioning program. But I'll tell you one thing: I can coach good players, but I can't do a damned thing with bad ones. *No* coach is that good at his job. Pat Flanagan says, 'In selling a piece of property, there are three important things: location, location, and location.' What I'm saying is, in coaching there are three important things: recruiting, recruiting, and recruiting."

Buck felt he had made his point. Johnny Hyspick would run a mean camp, and maybe a few of the marginal players would wash out. But he wanted to impress upon the coaches the added value of the off-season program — that it would be a recruiting tool, whereby recruits could see the level of talent, the training table, and the training room, as well as mingle with the current Rattlers and get a true feel of what it's like to be a Rattler. "Just don't bring in our two best quarterback prospects at the same time," Buck said, "because you're going to lose one of 'em. All right, let's do it."

Buck and his coaches left for the huge, tiered auditorium where nearly a hundred boys in all shapes and sizes were already gathered. Buck could see terror in the eyes of the players who knew what "off-season conditioning" meant. The seven-five Rattlers were supplemented by perhaps two dozen others who didn't have a prayer (although now and then a "walk-on" made it and even won a scholarship). Buck stood in front of the crowd and began his spiel, welcoming everybody and explaining how it was a "strictly voluntary" program. There were a few sniggers, and then a voice came hurtling down from the top row.

"What if we don't sign up?"

"Yeah," somebody else yelled, "do we get run off?"

Hyspick stepped to the microphone. "It's entirely voluntary."

"We don't *have* to do it?"

"It is an indication of your *attitude*, you *asshole*!" Hyspick was trying to restrain himself, but he wasn't doing a very good job of it. Buck stage-whispered, "Easy boy, easy."

"But what if we got labs and can't make it?"

"Yeah," said another, "I got a lab every afternoon."

Harry Ignarski, having survived his meeting with Buck and feeling as mean as ever, couldn't take it anymore. He grabbed the mike away from Hyspick and shouted his message: "You got any labs at 5:30 in the morning?" Silence. "Good. Dr. Ignarski will see you at four o'clock every afternoon. It's for your health."

Buck knew that the dissenters were most likely the slackers, the students, and that the seventy-five who were proven Rattlers wanted to win, wanted to benefit from the conditioning program. All they needed was direction and leadership. So after he had introduced the coaches, except for Hyspick, whom he saved for last since he would be in charge, Buck did his dance step.

"There are two kinds of people who play," he began. "There are those who play to win and there are those who are afraid to lose. People who play to win have fun and enjoy themselves while they're competing. They're not afraid to compliment the other person on a good play, because they recognize ability. They are the true competitors. Now, the person who is playing because he's afraid to lose is a terrible sport. He'll do anything to keep from losing. He'll cheat, he'll act like a baby, and he'll complain about everything."

Buck reached into his pocket and brought out a medal. It was from a box of Cracker Jack. "Men, this medal means more to me than any other medal I ever got. I won this for finishing third in a Golden Gloves tournament. Three buddies of mine went with me down to Memphis to fight in the state boxing championships. We were all pretty good in the little community we came from, so we decided to go on down to the big town." Buck held the medal up for all of them to get a quick look at. Just a flash. "We drew lots, and I was the first one to have to fight. I went into the ring with another 160-pounder. The only difference was his was a skinny 160 and mine was a pudgy 159. He knocked me down three times in the first round for a TKO. My other three buddies withdrew, and consequently I got third place."

Players slapped hands and punched one another on the shoulders as they laughed at Buck's story.

"I didn't think it was funny at the time, but the moral of that story is, you can't win or lose if you don't play. So, just so you'll understand the moral of that story, let me say that the purpose of our off-season program is to see who'll quit. We want you to quit now. We *don't* want you to quit in the fourth quarter next fall against the Hawks. DO YOU UNDERSTAND?" Buck screamed.

"HELL, YES!" was the answer.

With the place rocking and rolling now, Buck knew it was time to bring on his zealot, Johnny Hyspick. "Gentlemen, I'd like to introduce you to the man who'll be responsible for our off-season program, Coach Johnny Hyspick. Coach Hyspick, it's your show."

Hyspick got out of his chair very slowly. He stared at the squad for about five seconds, then suddenly screamed, "RATTLERS!" at the top of his lungs. In unison, the squad of seventy-five yelled back, "PRIDE!" Hyspick paused for effect. Then he screamed, "HAWKS!" In unison, the squad yelled, "SUCK!" Now the juices were flowing. Hyspick picked up his chair and smashed it against the wall. It splintered into little pieces. Then he picked up a football helmet, strapped it on, got a running start, and, with a banshee yell, stuck his head right through the wall. Of course, he had used a Hollywood stunt chair and had marked a spot on the wall where there was only sheetrock instead of studs. His act worked perfectly; the blood was up all over the room. Hyspick walked up to a frightened freshman, gave him the helmet, and said, "Butt me!" The frosh butted him right in the forehead, opening a small cut. Blood came down the middle of Hyspick's face and slowly dripped over his nose. When the animals saw it, they went into a full frenzy.

"You fucking pussy!" Hyspick shouted at the freshman. "Is that as hard as you can butt? You think the Hawks will hit like that? I'll tell you candy-asses one thing: Before we're through with you, you'll be in the best shape you've ever been in. No one will out-tough the Rattlers. RATTLERS!" screamed Hyspick.

"PRIDE!" yelled the mob.

As Hyspick strutted up and down in front of the squad in his tailored coach's shorts, Buck noticed a big bulge in his pubic area. Hyspick had stuffed a sock in his jock to give him a big look of masculinity. It was all part of the macho act.

Hyspick was preaching self-discipline to the crowd when suddenly he stopped and said, "How many of you prayed this morning? Hold up your hands." About twelve of the squad held up their hands. Before anyone could say anything, he began to pray: "Oh, great football coach in the sky, help those who cannot make it across the goal line of life to be strong. We ask thy help in making the Rattlers strong, so we can kick the shit out of the Hawks. For we ask it in Jesus' name. Amen."

Now it was time for Hyspick's finale. "I'll see you guys in the gym tomorrow at three in the afternoon. And don't be late." He turned and started for the door. There was a bucket at the end of the stage that Hyspick had placed there to kick as he walked past. It was great for effect — the bucket flying against the wall. But what he didn't know was that the other coaches had replaced the empty bucket with one filled with tar. It must have weighed twenty pounds. Hyspick kicked the bucket with his new white coaching shoes, expecting it to flying across the room, but it didn't move an inch.

"Son of a bitch! Cocksucker! I'll kill the motherfucker who did that!"

The coaches were rolling in laughter, but not one player even smiled as Hyspick limped out the door.

Buck moved to centerstage and said, "Coach Hyspick is right about prayer, so I want you all to pray for his toe tonight. OK, we'll begin tomorrow afternoon at three. One other thing: We'll be bringing by some of our prospects from time to time. We want y'all to help, so jump in and tell 'em what a great school we have."

* * *

As Buck walked back to his office, his mind a million miles away, a shadowy figure leaped from the bushes and landed right in front of him. Richard Culpepper had struck again.

"Dammit, Richard, you scared the crap out of me!" Buck yelled, trying to regain his composure.

"Coach Lee, I just want to work for you, that's all."

"Richard, I don't have a job for you now, but you can rest assured that when I do, I will certainly give you an interview. Now beat it."

As Richard disappeared around the corner, Buck could hear him saying, "Quitters never win, winners never quit. Quitters never win . . ." Buck felt his jock itch start to flare up again. He took the stairs to his office two at a time.

* * *

As Buck walked back into his office, his heart still racing from the encounter with Richard, Peggy followed him to his desk.

"Coach Lee, this nice young man has been waiting to see you for almost two hours. He says he is a representative of CALL."

"And what does CALL stand for, Peggy?"

"Christian Athletes Love Life. I know you're going to like his program for your players. He's so cute," she cooed.

"So bring him on in." The next thing Buck saw was a double-wide set of teeth. Behind the teeth followed a body that was covered by polyester.

"Coach Lee, I'd like to introduce myself. I'm Rusty Warren. I represent the organization CALL. I'm sure you've heard of us."

"Why certainly, Rusty. Have a seat." Buck had seen the Rusty Warrens of the world before — arrogant, self-righteous, and so sure they were right that they'd beat the devil out of you if you didn't agree with them.

Rusty slid his tight little body down on the sofa. He reached inside his briefcase and brought out several pamphlets. He put one on the coffee table and started to pass another to Buck.

"Just what is it you want me to do, Rusty?"

Stroking his wavy blond hair, Rusty said, "Coach Lee, our organization is based in Dallas, Texas, and what we try to do is to go by all the colleges in the country and sign up athletes for CALL. By the way, do you know what CALL stands for?"

"Of course, ah. . . ."

"Rusty. Rusty Warren. Rusty Warren of CALL."

Taking out what looked like about a hundred questionnaires from his briefcase, Rusty continued. "Coach Lee, I'd like for you to call a meeting of your squad so we can give out this questionnaire. It wouldn't take over an hour of their time, and we could do it right after dinner. I've got to catch a plane for Atlanta tonight."

Buck was irritated. This insipid Goody Two-Shoes thought if he came into the office and used the word *Christian*, Buck would stop everything and let him sign up players for some computer in Dallas.

"Rusty, I'd love to help you out, but I just can't."

"What do you mean, you *can't*?" asked Rusty. He rolled his eyes heavenward, as if searching for the lightning which surely would follow.

"I'll tell you why I can't. Last week the Muslims wanted to call a meeting, and I had to turn them down. The week before, the Jews wanted to have a meeting, and I refused their request, too. Now I hear the atheists want me to call a meeting so they can talk to our squad. Well, you know I can't do that, so I'm not going to call a meeting at all. It's just not my job to decide what religion a person should choose."

Rusty Warren's face flushed. "Do you mean that?"

"With all my heart."

"I'm deeply disappointed in you, Coach Lee."

"So's my mama."

"Well, last week Coach Shavers at West Alabama let us. . . ."

"Coach Shavers needs all the help he can get," said Buck. "Now look, you're testing my patience. If you want to sneak up on my players individually, I can't stop that. Be my guest. But I'm not in the business of saving souls. I'm in the business of saving my ass. Man of the turf, you might say, not a man of the cloth."

Rusty Warren of Christian Athletes Love Life knew where his friends weren't. He quickly gathered up his brochures and sped out of the football department, mumbling to himself. Buck stood in the outer office, beside Peggy's desk, and watched him leave. "One time when we got beat in college," he said to Peggy, "the other team's star told the press that they won because, 'The Lord was on *our* side.' I've been pissed ever since."

10

PEGGY, WOULD YOU COME into the office? I've got some telegrams and a letter to send." It had been a bad morning for Buck. Little Bucky had come home from school the day before with his clothes torn from fighting. The fact that Buck didn't get home from watching films in time to talk to the boy was bad news, according to Gail. Buck thought the bad news was that the kid had gotten the crap beat out of him. But the *worst* part of the whole thing was that once again Gail had gone to bed before he got home and left a chilly note: "I wouldn't trade you one twelve-year-old boy with a bloody nose," it read, "for seventy-five goons."

In the three months since coming to Eastern, Buck and Gail had begun to drift apart. As much as anything else, the problem was his absence at the supper table. They knew there was a growing problem, but they didn't quite know how to handle it. This was what they had always wanted — Buck Lee, Head Coach — but they were paying for it in recruiting trips, breakfast meetings, evening film sessions, speeches, and everything that went with the job.

"Coach Lee? Coach Lee? You with us?" It was Peggy with her note-pad.

"Oh, hi, Peg. Daydreaming again."

"Eaarnel?"

"Some of it," he said.

"Fast halfbacks, big offensive tackles, drink-of-water quarterbacks?"

"You're starting to catch on to this game."

"How could I miss? It's running out my ears."

"Actually," Buck said, "I was dreaming about Rattlerettes. I was just getting ready to make it with, ah, who's that cute little head Rattlerette? You know, the one with the. . . ."

"Cathy."

"Yeah, Cathy. Why'd you have to wake me up?"

Peggy pulled up her chair, crossed her legs, took out her pencil, and said, "You ought to be ashamed of yourself. She could be your daughter. Let's go. Dictate."

Buck leaned back in his swivel chair so he could relieve the pressure on his rash. "First, the telegrams. Send the same one to the athletes that I give you. You understand what I'm talking about?"

"To be totally honest and brutally frank, no, I don't understand you at all."

"OK, I'll speak real slowly. Now watch my lips. I'll give you a telegram to send. Then I will give you a lot of names of prospects. You will send the same wire to all the prospects. Got it?"

Peggy didn't answer immediately. If she had, she would have said something sarcastic, and today wasn't the day for it. She knew he had some personal problems when he came in, so she just kept her mouth shut. "I understand, now that you've made it so clear, Coach Lee. You can go ahead with the wire. I think I can handle it," she answered coolly.

"All right, here's the telegram. 'Dear Prospect: You are the No. 1 prospect we have in the state. Our program doesn't have anyone of your caliber. You can make the difference between a great year in recruiting and an average one. If there is anything I can do for you, let me know at any hour of the day or night. My home phone number is 205-231-0461. My wife, Gail, will be there to talk to your mother if she would like to talk about the food or the spiritual aspect of the community. You know, like where the churches are and who the minister is. Don't forget we need you! Buck Lee, East Alabama Head Coach.' "

"Just for the sake of asking, why do you always sign all your wires Buck Lee, Head Coach? They should know who you are."

"Most of the players we're after are so heavily recruited that they don't even pay attention to names. We had a player one time report to fall practice at Western and ask Shavers who he was. Shavers was so pissed he couldn't stand it. He looked directly at the player and said, 'If you weren't so damn good, I'd kick your ass off this team.' He didn't even know how funny that was." Peggy smiled a little in spite of herself. Buck felt guilty about putting her down earlier, so he went for another laugh . . . his way of apologizing.

"That story reminds me of the one about the coach who came home from work and found his star quarterback in bed with his wife. You heard this?" Peggy pulled out an emery board and started filing her long red nails ever-so-carefully. She answered like someone forced to watch a friend's three-year-old tap dancer perform. "No, I haven't heard it, Coach Lee."

"Well, anyway, when he walked in and found them in bed, he looked at the quarterback and said, 'If you didn't have one more year of eligibility, I'd shoot your ass." Buck laughed loudly at his own joke. Peggy only smiled and continued with her nails. She wasn't going to let him off the hook that easy.

"Do you have the names you want to send those wires to?"

Buck got the message and went back to work. "Here they are: Bobby Kicker, Hap Jones, Julian Lloyd, Robert Forbes, Chopper Ursey, Lightning Bolt Martin. Oh, hell, Peggy, why should I read off the names? You can copy them off the computer printout." Buck handed his list to Peggy. "Just copy the ones I have checks by. It's only about seventy-five names."

Peggy, who was used to such activities, calmly took the list, changed the sheet on her dictation pad, and waited for the letter.

"OK. This letter goes to Eaarnel Simpson. 'Dear Eaarnel: I recognize that you receive many letters each day, along with the phone calls and telegrams that come to your house. I haven't overloaded you with phone calls like some of the more zealous coaches who are chasing you. However, I do want to put down in writing how I feel about you as a person.'"

Buck paused to catch his breath. Peggy waited silently.

" 'You are a kind and decent person, and I know that if you decide to come to our school to get an education, we will be happy together. Our goals are the same, I'm sure, for your college career. We want you to get the best education that *money* can buy, the best food that *money* can buy, the best housing that *money* can buy, the best summer job for you making top *dollar*, and after graduation, the best job in pro football making the most *money*. Now, you will always have a job with our alums making a lot of *money* if you don't play pro ball, but it's ridiculous to even imply that you might not make the pros.

" 'Eaarnel, do you know how much easier it will be for your mother to get down to all our games than it would for her to get to West Alabama? Now, they might say that they're forty miles closer, but ours is all freeway. We have many more of our people driving down to the game because of the freeway than they do. Their roads are so bad going from your place to Western that your mother would have to get a new car every year to take the shock of driving on those bumpy old roads. Furthermore, we have much better roadside stops than they do. Our bathrooms are so much cleaner and the places to eat are so much cheaper and better that there's no comparison. Your mother's *money* would go much further if she didn't have to make the ride to Western.

" 'Great prospects like yourself are always concerned about spending *money* when they go off to school. Well, I can assure you that all our players usually have enough *money* supplied by their parents. I'm sure your mama will keep her son in enough *money* for him to enjoy college.

" 'Last, but certainly not least, is the most important thing for you to remember about going to college. It's like a marriage — sometimes great, sometimes turbulent. It can never survive if it's based only on *money*. Now, I know *money* is important, but a good relationship also must be based on friendship. If you come to play for the Rattlers, any time you want to come into my office and shut the door and talk about anything, you will always have an open door. Your friend, Buck Lee, Head Coach.' " Buck leaned back in his chair and looked over at Peggy for approval. Receiving none, he stood up and walked toward the open door.

"Is that all, Coach Lee?" Peggy asked as she closed her notepad.

"No, there's one more thing. I like that letter, so put it in the file and list it under form letters. Underline every reference to money. We'll use it again next year on some Hotshot Charlie."

* * *

"Coach Shavers, this is The Raven."

"I told you not to call me at home. And why do you have to use that silly name?"

"It might ruin my cover if someone had your phone tapped."

"Nobody has my phone tapped. I have the telephone company check every week."

"I have some news you might be interested in. Buck Lee wrote a long letter to that colored boy today. You know the one."

"I know who you're talking about, Raven. What's the big deal about some letter?"

"All I know is I just got a peek at the letter, and all Lee wrote about was money."

"Well, he'll have to work like hell to beat the master."

"Coach, I'll call back next week with some more inside poop. This is The Raven, signing off."

11

ROANOKE, ALABAMA, THE HOMETOWN of Eaarnel Simpson, was typical of the thousands of small farming communities dotting the undulating landscape of the Black Belt. It seemed as though there were a Roanoke every ten miles — a little cluster of a thousand people and one silvery water tower proclaiming the town's name. The Black Belt, which stretched for nearly a thousand miles from the piney woods of eastern South Carolina to the forbidding Big Thicket of eastern Texas, came by its name honestly. The bulk of its population was black — in many counties, eighty percent of the people were descendants of slaves — and the soil they worked was as black as their skin.

Consequently, Roanoke High, Buck observed as he mounted the steps to meet Eaarnel for the first time, was predominantly poor and black. Basketball was the name of the game here, even on this day in March, as evidenced by the banner hanging over the main entrance to the school ("DUNK DALTON") and the plethora of sneakers and Roanoke Panthers varsity basketball sweaters worn by saucy, Afroed girls. Football had forged into the spotlight during Eaarnel Simpson's four astonishing years — the football Panthers had won their region in two of those years, with Eaarnel averaging 12.4 yards per carry and scoring eighty-nine touchdowns in his forty games — but following his graduation, football was likely to go back into its shell.

Buck was reaching for the door to the old red-brick school, taking in the familiar sights and sounds of kids galloping and yelping in the yard in their tight blue jeans and suggestive T-shirts, when he heard a singsong female voice behind him.

"You lookin' for Eaarnel." It wasn't a question.

"How'd you know that?"

"See a white man in a suit, know he lookin' for Eaarnel."

"Well, you got it right. I'm Buck Lee, head coach at East Alabama."

"Say what?"

"East Alabama University. Up at Stanleyville. Football coach."

"Don't like that football," the girl said. "Too mean. We like basketball down here. They let girls play basketball."

"Well," said Buck, "you know where Eaarnel is right now?"

"He play basketball in the gym. Want me to show you?"

"I need to get permission from the principal first."

"I show you."

As Buck followed the girl down the grimy corridor, he was engulfed by a sense of depression. The interior of Roanoke High was a melange of grit and graffiti — discarded candy wrappers, rolled-up balls of notebook paper, broken pieces of chalk on the broken and unwaxed linoleum floor, obscene crayoned messages on the flaking walls, and the overpowering odor of cabbage being boiled somewhere in the caverns. It was as though "separate but unequal" were still alive. And the girl — pretty little thing, maybe sixteen, hair in pigtails, tight fanny wiggling beneath faded jeans, wrapping a lollipop and stuffing it into her pocket before a teacher saw her with it — what would happen to her in a world ruled by white people? It made Buck wish, however briefly, that he weren't the Great White Coach riding to the rescue in a suit costing enough to feed her family for a month.

The girl opened the door to the principal's office long enough to point out a Mrs. Morgan, a huge black woman wearing a flowered dress and glittery, rose-tinted glasses that hung around her neck with a string of pearls. Then the girl bolted and ran. Buck didn't think he would want to be caught in the presence of Mrs. Morgan, either, if he were still a high-schooler. He introduced himself to the woman, who turned out to be the assistant principal (meaning Chief Enforcer), and handed her his business card. She tried to read the card and deduce the purpose of his visit while kids swirled all about them.

"This is my first visit to your lovely school here, Mrs. Morgan."

"Hah," she snorted. "Lovely. I s'wanee. Humph."

"One of our coaches, Coach Perry Jackson, has been down here several times to visit with Eaarnel. But this is my first time. I was wanting to see if I could find him and talk to him."

"Well, Coach, ah" — she looked at Buck's card again — "Coach

Lee. You're going to have to get in line if you want to see that boy."

"Other coaches here today?"

"Lawd a-mercy. California, *Notra* Dame, Tennessee, everywhere."

"I'd really like to see the principal first."

"That would be Dr. Jones."

"I need to talk to him about Eaarnel's grades."

"Wonder that boy's got any grades at all, what with all this ruckus goin' on around him," said Mrs. Morgan. "Playin' sports, helpin' his mama, flyin' off to some college all the time. Boy gets home and they got coaches sittin' on the front porch waitin' for him. Boy tries to study and here comes another long-distance phone call. That boy's bright, Coach Lee, but his grades sho don't show it."

"Maybe we can do something about that, Mrs. Morgan."

She led Buck to the door marked PRINCIPAL, briefly introduced him to Dr. Jones, then softly shut the door to leave the two men to their own devices. Buck felt a giddy rush when he saw the principal. He was an angular, slightly graying black man, obviously an ex-jock — rather than some prim history major from Tuskegee — who would understand the situation.

"I'm Ramsey Jones," he said, extending his hand.

"Buck Lee, Dr. Jones. Head football coach at. . . ."

"Oh, I know, Coach Lee. I read the papers. Please have a seat."

The two men sat, Jones in a wooden swivel chair behind his desk and Buck in a metal folding chair on the other side. They were silent for a few seconds as they sized each other up. Buck scanned the walls and saw a framed diploma granting a graduate degree from Alabama A&I. Then he saw a silver trophy, topped by the statuette of a basketball player, sitting on a long table beneath a window overlooking the playground where kids were playing volleyball.

"You played basketball?" Buck asked, to break the silence.

"Over at A&I, yes sir. Couldn't go to Eastern in my day."

"Were you good?"

"Oh," Jones said, "I made all-Black Belt Conference one year. I wasn't bad. Got me an education, though. Don't let the 'Dr. Jones' fool you. I majored in physical education and then got a doctorate. Coached here for awhile, but then they made me principal."

Buck said, "Dr. Jones. . . ."

"Ramsey. Please."

"All right. Ramsey. If you'll call me Buck."

"Thank you."

"Well . . ." Buck didn't know whether to go into it or not. "Well, it's these kids. This town. This school. I don't mind telling you that sometimes I have mixed feelings about what I'm doing. White coach, big-time football school, coming down to places like this, trying to talk some poor black kid into leaving his mother and everything else he knows for some strange world. A hell of a lot of 'em can't cope with it, and it messes 'em up for life. Sometimes I think maybe it'd be better just to leave 'em alone. Eaarnel's the latest. Maybe I shouldn't have told you what I just did."

Buck thought it would take forever for Ramsey Jones to respond. Dr. Jones was clearly startled. He set the pipe he'd been holding down on his pipe rack, scratched the back of his head, flexed his bony shoulders, and eased up from the chair. For a moment, his back was turned as he gazed out the window at the kids on the playground. Then he turned to Buck and, silhouetted by the sun coming through the window, launched into a soliloquy.

"Let me tell you something," he said in a measured voice. "I was one of nine kids. Here it was, in the fifties, and we might as well have been slaves. Slaves, Buck, slaves, working those long hours in the sun. Sharecroppers, working for the white man, pulling things up out of the ground for him. Two of my brothers are in prison right now, and another got killed in Korea. A sister got pregnant when she was fourteen. Then I got pretty good at basketball, and I got a partial scholarship to A&I. Now, A&I was all black, and still is, but I couldn't get into most of the white schools back then anyway. But it was college; it was college, and look at me now. Dr. Ramsey Jones. All right. But that was a *black* college, you say, but what about, say, Eaarnel going off to a place like East Alabama University, where it's mostly white boys and girls? I'll say one thing about that. He's better off taking his chances than sticking with what he's got, because what he's got is a lifetime of helping his mama pick collard greens."

Dr. Jones sat back down in his swivel chair, relit his pipe, and leaned back to study Buck Lee's reaction. Buck wanted to applaud the man. He had gambled with this black, small-town, high school principal and won.

"The boy hasn't had *time* to study," Dr. Jones said.

"Mrs. Morgan told me."

"Bright boy, just been too busy."

"I can imagine," said Buck.

"Eaarnel's grades are *terrible*."

"I guessed as much."

"Why don't we take a look at 'em."

"That's what I'm here for."

"Been a while since I looked at Eaarnel's grades," Dr. Jones said, taking a few steps to a four-drawer filing cabinet, pulling out Eaarnel Simpson's folder and slapping it down on his desk. He invited Buck to bring his chair around to his side of the desk so they could inspect the records together. Dr. Jones opened the middle drawer of his desk and brought out a pencil with an eraser. Roanoke High's grades hadn't yet been fed to a countywide computer.

"That D in English, now," said Dr. Jones, "that's a mistake. His English teacher told me yesterday she was going to change it to a C. And this math grade can't be right. You ought to hear that boy do the multiplication tables. I think a C ought to go there, too, to be honest with you. And woodwork. I saw him make the prettiest table lamp for his mama that you ever saw. Worth at least a B on the lamp alone." Dr. Jones brushed away the eraser crumbs, then handed Buck the grade sheet, a pencil, and a piece of paper so that he could figure Eaarnel's average for himself. When Buck saw that Dr. Jones's handiwork had just made Eaarnel Simpson eligible to enter East Alabama University as a freshman in the fall, he grinned and gave the thumbs-up signal. Ramsey Jones, only a wry smile on his face, put the folder back in the filing cabinet and offered a handshake.

"How long do you think it would take him to make your team?" Dr. Jones asked.

"I figure two days," Buck told him.

"Why do you say two days?"

"First day's picture day."

* * *

Buck hustled over to the gym to see Eaarnel play basketball. As he walked into the arena, an Amazonian girl dribbled down the floor virtually unhindered to make a basket. He had come in on the girls' basketball game, being played in the afternoon while school was letting out. The boys' game would follow. His eyes roamed the gym looking for Eaarnel, who wasn't hard to find. About halfway up the stands near midcourt sat a large, handsome black man surrounded by six white males wearing coats of every color — green, red, blue, orange, black, white. Seldom had Buck seen so many plaid pants and white shoes in one place. Eaarnel was watching the game, as though he had something going with one of the girls on the floor, but the six white coaches never took their eyes off him.

Buck really had little choice. If he wanted to see Eaarnel, or at least let Eaarnel see him, he would have to walk up into the stands. He hated to, because it put him at such a disadvantage, joining them late and thus becoming just one more coach in the group. Then he had a better idea.

"Eaarnel! Eaarnel!" Buck screamed over the roar of the crowd as the big girl lumbered in for another basket. Eaarnel heard him yelling and looked over in his direction. So did the six men in plaid britches.

"Eaarnel, I need to talk to you," Buck yelled across the gym. He made a circular motion with his right hand and then pointed at the gigantic girl on the floor.

Eaarnel's curiosity was aroused. He excused himself from the six men and walked down to the entrance tunnel where Buck was standing. Buck introduced himself and shook hands with the specimen.

"Is that your girl, the tall one who keeps scoring all those goals?"

Eaarnel laughed. "Coach, that's Hannah the Hump. She can screw the whole team and not even work up a sweat. She can also whip about ninety percent of the guys in this school."

"Well, it scared the hell out of me. Coach, uh, I can't remember his name. The one up there in the red coat," Buck said.

"I think that's Coach Blasie from SMU."

"Yeah, well, he told me that Hannah was your girlfriend, and that whoever got you would have to take Hannah as a package deal. Now, I don't mind a package deal, but I didn't think we could afford to feed her. Now, we might give her a football scholarship, big as she is."

"He said *she* was my girl? *That* one is my girl," Eaarnel said, pointing out a little girl whom Big Hannah had just buried beneath the basket.

"Well, why don't you get that pretty little thing and let's go get some pizza, fried chicken, or steak and go over to your house and have a good time."

"Coach, I can't. I'm leaving tonight for a visit to Western. Coach Shavers is sending his private jet down to pick me up."

"That's OK, Eaarnel, I'll just take your girl over to your mother's and take them out."

"They're going with me to Western. Anyway, thanks for straightening me out on Big Hannah. My girlfriend!" Eaarnel was muttering as he walked toward the locker room.

Six coaches who hadn't taken their eyes off Eaarnel while he was with Buck sprinted toward the locker room. They all wanted to be the last one to tell him, "Have a good time at Western this weekend." Buck trailed along with the coaches. He couldn't afford to be the only one not to tell Eaarnel, with great sincerity, to have a great time.

12

A FTER DRIVING ONLY SIX of the ten miles from the Eastern campus to Orion High, Charlie Smith, en route to pick up Ed "The Hammer" Sledge, pulled over to call the office.

"Peggy. Any calls since I left?"

"Calls? You've only been gone ten minutes."

"I know, but I was expecting an important call about now."

"No calls."

"OK. I'm on my way to see a recruit."

"So *that's* where you are."

"Yep. On my way."

"Thank heavens. Coach Lee thought you were being interviewed."

"Funny, Peggy, very funny. I'll call back later."

Charlie climbed into his Ford LTD sedan and drove the other four miles. He pulled up to the curb beside the gym of the sprawling brick school, slid out of the car, and put on his best "You're-a-super-guy" smile. The Hammer, who had been waiting against his silver Trans-Am in his formfitting designer jeans and a shirt too small for his chest and arms, was swaggering toward Charlie.

"Big Ed," Charlie beamed. They shook hands. "How's school?"

"Ah, OK," said The Hammer. "Seniors got out early. I went to the weight room and worked out a couple of hours. Today was forearm day." Ed was admiring his swollen forearms when a candy-apple Pinto stuffed to the roof with sixteen-year-old girls drove by. The driver, a perky blonde, honked the horn, and all of the girls waved nervously to the star Orion High halfback as they screeched out of the parking lot. The Hammer acknowledged them with a cocked eyebrow.

Charlie cleared his throat. "Ed," he said, "knowing that you want to go to medical school and become a surgeon, I contacted Dr. Kinard yesterday. You may have heard of him. He's consulted on a lot of murder cases in the state. Dr. Lawrence Nathaniel Kinard. I told him the situation, and he said he'd love to talk to you about your career and answer any questions you might have."

"OK," said The Hammer.

"Hope you don't mind."

"Naw. I'd like to see what goes on."

They climbed into the LTD and drove away from the school.

"So," Charlie said, "I'm going to drive you by Dr. Kinard's office and introduce you. He's seen you play a few times and remembers that run you made against Beeson last fall. I still can't believe that one myself."

"You mean the one where I cut back across the field for about sixty on that screen pass and gained about forty of it with a bunch of people hanging on my back and legs?"

"I believe it was the screen. The one that went for the touchdown?"

"Could be," The Hammer said. "I don't remember hardly any of it. When I run, it's all on instinct. All I remember is Bucky, our center, crying and trying to kiss me through his face mask while we stood in the end zone. He went nuts."

"Excuse me, Ed," Charlie said as he wheeled the Ford off the road beside a phone booth at a Gulf station. "I've got to make a quick call to the office." Charlie leaped out of the car, the motor running and the door open, digging for a quarter to call Peggy one more time.

"Hi, Peg, me again. Any calls?"

"Yes, Coach. Your wife called to say Rusty's decided to play soccer this year instead of football, and that you shouldn't hit him when you get home."

"Why that little son of a bitch!" Charlie screamed.

"Don't yell at *me*. I don't want to get involved."

"I'll plow up every goddamn soccer field in Alabama!"

"What's the big deal, Coach? Soccer's a fine sport."

"Yeah," sputtered Charlie, "if you live in Argentina."

Charlie slammed the phone down, nearly ripping the receiver off the glass wall, and stormed back to the car snarling to himself. "Goddamn pinkos talked him into it . . . Might as well take up ping-pong or volleyball . . . Soccer, for Christ's sake. . . ."

"Something wrong, Coach?" asked The Hammer.

"Wrong? *Wrong*?"

"Well, I mean, on the phone. . . ."

"Oh, no, not really," Charlie said. "I just found out that my son thinks he'd rather play soccer than football. Christ! It's like finding out your kid's a faggot. I'll kill him."

"Yeah," The Hammer said, "that soccer's a pussy sport." Charlie drove on, glaring straight ahead, while The Hammer flexed his forearms.

* * *

Patrick Flanagan had to hurry before they got there. From a manila envelope just delivered by courier from his brother-in-law's print shop, he fished out the handsome parchment. He took the gold frame off the wall behind his walnut desk and removed his real estate license. In its place, he slid the diploma saying HARVARD MEDICAL SCHOOL. He hung the frame back in its place, slipped his real estate license into his desk drawer, then stood back to admire it. "Show time," he said.

And just in time. His secretary was buzzing him from the outer office. "Pat, ah, Dr. Kinard, Coach Smith and Mr. Sledge are here to see you." Patrick Flanagan closed the top button of the lab coat he had borrowed from his neighborhood butcher, hung a stethoscope (on loan from his family doctor) around his neck, straightened the medical magazines arrayed on his desk and the coffee table, and prepared for the curtain to rise. "Yes, Miss Pearlman," he said over the intercom in his finest Eastern accent, "please send the gentlemen in." The door opened and in came Charlie Smith and The Hammer.

"Dr. Kinard," Charlie said, shaking hands with Patrick.

"It's good to see you looking so good, Coach Smith. How's the wife?"

"Fine, thank you. She's up and about. Just like new."

"I don't mind telling you, brain surgery can be awfully tricky."

"It was a miracle, Dr. Kinard. You did wonders."

"Well, now, Coach," Patrick said, spreading his hands at the sight of Ed Sledge, "you don't have to tell me who this is. Ed Sledge. The one and only Hammer. I can't tell you how many times I've sneaked out of surgery on Friday nights, Ed, just to see you run for Orion High." The Hammer never had any problems with being worshipped. Nor did he have any difficulty noting that on the good doctor's desk was an Orion High football program from the previous season. It was next to a book, borrowed from Patrick's secretary, entitled *The Female Breast*. Charlie excused himself while "Dr. Kinard" and The Hammer sat down to kibitz about medical school and football.

After a few minutes, Patrick said, "Ed, I thought what we'd do is go down to St. Catherine's Hospital and watch some open-heart surgery."

"Open-heart surgery?" Ed Sledge gulped.

"Why not? Might as well get a real feel for medicine."

"You mean the *real thing*?"

"Sure, sure, why not?" Patrick, his stethoscope swinging from his neck as he bent over the intercom, asked his secretary if she had found out what the schedule was that afternoon at St. Catherine's. "Nothing in O.R. until midnight, Dr. Kinard," She told him.

"Such a shame, Ed," said Patrick. "I wanted you to see that."

"Yeah," said The Hammer, visibly relieved, "that sure would've been fun."

"Well, I tell you what. Since the veterinary school is just around the corner, it might be a good opportunity to pop in and get a first-hand look at how they castrate hogs. There are some new surgical procedures they're using over there that, quite frankly, I'd like to check up on myself. What say let's do that?" Before The Hammer could talk his way out, they were in Patrick's borrowed, yacht-class, black Lincoln Continental, headed for the vet school.

"I really wanted you to see some open-heart surgery or a brain operation, Ed, but there just wasn't anything happening. But you can't really see much from the observation room overlooking the operating table, anyway. It's frustrating as hell trying to see arteries being tied off or an especially tricky triple bypass maneuver. So, believe me, Ed, going down to the vet school every once in a while is good for a surgeon. Everything is in plain sight down here, and their techniques are just as skillful. Only difference is they're slicing up animals." He parked at the curb.

"Don't lock it," Pat said with a wave of his hand as they got out of the car. "Never worry about theft on this campus." Ed swung the massive door shut with a solid thump and walked beside Pat through the twin glass doors of the vet school. Pat, with his white coat and clipboard, looked like one of the researchers fresh from the old Shell Platformate commercial. Ed's confidence and enthusiasm were steadily rising. The more time he spent with Dr. Kinard, the more comfortable he felt. He was even considering talking to his parents about changing family doctors. He'd never liked that pale little redheaded doctor they had, anyway. Ed always thought he looked more like a hair stylist than a doctor.

Pat moved swiftly down several flights of stairs and through a dozen doors until finally they were standing on a concrete platform overlooking a well-populated hog pen.

"Boy, now that's a smell, isn't it, Ed?" said Pat, taking a deep breath. Ed had already buried his nose into the crook of his arm, trying to filter out the thick odor of fresh pig dung. "Yes, sir, I grew up on a farm, and there just aren't any smells like the natural ones." Ed moved his nose from the protection of his arm for a moment but quickly resumed his safe breathing position. "Here they come with a few now, Ed." Pat waved to the veterinarian who was holding a pair of hog testicles in his right hand while his assistant injected a local anesthetic into a squealing brown hog. The confused veterinarian waved back weakly to the man he had never seen before.

"OK, now, Ed, here comes the good part. You really have to know what you're doing here, or the hog ends up with a high-pitched grunt and an embarrassing scar. Look, he's giving the hog a local to kill the pain, just like a doctor would to a vasectomy patient or for a leg amputation." Ed was watching out of one eye through the crack of his fingers. A nauseous feeling began welling up in his stomach, and sweat popped out on his forehead and upper lip. "Now the vet is going to take the scalpel in his right hand, pull back the testicles with his left hand, and slice the tube connecting them to the penis."

In seconds the vet had severed the hog's testicles, tied off the tube, and Ed "The Hammer" Sledge had thrown up all over the platform.

"Well, Ed," Pat said, ignoring the uncontrolled vomiting, "do you want to go try our luck with some open-heart surgery, or would you like to hang around here and catch a few more castrations?"

* * *

"Coach Smith," Pat said, leaning back in his chair and speaking loudly into the phone. "I don't think The Hammer will be checking out any medical books from the library any time soon. He was pea-green when I took him home just now. Said he didn't feel too hot. I guess he just wasn't cut out to be a doctor. OK, Coach? Just holler if you need me again." Pat hung up the phone, replaced his real estate license on the panelled wall behind his desk, and began reading an unauthorized biography of Marlon Brando.

* * *

"Coach Lee, this is Coach Smith. Ed 'The Hammer' Sledge just finished his visit with the world-famous Dr. Kinard."

"How'd it go?"

"I don't think you'll be hearing anymore talk from The Hammer about being a doctor. I think you can concentrate on football."

Buck slapped his leg and broke out into a big grin. "I knew Patrick could help us. What time you bringing Ed over?"

"About an hour. He needs to rest for awhile."

"That's fine. I'll be waiting."

Buck still felt good about recruiting, except for Eaarnel. It'd take more than a trip to the vet school to land him. He'd be tough.

He remembered that he had an appointment with Cathy and buzzed Peggy to see if she had arrived.

"Yes, she's already here," snapped Peggy. "Shall I send her in?"

"Send her in, but leave the door open. I don't want you to think I've got anything but work on my mind."

"Hi, Coach Lee," Cathy said as she sashayed through the open door. She closed the door with her left hand and stuck out her right hand toward Buck. He jumped up from his feet-on-the-desk position, kicked the wastepaper basket over, and knocked the phone on the floor in an attempt to reach and shake hands with this gorgeous woman. Her grip was strong and firm, and she stared him down with eyes the color of pure jade. His eyes trailed down her pug nose to her pouty lips and perfect teeth, but they stopped dead when they reached her firm breasts.

"How-w-w *are* you, Cathy?" he stuttered. "It's a real pleasure to visit with you. We appreciate what you're doing for the program."

She stood tall and straight. "Coach Lee, I know you're a busy man, so I won't take up a lot of your time. I've got the pictures and resumes on all the girls who're going to be Rattlerettes. There's also the book of operating rules that we give all our girls. Can we sit so I can explain what I have for you?"

Buck motioned her over to the sofa. As soon as they sat down, the door opened and Peggy stuck her head in.

"Coach Smith is outside with Ed Sledge, and he says it's very important that he see you. *Right now*!"

"Just tell him I'll be through in about another five minutes. We've waited on The Hammer for two years; he can wait five minutes on me."

"Shall I leave the door open, or do you want it closed?" Peggy said icily, eyeing Cathy.

"You can close it, Peggy. We have some very important things to discuss."

Peggy slammed the door. Cathy turned her attention back to Buck. "Coach, is that a good prospect you were talking about, The Hammer?"

"Cathy, sweetheart, he's not a blue-chip player, but we'd like to have him. I think we've got a real good chance to get him. He's local and should come to school here if he's got any sense."

"That's terrific. My daddy will be so happy when I tell him about The Hammer. He reads all he can about recruiting, 'cause he knows how important it is. Why, if I'd been a boy, I know I would've played for the Rattlers. And I would've been easy to recruit."

Buck felt his crotch tingle. He couldn't tell if it was the rash or not. To be safe, he took the pictures and information sheets and laid them on his lap.

"Now, what I'm looking for, Cathy," Buck said, thumbing through the Polaroids, "what I'm looking for is. . . ."

Cathy reached over and selected a picture of one of the Rattlerettes off Buck's lap. She pointed to the picture of the coed and began to read off the back: "Denise Darling, 5′ 2″, 113 pounds, thirty-eight-inch bust, twenty-three-inch waist, thirty-five-inch hips. Loves quarterbacks with big hands. Has a great Southern accent, so would be real effective with yankee recruits."

"Have you done this with all your Rattlerettes?"

Cathy reached to Buck's lap again and began rummaging through the remaining Polaroids. Buck didn't dare help her look. She picked up several, holding them up for Buck to see.

"As you can see from the pictures, I've got nothing but good-looking gals. But unless you have a scouting report on each one of our gals, you won't know which one goes with which recruit. I believe in being organized, just like in coaching."

"Cathy, this is terrific. I can't tell you how much this'll help. But who on my staff do you want to coordinate this with?"

"Why, Coach Lee, it should be you and me. I'm like the head coach, and we should coordinate the prospect with the right girl."

Buck gulped. "Gee, I think that's great, Cathy, but my assistant coaches know much more than I do about each prospect. So why don't you work with them? I think that'll be a lot better."

Cathy smiled and said, "OK, but I'm going to leave all these pictures and our Standard Operating Procedure book with you. If you have any questions or changes you want to suggest, I'll be at the Phi Mu house. And if you change your mind about helping me coordinate, just call."

Peggy opened the door again and reminded Buck that Ed Sledge was still waiting outside.

"Thanks a lot, Cathy. We'll be in touch."

Peggy grimaced at Buck's pun, but Cathy just smiled.

* * *

The Hammer looked a little pale as he walked in the door, but otherwise he looked like a football player, even in his jeans. Buck had never thought he had the real good face, but it was acceptable. Sticking out his hand to The Hammer, Buck flashed his sincere, friendly look. He put his left hand over Ed's right hand as they shook, continuing to look The Hammer right in the eye. "It's great to see you again, Ed. We've missed you around here. Where've you been?"

"Busy traveling, Coach. When I became a heavily recruited athlete, I had no idea that I'd be gone so much from school. It's really affected my grades."

"That's why you've got to make a decision on where you're going to school, son, so you can concentrate on that education," Buck said, putting his arm around The Hammer and leading him over to the sofa. Ed plopped down. Buck pulled a straight-back chair over and sat right in front of The Hammer so they could talk face to face, man to man.

"Coach, I need to ask you a couple of questions."

"That's what I'm here for, Hammer, to help you make up your mind."

"Well, what position would I play?"

"What position do you *want* to play?"

"I don't want to play fullback. All they do is block. If you've ever seen me play, you know I'm a ball carrier. Now, I can block when I *have* to, but I like to have the football under my left arm, not in somebody else's hands." Hammer made a move like he had the football in his arm and was running for a touchdown.

"Hammer, why do you carry the ball in your left hand?"

Standing up, The Hammer snatched a throw pillow from the sofa and stuck it under his left arm. "See, this leaves my strongest hand free for the stiff-arm." He slammed his right hand into the wall. For the first time since coming into Buck's office, Sledge looked excited.

"That's great, Ed. Now, sit down while I answer your question. We'll play you at tailback, just like you want." Buck slid his chair closer to where The Hammer was sitting. He didn't want him getting up again. "What else can we do for you?"

Ed leaned back on the sofa, thought for a second, and suddenly leaned forward like he'd had a brilliant idea. "How about my high school jersey number? I'd like to wear it in college."

Buck didn't even know or care what The Hammer's number was, but he said, "Why, certainly. We'll work that out for you. Anything else? Any academic questions?"

"No, sir. They were all answered this morning."

"Then let me ask you one. How many schools have you got it narrowed down to?"

Turning his head up to look at the ceiling while playing with the top button on his shirt, The Hammer answered, "I've got it narrowed down to six schools: USC, Penn State, Oklahoma, UCLA, Notre Dame, and y'all."

"Do you know when you'll make up your mind? Eastern's been recruiting you for almost three years. You live close to the campus, your folks can see you play, and I know you like the campus and all our pretty women. So, tell me, what's holding you up?"

"I'm just not ready to make a commitment quite yet. It's a big decision."

Buck stood up and walked back over to his desk. He was trying not to show his anger at this run-of-the-mill player who had as much chance of playing at Notre Dame or Oklahoma as he had of catching the next space shuttle. He looked at his schedule on his desk and turned to The Hammer. "Ed, I'd love to visit with you some more, but I've got several more appointments today. Why don't you go with Coach Smith and get something to eat?"

Charlie came in and took Ed to lunch. When they left, Buck picked up the phone and called his old friend Bo Stiles, head coach at Western Mississippi.

"Bo, I know you're a busy man with your own problems," Buck told Stiles, "but I need a favor. We're recruiting this average running back, a local kid. He's a white fullback-type and not that great, but if we don't work our ass off on him, our local alumni will be all over us."

"You don't have to explain to me," said Bo. "I've had the same problem. I just wish we could all decide who the aces are and then recruit them like hell. Let the best man win. All the pissants, we would just flip a coin over."

"Exactly. Anyway, Bo, here's what I'd like you to do. Pick up the phone and call Ed Sledge. He likes to be called The Hammer. Tell him you want him to visit your campus. Give him the usual bullshit about how good he is and how much he would like your campus."

"I got that part. That's easy. What else?"

"He'll tell you he can't make the visit, that he's made his six visits. Then just say casually, 'Where are you going to school?' He'll tell you right off the bat. They always do. Here's his number: 205-456-8362. But you'll have to call him tomorrow. He's still on our campus today."

"I'll do it for my old drinking buddy. I'll call you back tomorrow."

* * *

"Peggy," Buck said into the intercom, "I'm expecting a very important call tomorrow from Coach Bo Stiles. No matter what I'm doing, call me. Unless I'm having another private meeting with Cathy."

"Very funny, Coach Lee." She was not amused.

13

IT HAD BEEN A long day, and Buck was ready for sleep. Dealing with Ed Sledge, visiting with Cathy Bennett, and checking the status of innumerable recruits had taken their toll. Gail was already in bed and sound asleep. He tiptoed into the bedroom, stripped down, and put his head on the pillow. He had just dozed off into the land of fast backs and beautiful women when the phone rang.

Buck fumbled for the receiver in the darkness until he finally knocked it off the stand. Groping on the floor, he found it just before falling out of bed. "Hello?"

"Coach Lee, this is Bobby Sexton. I didn't wake you up, did I?"

Propping the phone on the pillow so he wouldn't have to hold it, Buck answered sleepily. "What can I do for you, Mr. Sexton?"

Over the sound of Charley Pride singing in the background, Buck heard, "Coach, my son Bobby, Jr., is the best quarterback in the state. He's 6′ 1″, 184, runs a 4.6 forty, and can throw the football seventy yards. He hit seventy-one percent of his passes, and he makes straight A's."

"Great. We will surely follow up on your son. First thing in the morning. Now, if that's all, I'll go back to sleep."

"One more thing, Coach Lee!" he yelled over the background of loud country music. "Coach Lee, I want my boy to go to East Alabama, but if you don't want him, I'll let Coach Shavers have him," he said drunkenly.

"We'll certainly look at your boy, Mr. Sexton. Tomorrow morning."

"You still don't understand. My son's *great*. If you have a son that plays football, you know what I'm talking about."

Buck sat up in the bed and cleared his throat. "Mr. Sexton, my boy plays third string on the Stanleyville Junior High team. He should be first string, and I think the coach is stupid, but damned if I call him up at 2:00 A.M. to tell him so." There was a moment of silence except for Willie Nelson singing in the background. "Coach, I gotta go. My ride's leaving."

Buck's head hit the pillow again, and the lovely Cathy Bennett came into view. He dreamed he was in his office talking to Ignarski and Cathy danced through the door wearing a cancan outfit, doing high kicks. Ignarski was dragged out into the hall by a dozen Rattlerettes and raped. There was no justice. What should have been a sweet dream turned into a nightmare.

14

BUCK PARKED HIS CAR in the spot reserved for the head football coach and started for the office. It was a beautiful clear morning, and despite the drunken call in the middle of the night, he felt fresh and rejuvenated. He turned onto the walkway and hit the second chorus of "Oh, What a Beautiful Morning" when out from the bushes jumped Richard Culpepper.

"Great day, Coach Lee! Here's all the top prospects in Canada I've researched for you." He shoved a stack of paper at the dazed coach.

Buck, who almost went to his knees when Richard jumped out, screamed, "I'm telling you for the last time, don't scare me like that! Why can't you just drop these by the office like anybody else would?"

"I'm not *like* anybody else, Coach. They don't want a job with you like I do."

"All right, Richard, you've made your point. But try not to scare the crap out of me again, OK?" Richard nodded, and Buck ambled up the hill into his office.

"Get Hyspick in here as soon as possible," Buck told Peggy without so much as a "Good morning." He walked into his office, spent a few minutes looking through the list of Canadian prospects Culpepper had left him, and then waited for Hyspick.

"Coach Hyspick is here," Peggy said over the intercom. "And Coach Stiles called to say he still hasn't gotten hold of Ed Sledge, but as soon as he does, he'll call you back."

"OK. Send Coach Hyspick in." Buck positioned himself so he'd be looking directly at the door. Hyspick bounded into the room dressed in his coaching gear, not a hair was out of place.

"Yes, sir, Coach," he bubbled, standing directly in front of Buck's desk. His baseball cap with the big white Rattler on it was in his hands. "What can I do for you?" Buck tried to hide his irritation at Hyspick's attitude. He wasn't a bad guy, just a little overbearing.

"Coach Hyspick, tell me why Reed Sargent quit the off-season program."

Hyspick stood as firmly as a Marine D.I. "He couldn't take it. He's a pussy."

"Hyspick, do you know that Reed was the best high school shot-putter in the country two years ago? Do you know that I've worked my ass off to get him out for football, even though he's on a track scholarship? Did you know all that?"

"Yes, sir," Hyspick said.

"Do you know that he is 6′ 4″, weighs 267, bench-presses 511 pounds, and was the best defensive tackle in the country his senior year of high school?" Buck stood to face Hyspick eye to eye.

"I believe I've heard you mention that." Hyspick blushed.

Buck licked his lips to clear away the dryness, and slowly continued. "Do you know how hard it is to get a 6′ 4″, 267-pound gorilla out for football? And do you know how easy it is to hire a smart-ass, twenty-six-year-old weight coach?"

"Yes, sir, I guess so."

"I'll tell you one thing right now, Hyspick. If we don't get that gorilla back out, I'm gonna get another weight coach. Do you understand me?"

"I'll go find him, Coach. Right now." Hyspick spun in his tracks and left before Buck could say anything else.

Buck stomped over to the open door and yelled to Peggy.

"Peggy, send a telegram to Eaarnel, Ivie Buchanan, and Mr. Harold Johnson. 'Looking forward to having you on the campus. You are our No. 1 prospect. Will be in touch about detail of trip. Signed, Buck Lee.' Got it?"

"Got it. But why, if I may ask, are you sending the wire to Harold Johnson instead of to Grant? On my printout, Harold is the *father*."

"Don't ask, Peggy, just do it," Buck snapped as he turned and went back into his office.

* * *

"Coach Lee, Coach Lee," a voice said through the open door. It was a Cub Scoutmaster — a man in his forties with a little potbelly, wearing short pants and knee socks. "You don't remember me, do you?" the man asked.

Incredible. "No, I'm sorry, I don't," Buck said.

"You met me at the Ticonderoga High School football banquet ten years ago. You were the speaker."

"Your face is familiar, but I didn't catch your name." Buck stuck his hand out, but the man didn't notice. Instead he shouted, "Come on in, Scouts." Fourteen midgets came trooping through the door, followed by Peggy, who was trying to stem the tidal wave of Cub Scouts.

"Scouts, line up and stand at attention for Coach Lee if you want his autograph," bellowed the Scoutmaster.

"Stand at attention" apparently meant, "Let's tear up the first thing we can get our hands on." Cubbies were all over the room playing catch with every autographed football in Buck's office. Passes were zinging back and forth across the room, and Scouts in short pants were tackling one another on Buck's plush carpet.

"Hold it, fellows," Buck screamed. "If you want some autographed pictures, get in line."

That got it down to a small riot, while Buck called for Peggy to bring the pictures. Grabbing the first Cub by the neck, Buck asked, "What's your name, son?" A tough, little face with freckles and red hair topped by a beanie looked at Buck eyeball to eyeball. He wasn't going to be intimidated by anyone.

"Ernie, and I'm a Johnny Majors fan. Do you have a picture of him?"

"No, Ernie, I don't have a picture of Johnny Majors," Buck said. He wrote "Buck Lee, Best Wishes." After signing the remaining pictures and one for the Scoutmaster, who still hadn't given his name, Buck sent them on their way. This day was going nowhere in a hurry.

* * *

Buck took a bite of his lunch — a ham and cheese sandwich and potato chips he'd sent out for — and perused a report on Tnassip. He made a note to have Hildebrand in for a private meeting so they could discuss how Buck could help with Tnassip's recruiting.

"Coach Stiles on the phone," came Peggy's voice over the intercom.

"Got it." Buck picked up the phone and pushed the blinking light. "What'd you find out about The Hammer, Bo?"

"Well, we bullshitted for awhile about his visiting our place. After we figured out he couldn't, even though it was where he'd always wanted to go, I asked him where he was going to school. He said Penn State without a bit of hesitation."

"Penn State? You got to be kidding. Hell, *we* wouldn't even be recruiting him if he weren't a local kid."

"That's what he said, and when I asked him why not Eastern, he said it was too close. Wanted to get away from Stanleyville. In fact, Buck, he told me he'd already *signed* with Penn State. He signed last night."

"Why, that little cocksucker! That really pisses me off." Buck broke a pencil in half. "Thanks, anyway, Bo. I'll help you out sometime. May the wind always blow at your punter's back."

"You're welcome, Buck, and may the officials all wear purple underwear. See ya."

Buck was steaming. He snatched up the phone and called Charlie Smith. "Coach, get Ignarski, Barton, and Hyspick and bring 'em out to the big Caddy. We're going to see The Hammer. I'll explain when we meet. See you in ten minutes."

Buck picked up his ham and cheese sandwich and threw it across the office. Just as it splattered against the wall next to the door, J. A. walked in. It had barely missed his head. They looked at each other, J. A. with his pipe in his hand, Buck in a follow-through position. Buck looked at the mess on the wall and then said, "I told Peggy I didn't like mayonnaise on my ham sandwiches, J. A. I'm a mustard man."

J. A. puffed on his pipe and watched the smoke drift to the ceiling before he finally answered. "Just lost a prospect, I see. Well, I don't want a coach who takes losing a prospect lightly. Did I tell you about the time I was recruiting the best prospect in South Africa? He was a miler — of course, you know that I was a great miler myself — and we were way behind in the hunt for talent. Do you know what I had to do to get this boy in tow?"

"No, J. A., what'd you have to do?" Buck was working his way toward the door, trying to remember if he had heard this story five times or six.

J. A. blocked the door with his body and finished the tale. "Of course, I was a great deal younger then, although I could still probably run with most of 'em if I got myself back in shape. Well, anyway, I raced this great miler, and guess who won."

"I don't know, J. A., who won?"

Puffing on his pipe and filling the room with smoke, J. A. answered Buck rather matter-of-factly. "You're looking at the winner. That's what I had to do to sign him, beat him in the mile."

"That's great, J. A., but if you don't mind, I've got to see a prospect myself. I'll come by your office tomorrow if that's OK." Buck ducked under J. A.'s arm.

As he ran past Peggy, he said, "I dropped my sandwich. Have somebody clean it up."

He trotted to the parking lot where the coaches were waiting for him. "Get in, men, and I'll explain what we're going to do." Buck cranked the car, and they roared out of the parking lot and headed for Orion High.

Buck was furious. "We're going to get The Hammer out of class and find out why he lied to us. I don't care where the little turd goes to school, but it pisses me off that he wouldn't even tell us the truth. The little prick signed with Penn State last night right after he left our campus. We're going to have some fun."

Ignarski looked a little puzzled. "What are we going to do, beat the hell out of him?" He slammed his fist into his open hand.

"Nope. Better than that. We're going to get him in this car and watch him sweat. We're going to turn the heat on and savor his squirming while he answers our questions. The reason I wanted all of y'all along is that I want it crowded." Buck turned the corner on two wheels. His coaches, their thick necks incapable of whiplash, looked at each other in astonishment.

Slamming on the brakes and coming to a squealing halt in the school parking lot, Buck sent Charlie Smith dashing into the school to get The Hammer. The others waited in the car.

"Coach, it's hot in here. Can we roll down the windows?" said

Dave Barton. His face and armpits were starting to sweat profusely.

"Hell, no, you can't. I want it hot and stuffy in here." Buck felt the sweat start to pour around the rash on his thighs.

Charlie knocked on the steamy window, and Hyspick opened the door. The Hammer, who looked terrified, was shoved toward the car. Hyspick motioned for Sledge to get into the back. The Hammer climbed over Hyspick, who refused to budge, and squeezed himself between Ignarski and Hyspick.

Sledge looked uncomfortable between all that beef. He started to say something about the heat when Buck leaned over from the front seat and said, "Ed, have you made up your mind yet where you're going to school?"

The Hammer twisted around in the seat, his Levi's too tight, and wiped the sweat from his brow. "Coach, I haven't decided yet."

"Ed, I just got off the phone with Coach Stiles, and he tells me you're going to Penn State." Buck deliberately left out the fact that he had already signed. "Is that true?" Ten eyeballs stared at Ed, whose shirt with the alligator on it was now soaked.

"Yeah, I guess that's right." He said it as if he'd forgotten.

"Why Penn State? Everybody in town here knows you, and you'll be a big local favorite."

"Well, Coach Lee, that's why I'm going there. Everybody here knows me." Ed smiled at his own answer.

"We'll play you at tailback," Buck said. "You'll be a great one for us."

"They told me I'd be the only tailback they're recruiting," Ed boasted. "I'll be starting halfway through the season."

Leaning farther over the back seat, Buck said quietly, "Do you believe that? You're not the only back in the world, and there's more than one girl in the world."

The kid gulped and slumped down in the seat under the stress. "Coach Paterno said I could have his home phone number and call him any hour of the day or night."

Buck was now so close to The Hammer that he could smell the M&Ms on his breath. "Ed, you can have *my* home phone number and call *me* any time of the day or night."

Sitting up straight again, Ed let Buck have the real reason for his decision. "Coach Paterno told me I could call him Joe."

"Ed, this is my final offer." Buck put his right hand on The Hammer's shoulder. "You can call *me* Joe."

Everybody in the car broke out with laughter except Ed. He looked like his mother had just made him take a dose of castor oil. "I'd like to get back to school. I think I've been gone long enough." He was frantically looking for a way out of the car. Ignarski opened the door on his side and motioned for Ed to crawl over. Ignarski didn't make it easy for him to get out, but at least he didn't punch him. As Ed walked away from the car, his small ass clinging against his tight Levi's, Buck yelled out, "Congratulations, Ed. Good luck at Penn State." The big Caddy roared out of the parking lot as four coaches strapped themselves in.

"Can we open the windows now?" asked Barton, who looked like he'd been in a Turkish steambath.

"Hell, no!" Buck screamed. "We're going to punish ourselves for not getting that tight-ass."

After five minutes, as the sweat poured off their faces, Buck relented. "Ah, go ahead. But I want everybody to write Ed a letter and tell him how much you like him. He's got a five-year-old brother who's built like a fireplug. We might be recruiting him one day." The windows were down in a flash.

15

BUDDY SHAVERS' OFFICE WAS decorated almost entirely in black and gold — the two sofas, the four throw pillows with the word HAWKS stitched on each one, the chairs, the carpets, the drapes. The panelled walls were cluttered with pictures of former all-American players or pictures of Shavers shaking hands with everybody from former presidents to Mickey Mouse at Disneyland. His desk, conversely, was neat and clean. The only things on it were Rotary, Lions Club, and Knights of Columbus paperweights, and two phones — one for the secretary to call him on and the other a private line he used to tape his conversations. There was a film projector, brand-new, on a small table right next to his desk. Shavers never used it, but it looked good when prospects and rich alums came in. The screen in front of the projector was up in its casing so as not to obstruct the diagrammed plays on the small blackboard behind it. The stage was set.

Shavers reacted quickly to the buzzer. "What is it?"

"Coach Shavers, Eaarnel is here," said Adelle Muncie.

"Tell him to come on in, Mrs. Muncie." Shavers got out of his chair, walked over to his private bathroom, and looked at himself in the mirror to be sure his gold and black tie was on straight. The tie looked good, he thought, and so did he for a man of fifty-five. He wished he didn't have such a heavy beard, but his slightly graying hair gave him the touch of maturity that parents liked. And he wished his face weren't flushed all the time, like he'd been drinking too much, but he kept the color pretty much under control by using pancake makeup. There was nothing he could do about the ear. He heard a knock on the door and Coach Blackwell saying, "Can we come in, Coach Shavers?"

"Come on in, Coach, I'm looking forward to seeing Eaarnel." The door opened and there stood the finest-looking specimen Shavers had seen in twenty-five years of coaching: tall, lean, big buttocks, great thighs, arms that looked like the man on Arm and Hammer baking soda boxes, and a big smile on his broad face.

Blackwell was grinning from ear to ear. He looked like he had just walked into the coaches' convention with the best-looking woman in America. "Coach Shavers, this is Eaarnel," he said with the emphasis on *Ear*, which was the proper pronunciation.

Shavers blushed at the emphasis and turned slightly to his left. "Eaarnel, it's great having you on the campus of the Western Black and Gold Fightin' Hawks," he said. "I know you've been here before, but this is the first time you and I have gotten to visit in my office. I trust you've had a good time on campus."

Shavers grabbed one of the gold and black chairs beside his desk and pulled it over to the sofa where Coach Blackwell was motioning for Eaarnel to sit. Shavers pulled himself up to a position right in front of Eaarnel. The cigar smell was awful, and Eaarnel's nose twitched slightly as the scent reached him. If Shavers had one weakness in recruiting, it was that he smoked cigars constantly, and his clothes reeked of their smell.

"Eaarnel, let's be honest with one another. What will it take for you to sign a Western scholarship?" Blackwell squirmed. He'd heard Shavers use this direct approach a thousand times, but it still worried him. Shavers always argued that if you dealt in cash, you never got caught. The NCAA caught only coaches who did stupid things, like giving a player a T-shirt, helping him sell his tickets, or letting him use the school phone to call home.

Eaarnel just looked at Shavers, smiled, and didn't say a word. Shavers stood up, took a key out of his pocket, walked over to his desk, and opened the top, righthand drawer. He slowly pulled out a Tampa Nugget cigar box, fondled it, and then walked back over to where Eaarnel was sitting.

"Eaarnel, do you know the one thing money won't buy?" He still didn't get an answer from Eaarnel, who just kept sitting there staring at Shavers with those dark, penetrating eyes. "Well, I'll tell you what it won't buy, Eaarnel. It won't buy poverty."

When there was still no answer from Eaarnel and Blackwell began to move around in his seat like he had hemorrhoids, Shavers decided to push on. This dumb-ass is probably too stupid to know what I'm talking about, Shavers was thinking.

"Eaarnel, listen to me. I'm going to get you here one way or the other. You hear? You're not going to get away from me. Now, let me give you your choices." Shavers opened his cigar box, reached inside with his pudgy left hand, and pulled out a stack of $100 bills. He stared at the money for about thirty seconds to make sure Eaarnel noticed how big the stack was.

"Let's see, Eaarnel, it's about four hundred miles round-trip to your house from here. The school pays us twenty cents a mile when we use our cars to recruit. Me and my assistant coaches will probably make about forty trips down to see you. Let's see, now, four hundred multiplied by twenty cents comes out to $80. Now we multiply that by forty, and that comes out to be $3,200." Shavers slowly counted out thirty-two $100 bills on the sofa right next to where Eaarnel was sitting.

"We'll have to stay in a motel while we're there, and that'll cost about $40 to $50 a night. Let's just use fifty. Forty nights at $50 is $2,000." Shavers counted out more bills.

"We've got to eat don't we, Coach Blackwell? All of our coaches like to eat well, so that's another $40 or $50 a day. That comes out to another $2,000. Wait a minute. Coach Blackwell, we always tip well, don't we? So that's another $300." Shavers slowly counted out twenty-three $100 bills. Eaarnel wasn't about to say anything. He just kept his mouth shut and glared at the money. He couldn't wait to get home to tell his mama.

"Now, Eaarnel, Coach Blackwell can tell you that when I make up my mind to get someone, I get him. Isn't that right, Coach Blackwell?"

"I've never seen you fail to get one, Coach, that you really wanted." Blackwell was trying to say as little as possible.

"Here are the two choices, Eaarnel. I can spend all the money that you see in front of you driving back and forth to sign you, or you can save us both a lot of work by just taking this money I'm going to spend anyway and saying you're going to be a Hawk. It makes no difference to me; either way, I'm going to get you." Shavers picked up the seventy-five $100 bills and handed them to Eaarnel.

Eaarnel took the money, looked at it, and stuck it deep in his hip pocket. "Coach," he said, "I'll keep the money if you want me to, but I haven't made up my mind yet about what I'm going to do. I've got it narrowed down to USC, Michigan, Ohio State, Notre Dame, y'all, and the Eastern Rattlers. When I get ready to make a decision, we'll talk again." He stood up and stuck out his hand to Shavers, who tried clumsily to give Eaarnel a soul brother shake. Eaarnel just ignored it and shook hands the way fifty-five-year-old men shake hands all over the country. There was a moment of awkward silence, and then Blackwell said, "Coach, I've got to take Eaarnel to get something to eat. He's a growing man." He emphasized the *man*.

"Don't forget to add the cost of the meal to that $7,500, Eaarnel. I forgot to add that on," Shavers said as Eaarnel and Blackwell left the office.

The door closed and Shavers turned livid. He stormed into the bathroom and started tearing off his clothes. He needed a shower bad. "Shit! Goddammit! That black bastard took my money and didn't sign!" Shavers yelled as the hot water pounded against his body. "I'll kill that stupid Blackwell."

* * *

After finishing his shower and donning clean clothes, Shavers picked up his private line and dialed 205-237-4387. While the phone rang, he reached into his gold-plated humidor and pulled out a long, black, Cuban cigar. He picked up the gold lighter that the Cartersville Quarterback Club had given him and flipped the top.

"Hello, Roanoke Clothing Store."

"May I speak to Harold Gold? This is Buddy Shavers calling."

"Yes, sir, Coach Shavers, I'll go get him," an excited female voice said. "Coach Shavers, before I go, I'll have to tell you my daddy played for you. Frank Watson. Do you remember him?"

"Why, *sure* I remember your daddy, honey," Shavers said as he quickly flipped through his Rolodex to the W's. He found Frank Watson's card.

"He played, I believe, in 1958. From Roanoke. He was a defensive tackle and earned one letter. You must be his daughter, Sally. Why, I remember when you were born." The girl giggled with pride.

Shavers lit his cigar while waiting for Gold to come to the phone. As the smoke drifted lazily toward the ceiling, he made a note to see if a computer might not be better than the Rolodex. That way, when somebody asked if he remembered some asshole who used to play for him, he could just punch a button and get all the information to make 'em think he remembered.

"Hello, Coach Shavers, this is Harold Gold. It's a real pleasure to hear from you. What can I do for you?"

"Mr. Gold, as you know, we think Eaarnel Simpson is the No. 1 prospect in the state, maybe in the country. Now, his mama don't have enough to go around, so if you could help the boy out with some nice clothes, I'd sure appreciate it."

"Coach Shavers, we haven't had a lot of good players in Roanoke, and I don't rightly know what you mean. Do you want me to give him a part-time job so he can buy clothes at discount?"

"Let me explain something to you, Mr. Gold. If, let's say, Eaarnel's name was Marilyn, and Marilyn was 5′ 4″, weighed 120, had beautiful hair, teeth, legs, skin, face, and a pair of knockers that would pop your eyes out, would you give her a part-time job, or would you just let her have the clothes?"

"It's just according to what she'd do for me," Gold said.

"You got it, Mr. Gold. Tell Eaarnel you're going to open up a charge account for him. When he asks how he'll pay for it, you just say Coach Shavers is a good friend of yours. That's all you have to do."

"Just one more question, Coach Shavers. What if he signs with East Alabama?"

"Then you send the son of a bitch the bill."

16

THE FIELD HOUSE AT Eastern was musty, cavernous, and usually full of students either playing basketball on the new 3M floor or jogging around the track with faculty members or spouses. When you walked into the building, the first thing you noticed were the pennants hanging from the rafters. The many championships that Coach Ashford Roberts' basketball teams had won were there for all to see. It reminded Buck that at least for the time being, like at the University of Kentucky, this was a basketball school rather than a football school.

As he worked his way across the arena, Buck spotted Ignarski and Stone jogging around the track. Their chubby bodies huffed and puffed as they tried to keep up with a couple of overweight housewives. Ignarski ran like he did everything else: He tried to beat the hell out of the ground. Buck waved as he continued on toward the handball courts, where Hyspick was holding the off-season workouts.

"Coach Lee," Buck heard as he started to open the narrow door to the handball courts. Coming up behind him, smoking his ever-present pipe, was J. A.

"How are you, Buck. I haven't seen you in awhile. Hope you've been signing up some good 'uns."

"We're doing OK, J. A., but you know how tough it is to go against the Hawks. That son of a bitch is the toughest damn coach in the country to beat when you're one-on-one with him over a biggie like Eaarnel. He'll do anything, and I mean *anything*. I should know. I worked for him."

J. A. puffed on his pipe, saw it was out, and reached into his coat pocket for his lighter. He held the pipe with his left hand, and flicking the large lighter with his right, created a flame that should have set off an alarm. He sucked in until blue smoke began to rise from the pipe.

"When I was track coach," J. A. said, "it was a constant fight with Rufus Hearn over at Western. I was a much better coach, but as you know, even a great coach needs *some* talent."

"Do I know that!"

"Well, anyway, we were after this great shot-putter from Butte, Montana. At the time, our campus wasn't very big or very pretty, while the campus at Western was a much better place to show off. Know how your athletic director got that lad to sign with us?"

Fidgeting with the change in his pocket, Buck answered simply, "No, how'd you do it?"

J. A. savored the moment, as though remembering the first time he ever made love to a woman. "Buck, here's what I did. When this lad got off the plane and got settled down, I took him over to the Rogers Plantation. That's the one where they have the gates, and you have to have a password to get in. The big house that sits up on top of the hill. Looks like Tara from *Gone With the Wind*."

"Yeah, I remember. It belonged to Clyde Rogers. The millionaire."

"Right," said J. A., knocking the ashes out of his pipe. "Well, I took this lad over to the plantation and told him that was where we housed our track people at Eastern. His eyes got as big as saucers, and he wanted to know if he could see his room. I looked at him real serious-like, Buck, and told him we couldn't go in right then because it was Sorority Day at the house, and all the girls from the sororities were there. I didn't have to tell him any more. The next day he signed on with your athletic director."

"That's a helluva story, J. A., but I gotta run now. Gotta meet Coach Hyspick and tell him how many prospects we have coming in this weekend. We'll need some of our own guys to show 'em around."

J. A. refilled his pipe with Sail tobacco, still reveling in his story, and started to leave. "Oh, yeah, Buck, one more thing. Tell Hyspick not to make so much noise in the handball court. That nosey Meecham might come around and have a heart attack if he sees all those fine, clean-cut young boys knocking the shit out of one another." J. A. turned and left.

Buck opened the door to the brightly lit handball court and walked in. There were about sixty-five players, in sweat clothes with weights around their ankles, engaging in combat with a weapon called the *batacca*. The *batacca* was something Hyspick had picked up at last year's coaches' convention. It was about two feet in length and had a foam rubber pad at the end of a stick. The stick had a grip on the other end, so the gladiator could hold it without being afraid it would slip out of his hand. Its purpose was to let the players know what it felt like to be hit up 'side the head by a stick with foam rubber on the end of it. The temperature must have been at least a hundred degrees in the room meant to be shared by four rather than sixty-five. The high ceiling gave it the appearance of being bigger than it actually was, but the bodies barely had room to move, much less to knock the hell out of one another with *bataccas*.

Hyspick didn't see Buck when he first came in. He was too busy yelling commands to his sweaty warriors. "Hit him! Knock his dick off!" he screamed. "Don't quit, you pussy. What do you think this is, a class for old ladies and faggots? That's it. Nail him! Don't let a little blood bother you, just remember the Hawks are your enemy. We have to kill their ass. It's only 125 days until we line up against 'em. Get your asses in gear!" Hyspick continued ranting and screaming at sixty-five players who were too tired to even swing the sticks at each other. Then he spotted Buck in the room, and without missing a beat, roared, "*Rattlers*!" Sixty-five football players dropped their *bataccas* and assumed a football hitting position, knees bent, backs straight, and arms with fists clenched and ready to strike. They screamed back, "*Pride*!"

"*Hawks*!" screamed Hyspick.

"*Suck*!" replied sixty-five maniacs.

"Now, let's give the head coach a big fifteen."

Clap, Clap, Clap, Clap, Clap.

Clap, Clap, Clap, Clap, Clap.

Clap, Clap, Clap, Clap, Clap.

Buck looked at the faces of the sixty-five young men who were going to represent the Rattlers on the field of battle and felt a great sense of pride. There was a lot of bullshit in the recruiting, more than he could stomach sometimes, but when he saw how hard players worked because they wanted to win, he got all choked up. Hell, he figured half the kids out here would never see the field on Saturday except from the sidelines or maybe even the stands. But they were willing to go through all this gore just for the fun of being a participant in the greatest game of them all — football. There was snot running from their noses and blood coming from their ears, lips, and foreheads from the *batacca* blows. Buck walked over and motioned for them to gather around and take a rest. He could see the relief in their eyes as they dropped to one knee.

"Great spirit, men. I can see by what you're doing here that you'll be ready when we start football practice." Buck slapped hands with players as he praised them for their positive attitude. He stopped when he heard a retching noise from the corner of the room. Big Johnny Grayson, all 255 pounds of him, was throwing up in the corner of the court. Hyspick had prepared for this by having sandboxes placed in every corner. Nobody else paid any attention, so Buck ignored the sound and continued.

"Men, we've got a great group of prospects coming in this weekend, and we need your help. The assistant coaches will be asking some of you to act as hosts this weekend for a prospect. So please do your best. We give Christmas bonuses for the player who does the best job of showing the prospect a good time — *if* the kid signs with us because he had fun while he was here. Remember, we can't have a top-notch football team unless you help us."

The little rest did wonders for most of the players — except for Grayson, who was still throwing up in the box — and they were starting to feel feisty again.

"How about a date with one of those Rattlerettes, Coach Lee, as a bonus for getting one of these prospects to sign with us?" Dave Bledsoe's sweat clothes were two sizes too large for him and were soaking wet, but his interest was up.

"Can't a big stud like you get a date on his own?" Buck asked.

Rubbing his hand across his closely cropped scalp, Bledsoe looked directly at Buck, avoiding the hostile stare that Hyspick was giving him, and said, "Coach Lee, the gals don't like guys with hair this short. It's not in style."

"He's right, Coach," seconded another.

"Right on," said a third.

"OK, guys, you help us and we'll help you. After this weekend, Coach Hyspick and I will sit down and discuss the length of your hair. Is that fair enough?"

In unison they yelled, "*Rattlers*!"

The spontaneous emotion was starting to get Buck fired up, too. The closeness of the players in the handball court made him feel like a warrior again. His jaw got tight, his eyes became slits, and his neck tightened as he got ready to speak.

"We're going to get after that bunch of candy-asses over at Western like they've never been gotten after in recruiting! We're gonna knock their asses off this weekend. Anybody who doesn't want to compete against that Hawk who's showing around the same prospect next weekend at Western better get out now!" Buck was screaming.

"If you don't have the Rattler spirit, then go play for some half-ass program where they talk about everything except winning. If you don't want to be a Rattler and don't want to play to be No. 1, then get out of this school. Love it or leave it!" Buck was drooling at the mouth and his heart was pumping wildly. He was ready. He screamed at the top of his lungs, "*Rattlers*!" Every man there leaped to his feet and screamed back, "*Pride*!"

Buck instantly dropped into a hitting position and slammed his fist into the concrete wall. He really didn't intend to hit it quite as hard as he did, but when his fist struck the wall, blood spurted from his knuckles. Buck stared at his hand, grimaced, then began to rage anew. "Goddammit! You dumb asshole!" he screamed at himself as blood poured down his hand.

"You OK, Coach Lee?" said Hyspick. His voice was the only sound in the room. The players just stared at Buck Lee's hand full of blood.

"I must apologize, men, for my language," Buck said. He was surprised at his calm. "I'm not a member of the FCA, or, as it's better known, the Fellowship of Christian Athletes. But I *am* president and founder of the SBA." Silence. Blood dripped from his hand onto the floor. "SBA, in case you didn't know, stands for Save Buck's Ass!"

The players, buoyed by this fanatical display, forgot all about their soreness and their aches. They began to chant, "*Rattlers! Rattlers! Rattlers!*" until the walls were vibrating. Then, as Buck held up his bloody hand for quiet, they hushed.

"I want to leave you with one thought," Buck said. "Pride is everything in life. Have pride in yourself, your team, and your school. Now, when we bring those hotshots over to watch you work out, I want you to show them Rattler pride. Have pride! I want you to act like you're walking around the shower room with a twelve-inch cock. Now *that's* pride!"

Cheers echoed throughout the court as the players punched and gave the high-five.

"*Rattlers*!" screamed Buck.

"*Pride*!" came the response.

As he turned to leave the room, Buck heard Hyspick say, "How many of you went to church last Sunday? Hold up your hands."

All Buck could think about was getting his hand in some ice. He was sure it wasn't broken, but it hurt like hell. He started to grin as he went into the training room for some ice. This will probably help in recruiting, he thought. All the prospects will assume I've been in a fight. Better yet, every week we'll have one coach bandaged up like he's been in a fight. Hell, yes, great idea.

17

WHEN BUCK HEARD PEGGY'S distinctive high-heeled footsteps marching toward his half-open office door, he quickly slipped the dozen Polaroid pictures of the Rattlerettes into his desk drawer. Even though he had semi-legitimate reasons for sitting alone in his office drooling over close-ups of nineteen- and twenty-year-olds, he felt like a peeping Tom caught in the act.

"Coach Lee, you've got to go up to the hill right away," Peggy said. "It seems somebody's turned us in."

Oh, God, no, Buck thought. The Baptist Student Union has found out about the Rattlerettes.

"What are you talking about, Peggy? Who's turned us in and for what?"

"It's about recruiting violations, I think. All I know is that Dr. Lowe's secretary called and said for you to get over there. Dr. Lowe, J. A. Symington, and Dr. Meecham are waiting for you."

"OK, Peggy," Buck said. "I'll just put on my innocent face and mosey on up." Better to face the NCAA than the Baptist Student Union, he thought. "Ah, Peggy, I'm expecting a call from Kirk Battle. If I don't get back before he calls, get his number and tell him I'll call later."

"Right, Coach."

"*If* I come back," Buck said, feeling his rash flare up again. He grabbed a can of Cruex out of his drawer and wobbled to the bathroom. As he leaned against the sink dousing his stinging pubic area, the toilet in the first stall flushed and out jumped Richard Culpepper.

"Coach Lee! Got the crud?"

Buck, startled, jerked his arm up and sent powder flying all over himself and Richard.

"Naw, I'm starting a ski slope on my balls, and this is artificial snow."

"Geez, Coach Lee, I'm sorry. I didn't mean to scare you. Let me help you dust some of this off. . . ."

"Get the hell away from me!" Buck blurted. "I'll take care of my own damned jock itch!"

Buck pulled up his coaching shorts and turned to the mirror to zip up. He saw Richard's grinning reflection. "You still want a job? That it?"

"You bet, Coach Lee. I want to work for you. What do you say?"

Buck turned around, studied him for a moment, then walked toward the door. "Richard," he said as he opened the door, "you've got jock powder on your face. Better wipe if off before you leave the bathroom. If you ever *do* work for me, I don't want anybody saying you slept with me to get the job."

* * *

Buck drove slowly up the tree-lined street, past the guard to the president's office in the old administration building. He thought how strange it was that this had happened so quickly. Recruiting wasn't easy, but Buck had always felt that he was good at it. Getting called on the carpet this soon was embarrassing. He'd seen too many schools put on probation during the past ten years. Funny thing was, he thought, the coaches break the rules but the school takes the heat. Then while the school's on probation, the coach goes on to the pros and makes $200,000 a year.

"I think Dr. Lowe wants to see me," Buck told Lowe's secretary.

"They're expecting you." The secretary, Ann Sletchbaum, never glanced up from her *New York Times* crossword puzzle. She seemed to be stumped.

"What's the clue?" Buck asked, as he walked to the side of her uncluttered desk.

"Excuse me?"

"What's your clue there? Maybe I can help."

"I *doubt* it," she said. "But it's a four-letter word meaning 'to compromise.'"

Buck walked to the president's door, opened it, stepped halfway into the office, and stopped. "Rape!" he shouted. "Try *rape*, Miz Sletchbaum." Her eyes smouldered while her legs pressed tightly together under her desk.

The plush, masculine smells of expensive leather and pipe tobacco filled Buck's nostrils as he entered the spacious, book-lined office. The pipe smoke he recognized as J. A.'s. The leather was unmistakably presidential.

"Coach Lee," Dr. Lowe greeted him from behind his huge desk, which seemed too big for the little man. Buck walked over and politely gripped his hand. It felt like the hand of a pale child who'd been bedridden for years.

"Hello, Buck," J. A. said from the shadows in his usual serious tone. "You remember Dr. Meecham here, I'm sure — our faculty rep."

"Of course, I do," Buck said. Who could forget such a slob? he thought. "Good to see you again, Dr. Meecham." Buck gripped his chubby, greasy hand and resisted an urge to wipe his palm on his shorts.

"I know this is not going to be very pleasant," Dr. Lowe said. "But we've had some very unpleasant charges brought against our program."

Buck glanced around the office and noticed that, aside from two or three framed degrees, the only things on Dr. Lowe's walls were several black and white photographs of a sickly kid in an East Alabama track uniform. In one of the pictures, Clarke Lowe had his arm around an older, white-haired man wearing a whistle. It was J. A. Buck knew that J. A. had been a big track man, but he never knew that he had coached Clarke Lowe. Every ornament in the office was track-related. There were dozens of small, cheap trophies stashed between volumes of leather-bound books with gold printing. A pair of decaying track shoes hung from a nail between the shelves, and a tiny bust of Jesse Owens rested on the glass table beside the high-backed leather couch. And as Dr. Lowe spoke, he held his glass paperweight up to the light and watched a tiny track man jogging through flecks of white snow swirling around inside the bubble.

"He said, some very serious charges have been brought against the program" repeated Dr. Meecham.

"Yes, and I'd like to hear your answers before we continue with the investigation," said Dr. Lowe. He vigorously shook the paperweight and set it down on his desk.

"I'd like to hear the questions," Buck said.

"Dr. Meecham," said Clarke Lowe, nodding.

"There are several charges, Coach Lee, which we discovered through a very reliable source. The first charge is that Coach Driscoll is allowing players to use his phone to call home. He even allowed one player to use his credit card, and that player, in turn, let everyone at the Sigma Nu fraternity house call on the credit card." J. A. relit his pipe and looked uncomfortable. "The phone bill amounted to over a thousand dollars — $1,012 to be exact."

"Coach Lee, you know it's against the rules to allow a player to use a school phone," Dr. Lowe said.

Dr. Meecham put away his notes and looked very proud of himself. Buck considered the consequences of strangling this wimp, who didn't know the first thing about athletics, but decided it would be too difficult to get a good grip under his three sagging chins. Meecham didn't understand that it was a humanitarian gesture to let some homesick youngster, who was busting his ass for you on the field, use the office phone to call his girlfriend or mother.

"Dr. Lowe," said Buck. "You are one hundred percent right. I'll certainly talk with Coach Driscoll about the phone. We'll take the money out of the scholarship allowance that the guilty player gets and pay off the phone bill. I'll also insist that the fraternity pay its share of the phone bill. I'll make sure that they pay what they charged on Coach Driscoll's credit card." Buck leaned back in the comfortable sofa and hoped that would appease Lowe.

"Coach Lee," Meecham said before Dr. Lowe could react, "we've also had some complaints about the transcripts of some of our student-athletes. They don't seem to meet the requirements set down by the university." Buck made an effort to give Meecham his full attention, but the condescending tone of voice and his upturned nose made it difficult. "In fact," Meecham continued, "it looks as if some of the courses for which they have been given credit do not even *exist*. How do you explain junior college courses on a high school transcript?"

J. A. raised a concerned eyebrow, and Dr. Lowe leaned forward in his chair until the knot in his tie was pressing against the edge of his desk.

"Dr. Meecham," Buck said with outward calm, "I'm sure there's an explanation for that. They were probably in the junior college area last summer and took the courses while visiting a friend or relative. I'm sure you could check it out with the junior college instructor."

Buck eyed Meecham, who suddenly realized that he didn't have the ammunition to raise a lingering stink.

J. A. sprang from the couch beside Buck and spoke up for the first time. "Meecham, why don't we just forget all that crap you've just laid on us? I don't see one thing that implicates any of our coaches in anything illegal. Buck runs an honest ship. You'd better have more than phone calls and other petty bullshit before you bring us up here for a hanging party. And if you do, Dr. Meecham, I'll be the one taking responsibility for my coaches."

"I'll have to agree with J. A., Dr. Meecham," said Clarke Lowe. "I think Coach Lee has answered your questions satisfactorily. Now, Coach Lee, if you'll take care of those problems we just mentioned, we'll go on about the business of running an academic institution and leave the sports to you and your staff."

"Thank you, Dr. Lowe," said J. A., remembering to address him formally when in the presence of others. "I can assure you that Coach Lee and all our coaches will abide by what we have in the NCAA manual."

Buck and J. A. excused themselves and headed for the door, but Buck stopped for a moment to examine a photo of a much younger Dr. Lowe shaking hands with a lean and hard-looking J. A. Symington. At the bottom of the picture was typed, "Coach J. A. Symington giving last-minute tip before 440 relay."

J. A. winked at Buck, who knew there was more to the story of the track coach who becomes athletic director and the student who becomes university president. Buck figured J. A. would tell him the story when the time was right.

"Well, Ann, was it *rape*?" Buck asked as he passed the secretary's desk. J. A.'s ears perked up. He figured whoever raped *her* must have been either a necrophile or a Sigma Nu with very bad grades.

"No, Coach Lee, it wasn't," she snapped. "But it's amazing how quickly the word occurred to you. You have an amazing vocabulary."

"Well, thank you Miz Sletchbaum," Buck said, enjoying the repartee. "I'm sure you will figure it out sooner or later. Have a nice day." J. A. just scratched his head.

"Well, well, well," J. A. said as they approached their cars parked along the yellow curb. "That wasn't so tough was it?"

"No, it wasn't, J. A.," said Buck. "But it really is silly having a rule that forbids us paying a $6 phone bill for an eighteen-year-old boy to call his mother after we've spent $10,000 to recruit him. 'I'm sorry, son, I realize you're homesick, your father is in the hospital, and your mother is near a nervous breakdown, but you can't use my phone unless you can pay for it. It's against the rules.'"

"Buck, I don't make the rules," J. A. said. "Just do me a favor. Don't tell me what you're doing. I just don't need to know all that. You know what I mean?"

"I believe I do."

"But remember what I've always said: If we're going to bend the rules, he'd better be good!"

"They'll be good ones, J. A.," Buck promised.

J. A., evidently pumped up by winning the war against Meecham, screeched away from the curb and promptly smashed his Porsche through the black-and-white striped wooden traffic barrier at the guard gate. The young security guard ran out of his little white booth, not knowing whether to draw his gun, write down the tag number, or just cuss.

As Buck slid behind the wheel of his car, proud of the support J. A. had just given him, he felt a twinge of regret about not being able to tell J. A. the truth about the transcripts — about how the prospects actually had been enrolled in junior college classes while they were working in their hometowns. That would have been perfectly legal, except for the fact that the junior college was at least a thousand miles away in Northern Colorado. A friend of Buck's at the junior college had enrolled the prospects as if they were there. At the end of the summer session, they got several A's and Buck's friend got $200 per A. All in the name of school spirit, of course.

"Did you get the tag number of that maniac?" Buck asked as he rolled up to the guard.

"Hell, naw!" He was spitting mad. "But we'll find the crazy son of a bitch."

"Well, I think I know who it was," Buck said. The red-faced guard came closer.

"Who?"

"I'm almost positive it was a faculty member."

"*Faculty* member?"

"Yeah. I'm almost positive it was Dr. Meecham."

"Dr. Meecham? The fat-ass?"

"Yep."

"Oh, boy! He's gonna pay for this. It's gonna be too wet to plow for that crazy lard-ass."

Buck nodded goodbye to the guard, now rocking back and forth on his heels, and headed for the office.

18

DAVE, I WANT SOME more information on Grant Johnson," Buck said to Barton as he walked into the office. "You really only gave us the bare essentials in our last meeting. I need to know what it'll take to get him. This kid's our quarterback."

Dave leaned forward and placed his hands on Buck's desk. "Coach, it's like we suspected all along, the dad is the key. The boy is like a mute. The mother, all she does is play tennis and smoke menthols. If we're going to sign this kid, we've got to work on the father."

"What do we do, give him some money? I'm not going to play that game. It's bad enough to have to do things for players, but I'll be damned if I'll buy a dad," Buck said.

"I've set up a meeting with the family in Birmingham next week. I think if we get into the house, we'll have a chance. Otherwise, we're out of it," Barton said. "Everybody in the country is recruiting Mr. Johnson. I mean everybody. That old man's been sending out statistics on his kid to everybody for three years."

"You're kidding. I thought we were the only one."

"That's what he wrote on every letter, that they were the only school his son was interested in. Consequently, every school is in on the hunt."

"Why Dave, that's not *fair*," said Buck.

"That's the way they're working it these days, Coach."

"I never heard of such shenanigans. It's, why, it's *cheating*."

"I know, but the fathers, they've . . ." Barton blushed as he finally realized he had been had. "Shit, Coach."

"Had you going there, didn't I?" said Buck. "Set something up for next week. I might learn some tricks from Mr. Johnson."

* * *

The ride to Birmingham was cool and pleasant. Buck and Dave solved all the world's problems while driving the three-hour stretch through rural Alabama. As they approached the city limits of the state's only real city and started out into the suburbs, the talk returned to Grant Johnson.

"This one's a weird case," Barton said. "The old man does everything for the boy. He does all the talking and all the planning. He's the one who'll make the decision about where the boy will go to school."

Buck turned the Cadillac down Shady Lane Avenue onto a row of homes that all looked alike. Ticky-tacky boxes, all in a row. As he looked for Shady Lane Terrace, he said, "What about the mother? What say-so does she have?"

"Nothing important. She sits there in her tennis dress and nods her head at whatever Harold, that's the dad, says."

Turning onto Shady Lane Terrace, Buck began to slow down, looking for 2811. "What do you think our approach should be with the dad? Should we talk academics, football, job after graduation, or talk about *him*?"

"There's 2811 on this side. It's the one with the 'Yard of the Month' sign on the lawn. Anyway, talk is what you'll get from him. I doubt that you'll get a lot of your sales pitch in." Dave reached back for his briefcase and thumbed through his notes on the Johnsons one more time. He didn't want to make a mistake on the head coach's first trip into the Johnson home. "Buck," he said, "there *is* one thing I've forgotten to mention. They *do* have a dog."

"A *dog*?" Buck stopped the car in the driveway. "Why didn't you tell me that before? I would've worn my boots."

"He's really harmless. He's an old Irish setter that the family dearly loves. Probably ten years old. Just gums, no teeth."

Buck fixed his tie in the mirror and tried to calm himself. "OK. Give me your briefcase. I want something to defend myself with in case I'm attacked." Barton handed over his briefcase and got out of the car first. He knew Buck was waiting to see if the dog were going to charge. Dave stood there for a minute while Buck fiddled with his hair, coat, tie, and car keys. Finally, when there was no ferocious dog attack, Buck got out of the car.

As they started for the front door, they heard the sound of young girls screaming. They looked across the street to a playground where the screams were coming from and almost dropped their teeth. Grant Johnson, high school all-American quarterback, was throwing passes to a fat little girl while a taller and skinnier one was jumping up and down in front of him, trying to block the passes.

"What the hell's going on over there?" Buck asked, one eye on Grant Johnson and the other on lookout for the dog.

"It's a regular routine for Grant and his sisters — part of the training program. The fat sister has the better hands, so she catches the passes. The skinny kid makes it tougher for Grant because she's taller and faster."

The front door opened and Harold Johnson stood there. His short, pudgy body was not adaptable to clothes. He looked like he had been sleeping in his shirt for a week. His face was well-lined, even though Buck knew he couldn't be over forty. The cigarette in his right hand was down to the filter, and the ashes were as long as the original cigarette. His tie hung down below his belt, and his pants were full of cigarette holes. His beady little eyes were set back in his head and his skin color was platinum.

"How are you, Mr. Johnson? In case you don't remember me, I'm Coach Barton. And this is Coach Buck Lee."

"Sure, I remember you, Dave. We've had lots of nice talks. And you're Buck Lee. How are you, Buck?"

"Well, it's certainly a pleasure to meet you, Mr. Johnson. I've heard so much about your son." Buck was still looking for the dog.

Harold Johnson turned to Buck and pointed out across the field to where Grant was throwing passes. "Grant won't be able to visit with us tonight. He has to throw against the rush for an hour, then lift weights with his throwing arm for another hour. Then he's got to go to his room and read up on football strategy before he does his school work."

"That's OK, Mr. Johnson. We wanted to talk with you and your wife about Grant's education, anyway," Buck said. He followed Mr. Johnson and Dave into the musty house, looking left and right for the lurking dog, clutching the briefcase as a shield.

"I must apologize for not hearing you arrive, but I was on the phone with Barry," said Johnson.

"Switzer?"

"Yeah, Oklahoma."

"Oh, *that* Barry," said Buck.

As they headed for the back of the house, Buck wondered where the trophies and awards were. He hadn't spotted them yet, but he knew they were here. Johnson opened a door and motioned for Buck and Dave to follow. They all walked down into the basement, which had been made into a den.

"Buck, I want you to meet my wife, Madeline." Buck reached out to shake the hand of the skinniest woman he had ever seen in tennis clothes. Her legs looked like matches. Her dyed-blonde hair was covered by a droopy headband, and she had sweatbands dangling on both wrists and a cigarette in her yellowish left hand.

"Hello, Buck. I have to apologize for my appearance, but this was tennis day. Now, if you had caught me on garden club day, I'd be dressed much nicer."

"You look lovely in your tennis clothes, Mrs. Johnson. I don't know if I could stand the garden clothes if you looked any better. And did you meet my assistant coach, Dave Barton?"

Harold Johnson answered for her. "She's met him. Now, Buck, I want you to meet the *real* star of our family. We really love him." Johnson opened another door and released the ugliest red dog Buck had ever dreamed of. "Red, this is Buck." The setter was up in his face, licking him, before Buck could move. He backpeddled until the dog's paws hit the floor.

"He's a great dog, Mr. Johnson. Wish I had one just like him." Please, God, don't let there be a litter of little Reds, Buck thought.

Dave quickly started petting the dog and pulled him away. Buck looked for a place to sit so he could get this meeting started. Without waiting for an invitation, he sat down in one of the two Naugahyde La-Z-Boy chairs. Keeping one eye on the dog, Buck looked around the room and spotted all the trophies and autographed pictures of coaches. It looked like an alcove of the Hall of Fame in Canton, Ohio.

"Buck," Harold Johnson said, "let's get down to business. Barry was over here the other night and said he could make my kid an all-American. My first question is, can *you*?" Johnson commandeered the other recliner. He ignored his wife and Dave.

"We have one rule at our school, Mr. Johnson: If the other coach says he can make your son an all-American, we say we can, too." Red ambled over and put his head in Buck's lap.

"Isn't that cute, Daddy? Red really likes Buck," Madeline said as she fired up another cigarette. Smoke already clung to the ceiling and permeated everything.

"Question No. 2," said Harold Johnson. "I talked with Pat the other day, and he said he'd change his offense to fit Grant's talent. How do you feel about that?"

"Would you like some dip and chip?" said Madeline.

"No, ma'am," said Buck. "I'm playing with the dog right now."

"Don't bother us, Madeline, we're talking business," Johnson shouted. "Now. You didn't answer my question, Buck." Harold Johnson stared at Buck and took a notepad from the magazine pouch of the La-Z-Boy. "Excuse me for looking at my notes, but I like to be fair. I want to ask you the same questions I asked everyone else. Now, go ahead and answer my question."

"I don't think we have to change our offense for your son," Buck said. "When I took the job, I told Coach Barton over there to install the offense that would help us get the best quarterback in the country. He's done it. Now all we have to do is get Grant to come run his offense."

Harold Johnson grinned like a Cheshire cat. He liked that answer. He continued down his checklist. "What kind of linemen will you have to protect us? I mean, we don't want to get back there and have no protection."

Madeline Johnson interrupted again. "Meg, you come down here right now and meet Coach Buck Lee. Don't sit up there on the steps, come on down *here*. And don't stick your lip out at me, young lady, or I'll bust your behind."

"Madeline, goddammit, if you bust in on us again, I'll bust *your* behind," shouted Johnson. "Meg, say hello to Buck."

The fat little girl who had been catching passes across the street came slowly down the stairs. Her lip was cut and her clothes were filthy. "Daddy," she whined, "why do I have to be the pass-catcher all the time? Why can't I rush Grant like Marjoe? Look at my lip where he hit me with the ball."

"You know the answer to that, Meg. She's taller and faster than you are. It makes it harder for Grant to throw over her, and he has to work harder practicing his scrambling, like Fran Tarkenton, because of her speed. Now, say hello to Buck."

"Hi," she said without looking at Buck and Dave. "But Daddy, why do I have to dive for all the balls? Look at my clothes."

"That's how we make Grant better. Now, go up to your room, clean up, and study." Harold returned to his notes. "Did you get the question, Buck?"

"Well, I. . . ."

Madeline Johnson yelled, "Meg, after you shower, bring down the guest book. Buck hasn't signed it yet."

"Goddammit, Madeline, *shut up*! I want to hear what Buck's got to say." Harold was livid, but Madeline didn't pay any attention to him. She just picked up her tennis racket and started hitting imaginary backhands.

"What was the question?" Buck said.

"Let's see. No. 3. Offensive line."

Buck felt his jock itch returning. "Every lineman we've recruited has been the best. Coach Barton has even invented a new block. It's called the Rooster block." Buck saw Dave blushing. He obviously hadn't forgotten how Ignarski knocked him on his butt when he tried it. "This block will absolutely guarantee maximum protection for your son. Why, we wouldn't let anybody get close to him."

Suddenly there was a loud crash. Madeline had knocked over a lamp — the one with the football helmet for a base — with one of her backhands. The dog jumped straight up, Buck yelled, and Dave laughed hysterically.

"Ah, shit, I can't stand it any longer," Johnson screamed. "Madeline, get your skinny ass out of here and let us men work. And take Red with you. Buck's tired of playing with him." Buck wanted to applaud.

Madeline took the dog by the collar and excused herself. "I'll be in the back yard hitting tennis balls up against the wall. Nice seeing you two. Don't forget to sign the guest book before you leave." As she started out the back door with Big Red, she turned back to Harold. "Sugar, by the way, Vince called and wanted to know if you would call him back as soon as possible."

"Excuse me, Buck, I'll only be a second," Harold said as he got up to leave the room. "It's not that Vince and I would say anything important about Grant, understand, but I think it's important that we say it in private."

"That's fine, we understand," Buck said as Johnson disappeared up the steps. What a zoo, he thought. Buck looked over at Barton and asked, "How'm I doing, Coach?"

"Great, what with the dog, the indoor tennis match, and the girl receiver. Can you believe this shit? What we won't do for a football player." Dave stood up and pulled the rear of his trousers from his sweaty butt.

"Just part of the job, I guess. But do we ever get to see the kid? Where's Grant?"

"Grant isn't allowed to come down during the school week to see coaches. That's why the old man likes to have coaches come over during the week. He can run the whole show then."

Johnson came back. "Vince said to tell you hello, Buck. He also said you didn't have a chance to get Grant." Before Buck could answer, Johnson sat down and picked up his notes. "Now, No. 4. How much input will we have in the game plan? I should tell you that Buddy gave the best answer of all the coaches."

Buck looked directly at Harold with the most sincere look he could muster. "Mr. Johnson, what we'll do is give Grant a chance to contribute his thoughts to our plan. Personally, I'd let Grant do it all, but I *do* have assistant coaches who'd have to be consulted about giving Grant all the responsibility. I'm sure after they all meet him and you, they'll come around to *my* way of thinking." Buck gritted his teeth to emphasize his sincerity.

"Next question. How many tickets will I get to each game? You know that when Grant and I get over there, the stands will fill up every game and tickets will be damned hard to get, so I want mine before the season starts. And I want a lot of 'em."

"Mr. Johnson, we'll take care of your needs. You can count on that." Buck winked at Johnson and reached for a Frito and some dip.

"Last question. Biggest one. Will you push my son for the Heisman? Hot damn, I've always wanted to go to New York and meet all those former Heismans like Glenn Davis, Paul Hornung, and O. J. Simpson." Harold Johnson was getting fired up. He was out of his chair, accepting the Heisman Trophy "for my son, who couldn't be here today."

"I can assure you we'll do everything in our power to make your trip to New York for the award ceremony fun, Mr. Johnson." Buck stood up, grabbed Mr. Johnson's hand, and raised it over his head like a prizefighter. "The father responsible for the Heisman Trophy winner, *Harold Johnson*!"

"Now you're talking. OK. When are we coming down to visit your school? Is it this weekend?"

Buck turned and looked at Dave. "Mr. Johnson, we've got you scheduled for this weekend. We'll have everything arranged for you." They were Barton's first words of the meeting.

"And you and I," said Buck, "we'll sit down and talk about your business while Grant is seeing the campus. Is Mrs. Johnson coming with you?"

"No. She's got some goddamn tennis match or something. It'll just be Grant and me."

As Buck and Dave started up the stairs, they bumped into Meg. She was sitting at the top of the stairs with the guest book. "I thought I told you to go to your room," Johnson said. "Oh, well, give me the book. Buck, you sign right here, right after Charlie. Dave, I'm sorry, but we don't have any assistant coaches' names in here. It's for head coaches only." Buck took the book, placed it on his knee, and signed "Buck Lee, East Alabama."

"Boy," said Buck, "you've got *everybody* in here. Let's see. Howard, Lou, Bo, Johnny, Vince, Barry. They've all been here. Plus a lot more I can't make out."

Harold Johnson took the book back from Buck like it was the Holy Bible. His face took on the look of a most contented man. "Buck, this has been the greatest year of my life. Madeline and I just love socializing with all you coaches. It won't matter who we sign with, because all the coaches and their wives have become dear friends of ours, and they said it really didn't matter where Grant went to school, that they just wanted him to be happy. Would you believe that each coach's wife has written my wife and told her that she had a home away from home if Grant plays for their husband?"

Buck took Mr. Johnson's hand one more time and put his arm around Johnson's shoulders. He pulled him closer and gently said, "That's exactly what my wife told me to tell y'all. You can stay at our house anytime you're in town. Now, I don't just mean if your son is playing for *us*, Mr. Johnson, I mean even if he's playing for Coach Shavers. That's how much we think of your son and you people."

Small tears welled in the corners of Harold Johnson's eyes. He put his arms around Buck and said, "That's the nicest thing I've ever heard. It'd save us a lot of money if Grant decides to play for Buddy and the game is played at your place."

Buck and Dave got into the Caddy, finally, and pulled away from the house. They looked at each other and began to howl and do imitations of Harold and Madeline Johnson. Between laughs, Dave said, "Bo, Barry, Vince — Buck, this son of a bitch is *everybody's* asshole buddy." They headed for the first Magic Mart they could find. They needed a six-pack for the 150-mile ride. The Buck and Dave Show was going home.

19

MISS MUNCIE, GET HAROLD Johnson on the phone for me. He'll be at home." Shavers liked being able to make calls from the private shower in his office. Feeling the warm water run over his body not only soothed him but made him think better.

Within a minute, Adelle Muncie was back on the intercom. "Coach Shavers, I've got Mr. Johnson for you."

"Mr. Johnson? Things going along OK for you and your family?" Shavers cleaned his toes as he spoke.

"Coach Shavers," Johnson said from Birmingham, "to be totally honest with you, things aren't so hot. My business has been bad and it's my fault. The reason is I've been devoting most of my time to Grant. Training a boy to be the greatest quarterback in the country isn't exactly easy. It requires dedication from the whole family. Particularly the daddy. We've had to sacrifice a lot."

Shavers propped the phone on his shoulder and washed under his arms. "Mr. Johnson, that's what I need to talk to you about. When can we meet? Just the two of us."

"Well, I'm gonna be busy this weekend. But if you'll call me back next week, we'll sit down and talk."

"You're not going to visit *Eastern* this weekend are you?" asked Shavers as the soap slipped from his hands.

"Buddy, we're visiting a lot of schools, but you can rest assured you'll have your chance to come up with a package."

Struggling to regain his composure, as well as the soap, Shavers grunted, "I'll be in touch next week. Now, don't you do anything, you hear? I'll be in touch."

"I gotta go now, Buddy. I'll see you."

Shavers waddled out of the shower and over to the desk, dripping on the plush carpet. He jabbed the intercom button. "Miss Muncie, send a wire to Harold Johnson. 'Dear Mr. Johnson: Just talked with Buddy Shavers and he tells me you are the best insurance salesman in the state. He also informs me that you have been so busy training your son to be another Fran Tarkenton that your business has suffered. As president of the biggest buyer of insurance in this state, I want you to know that we will not forget you. Signed, Fred M. Smith, President, Blues Mutual."

"Is that all?"

"No. Call the laundry room and have them send up a dozen fresh towels."

20

PATRICK FLANAGAN WAS STUDYING the catalogue from Eastern's School of Aeronautical Engineering, boning up so he could do his best number on young Grant Johnson, when the phone rang at his real estate office. It was Dave Barton, Buck's most valuable and trustworthy assistant coach. He wanted to know if he could drop by the office for a "little chat." Flanagan had no idea what was up — another scam, some gossip, some dirt on Buddy Shavers at WAS? — but he was curious enough to virtually beg Barton to come on over. Flanagan was a sucker for intrigue, and this reeked of it.

But when Barton dragged into his office an hour later, Flanagan knew there would be no excitement this day. Dave — normally the happy-go-lucky, tobacco-chewing, hell-raising, good ol' boy of the bunch — looked like he had just lost his favorite 'coon dog to a Mack truck. He practically limped into the office, shoulders hunched, and fell onto the sofa opposite Flanagan's desk. He hadn't shaved or even bothered to brush his hair.

"What the hell happened to you?" Patrick said. "Knock up a Rattlerette or something?"

"Nothing happened," Barton told him. "Maybe that's the problem."

"What can I do for you, then?"

"Aw, hell, Pat, I don't know. I don't even know why I called."

"Trouble at home?"

"No more than any other coach has."

"Ah-hah," said Flanagan. "So that's it."

"What's what?"

"Severe coachitis. Nausea, guilt, old age creeping up."

Barton crammed a chaw of Red Man into his jaw. "How'd you know?"

"It's always just a matter of time, Dave, a matter of time."

"Well, it finally caught up with me."

"What did it?"

"I don't know exactly," Barton told him. "The Johnson kid, maybe. Good kid. Hell of a player. Got all the tools. But he's also got an asshole for an old man, and the old man's trying to get his jollies by living his life through his boy. Gonna screw up that kid sure as we're sitting here. That's Grant Johnson, and then there's poor Eaarnel. Jesus Christ, what a football player, but now he's been thrown into an orbit he'll never get out of. How the hell is Eaarnel Simpson going to cope with all of the shit that's ahead of him? Poor black kid from the sticks of Alabama."

"Well," Patrick said, "either you get him or somebody like Buddy Shavers does."

"But all of those promises we have to make, Pat."

"Shavers is doing the same thing. You know that."

"Aw *sure* he is. So's Schembechler and Macabe and all of us. Bunch of grown men running around lying to teen-age boys and their parents, and most of all, to ourselves. That's what gets me down the most. Sometimes even I start believing my own bullshit. You got a place I can spit?"

"Wastebasket there," said Flanagan, pointing to the corner. "That stuff any good?"

"What?"

"Chewing tobacco. I never tried it."

"Don't. Messy as hell."

Flanagan figured he did, after all, have a role to play today — father confessor and vocational counselor. Time for the soapbox. "You don't want to coach college football anymore, do you?" he said to Barton.

"Nope."

"Thinking about selling insurance? Or real estate, like me?"

"Yep."

"OK," said Flanagan, "I'll give you my two-bit lecture. What makes you think that selling real estate, or insurance, or even encyclopedias, is any different from selling teen-age quarterbacks and their parents? Sometimes when I've made a sale, lying through my teeth, I have to go straight home and take a long shower to get the grime off. I have to put up with customers and stroke their egos. I've kissed a customer's ass for six months and then seen him run off and sign with somebody else."

"Yeah, Pat but. . . ."

"Wait a minute. I'm not through." Patrick was surprised to find that he was getting a little put-out with Dave Barton's whimpering. "What you people tend to forget is that ninety-nine percent of the men in American would run you over with a Greyhound bus if they could have your job. The money's OK. You get your picture in the paper now and then. You work outdoors. You get every kind of perk in the world, from a staff car to a big expense account. And then there's the biggie: On Saturday afternoon, when some poor salesman, who's come in from a week on the road, finds himself cutting the grass and catching hell from his wife, you're running out onto a football field and sixty thousand people are actually *cheering* you for playing dirty."

"You asshole," Dave Barton said.

"I thought you'd see it my way," said Flanagan.

21

HERE'S WHAT I NEED you to do," Buck told Flanagan. "Go down to Roanoke and work out a deal for Eaarnel's mother so she can get some meat at the local butcher shop. I don't know what Shavers is doing for Eaarnel and his family, but you can bet it's something big. We can't compete on the big things, so we need to do something for the family to show we care." Buck rubbed his damaged hand, the one he had smashed against the wall, hoping that Patrick would ask how he hurt himself so he could say he punched somebody out.

"So go down to Roanoke," Buck said again. He got up from his desk and shadow-boxed around the room, hoping Pat would notice the swollen fist. "When you get there, call Mrs. Simpson and ask her to come by the shop where you'll be working. It's a friend's butcher shop, but you'll do all the talking. Then, after you're gone, he'll follow up on the deal. So make her one she can't refuse.

"I love it. I'll leave tomorrow. One thing I particularly like about this one."

"What's that?" Buck continued bobbing and weaving.

"No incriminating evidence. She'll eat it all." Patrick started out the door, then hesitated for a second. "Might check that hand, Coach. Could be broken."

* * *

"Hey, Patrick," Butch Henderson whispered. "Here she comes."

Patrick Flanagan slipped on the bloodstained apron, put a grease pencil behind his ear, and stepped out from the meat locker in the rear of Butch's Butcher Shop as if he were walking onto a stage. He had spent the last fifty-five minutes in the cold-storage locker waiting for Mrs. Simpson to arrive. By the time he emerged to greet Eaarnel's mother, he looked like a butcher, smelled like a butcher, felt like a butcher, and was as cold as a corpse.

"Mrs. Simpson," Flanagan said with a stammer and a smile, "I'm Mike Henderson, Butch's brother. I'm so glad you could come down to the store today."

"You the man what called this morning?" Mrs. Simpson asked suspiciously.

Flanagan could feel the strength and authority of the woman in front of him. She outweighed every other woman in the store by at least forty pounds. Her biceps bulged and strained at the sleeve of her print dress under the weight of her suitcase-sized handbag. She held her big bosom and wide shoulders erect and looked Flanagan right in the eye. Patrick pictured her wearing shoulder pads and a helmet and imagined her lowering her shoulder, turning the corner, running slap-dab over a linebacker, and spiking her purse in the end zone. She was Eaarnel's mother, all right.

"Yes, ma'am, I asked you to come down because there's something we'd like to do for you."

"Well, I ain't got a lot of time for no foolishness, you hear?" she said. "My church is having a covered dish supper tonight, and I can't be late."

"Right, Mrs. Simpson, so if you'll just step around the counter here, this won't take but a jiffy."

Flanagan wiped his hands on his apron as Mrs. Simpson stood big-eyed behind the counter. She'd never seen so much meat in her life. He slapped a side of pork on the butcher's block and quickly sliced off twenty-two thick pork chops. He then cup up eight pounds of juicy spare ribs and four of the thickest sirloins Mrs. Simpson could possibly have seen. Butch Henderson looked over from his customer at the counter and mumbled to himself, "Jesus, he's going to give away the store."

Flanagan stacked the meat, wiped his hands on his apron again, and smiled. "Mrs. Simpson," he said, "what do you think about having all this meat every week for your family?"

"What you talking about? All that meat for me?"

"All this for you, Mrs. Simpson."

"What I got to do for it?"

"Not a thing. All we want is for you to know how much we care about you and your family. Just come by every week and pick it up."

Mrs. Simpson, even though she was still a little suspicious, reached over and felt the meat. She couldn't resist touching it.

"You see," said Flanagan, "Butch and I just happen to be friends of the coach over at Eastern, Buck Lee. We think he's a great man, and if we had kids, we'd want our sons to play football for Coach Lee. We didn't even go to school there, but he's just a great man."

"Well, if this ain't just the most."

"We're just glad to help out." Flanagan wrapped the huge clump of meat and handed it to Mrs. Simpson. "You just come by and pick up the meat every Tuesday."

Mrs. Simpson cradled the twenty-pound load in one arm and walked around to the front of the counter. She was dumbfounded, but not dumb. If all these white folks wanted to give her things for her family because of Eaarnel, then she'd take it. Before she reached the door, Flanagan added, "If you ever need a little extra for your church suppers, you just call us now, you hear? We'll take care of you."

Butch Henderson shook his head and reached for the phone to call his accountant. Feeding Eaarnel was going to be more expensive than he had anticipated.

22

BUCK, I DON'T CARE if you do have to drive down to Roanoke to see Eaarnel play basketball. You need to take Bucky over to the PeeWee football meeting. Most of his friends probably think he doesn't even have a father." Gail wasn't kidding. Buck knew he'd better plan on making the halftime show of the basketball game in Roanoke instead of the first half.

"All right, I'll go," he said, "but it always pisses me off when I get to these meetings and listen to the parents talk about their sons. Have you ever heard 'em bitch about the coach not playing their kid? They think winning's the only good that comes out of PeeWee football. Just playing should be the idea." He pushed his dinner around his plate.

"Buck," answered Gail in her motherly voice, "I don't care what happened last year. I want Bucky to go and you to go with him. He's in his room right now getting on his football shoes and jersey. You can go see Eaarnel after the meeting. And don't forget, Coach Lee, there will be at least five hundred potential prospects there."

Buck stood up from the table and tossed his napkin down on the plate. "OK, on the five hundred potentials. But, dammit, they ought to let the kids have fun."

"Who said football's fun, Coach?"

There was a whoop and a holler, and in clomped Bucky wearing his jersey and his cleated football shoes. He was so excited and looked so cute that Buck reached down and hoisted him onto his shoulders. "OK, Tiger, let's go get 'em," Buck said, heading for the garage with Bucky sitting proudly on his shoulders. He threw Bucky into the back seat of his Caddy, cranked it, and backed out of the garage.

Gail stood in the back door and waved. "Have a good time, laddies."

"I'll drop Bucky off after the meeting. Then I'll go to see Eaarnel. Catch you later."

* * *

As Bucky ran ahead to join his friends, Buck surveyed the room in amazement. There were at least five hundred kids in football jerseys and shoes running everywhere. Never mind that the first game was a month away — they were ready.

Buck found himself a seat where he would be as inconspicuous as possible and looked over the festivities. He spotted his son in one corner with his team, the Eagles. They were all decked out in Philadelphia Eagles green. Their coach, a middle-aged businessman whom Buck recognized, had on baggy sweatpants, a coaching shirt with *Eagles* on it, a baseball cap, and a whistle around his neck. He was teaching Bucky and his teammates one of the most important lessons of PeeWee football — how to yell, "Yes, *Sir*!" The coach gathered all of the little Eagles around him in a big circle and yelled, "Are we the best?" The kids screamed, "Yes, *Sir*!"

Without pausing, the tall man in sweatpants yelled back, "I can't hear you."

"Yes, *Sir*!" forty voices screamed louder than before.

"I still can't hear you," the tall man yelled.

"Yes, *Sir*!" came the scream from faces so strained that veins were bulging on little necks. Before the coach could yell again, the head of the PeeWee association called everyone to attention.

"Before we get started with the program, let's have the invocation," he said. "We have asked the most noble of them all to give us the benefit of his wisdom. Let's hear it for Coach Noble Rockwell."

Buck noticed that all the parents over forty-five cheered, but the kids just kept on playing grab-ass. He looked over at the dais and saw Noble Rockwell in his coaching gear getting up and approaching the microphone. He teetered slightly as he grabbed for the mike, but Buck figured that was just age taking over.

"Please bow you head," Rockwell said. Buck couldn't believe what he'd just heard. Please bow *you* head? He had to be kidding or drunk.

"Father, in heaven," Rockwell said, "make each one of these little kids a good Christian. We can stand some help." He paused, looked out over the audience, realized he was talking to five hundred kids who were not listening to him, and decided to cut it short. "Amen." Rockwell sat down and closed his eyes. Buck wasn't sure whether he was still praying or napping. Either way, it was the shortest prayer he'd ever heard.

"Now we will have 'The Star-Spangled Banner' sung by Matilda Preston. Matilda is a sixth-grader at Lovell Elementary School," the master of ceremonies announced. Buck scanned the room for a celebrity. This program was so elaborate that they had to have some biggie waiting in the wings.

As Matilda squeaked out "The Star-Spangled Banner," Buck again began to question the value of youth football. How could playing high school ball not be anticlimactic after all this? The top PeeWee player would get a bigger trophy than the high school star got. The uniforms the kids wore in this league were better than those provided in high school. And half of them would be burned out from yelling, "Yes, *Sir*!" ten thousand times before they ever reached high school.

"Now we're going to hear from one of our local council members, Reuben Flask," said the emcee. "As you all might or might not know, Mr. Flask was a star linebacker for Coach Noble Rockwell, and he's consented to talk for a few minutes about the great game of football and how it made him a success in politics. I'd like to introduce Councilman Flask."

There was scattered applause as a red-faced, balding councilman with a protruding belly stood up to talk. He raved on about the American way and how football was a maker of men, and how without the lessons learned from his old coach, he would have quit politics when he was behind. The speech riled Buck. He loved football as much as anybody, but it was a travesty to imply to kids that they had to play football to be a success. Finally, Flask turned the mike back over to the emcee.

"All right, fans, it's time to introduce all our teams and players. First the Raiders. At quarterback, Charles Falsworth." A little 4′ 2″, ten-year-old midget wearing a big Oakland Raider jersey raced across the gym signalling No. 1 with his right hand. He planted himself in front of the crowd of parents and friends and waited for his teammates. "At left halfback, Bobby Gunn." Bobby also sprinted across the gym holding up one finger. Buck looked at his watch and headed for the nearest pay phone.

He dialed Kyle's home number. "Kyle. Buck. Listen, I want you to get two or three of the coaches and go down to Roanoke and watch Eaarnel play basketball. I was going, but I'm stuck over here at the PeeWee meeting. Christ, they're introducing every kid like it's the Super Bowl. There must be at least five hundred of the little buggers, one of which is my son, so it's gonna take awhile."

"Glad to, but you can do me a favor, too," said Kyle. "How about sending Ivie Buchanan a wire tomorrow congratulating him on being named Amateur Athlete of the Year in New Jersey."

Buck reached into his pocket and pulled out his notepad. "I'll do it first thing tomorrow. If you imagine it's gonna take a long time to introduce the players, just imagine how long it's going to take to introduce the coaches and a hundred cheerleaders. I'll be here all night."

"Have fun, Coach. See you later."

Buck returned to the room just as the Eagles were being introduced. ". . . also at halfback, Bucky Leeeee!" As Buck watched his little boy running out in front of the crowd, he was surprised, even slightly embarrassed, by the tingle down his spine and the glaze in his eyes. His own little boy in that grown-up uniform. Maybe I'm no different from the rest, he thought. An Eagle Father.

* * *

It was all downhill when he and Bucky got home. Gail was waiting up and was surprised, of course, to hear that he wasn't going to Roanoke for Eaarnel's basketball game. She fussed over Bucky but paid no attention to Buck. He poured himself a glass of milk, grabbed a handful of chocolate-chip cookies, and retired to the bedroom. It was too late to get on the phone and make his nightly courtesy calls to prospects and alumni, so he stripped and laid up in bed to catch the tail-end of the eleven o'clock news.

"I swear, it's the same old shit everyday," he said about the news as Gail came in for bed.

"What, this marriage?" she snapped.

"Now, what the hell do you mean by that?"

"You can look it up, Coach."

"Wait a minute. I could be in Roanoke right now."

"So go," Gail said. "Eaarnel's going to be terribly disappointed."

She put on her gown, threw the covers over her body, and turned her back on Buck. That made eighteen nights in a row.

23

THE GYMNASIUM WAS PACKED and the crowd was going wild as Kyle Moore and Harry Ignarski walked in. They, along with ten other scouts from various colleges, had come to Roanoke to watch Eaarnel play basketball. It made little difference that Eaarnel, in this basketball hotbed, was not even a first-team player. All that counted was being there to show Eaarnel that you loved him as much as the coach from the other school.

"Gimme an E! Gimme an A! Gimme another A!" the cheerleaders yelled when the Roanoke High coach patted his star substitute on the shoulder midway through the first period and told him to go in.

The crowd roared as the school's biggest hero ever ran into the game. The first to stand and yell for Eaarnel were the college coaches sitting behind the Panther bench. Eastern's Ignarski and Moore clapped and cheered with the others when this beautifully built, brown-skinned god ran into the game. Raquel Welch in a two-piece couldn't have evoked any more feeling in the coaches than Eaarnel, in short pants, leaping above the rim and pulling down a rebound.

Ignarski, above the noise of the crowd, asked Kyle, "Where's Perry? He was supposed to meet us here."

"I don't know where he is. He's been living down here the last two weeks. Maybe he's gone stir-crazy."

Every coach in the gym cheered loudly whenever Eaarnel moved. The score was irrelevant to the group of nattily dressed men from colleges across the country. They weren't there to see the game. In fact, they weren't even there to watch Eaarnel. They were there to be *seen* by him.

Finally it was halftime, and the teams went into the locker rooms for their Coca-Colas and pep talks. Ignarski and Kyle walked outside the gym to get a breath of fresh air and to see if they could find Perry Jackson. The faint smell of marijuana was in the air as students used halftime for a smoke. Others slipped into parked cars for a little halftime necking.

Kyle spotted Perry running across the street toward the gym. "Perry, over here," he yelled. "Next to the guy with lots of hair."

"Very funny, Moore, you're a regular Toots Shor," said Ignarski. "We'll see how much you laugh when . . ." He stopped in mid-sentence when he saw the look on Perry's face. "What happened, Coach? You look pissed off."

Perry was steaming. "I'll kill that son of a bitch. I'll kill him."

"You get mugged or something?"

Perry slowed down and caught his breath. "I was waiting this afternoon for Eaarnel to get out of class so I could walk home with him and carry his books. Just as Eaarnel came out of the school, Big Hawg Curley — you know, that fat bastard from Clemson. Must weigh 275 if he weighs a pound . . ."

"What happened? Tell me." Ignarski was smacking his right fist into his open left hand.

"Hawg was blocking my way to Eaarnel. Said *he* was going to carry Eaarnel's books today. I stood up to him and said, 'I'll be damned if you are,' and I reached for Eaarnel's books."

"You knock him on his ass?" Now Ignarski was slugging Kyle on the arm.

"Cut it out, Harry, let's hear the story," said Kyle.

"Before I could do anything," Perry said, "he took that fat belly of his and knocked me over that hedge in the front of the school. There I was, upside down in that fuckin' hedge, while he walked off with Eaarnel and the books *I* was supposed to carry. I had to go back to the motel and change clothes. Got grass stains all over me. I'll kill him!"

Kyle and Ignarski looked at Perry, still sizzling, then at one another. Then they started laughing.

"I don't think that's funny, man. You let some big hawg knock you over a hedge and see how funny it is." Perry was still livid.

"So he belly-whipped you, huh? I think that's funny as hell, if you ask me," said Ignarski, sticking his gut out at Perry. Soon Perry cooled down and even started laughing about it. Before long, all three were stumbling in the grass, laughing like hell at what had happened, and practicing belly-butts.

"Just remember one thing, Perry," Kyle said as the crowd started back in for the second half. "If you see him at the end of the game, don't start anything. I don't want to get arrested in Roanoke for killing a hawg."

* * *

The game ended with the Roanoke Panthers on the short end of the score. Eaarnel had played most of the second half, until he was ejected for tackling a player who broke free for a layup. The college coaches had stood up and yelled like they were at a football game: "Dee-fense, Dee-fense, Dee-fense!"

As the crowd made its way out, the coaches made a beeline for the dressing room. There they fought for position to shake Eaarnel's hand as he left the gym. The line stretched down the entire hall. The visiting coaches were joined by alumni from the different schools, who would slip $100 bills into Eaarnel's hand as they shook it.

The small talk among the waiting coaches ranged from, "That Ralph Hays, he's a good 'un," to "I don't think that big hog can play." In the midst of such prattle, Coach Zeke Bradbury of West Alabama sidled over to Kyle. He fumbled around and then finally said, "Coach, I know this is unusual, but if you help me out on this, I'll be your friend for life. Coach Shavers has been all over our case about some great prospect named Tnassip. I can't find out anything about him. Are y'all recruiting him?"

Kyle stepped lightly on Ignarski's leg. "Tnassip? Are you kidding? He might not be as good as Eaarnel, but who is? Besides that, he's a white running back, and you know how hard they are to find." The tap on Ignarski's toe hadn't gotten his attention, so Kyle punched him in the side. Finally, he joined in.

"Yeah, that Tnassip is so tough, I'd like to use him on defense when he's resting from offense."

Bradbury was pleading. "Help me out, would you? You're the only ones who know about Tnassip. The rest of the coaches here never heard of him."

Suddenly their attention was diverted to the front as Eaarnel opened the door to come out. Kyle turned to Bradbury and said, "I'd like to help you, but Coach Lee would kill us if we divulged that information. Sorry."

Eaarnel made his way down the row of coaches and alumni who shook his hand as he sauntered by.

"Good game, Stud!"

"What do you say, Stallion?"

"How you, Hoss?"

"Good game, Bubba!"

"Way to get after 'em, Big'un!"

"You got it, Racehorse!"

"Way to go, Big Cat!"

Eaarnel finally made it through the crowd to his girlfriend's side, and they left the building. Forty men, all over the age of thirty and most over forty, were left standing there like groupies at a rock concert. The competition was over for now, and it was time to go. Most would make the long drive home with only a six-pack of beer to keep them company. Then first thing in the morning they would sit down and write Eaarnel a note telling him how great he is.

"It's the shits, Ignarski — standing in line to shake the hand of a seventeen-year-old who really didn't even know we were there," Kyle said as they drove along the deserted road through the cool night air. "But, what the hell? If we get the big man, we can strut around the coaches' convention like we know more football than the dumb-asses who didn't get him. Right?" Kyle turned to Ignarski for a reply, but it was no use. He was sound asleep.

* * *

"Coach Shavers, this is Bradbury."

"Who?" answered the sleepy voice.

"It's Coach Bradbury. I'm down watching the basketball game between Roanoke and Johnson County."

"What in the hell are you doing waking me up to tell me about a basketball game?"

"You asked us to find out about that back, Tnassip."

"Oh, yeah. Go ahead, I'm listening."

"Well, I talked to two coaches from Eastern, and they said he's fantastic. Could play either offense or defense."

"What else did they say? Where's he from? How do we get in touch with him?"

"They wouldn't tell me. All they said was that he's great."

"You woke me up just to tell me what I already know? If you want to keep coaching, you better follow up and find out where he is and how we can get in touch with him!" *Click*.

Bradbury hung up the phone and started back toward his car. That old asshole, he thought. Here I am trying to find out something that'll help him pay for that big house he lives in, and he chews my butt out. He jerked the door open, climbed inside, slammed the door, revved the engine, and roared off into the night. *Tnassip, Tnassip, Tnassip*. It was all he could think about.

24

GAIL COULDN'T BELIEVE HER eyes and ears. Here it was six o'clock on a Sunday morning, the first pale dawn light barely filtering into the bedroom, and Buck had already showered and shaved and now stood in front of the mirror singing "Amazing Grace" while knotting his white tie. He was wearing his three-piece striped charcoal suit, the one reserved for funerals and banquets, with his black wingtips. Gail sat up groggily, wondering if she were in the right house.

"That's a hell of a golfing outfit, Coach," she said.

"Wrong," said Buck. "Church."

"Church? Christ, you didn't even get *married* in church! You been born again? That kid from CALL finally get to you?"

"Eaarnel got to me."

"What's Eaarnel got to do with it?"

"I'm going to church with his mama. They're taking up a special collection this morning for some new robes for the deacons. I'm gonna help 'em out."

"You're driving all the way to Roanoke for some deacons' robes?"

"I got six hundred dollars in East Alabama bills that says I am."

"Well, Hallelujah! Buck Lee turns spiritual."

"You got pretty spiritual yourself last night. Kept saying, 'Oh, God, oh, God.'" The drought, thanks in part to Jack Daniel, had finally been broken.

"I know, I know. And your response was so cute — 'Around the house, you can call me Buck.'"

Buck took one more look at himself — even he couldn't believe what he saw — and bent over the rumpled bed to kiss Gail. "In the name of the Father, the Son, and Eaarnel Simpson," he said.

"Hit the road, Coach, or we're going to have our own revival right here."

* * *

The front yard of the white wooden church was filled with South Roanoke's finest black citizens. Most of the women wore shiny high heels, white gloves, big hats, and floral print dresses. The men were dressed in white or navy suits, had flowers in their lapels, and wore two-toned shoes. As the big bell in the steeple began to chime, announcing the start of church, everybody crowded inside and looked for a seat.

Buck drove up just as the crowd headed into the church. Making sure that he parked the Caddy right out front so Mama Simpson could see it when she came out, he rushed inside and scanned the crowd for her. He was surprised to see another white man sitting near the front of the church. From the rear Buck could see the cauliflower ear — Shavers. To make matters worse, he was sitting right next to Mrs. Simpson. No need to be bashful at this point. Having driven almost a hundred miles to get here, he wasn't about to sit by himself.

"Excuse me, excuse me," Buck said, crawling over people to get to Mrs. Simpson. He sat down beside her just as the choir broke into its first hymn of the day. *Amazing Grace, how sweet the sound, that saved a wretch like me. . . .*

As they all stood to sing along with the choir of big-breasted women in dresses of pink or yellow, Buck noticed that there were more people in the choir than there were in the congregation. There must have been at least a hundred singers belting out "Amazing Grace." Buck glanced out of the corner of his eye at Shavers, his hymnal in front of him, singing with great solemnity. It didn't take Buck long to figure out that he should try to out-sing Shavers. He reached down for a little extra and sang with great gusto, "*I once was lost, but now am found. . . .*" A loud voice bellowed from the right. Shavers was fighting back. When the hymn ended, the Reverend Charles H. Griffin took the rostrum.

"All right ladies and gentlemen, and you two white folks in the congregation, turn to page 195. We'll sing the first and last verses." Buck quickly turned to page 195 and got ready for the next round in this competition. Damned if Shavers was going to sing louder than he did. Buck glanced to his right again and saw Shavers looking at him and gritting his teeth.

The choir broke out in "Rock of Ages." Mrs. Simpson, sitting between Shavers and Buck, sang as loudly as anybody. When the choir finished the hymn and sat down, Mrs. Simpson turned to both men and said, "You all are some kind of religious folks. I ain't heard singing like that since I joined this church."

Suddenly there was complete silence as the Reverend Griffin prepared to speak. He strutted up and down in front of the congregation for a minute or so, then he stopped and began to pray. "As we gather here in the house of the Lord, let us remember what day it is. It's a day of giving. Now, Lord, we need some new robes for our deacons because their old ones are ragged and torn. Now, Lord, I don't need none for myself, 'cause I got all I need. So I ask You to whisper in the ear of each one here, and tell 'em not to be putting money in the collection plate that makes noise. Lord, let's have the kind that don't make no sound when it hits the bottom. For we ask it in Jesus' name, Amen!"

Buck wanted to clap and cheer. The preacher was one hell of a fund-raiser. He'd just gotten the Lord to ask for the collection. No way anyone could turn *Him* down.

"Now, I don't know how much longer I'll be with you folks," continued the Reverend Griffin. "They might have to carry me out of this place on a stretcher, but I'll still be kicking at the Devil." Buck, who'd never been in a black church before, was surprised to hear the congregation go, "Umm, a-umm." Shavers looked confused, too. "If I can't kick him because I'm too feeble," said the Reverend, "I'll bite him."

"Umm, a-umm."

"And if I'm too old and tired to bite him, I'll *spit* on him."

Buck was ready this time. "UMM, A-UMM." He had out-"umm, a-ummed" Shavers.

"And after all that, brothers and sisters," the Reverend Griffin implored, holding both arms up to the heavens, "if I can't spit on him because I'm too weak, I'll *glare* him to death."

Out of sync with the rest of the congregation, Shavers yelled out, "Ugg-a-ugg-ugg." Every eye in the place turned to look at this man who had yelled in church, "Ugg-a-ugg-ugg." Buck smiled. At least he had more soul than Shavers.

"There was this runner who said, 'I am the fastest runner in the world.'" The Reverend paused for a second, looked over the congregation, then continued. "One day an old man came up to the fastest runner in the world and said, 'I can catch you, Fastest Runner in the World.'"

The Reverend started walking up and down in front of the congregation. Buck was spellbound by his showmanship and his boundless energy. He cut his eyes to the side and saw Mrs. Simpson, her hands clasped over her Bible, listening with undivided attention. Shavers held his Bible in exactly the same position.

" 'You can't beat me, old man. I'm the fastest runner in the world.'"

" 'Let's race,' said the old man. Well, now, brothers and sisters, the Fastest Runner in the World took off and started running." The Reverend imitated a runner by pumping his arms. He pumped them furiously for the Fastest Runner, and very slowly for the old man.

"The Fastest Runner in the World ran about three-quarter speed, thinking that would be fast enough to beat the old man. But he looked back and there was the old man on his shoulder." The Reverend looked over his right shoulder, then did a double take. "The Fastest Runner in the World speeded up, thinking now he'd lose the old man. Again, he looked over his shoulder and guess who he saw." Again he did a double take over his right shoulder. "Now the Fastest Runner was really mad. He turned it on and give it everything he had, but there was no way he could shake the old man. Finally, after four laps and a half, the old man passed the Fastest Runner in the World." The Reverend had the congregation in his hands, and he had Buck on the edge of his seat. "The Fastest Runner in the World turned to the old man and asked him, 'How did you beat me? Who are you?'" The Reverend paused and stared out into the audience. He was waiting for the right moment for the punch line. His timing was perfect. You could hear a pin drop as the Reverend Griffin began to speak.

" 'Don't you know who I am?' the old man said. 'I'm Death. I catch 'em all sooner or later.'"

"Umm, a-umm" went the chant from the audience. This time Shavers kept his mouth shut.

The Reverend suddenly screamed at the congregation, "That's why, brothers and sisters, it's important to live the right kind of life down on this Earth, so when that old man catches us, we'll be ready." Just then the choir began to sing, "Just As I Am," and the ushers handed out the collection plate to be passed.

Buck reached into his pocket and took out all the bills he had. He wanted to be ready to look good in front of Mrs. Simpson. The collection plate was coming from his right and would pass by Shavers first. Buck liked that, because he'd have a chance to see what Shavers gave before he put his money in. Shavers grabbed the plate and stuck a brand-new $100 bill in. Mrs. Simpson looked at the bill and said, "Mercy, mercy." Buck reached over Mrs. Simpson and grabbed the plate. He put *two* $100 bills in the plate. "Hallelujah, save my soul," was all Mrs. Simpson could say.

"We ask your benevolence today. Our Lord needs the money," said the Reverend Griffin. Shavers, scowling at Buck, reached over Mrs. Simpson, grabbed the plate back from Buck, and added three more $100 bills to the collection.

"We got some real benevolent folks on this row today, Lord. Praise the Lord!" said Mrs. Simpson.

Buck stood up, grabbed the collection tray back, and counted off, "One, two, three, *four* hundred dollars." Before Shavers could do anything, Buck walked down to the end of the row and gave the plate to one of the shocked elders. As Buck walked back to his seat, he grinned at Shavers, who was so angry the veins in his head looked like they were going to explode. "Bless you, Brother Shavers," Buck said as he sat down.

"If you all ain't the most Christian men I ever did see. God bless both of you," Mrs. Simpson said as the choir sang the last hymn of the day and the congregation filed out the door.

Shavers and Buck walked on either side of Mrs. Simpson like two escorts at a debutante ball. She could hardly move, they were so close. As they came out into the bright sunlight, Mrs. Simpson excused herself, saying she had to go visit some sick church members. Buck and Shavers were left staring at one another.

"I'm gonna get that boy, you cocksucker."

"We'll see, you crimp-eared son of a bitch."

"He won't get away from me, Jock Itch. Or is it the crabs you've got?"

"You'd better go home and take another shower, Shavers. You stink."

"Watch out for that poodle. He might bite you, tough guy."

"Shavers, do you like to fly?" When Shavers didn't answer, Buck went on. "Do you like sex?" Still nothing but a glare. "Well, if you do, why don't you go find yourself a runway and fuck off." Buck turned and headed toward his car, leaving Shavers standing in the churchyard.

Shavers started after him. "Buck Lee, you can put this down in your little black book. I'm gonna get Eaarnel, and then I'm gonna kick your ass all over the football field next year." As Buck pulled away, he waved at the crowd of churchgoers. They all waved back.

25

SHAVERS SLAMMED THE CAR door and slung gravel as he left the church parking lot. Buck had absolutely driven him to the limit. No more Mister Nice Guy. He was determined to close the deal on Eaarnel today. As he turned the corner and headed down Eaarnel's street, he saw the big limo of Judson P. Higgenbotham, the richest man in Atchison County. As usual, Mr. Higgenbotham was right on time. Shavers pulled his rented Lincoln Continental up beside the limo and got out. A driver opened the door, and Shavers stepped into the back with Higgenbotham.

"How you doing, Buddy?"

"Fine, Mr. Higgenbotham."

"Now, who's this nigger you want me to get for you?"

"Eaarnel Simpson. He's the best football player in the state. Maybe in the country."

"How much money'd you offer him the first time?"

"About seven thousand dollars."

"Buddy, you ought to know better than that. Don't ever lowball a nigger or a man who's selling a good bull. Give 'em what you think they're worth, and don't hassle. If it ain't good enough, go on home and get the next one. Who's our competition?"

"Buck Lee and Eastern. But, Mr. Higgenbotham, with your help, we can get this boy."

"Let's go see what he looks like."

Shavers directed the driver to the small wooden house that Eaarnel and his mother and twelve brothers and sisters lived in. The street was deserted, since almost everyone in the community was involved with the church on Sunday. Shavers knew that Eaarnel was there because he had told Eaarnel's best friend, who was also going to be a Hawk if Eaarnel signed with Shavers, to alert Eaarnel that he was coming by with a very important man.

Shavers went up to the door and knocked while Judson P. Higgenbotham waited in the car. The door opened slightly, and Eaarnel peeked out through the crack. "Oh, it's you, Coach Shavers," he said in his deep Southern drawl. "Mama told me not to open the door, 'cause it might be one of those insurance salesmen."

"That's good thinking, Eaarnel," Shavers said. He motioned for Higgenbotham to get out of the car. Instead, the chauffeur got out and, in his most proper voice, said, "Mr. Simpson and Coach Shavers, Mr. Judson P. Higgenbotham would like for y'all to join him in his car." Eaarnel and Shavers looked at each other and walked over to the limo.

"Mr. Higgenbotham, this is Eaarnel Simpson, the finest running back in the country. We want to make him a Hawk."

Flashing the grin that had sold a million encyclopedias in one year, Judson Higgenbotham grabbed Eaarnel's hand and squeezed it. "You are a fine-looking boy, aren't you? How'd you like to take a ride in my Lear jet? Driver, the airport." Before Eaarnel could protest, the limo was rolling down the street. Taking a ride in a jet didn't sound too bad to Eaarnel. Anyway, he'd be back long before his mama got home from church and visiting the sick.

As the limo zipped through the streets toward the airport, Shavers tried to carry on a conversation with Eaarnel.

"How's your family?"

"OK."

"How's your girlfriend?"

"OK."

"Have you made up your mind on a school?"

"Nope."

"Do you know when you'll be ready to make a decision?"

"Nope."

"What can we do to make your mind up for you?"

"I don't know."

Suddenly Judson P. Higgenbotham interrupted Shavers' monologue. He pointed a big finger out the window at the Lear jet that was being primed for takeoff. "Let's hold the conversation down until I get a chance to talk to Eaarnel. He and I both need to find out just what it is he wants." The door to the limo opened, and the two white men and the young black man stepped out and went up the steps into the

Lear. The whine of the jet engines had Eaarnel wide-eyed and staring at things that only big money could buy. It was old stuff to Shavers. He'd pulled this routine on every top athlete in the state for the last ten years. It had never failed.

The doors of the jet were closed and locked, and the seat belts were strapped. The Lear taxied out to the end of the runway, was cleared, and the throttles were thrown to the floor. Eaarnel was pushed back against his seat as the jet picked up speed and the mini-"G" force took over. Suddenly the plane lifted off the ground, and they soared up into the heaven. Eaarnel looked out the window nervously from his seat near the rear of the plane. All he could see was soft white clouds flashing by as the plane climbed.

"How you like this, boy?" asked Higgenbotham, who was lighting up the longest cigar Eaarnel had ever seen. Eaarnel just nodded and continued looking out the window at the clouds. Higgenbotham passed one of his expensive cigars to Shavers. The cabin of the Lear soon was full of smoke, and Eaarnel coughed a couple of times.

"You having a good time, Eaarnel?" asked Shavers. Eaarnel again just nodded. He knew that the best thing to do in a strange environment, and when a man was going to offer you something, was to keep your mouth shut.

The Lear finally leveled off, and Higgenbotham and Shavers carried on a private conversation in the front of the plane. Suddenly the Lear did a wingover and started toward the ground. The seat belt warning light went on and the plane began to descend rapidly. Eaarnel looked at his watch and saw they had been flying for less than an hour. No problem getting home before his mama. But then Eaarnel saw water as the plane started coming over the end of the runway for its approach. "There ain't no water in Roanoke," he said. "Where are we?"

Judson P. Higgenbotham put out his cigar and coughed. "Hilton Head, South Carolina, boy. We're just going to have a bite to eat on my plantation before we take you back. Might do a little quail shooting. You like to hunt quail?"

"I'd better call my mama. She don't know where I am," Eaarnel said. He had begun to panic. The Lear's wheels touched the ground, bounced, and came back to earth. The reverse throttle was shoved forward, and the noise was so loud that nobody could answer Eaarnel.

When the plane slowed down and the noise subsided, Shavers said, "Eaarnel, we're just going to have a little buffet and do a little talking about your career and your future. Mr. Higgenbotham here can ensure the financial security for you and your family forever. Now, you don't want to pass up the opportunity to help your mama, do you?"

Before Eaarnel could answer, the door opened and there was another chauffeur and another big limo. They all walked out into the bright sunshine of Hilton Head and headed for the Higgenbotham Plantation.

* * *

"Mrs. Simpson, this is Coach Lee. How are you?"

"Coach Lee, they done kidnapped my baby!"

"Now, slow down, Mrs. Simpson. What are you talking about? Where's Eaarnel? Wasn't he at home when you got there?" Buck was frantically waving at Gail in the kitchen with his left hand, trying to get her attention.

"Coach Lee, all I know is that when I come home, my baby was gone. Some of the kids down the street told me a big black car with two fancy white men in it come by and took my baby."

By this time, Gail had gotten the signal from Buck and called J. A. on the other line. "Now, just calm down Mrs. Simpson," Buck said. "I'm sure he's all right. If you'll just sit by the phone, I'll call you back as soon as I find Eaarnel." Buck hung up and grabbed the other line.

"J. A., we've got a real problem. Shavers and one of his bag men got Eaarnel. It's probably that big buffoon with all the money, that Judson Higgenbotham. When I worked for Shavers, he was always the one he'd call out on the biggies. He's got a Lear jet, and what he does is take 'em off and blitz 'em into signing. I'm not sure he can do that to Eaarnel, but he's tough."

"You just leave everything to your ath-uh-let-ic di-rec-tor. I'll call back in less than an hour."

* * *

"Hello. May I speak to Hubert Stinson? This is J. A. Symington, athletic director at Eastern, and I want to speak with your A. D. right now." J. A. hated being disturbed at home on Sunday afternoon. It was his favorite day of the week, when he got to play with his German shepherd and his Siamese cat. He had been wrestling around on the floor, just about to pin the big shepherd, when Buck had called.

"Hello."

"Stinson. This J. A."

After the usual formalities, in which Stinson asked about J. A.'s family, job, and new coach, J. A. interrupted him. "Stinson, I don't have a lot of time for this bullshit. I want to tell you the facts of life. If that weaselly-eared, son of a bitch coach of yours doesn't get that Eaarnel Simpson boy back home in the next two hours, I'm personally going to drive to Roanoke and kick the shit out of Shavers when he does get back."

Holding the phone with his shoulder so he could continue playing with the dog, J. A. listened to Stinson explain that he didn't know anything about Eaarnel.

"Stinson, this is the A. D. at Eastern speaking. I don't care how you get hold of Shavers, but you find him and get that boy home." J. A. slammed the phone down and dropped back onto the floor so he could continue wrestling with his pets. As he twisted the big dog's head, he realized he'd forgotten to call Buck.

"Sweetheart, Poopsy-Pie," J. A. yelled into the other room to his gorgeous, young second wife, "would you call Buck for me and tell him everything is OK, and that I took care of his problem?"

"Do it yourself. I'm watching 'Gilligan's Island.'"

He picked up the phone and muttered under his breath, "Doesn't she know who I am?"

* * *

"That was really a nice meal, but I'd better get back home. My mama will be worried about me," said Eaarnel.

"Now, don't you worry about a thing. Before we go back, we've got some business to take care of." Judson P. Higgenbotham took a big satchel from a closet. Eaarnel's eyes popped out like hardboiled eggs as he watched J. P. open the satchel. There were crisp green bills from latch to lock. Before either one of them could speak, however, one of the fourteen servants who cared for the thirty-five room mansion entered the room.

"Coach Shavers, there's a phone call for you in the den. They say it's very important."

"Thank you, Moses. I'll be right back, Eaarnel. You need to talk to Mr. Higgenbotham by yourself, anyway. I might go to the bathroom and clean up after the call, so y'all have a good visit."

Higgenbotham went to work as soon as Shavers closed the door. "Eaarnel, I'm going to buy your tickets in advance for the next four years," he said. "For each game — for you, now, not counting what you get for your family — I'll pay you $250 a ticket, which comes out to $1,000 a game. There are eleven games, plus the bowl, so that's $12,000 a year. You will play four years of football, so that's $48,000." Higgenbotham counted off the bills and placed them in front of Eaarnel in a neat little stack.

"Now, everybody needs a car while they're in school. I'm going to take you over to the bank that a friend of mine owns in Roanoke, and we're going to take out a loan for $10,000. You'll sign the note yourself, because you'll be able to pay the note off when you play professional football. It's all set. Don't even worry about it. Now, to make sure your mother'll have plenty of money to take care of the kids and maybe even move over to where you're gonna play ball, we've taken care of that, too. Your mother will become the special food consultant for the training table at Western. We need somebody to make sure the black athletes in school are getting enough of that 'soul food.'"

The stack of money kept getting bigger, and Eaarnel's heart began to thump louder, when suddenly they were interrupted by Shavers. He was panicked.

"We've gotta go. Eaarnel's mother thinks we've kidnapped him. We'll have to take him back right now, or they'll send the police after him."

"But Eaarnel and I haven't made a deal," said Higgenbotham.

"How's it look to you, boy? It's all yours. All you got to do is reach down with one hand and take the money and sign the scholarship with the other hand."

"Could I have a few more days to think about it? I need to talk to my mama," Eaarnel stammered. He wet his lips, dry from seeing all that money.

"We gotta go, we gotta go," said Shavers, spraying spit all over everybody. "They'll be looking for us."

Judson P. Higgenbotham stood up to his full 6′ 3″ and looked at Eaarnel. He jingled the coins in his pocket while he thought. "Eaarnel, here's what we're gonna do. We're gonna take you back to Roanoke and let you talk to your mama. After you've had a chance to talk to her, you're gonna tell us yes or no. You understand that, boy?"

"I don't know, Mr. Higgenbotham," said Eaarnel. "I just need some time to think."

* * *

As the Lear approached the Roanoke airport, Shavers suddenly remembered something very important. Reaching across the aisle, he grabbed Eaarnel by the arm, looked into his eyes, and with great sincerity said, "Eaarnel, don't forget this. If the NCAA asks how you got down to Hilton Head in the jet, just remember to tell 'em you paid for half the gas."

26

COACH LEE, MR. JOHNSON is on the phone from Birmingham, and he really sounds excited," Peggy blurted as she broke into the staff meeting. "I hate to interrupt like this, but I know how much you want Grant." Buck leaped out of his chair and raced for the upstairs phone. He knew he didn't have to explain the emergency to his coaches.

"Mr. Johnson? Buck Lee. What can I do for you?"

"Can you get up here by four o'clock with your purple blazer and an Eastern grant-in-aid?"

"Are you serious?"

"Of course I'm serious."

"You bet I can. I'll be there in two hours. Just put the coffee on the stove and save me a cup." Buck hung up and raced out the door. He'd have to run by the house and pick up his jacket and tie. Halfway to the car, however, he realized he'd forgotten the grant-in-aid form. Racing back into the office, he spotted Kyle in the hallway.

"Kyle, tell all the coaches we're going to sign Grant. His old man called and said for me to hurry up with my blazer on and a scholarship in my hands." Buck went back into the office, grabbed a grant-in-aid form from Peggy, and told her to call Gail and have her waiting out front of the house with his purple blazer and tie. He was off to sign the quarterback who would show them the way to the Sugar Bowl.

* * *

"Hey," Kyle yelled as he re-entered the staff room, "Buck's gone to Birmingham to sign Grant. Or maybe I ought to say to sign Harold Johnson. Anyway, the old man told Buck to hurry and to bring a scholarship and wear his purple blazer. If that doesn't sound like he's ready, I don't know what does."

"I'll believe it when I see it," said Barton.

"Well, in the meantime, Buck said to go ahead with the slide show of the prospects coming in this weekend. And since I'm the prettiest," said Kyle, "I'll run the projector." Despite a series of hoots, he flashed up the next slide.

"OK, here we go. Ignarski. Who's that?"

"Jack Rhea. Union, Alabama. 6′ 1″, 185. Inside safety. 4.7 forty. Likes to be called The Laser. Loves hot cars, country music, and he'll knock your cock off."

Snap. Click. "How about it, Chuck?"

"That looks like Greg Melton. Nose guard from Ontario, Alabama. Plays basketball; puts the shot. His dad's a real asshole and thinks his kid oughta be a fullback. His mother's terrific, and his sister's gonna be a key in getting him. She's a little tenth-grade baton twirler and wants a scholarship in two years. Greg likes to be called Bulletman."

Snap. Click. "OK. Billy Tom."

"This hog's name is Rufus William Jackson. He likes to be called Sugar Daddy. Thinks he's a big swordsman — always wants somebody to fix him up. Weighs about 275, but he's still a pussy as far as I'm concerned. I watched him play, and all he did was stand around all night long. I personally can't stand the pissant, but we've got to recruit him because of his size."

Snap. Click. "How about this one, Perry?"

"That's Billy 'Hitman' Carroll. He's visiting us from Houston, Texas. He's 6′ 1″, weighs 200, plays fullback and outside linebacker. If you look at his face, you can tell why they call him Hitman. You ever seen a face that's been used as a weapon like his? He's got a beautiful mother who's divorced. That means the head coach gets to recruit Hitman."

Kyle finished running through the list of prospects coming in over the weekend. Bubba, Butch, Willie, Tex, Killer Truck, Stud, and all the other macho names. "The big coach will be real proud of us. Maybe we won't even have to use any name tags this weekend."

* * *

Buck drove across Stanleyville faster than he'd ever driven in town. He turned onto his street and spotted Gail standing in the front yard with his purple blazer. Slamming on the brakes, he reached out the window for the clothes. "Thanks, honey. I ought to be home with the kid's signature tonight, if everything goes right. I'll call if we sign him, and you can ice the champagne." Buck wheeled the Caddy around and careened for Birmingham.

An hour and a half later, he turned into the Johnsons' street at a very leisurely pace. He didn't want to give the impression that a prospect was worth killing himself for, even though he'd almost done just that on the way over. It was time to act relaxed and in control. As he neared the Johnson house, it occurred to him that there were a hell of a lot of cars parked in front. Harold Johnson probably called all the media, he figured. Buck finally found a spot about a half-block from the house and pulled in. He got out of the car, put on his purple blazer, and looked up to see Harold Johnson standing triumphantly in his front yard. "Buck, over here. Hurry up. Everybody's here but you. Come on. We want to take the picture in the back yard."

When they turned the corner of the house, Buck almost passed out. At least twenty-five of the nation's leading coaches were lolling around the back yard, trying to make small talk with one another. Vince, Lou, Pat, Charlie, Jackie, Howard, all of them, all dressed in their colorful school blazers. And all of them, like Buck, had come with a scholarship form to be signed by Harold Johnson's son.

Johnson pulled out a whistle and blew for attention. Twenty-five coaches stopped in their tracks. "All right, coaches, it's great of you all to come over. I thought it'd be real nice if we got a picture of all the head coaches, the ones who're recruiting us, in their school blazers holding a scholarship."

"Mr. Johnson, could we get on with this," said the acned young photographer with a prissy voice. "My mother's expecting me home for dinner. If you'd help me get everybody lined up by color, I'd appreciate it."

"I'd like for all you coaches to meet my next-door neighbor, Bruce Lefleur," said Johnson, pointing to the wimp in Bermuda shorts.

"Bruce is a great photographer and is going to try and take such a beautiful picture that maybe *US* or *People* magazines will buy it."

None of the coaches dared to say what they were thinking. The Johnson kid still wasn't signed.

"Over here, fellas, up against the fence," said Bruce. "Some will have to stand on the lawn chairs. You're all so close in height that we have to use the chairs."

"OK, Buck, you're there," Johnson said. He placed Buck on one end. "Lou, you're next. Bo, you're next to Johnny. Stand on the chair, Vince. Joe, you're the shortest, so you get out front."

"Wait a minute, Mr. Johnson," Bruce said as he put his hands on his hips. "We don't want these colors to clash. They'll look so much more appealing if they're color-coordinated."

"Go ahead, Bruce, line 'em up the way you want. Let me know when you're ready."

Bruce looked lovingly at the coaches with his head cocked and one eye closed. He was studying their colors like a jeweler inspecting a rare diamond. "Now, if you all will just trust my taste, we'll get started. Please, purple, over there. All right, green, you'll be so much more appealing if you're tucked in between the fella with the bad ear, the Sunkist gold, and the one in mushroom beige."

"I want to be at the other end," Buddy Shavers said. Buck started laughing; no way Shavers was going to let him photograph his bad side. "Let Buddy move to the other end, Bruce," said Harold Johnson. He didn't want to make Shavers mad. They still had to talk business.

"If you say so, Mr. Johnson, but I liked the scheme the way I first had it. Let's see now. Passionate pink, you get between orange and that beautiful sky blue the little short fella has on. I want the complementary colors, yellow and violet, directly opposite one another. Now, you all look smashing." Bruce clapped his hands together and sighed.

Harold Johnson, seeing that Bruce was through, began giving instructions. "All right, coaches, take your scholarship papers and hold 'em out in front of you. That's good, Barry. A little lower, Joe. Now we've got it." After his final instruction to the coaches, Harold Johnson positioned himself in front of them, a football under his arm, and motioned for Bruce to take the picture.

"Now, hold up that football, Mr. Johnson. Pretend you're passing. That's it. Teeth, everyone! This is *it*!" Bruce snapped the picture and clapped his hands joyously.

"I'll have a copy of the picture sent to each one of you for your wall. You fellas have been terrific. Thanks a lot," Johnson said.

Buck and the other coaches just smiled at Harold Johnson and headed for their cars.

* * *

"This is The Raven."

"This is Shavers. What do you have for me?"

"The Johnsons will be on the Eastern campus this weekend."

"Where are they staying, Raven?"

"The new Downtowner Motel. I personally think that's a waste of money."

"Slip over there and leave a message for the Johnsons. No, I mean just for the old man. I want you to slip it under his door. Don't leave it with the front desk, because then they won't give it to him. Tell him to call me Saturday night at exactly 10:30."

"What's your phone number?"

"You idiot, you know my number. You just called me."

"Right. I do know your number. This is The Raven, signing off."

"Raven, you better be giving me the right poop. You fuck this up and you don't get those new golf shoes you wanted."

"I understand, Mr. Shavers. I'll do a good job."

27

THE PURPLE AND WHITE Cessna with the Rattler coiled around the nose approached the Stanleyville airport from the north. As Buck watched the plane drop its landing gear and flaps and start its final approach, he thought how absurd it was that the Johnsons hadn't driven down. It was only a hundred miles, and a car ride would have been a lot less trouble for everybody, but old man Johnson insisted on having a plane sent for him and Grant.

Buck quickly checked out everything as the plane touched down and taxied toward the crowd. The signs proclaiming today as "Harold and Grant Johnson Day" at East Alabama were hung from the fence. Cathy had six of her most voluptuous Rattlerettes out in their purple and white sweaters. The pep band was playing the school fight song. Buck, all of his coaches, and even Patrick Flanagan were there.

The door to the plane opened, and Harold Johnson stepped out waving to the crowd like a politician. Grant followed behind. Despite Harold Johnson, Buck liked the way the kid looked. He had that all-American presence and he *did* have the good face.

"How are you, Mr. Johnson? How was the plane ride?" Buck said. He shook hands with the dad first.

"A little bumpy, Buck. I was afraid Grant was going to get sick. Don't y'all have a bigger plane like the Hawks?"

"I'm sorry, we don't, Mr. Johnson, but if we can get this fine youngster over here to come play for us, we'll be able to afford a bigger plane." Buck reached out and took Grant's hand. The boy's handshake was firm and strong. He looked Buck in the eye and acknowledged how glad he was to be there. "Grant, I'd like you to meet our coaches. They've all heard so much about you that they wanted to be here when you landed. Men, introduce yourselves to Mr. Johnson and Grant."

Each coach on the staff walked over to the Johnsons and said, "Hi,

Mr. Johnson, I'm coach. . . ." Harold Johnson was like a king receiving his subjects, but Grant was appropriately humble about all the attention he was receiving. Buck was impressed.

"Grant, I'd like you to meet Professor Albert O'Neal. We know how interested you are in aeronautical engineering, so Dr. O'Neal will be showing you around the department." Buck introduced Patrick Flanagan, who was dressed in a flying suit with thunderbolt patches on each sleeve.

Patrick beamed from ear to ear. "How are you, my lad? We'll get together tomorrow and talk about the flying business. I understand you want to be an astronaut."

"I don't know if that's true or not, Dr. O'Neal," Harold Johnson said. "We've got a pro football career to worry about first. After that, he can be whatever he wants to be."

"Well, anyway, Grant, you and I will have a nice visit tomorrow." Patrick turned to walk away and was almost knocked down by Cathy and her six Rattlerettes who were now rushing over to see Grant. They formed a tight circle around him.

"Grant, my name's Cathy, and we're the Rattlerettes. This is Barbsy, Betty Sue, Mary Jane, Bobbie Candy, Sunny, and Dinah. We want you to know that we'll do *anything* to make your stay here a pleasant one. If you want one of us to show you the campus tomorrow, we'll be at your beck and call."

Harold Johnson broke through the circle. "Girls, Grant's going to be too busy to have time for a date. He's got to look at films with Coach Lee and his quarterback coach. Then he's got to talk academics with Dr. O'Neal. He just won't have any time."

"Well, if you do want to come to a party tonight," Cathy said to Grant, "we're having one over at the Phi Mu house. One of the girls will come over and pick you up."

Again Harold Johnson answered before Grant could speak. "Sorry, ladies, he just won't have time."

Buck, figuring the girls had done as much as they could, loaded up father and son and headed toward the motel.

* * *

"Welcome Mr. Harold Johnson and Grant to Rattler Country," read the sign out front of the new Downtowner Motel. The sign was gaudy, but Buck appreciated the motel's effort.

"So, did you have a nice trip last week to Western?" Buck said, trying to get a feel for what the old man was thinking.

"*They* had an airplane fying over with a big banner welcoming me and Grant," said Johnson.

Buck opened the trunk and grabbed the Johnsons' bags. Neither of them offered to help, so Buck lugged the baggage into the motel while the Johnsons walked ahead. The lobby was spacious, clean, and full of people from town whom Buck had planted there to meet them.

"Mr. Johnson," a portly man in a business suit said as he stuck out an oversized hand. "I'm Bill Ross, the Cadillac dealer here in town." Before Johnson could respond, a tall, skinny man in a classy sport coat stuck out his hand. "I'm Harvey Fleishman of the Dandy Dud store." Standing right behind Harvey was John English, owner of the local pub. Then came Tommy Skelton, owner of the jewelry store. They were all there — the teases, the come-ons, anything to make the old man think of Eastern as a good place for him to spend his weekends and for his kid to go to school.

After finishing with the well-wishers, Buck led the Johnsons over to the desk clerk. "We've got a nice suite for you, Mr. Johnson, and a nice double for your son." The clerk was smiling but Johnson wasn't.

"Grant is going to stay in the room with me. You can send up a cot if you don't have another bed in the room."

Buck glanced at Grant as the desk clerk changed the rooms. The kid looked embarrassed but didn't say a word. Buck winked at him and turned to Johnson. "Harold, why don't you and I have dinner tonight and talk some business. I'm sure Grant will be OK in the room. Let him stay by himself so he can look at some of our films from last year. I'll send over a coach with a projector."

Johnson's face lit up. "That's great, Buck. That's exactly what Grant wants to do, don't you, son?"

Grant, catching another wink from Buck while his father wasn't looking, smiled and reached down for the bags. "If you say so,

Daddy." Grant grabbed the bags and started toward the elevator. He stopped, turned back and asked, "Coach Lee, what time will you send the coach over with the films?"

"I'll pick up your dad at seven o'clock. The coach will be over at about seven-thirty. See you at seven, Mr. Johnson."

Harold Johnson reached out and gave Buck's hand a big squeeze. "I can't wait to talk some business with you, Buck. See you at seven."

* * *

Just as planned, the four-door, purple Ford Fairlane pulled up under the motel canopy precisely at 7:30. Dave Bledsoe, starting quarterback for the Rattlers, handed a can of beer out the window to Grant and said, "The Big Purple Machine has arrived!" Grant, dressed in brown corduroy slacks, brown crepe-soled loafers, and a brown and white knit shirt, smiled and jumped into the back seat. He wanted to get out of here as quickly as possible before his father came back and spoiled the fun.

"Grant," said Dave, "this is Sally Porter."

Grant leered at the blonde vision sitting beside him and managed a nod.

"Hello, Grant. I've heard a great deal about you." Sally flashed her perfect teeth and gently brushed the hair from her beautiful face. "Why, you're even better looking than your picture." She winked and playfully touched Grant on the shoulder.

Grant blushed and stammered, "Yeah, thanks, well, you look good enough to — you look pretty damn good yourself."

"And this is my girlfriend, Mary Harmon," said Dave. "She'll show you around the campus tomorrow."

"Hi, Mary." Grant reached over the front seat and shook her hand.

"Good to see you, Grant," Mary said. "Are you enjoying your visit so far?"

"Oh, yeah, Coach Lee drove us around the campus this afternoon, and we stopped and met most of the deans and doctors along the way." Grant stole a look at Sally — she was loaded, and she had to be loose because she had already touched him. Oh, why did he have to be staying in the same room with his dad?

"OK, guys and dolls," Dave said, "what's on for tonight?"

"How about an orgy?" piped up Mary.

Dave slammed on the brakes and said, "You got it!"

A hot flash went through Grant as he thought about an orgy. This could get wild. These chicks were big-league!

"Just kidding, big boy." Mary laughed.

"You want to go to Bobby McCurdy's party?" Dave tried to leave the decision to the others. "Maybe a movie or something?"

"I don't know, what do you want to do, Sally?" asked Mary as she leaned over into the back seat. Grant's eyes bulged and his glands tingled as he looked at Mary with one eye and Sally with the other. God, they're both stacked like brick shit-houses, he thought.

"Anything goes with me," Sally said, brushing lint off her sweater.

"I know what." Mary's husky voice snapped Grant out of his breast-induced trance. "Grant, have you seen 'Doctor Zhivago' yet?"

Grant leaned back and crossed his arms, trying to appear cool. "To tell the truth, I've met so many deans since I've been here, I'm not sure whether I've seen that one or not." Dave, Mary, and Sally burst out laughing. Grant wasn't sure what the joke was, but he joined in the laughter anyway.

Dave finally said, "I like the first suggestion. Let's go get drunk and screw."

"Well, we can at least do one of the two," Sally said. She winked and touched Grant on the shoulder again.

"Let's go to the Rattler's Den," yelled Dave.

"Coach Lee won't take my dad there, will he?" Grant opened the window and gulped in some fresh air, wondering if the "Mister Macho" aftershave he'd splashed on his crotch would last until midnight.

* * *

"Coach Lee, Grant Johnson and Mr. Johnson are here. Shall I send them in?"

"Just a second, Peggy. I'll be right with you." Buck reached up and turned on the spotlight above Grant's picture on the wall behind his desk. The soft light shining on the portrait gave it an almost-mystical look. The face was that of Grant pasted over the uniform of one of Buck's players who wore the same number as Grant. Beneath the picture was a phony newspaper clipping Buck had made up. In bold letters on the front page of the paper it said "Harold Johnson's Son Wins Heisman." Buck switched on a tape of the school fight song and turned it down, so it was barely audible in the background.

"OK, Peggy, send in the Johnsons." Buck moved over beside the door so he could see Harold Johnson's reaction when he came in. The response was just what he had hoped for — Harold Johnson saw the picture and swelled up like a toad. Even Grant, despite his bloodshot eyes, managed to smile. The sound of the fight song in the background was so stirring that Buck felt like returning the opening kickoff of the season himself.

"How do you like that, Mr. Johnson? Doesn't that look great? Don't you think that could be possible if Grant came to Eastern?" Buck stood by Harold Johnson, expecting some positive reaction, but didn't get it.

"Coach Lee, we've had a great time, but I think we ought to head back home. Grant has seen all of the campus he needs to, and he stayed up pretty late last night watching films. On top of that, my little gal Meg is wrestling tonight."

"Why, you haven't even had a chance to see the press box where you're going to sit while Grant's playing. And Billy Tom's supposed to take you down to the trophy room so you can see the spot we've reserved for Grant's trophies." Buck needed to stall for time. He sensed he was losing Grant, but he didn't know why. "Grant, did you get a chance to talk to the head of the School of Aeronautical Engineering? He's a former astronaut and should be able to help you."

"He's already talked to the dean," said Johnson, "so what else can he do? He's seen everything." Harold Johnson got up to leave.

"Mr. Johnson, why don't you and I talk again for a few minutes by ourselves? I think if we spend a few minutes alone, we can resolve any problem you might have. If not, then you can go on back to Birmingham." Johnson started to sweat around his lips. Buck knew that no matter what kind of deal Johnson had, he'd listen to another.

"Son, why don't you wait out in the hall for me. I'll be out in a minute." Grant got up without a word and left.

"Mr. Johnson, what can I do for you to make you reconsider Eastern? Just tell me. I might be able to do it, but I can't unless I know where you stand." The two men faced each other — one wanting the body of a seventeen-year-old, the other selling it.

Harold Johnson stammered for a moment before finally speaking. "Buck, my business has been bad, what with me devoting all my time to Grant. I really haven't had time to get out and sell as much insurance as I would have liked to. So, times haven't been real good for us financially. What I need is somebody to help me out with a big purchase of insurance." Now that he had gotten it out, he felt good. He smiled, licked the sweat off his lips, and waited for Buck's reply.

Buck knew he couldn't bluff on something like this. He'd have to have facts and figures. "Mr. Johnson, if you'll give me about another day, maybe I can come up with a big account for you. I don't know what I can do today, but I might be able to find out something tomorrow. Can you stay over tonight?"

Harold Johnson thought for a minute. "All right. We'll stay tonight and watch the basketball game. I've always wanted to watch UCLA play, anyway."

"Great. We'll watch the game tonight, and then tomorrow we can talk again." Having stalled a decision for at least twenty-four hours, Buck walked Harold Johnson to the door. He motioned for Chuck Driscoll to come over and escort Grant and his dad back to the motel. Then Buck picked up the phone and dialed Patrick Flanagan.

* * *

"Mr. Johnson? Buck Lee. If you'll meet me in the lobby, I've got something I want to talk with you about. It's in reference to the conversation that we had earlier this afternoon. I'll be in the lounge waiting for you." Buck hung up the phone and walked back to where Patrick Flanagan was sitting in the booth. They had chosen the corner booth where it was darkest and most inconspicuous.

"Buck, are you sure he won't recognize me? Hell, all I've done is put on a cowboy hat and some shades."

"Patrick, you still don't understand parents like Harold Johnson. They don't even *see* you when you're not important to them. Hell, yesterday when you met the old man as O'Neal, head of the School of Aeronautical Engineering, he didn't even look at you. But now that you're going to offer him a deal to make some money, he'll know you for the rest of his life. OK, here he comes. Get ready."

Buck stood up and went to meet Johnson before he could get to the booth. He left Patrick sitting there with his cowboy hat on and his sunglasses slightly down over his nose. Buck put his arm around Johnson, gently turned him toward where Patrick was sitting, and whispered, "Don't stare, but he's here to talk to you about your insurance programs. Now, when we walk over to the booth, I'll introduce him as Bill Smith. That's just an alias, of course." Johnson, a little intimidated, still hadn't said a word.

Patrick Flanagan stood up and stuck out his hand. His cowboy boots, with the super-high heels, made him three inches taller than he normally was. He was an imposing sight. "Well, how are y'all, Mr. Johnson. I'm Billy Bob Smith from Odessa, Texas. It's where the men are men and the women are women, and the men are damned glad of it. Whoops. Sorry about that 'damn.' My mama wouldn't like that, rest her soul. Passed away last spring." Patrick took off his hat and put it over his heart.

Buck, standing slightly to the rear, mouthed slowly, *You're overdoing it*. "Well," said Patrick, "let's sit down and talk some insurance." Before Johnson could speak, Patrick whipped out a contract and laid it on the table. Harold Johnson snatched it up like a kid grabbing a sucker from his little sister. In the dim light of the bar, he looked over the contract to make sure everything was covered.

Suddenly, Texas Billy Bob reached over and grabbed the contract. "Mr. Johnson, now down in Texas, we make a deal and we stand by it. Here's the deal I want to offer you. You can see how much money you'll make in the insurance business if you sign this contract. But my problem is this: Before we can close our deal, I need to see the contract that Biddy or Buddy whatever-his-name-is has offered you. When I see his contract, I'll give you this one to sign. I just want to make sure that you really have a contract with that other fella." Billy Bob stuck the contract back in his coat pocket, leaned back, and smiled.

"Buck," said Johnson, "you and Billy Bob will have my answer as soon as I get home tomorrow. I'll get the contract from Buddy and let you see it. Then we can make a deal. OK?"

"You got it, Bubba." Billy Bob stood, grabbed Johnson's hand, and pulled him up. "I'll be expecting to hear from you Monday at the latest, you heah?"

Buck thought the game had gone far enough, so he guided Johnson to the door of the lounge and turned him loose. "Have a good time at the basketball game tonight, and I'll see you tomorrow." As Johnson waddled out the door, Buck spun around and bumped into someone holding a beer. He felt the cool liquid soaking into his pants leg. It was Richard Culpepper.

"Beer, Coach? Pabst. Your favorite."

"I don't know what to do with you, Richard. I've never seen anybody so persistent. At least you didn't scare the hell out of me this time." Buck tried not to laugh. It might be construed as encouragement.

"I just want to work for you, Coach. I could get that Johnson boy for you. He wouldn't get away from me."

Buck patted Richard on the shoulder. He really felt sorry for him. "I don't have a job for you, Richard, but I don't think you'll give up. I promise you, as soon as I have something, I'll call you — don't call me. Gotta run. See you later." Buck left Richard Culpepper standing at the bar holding two beers and walked back to the corner booth.

"How was I, boss? Fantastic as usual?" asked Flanagan.

"You overplayed the part ever so slightly, but I think it worked. Now, if he can get Shavers to give him something in writing before the kid signs, we can nail Biddy. I like that — Biddy."

"You don't think Shavers is that stupid, do you? He'd have to be crazy to write down what he's going to do for the old man. Nobody's that dumb."

"I never did think Shavers would write it down. I was just trying to show the old man that it was all promise and no show. We'll see what happens."

* * *

The long black limo pulled into the parking lot of the Downtowner Motel. Buddy Shavers looked out the rear window, treated so you could see out but not in, and spotted Harold Johnson beneath the awning over the side entrance to the bar. "Driver, pull over there," Shavers said.

The limo came to a stop, and Harold Johnson got in the back seat. He nervously fingered his tie. "It's a good thing I called you, or I never would have heard from you. They were blocking my in-coming calls."

Shavers took a big puff off his Cuban cigar and smiled. "If they think they can fool the old master, they're wrong. I knew when you came down here that they'd try that. That's why I told you to call me at exactly 10:30." Shavers reached over and patted his car phone like it was a secret weapon. "Now, tell me. What's their deal?"

Harold Johnson looked across the darkened car and tried to read the look on Shavers' face. He wasn't sure whether he should bluff it or tell the truth. "Buddy, here's the deal. They had a big alum tell me that whatever your best deal was, they'd top it. All I have to do is to get yours in writing, and they'll beat it. So. What's your best offer?"

"I hate to say this to the father of the best quarterback in America, Harold, but you're not very smart." Shavers reached over and picked up his briefcase. "All they want to do is trap your son and make him ineligible. If I wrote down what we're going to do for you, they'd take that and turn it in to the NCAA. We can't do that. That's an old trick. Eastern plays dirty."

"But I thought they were trying to *help* me. I thought they *liked* me. I didn't know they were trying to get Grant put on probation." Johnson was whining. Shavers just sat there with his good side showing and a benevolent smile on his lips. Then he opened his briefcase.

"Mr. Johnson, here's a contract. It's a group life insurance policy for the Blues Mutual Company. The contract is worth about $250,000 to you in premiums. As soon as your son signs the scholarship tomorrow, you can sign this. If your kid doesn't sign tomorrow, I've got another father in the insurance business who wants this deal."

Harold Johnson tried to figure how much money he would make per month, but he never was very good at division. "Look, Buddy, this is fine, but can we get out of here? I don't want to stay here another night. Buck might come back by the motel, and I'd like to be gone before they come tomorrow."

"You go get the boy and I'll wait for you. Just pack your bags and don't worry about checking out. They'll take care of that. Lee loves to pay the bill."

28

BUDDY SHAVERS ROLLED OUT of bed, making the springs bounce like a car with worn-out shocks.

"Honey, where are you going? It's almost midnight," said Gertrude, his petite wife.

"I've got to make a couple of phone calls. Just go on back to sleep."

Shavers walked down the hall to the den where he liked to work at night. The room was filled with photos and memorabilia, each of which signified a victory; the defeats weren't worth remembering. He turned on the desk lamp and began to dial long distance. After seven rings, a sleepy voice said, "Hello."

"Mrs. Simpson, I just couldn't sleep and I had to talk with Eaarnel. Is he in the bed?" Shavers slurred his words as if half-drunk.

"Who's this calling at this hour of the night?" said Mrs. Simpson. "Eaarnel needs his sleep, you hear? So don't you be calling no more."

"Wait. This is Coach Buck Lee, Mrs. Simpson. I hope I didn't make you mad."

"Well, I don't care if you is the Lord hisself. Don't be calling me at this hour."

"Mrs. Simpson, don't hang. . . ." She slammed down the phone. Rats, thought Shavers. I wish I'd had time to say Lee's name one more time. She might forget it by morning. He looked in his little recruiting book for another prospect to call.

"Hello, Mrs. Buchanan," Shavers mumbled into the phone, "this is Coach Buck Lee."

* * *

Buck was trapped inside a kennel. Thousands of ugly dogs tore at his pants legs. He spotted a fire alarm on the wall and lunged for it. As the bell clanged, signalling distress, Buck slapped at the dogs. He woke up as the phone hit the floor.

"Hello," Buck said softly, wiping the cold sweat from his brow. Gail was purring away, oblivious to his fleeting terror.

"Buck, Dave Barton. The Johnsons have checked out of the motel and gone home. Someone said they saw Mr. Johnson get in a big limo earlier in the evening, and they haven't seen him since."

"Ah, shit. Did you check the calls that went out? We had the incoming calls blocked, so he must have called out."

"Yeah, he called Buddy Shavers at 10:30. It must have been Shavers' limo. So what do we do now?"

Buck looked at the clock — 6 A.M. "Come on over in twenty minutes. We're going to drive to Birminghan and at least be there when he signs. Maybe we can even talk him out of it. Anyway, be here in twenty minutes."

* * *

The purple Caddy rolled down the highway as if it knew the way to Grant Johnson's house. The sun was up, but the early-morning fog made driving a little more hazardous than usual. As they sped past farmhouses and churches on this Sunday morning, Buck wondered if they would at least wait until after church for the signing. No, not if Shavers could help it. He was like a panther: Once he sensed the kill, he didn't go away.

Buck's trance and a long silence were broken by Dave's pitiful plea. "What'd I do wrong on Grant? I thought I covered every base, opened every door, and looked under every rug. Where'd I go wrong?"

"Only thing we did wrong was not to sit outside the old man's door all night, Dave. You just can't trust 'em to do what they say they're gonna do. If we could've flown back with Johnson, we could've stayed right with him until the boy signed. He's gonna sign with the last one who's with him."

* * *

The three television trucks were leaving the Johnson house as Buck and Dave pulled into the driveway. Shavers' limo was still in the front yard, next to Johnson's '76 Ford. Buck motioned for Dave to lead the way. "I'm sure as hell not gonna get bit by that big dog after the boy's already signed," he said.

Buck knocked and waited for somebody to answer. The door swung open to reveal Buddy Shavers in all his splendor — black coat, gold tie embellished with a Hawk poised to strike, Cheshire-cat grin on his face, and big cigar in his hand. "Come on in, boys, and join the party."

"First of all, crimp-ear," Buck said, "we're not your 'boys.' I've told you before — call me Buck, Coach, or Coach Lee, but don't call me *boy*."

Harold Johnson, dressed in a black double-knit leisure suit, appeared in the doorway beside Shavers. "Come on in, Buck, we're having some punch to celebrate Grant's signing with the Hawks. Everybody's here — television, radio, all the newspapers. Even the *Atlanta Journal*. I'm glad y'all could make it."

"We certainly didn't want to miss this great occasion," said Buck. "Where's Mrs. Johnson? She out playing tennis?"

"Not today. She's over with Buddy's wife playing golf at the country club in Evergreen. It was damned nice of Gertrude to call and ask her, seeing as how my wife has never played golf. But Gertrude said it didn't matter, it was just the good company she really wanted. Ain't that the warmest thing you ever heard of?"

Johnson kept looking past Buck toward the front door, trying to see if any of the other coaches he'd called to be there for the signing had shown up. "And Grant," asked Buck, "where's Grant? We'd like to congratulate him."

"Oh, I gave him the afternoon off. Soon as he signed the scholarship papers, he took off for the movies. I told him he should go see the old movie that's playing at the Ritz. You remember the movie where Ronald Reagan played the Gipper. Great president. Great actor."

Buck and Dave said good-bye quickly and walked in honorable

retreat back to the car. Neither man said a word, but each was boiling mad. Buck looked at Dave and gritted his teeth. "I'd like to kick the shit outta old man Johnson." Dave didn't answer. He just opened the door to the Cadillac and punched the front seat with a right that would have floored a mule. Buck cocked his knee to kick the front tire, but as he did, a big German shepherd appeared out of nowhere and growled menacingly. Buck reached down, grabbed the dog by his choker collar, and lifted him up off the ground. Gurgling sounds came from the dog's mouth as he gasped for air. Buck tossed him aside, and the dog ran away yelping.

Dave couldn't believe his eyes. "Do you know what you just did, Coach?"

"Let's get out of here," Buck said, "before that dog realizes I was temporarily insane."

29

COACH HILDEBRAND, THIS IS Mugsy Harmon calling about Tnassip." Larry put his hand over the phone and turned to Noble Rockwell, who was trying on the new tennis shoes Sarge had just brought up to him. "Coach," he whispered, "this is my contact who's helping me with Tnassip."

"Damn, Sarge never gets the right size," said Rockwell, trying to squeeze his size-nine foot into an eight.

Hildebrand returned to the phone. "Great hearing from you, Mr. Harmon. I've heard a lot about Tnassip, and I'm real glad you're gonna help me sign him."

"Coach Hildebrand, this boy is one of the finest athletes I've seen. As you know, they're in spring practice now, so I'll have a chance to see him play in the spring game next week. He gained over two hundred yards in the last scrimmage."

"He's a great one, Coach," Hildebrand whispered to Noble Rockwell, who was now trying on a new nylon windbreaker.

"And the goddamn windbreaker's been worn," said Rockwell.

"Mr. Harmon, if you would go out and watch him play, I'd really appreciate it. I'd be there myself, but my wife has to go into the hospital."

"You can count on me, Coach Hildebrand. I'll be in touch the minute the game is over."

"I'll be waiting for your call. Thanks again."

Patrick Flanagan smiled and immediately phoned Dave Barton to give a report on his first call to Hildebrand.

Hildebrand, meanwhile, grabbed a piece of pink chalk and scribbled *Tnassip, No. 1 Prospect* on the blackboard. Then he pulled out his memo pad and sat down to write.

Attention: Coach Lee

We are making great progress on Tnassip. I have made personal contact with the boy as well as an alumnus, Mugsy Harmon, who is going to help us with Tnassip. I have also enlisted the help of Coach Noble Rockwell. The Coach thinks he might know the parents. I will have him down for a visit so you can get a personal look at him. I really don't need any help at the present time as we are in good shape.

Larry Hildebrand
Assistant Coach

P.S. I will do my best to compete in the coaches' relay race, but could you shorten it a little? Thanks.

Hildebrand carefully placed the memo in an envelope, sealed it, and put it in his OUT box. He looked at his watch — 4:30. There was still time enough to meet the boys for a drink at the Elks Club before he went home.

30

BUCK HAD SPENT ALL afternoon preparing his office for the arrival of Eaarnel Simpson. This was the big weekend for prospects to visit the campus, and there could be no bigger catch than Eaarnel. He dusted the framed picture hanging behind his desk and adjusted the spotlight which shone on it. The picture was of Eaarnel's face on the body of P. J. "Prune Juice" Butler, Eastern's last all-American, who was now a star for the Chicago Bears. Buck knew that Eaarnel wore P. J.'s number and idolized him as a player and a person. He also knew that Eaarnel would be flattered by the comparison. Beneath the picture in big, bold letters was *Eaarnel Simpson — Heisman Trophy — EAU*. The school fight song was playing softly in the background. The hook was baited. The Buck Lee Show was on the road again.

"Coach?" Peggy's voice on the intercom was like a cue call for Buck. "Coach Jackson and Eaarnel Simpson are here. Should I send them in?"

"No," Buck said. "Put Coach Jackson on the phone before you send Eaarnel in, and make sure Eaarnel can't hear our conversation."

Buck checked the room to see that all the game balls and trophies from great victories in the past were in the right places. Everything looked great.

"Coach Lee, this is Coach Jackson."

"Look, Perry, here's what I want you to do. In ten minutes, pick up the phone in Peggy's office and call me. No matter what I say, you just listen. And most of all, don't hang up until I say good-bye. You got it?"

"I don't understand," said Perry, "but I got it. You want me to send Eaarnel in?"

"Send him in." Buck straightened his tie and walked to the door to greet the boy wonder. Eaarnel was dressed in Levi's and a T-shirt that clung to his body like a wet suit. His new Nikes were obviously a gift from somebody's equipment room. His strong jaws ground a wad of gum. Without saying a word, he slowly walked over to the doctored picture of himself and studied the inscription beneath it.

"Do you really think I can win the Heisman if I come to Eastern?" he said. "Coach Shavers said I had a better chance of winning if I came to West Alabama and played for him. Which is true?"

Buck thought for a minute, reached out, and took Eaarnel's hand. "Eaarnel, would I lie to you?" Buck stared directly at his wide, expressionless face. "If I did and you came to school here and didn't win the Heisman, you'd blame me for the rest of your life. I like you and your mother too much to have that burden on me."

"Coach Lee, somebody else told me you got fired as Coach Shavers' backfield coach because you didn't like blacks."

"Eaarnel, that's not true and you know it. Ask any of the blacks who played at Western when I was there. That's just a bunch of hogwash that somebody's spreading, so don't you believe it."

"Another question, Coach Lee." Eaarnel blew a big bubble, then sucked it in flawlessly. "How many tickets will I get to take care of my family and friends?"

"How many do you need?" Buck reached for his notepad.

"Let's see. I have twelve brothers and sisters, eighteen aunts and uncles, the preacher and his wife, my high school coach and his staff of four, and Willie Brown. He's a little kid down the street that I like a lot."

"OK," Buck said, adding up the numbers on his notepad. "That comes to thirty-eight. No big deal."

Eaarnel snapped his fingers. "I forgot my mama. Can you get her a ticket?"

"You don't have to worry about a ticket for your mama, Eaarnel. She can sit up in the press box with my wife. Now, if she doesn't *want* to sit up there, I'll get her another ticket in the stands."

Before Eaarnel could respond, the purple phone rang. "Excuse me, Eaarnel," Buck said, moving behind his desk. "Yes?"

"It's me, Coach Jackson."

Buck put his left hand over the phone and turned to Eaarnel. "This is one of our very wealthy alumni, Fred Carson from Centerville. Just down the road from where you live." Eaarnel smiled and sat down. Buck leaned back in his chair and pretended to listen. "Uh . . . uh-uh . . . uh-uh." Buck put his hand over the phone and said, "Big friend of ours. He loves you."

Eaarnel sat up and quit blowing bubbles. He began to get a little more interested. "You'd do what for Eaarnel?" Buck said. "I can't believe you'd do all that for one person. That's fantastic." With his hand still over the mouthpiece, Buck whispered, "Eaarnel, I can't believe all the things he wants to do for you. He really loves you."

Buck could see that Eaarnel was really enjoying himself, so he continued his phony conversation, setting the hook a little deeper. "A brand-new *what*? That's great. You don't mean you'd really do all that for Eaarnel?" Eaarnel walked over and stood in front of Buck's desk. With his voice only slightly above a whisper, Buck said, "One of our *big* alums, Eaarnel. He loves you better than anybody else." Eaarnel rubbed his clammy hands on his Levi's as he tried to imagine the other side of the conversation.

Realizing that he had pricked Eaarnel's interest, Buck decided it was time to end the charade. It had served its purpose. "Thanks a lot, Mr. Carson. We really appreciate your help. If Eaarnel decides to sign with us, I know all those things we've talked about will make him very happy. Bye now."

Buck stood up and walked around the desk to where Eaarnel was standing. The two just stared at each other until Buck finally broke the silence. "Eaarnel, this is great. If you decide you want to become a Rattler, you'll have a friend for life in Mr. Carson. He loves you. If it weren't illegal, I'd like to tell you all the things he plans to do for you. But you can take my word for it — you and your family won't ever have to worry about a thing if you come to school here."

Eaarnel smiled broadly. "That answers a lot of questions for me, Coach. You know, I'm real concerned about my family."

"I know that, Eaarnel, and I hope I've helped you. Now, let's get you out of here so you can meet with Father O'Brien, the team chaplain. He's been asking about you."

As soon as Eaarnel had gone, Buck went to his closet and took out the picture of Tiger Clements with Ivie Buchanan's face pasted over Tiger's. He replaced the picture of Eaarnel with the picture of Ivie.

The inscription below the photo read *Ivie Buchanan — Eastern's first Heisman*.

"Peggy, send in Ivie. But put Coach Moore on the phone first." Buck waited until Kyle was on the phone. "Kyle, I want you to call me in ten minutes," Buck said. "Don't say anything. Just listen."

31

GAIL LEE DREW THE curtains, dimmed the living-room lights, and switched on the carousel projector pointed against the wall where the team picture usually hung. She depressed the remote-control button and began her interrogation.

"OK, Doris, tell me everything you know about this prospect."

Doris Smith was rinsing down a mouthful of Gouda cheese and cracker with sherry. "Well, he's cute," she said. Several of the women snickered.

"Yes, I *know* he's cute, Doris," said Gail, "and he's probably hung like Trigger. But who *is* he?"

"Oh, Bubba something."

"Dammit, Doris, this is Chip Mauldin! It rhymes with *balled him*. Now, who is it, everybody?"

"Chip Maul-din," the coaches' wives said in unison.

Gail pressed for the next slide. It appeared on the wall upside down.

"That's Mike 'The Bat' Carter," said Janet Stone. "He loves to kill quarterbacks and hang upside down."

"That's real funny, Janet, but this happens to be a blue-chipper. You should be able to recognize him in any position."

Gail corrected the slide, and Doris, Janet, Laverne, Harriet, Bobbie Sue, Francine, Delores, and Pamela put on their thinking caps.

"Isn't that the guy from St. Louis that plays tackle or something?" said Harriet Ignarski. "Harry says he's meaner than pig shit."

"OK, that's right. This is Larry 'Bird Man' Luchi. Larry Luchi. He plays defensive tackle, has a girlfriend named Praline, and he bench presses 450 pounds. Remember, his last name rhymes with 'Gucci.' Got it?"

"Got it," chimed the gang.

Gail pressed for the next slide. "Francie, who's this and what position does he play?"

Francine Moore pulled her tight dress down, felt her pierced earrings, and put down her sherry to stall for time. "Hell, I don't know. Give me a hint."

Harriet Ignarski slammed her can of Budweiser down on the coffee table. A stream of foam covered her hairy forearm. "Goddamn it, Francine, that's Eaarnel Simpson! The coon that's on the front of the sports section everyday!"

Pamela Jackson stiffened. Her chocolate skin reddened slightly around the cheeks.

"Sorry, Pamela," said Harriet, "but everybody in the country knows this dude. He plays tailback, runs a 4.5 forty, averages about thirteen yards per carry, and likes poetry."

"OK, Francine, you got it?" asked Gail.

"Got it."

Gail took a deep breath. "Buck's going to be pissed if we call some kid by the wrong name or call a quarterback a lineman. So we're staying here this afternoon until you learn 'em."

"But I've got a tennis lesson at four," said Laverne Hildebrand.

"Tough, Laverne," Gail said, switching to the next slide.

"Who's this, Bobbie Sue?"

"That's Fred Foreman."

"Wrong," said Gail, sounding like a game-show host.

"Well, he *looks* like Fred Foreman with those skinny little lips and that big nose. And what's wrong with his neck?"

"What do you mean?" asked Bobbie Sue Harris.

"It looks like he's got the mumps."

"Yeah, he does," said Delores Barton.

"Nothing is wrong with his damn neck," Gail said. "He's just a hard-hitting stud who'll put his face on anything."

They all looked at each other. "Anything?" said Bobbie Sue.

32

PATRICK FLANAGAN PATIENTLY WAITED for Perry Jackson and Eaarnel Simpson to arrive so they could discuss the church's role in athletics. Patrick was decked out in the priest's outfit he had rented from the local costume shop. He looked at himself in the mirror and felt almost spiritual. He had thought at one time about being a priest, but he discovered that he liked women and money too much to be celibate and poor. Of course, the Pope wasn't poor, he knew, but not everybody could make it to the Vatican. Patrick heard a car approaching and recognized the sound of Perry's 1972 Dodge Dart. He left his office and walked outside to greet them.

Patrick was waiting as the car pulled into the gravel driveway, and opened the door for Eaarnel. "Welcome to Stanleyville, my son. I'm Father O'Brien, chaplain for the Rattlers. We're delighted to have you visit us. My, you *are* a handsome young man, aren't you? I can see now why all the schools are after you — including Notre Dame, my alma mater."

Eaarnel reached out and accepted the limp-fish handshake Patrick offered him. Smiling benignly, he said, "I'm glad to meet you, Father."

"Why don't we go and talk where we can be completely open and honest with each other? This is where you and I can get to know one another," Patrick said as he led Eaarnel into the woods behind the office.

Perry waited at the car. They didn't need him and he didn't want to go, anyway. Being Catholic, he was a little uneasy seeing Flanagan dressed up like a priest. So he scanned the radio dial in search of some bluesy music.

Patrick and Eaarnel walked deep into the woods until there was no sound except for frogs croaking and crickets chirping. They sat down on a big rock near the water, and Patrick Flanagan began his spiel.

"My son, are you considering going to a Catholic school such as Notre Dame or Boston College?"

"Yes, Father," said Eaarnel, who had never been this close to a priest before and didn't know if he was supposed to act the same around one as he did around his Baptist preacher.

"Well, that's wonderful. Even though I'm the chaplain here, I still have a deep allegiance to the Catholic schools. You *are* a Catholic, aren't you, my son?"

"No, Father, I'm a Baptist just like my mama."

Flanagan reached over and put his hand on Eaarnel's hand. "Then why are you considering going to a Catholic school to play football, my son?"

"I don't know, it just seems like a good deal to me to go to Notre Dame. They're on television all the time, and they've had more all-Americans than anybody else. At least, that's what they say."

"Well, then, you must start going to the Catholic church so you can become a Catholic, my son. We can't have a Baptist scoring all those touchdowns for the church. What would the Pope say? So you go home and tell your mother that I will call the diocese and have them contact you and her about taking the Holy Sacraments."

A frightened look swept across Eaarnel's face. "Father, I don't know nothing about no die-a-cese or those sack-ra-ments, but I think I'd better get on back. I got to call my mama."

"Bless you, my son."

* * *

Patrick Flanagan pulled off his collar and phoned Buck. "Coach, I don't think Eaarnel will be genuflecting any time soon."

"Thanks, Pat," said Buck. "So much for Notre Dame."

33

ALL ELEVEN MEMBERS OF the Rattler coaching staff trudged wearily down the hall and entered the staff meeting room to wait for Buck. It had been a long, hard weekend, what with forty prospects and their parents in town expecting to be entertained, and it wasn't over yet.

Friday night they'd had a banquet at Bobby's Great American Steak House on the outskirts of Stanleyville. From the restaurant they'd gone to the basketball game between Eastern and Gulf Shores University. At halftime, Buck introduced each of the players and parents without forgetting a name.

Then Ignarski and Barton had spent half the night at the Ramada Inn, where several prospects had torn the phones off the walls and used them for battering rams against the doors of a suite containing a half-dozen, terrified stewardesses on layover. To top it off, a rabble of Shriners had taken fire extinguishers and fought the kids brandishing the telephones. It had turned into a battle royal between America's finest. On one side were the high school seniors, being recruited to represent the university of their choice. On the other side were the chivalrous Shriners, who had been celebrating a new shipment of fez hats when they heard the banging and the stews' cries for help. Everybody was soaking wet and there were dimes and quarters all over the motel when Ignarski and Barton arrived to break it up.

All day Saturday, the coaches had conducted campus tours and answered a deluge of questions from the parents. It had been the longest weekend any of them could remember, and they still had half a day to go.

Conversation in the meeting room stopped as Dave Barton stood up, cleared his throat, and asked for everybody's attention. "Well, men, our weekend is almost over. In about ten minutes, Coach Lee's gonna walk in here and give us another pep talk about getting up for this afternoon's pool party." The coaches groaned and faked exhaustion. "And I guarantee you," Dave said, "this is what the man's going to say to us." Barton loved to do his Buck Lee imitation, and the coaches usually enjoyed it, too. He was urged on by several whistles, a smattering of applause, and one "All right!" from Johnny Hyspick.

Kyle Moore handed him a purple baseball cap with a big rattler on the front and said, "All Buck Lees wear a coach's hat." Barton curtsied, took the hat from Kyle, and began the show.

"This here pool pawty is gon' be fun as shee-it, coaches," he said in his deepest Southern drawl. "We gon' have a who-laht mouth-waterin' barbecue chicken, awlem great prospects, and awlem beautiful, sexy Rattlerettes. But they's a coupla thangs I'd like to tawk about 'fore we mosey ova they-ah to see awlose purty bawdies. Firs of awl, check out their butts. Y'all know that unless they got great cookies, they juss ain't got it. Next, you look at the laigs an' ankles of each of the bawdies there. If them little ankles are too thick, foget 'um! Next, you look agin at the legs. If y'all spot any of 'em with big, sawft, fleshy-lookin' thighs, fowget dem, too! Now, one of the most impawtant thangs is to look at their chests. We like to have them big ol' boobs. No little 'uns fo' us. Now, after y'all finish lookin' at awl the football prospects in their bathin' suits, y'all can check out the girls in theirs."

The room exploded in laughter. They all needed a break before they had to get serious again.

"I'd like to remind y'all of a couple of thangs 'fore we slide outa here and go on over to the pool," Dave continued with the act. "First of all, Ignarski, I don't wawnt you wearin' no bathing suit. It might scare the livin' monkey crap out o' th' prospects. I know damn well it'll frighten the gals with awlat hair on yo' back and elbows." Dave hiked his right leg up on the table and began to perform an exaggerated version of Buck scratching his jock itch. The coaches were pounding each other and gasping for air. Dave even had Buck's facial expression down perfectly — the eyes shut tight, the eyebrows pulled together, and the lips parted slightly with the tip of the tongue poking out of the corner.

"I'm taller'n all you coaches. That's why I'm the head coach. But y'all don't have to cawl me God. Just cawl me Co-ach Lee. Now men, listen carefully. You ova theah, Coach Smith. You caint have mah job today. What's that Coach Smith? Say you don't *want* my job? You just want *J. A.*'s job?" The guffaws and back pounding continued as Charlie turned beet red.

"I don't think that's funny, Dave," Smith said. "I hope Buck comes into the room and catches you." Smith took his gold Cross pen from his pocket and started scribbling notes. He wanted to look studious when Buck finally came in and found the rest of the staff goofing off.

But Dave Barton's "Buck Lee Revue" continued for another twenty minutes, and he didn't miss many nerves. He stuck a Coke bottle in his pocket and limped around to emulate Buck, at full erection, coming out of a meeting with Cathy the Rattlerette. He played on Buck's fear of dogs ("I doan cay-uh if it *is* just six weeks old, Miz Fletcher, them poodles are killahs!"). He ridiculed Hyspick's curious blend of barbarism and Christianity ("A real *Jew* showed up for a tryout? Won't they ever learn?"), and even wandered off onto J. A.'s reminiscing about his good old days ("Ran the mile in 3:45 but the idiots forgot to clock me."). He was needling Billy Tom Harris ("Whadda you mean, you can't attend the coaches' meeting 'cause you have to go home and make love to yo' wife? Oh, I see, she goes to the hair dresser tomorrow.") when the coaches abruptly stopped laughing. Buck was standing in the door.

"Oh, shit," said Barton, almost in shock. "How long you been there?"

"Aw, might-neah a half-houah, ah'd say." Buck suppressed his grin.

"Well, hell, Coach, you know how it is."

"I got an assignment for you, Dave."

"Yeah?"

"From now on, I'm gonna let *you* make my phone calls. You do me better than I do."

The coaches erupted in laughter again . . . except for Larry Hildebrand, who was asleep in the corner. Buck spotted him and decided to rattle his cage. "Coach Hildebrand!" he shouted. "How we doing on Tnassip? You told me you'd have him down for this weekend, but he didn't show. Where is he?"

Hildebrand shook his head and wiped the sleep from his bloodshot eyes. "Coach Rockwell and I are working on him, Coach, and we're in good shape. I've got an alum who's keeping in touch and telling me how he's doing."

"How he's doing? Coach, the season's been over for weeks. Where the hell's he from, Australia?"

Hildebrand grasped for words. "Coach, all I know is that Mugsy Harmon calls me every week and gives me his stats. I saw him late last season and he looked great. He's a real prospect."

"You better get on the ball and give me more than you've given so far, if you want us to give Tnassip a scholarship." Hildebrand nodded twice and dozed off again.

34

WHEN THE WEATHER TURNED damp and dreary, the afternoon pool party was moved indoors to the new Campbell Student Complex. The scene was a series of incongruities: Green water reflecting off the aqua-colored tile walls clashed with the dark skies visible through large windows surrounding the pool; forty muscle-bound, hairy prospects seemed miscast among the forty-five silky smooth, curvaceous Rattlerettes; and the smell of chlorine mixed unappetizingly with the smell of barbecue, which had been brought in to feed the horde.

Buck and his staff walked into this visual and sensual hodgepodge just in time to see one of their star recruits go off the high board and hit the water spread-eagled. The sound from the impact echoed through the room. The kid may have been graceful on the football field, but his diving style was just short of spastic. As Buck watched to see if the boy had survived, he heard someone calling his name. "Coach Lee, Coach Lee, over here. It's me, Cathy!"

He scanned the pool for the source of the voice and finally spotted her coming out of the water. She propped both elbows up on the side, shook her hair out of her eyes, and lifted herself out of the pool. As she emerged, water filled the top of her suit, pulling it down and exposing two beautiful breasts to Buck and his coaches. If eyes could have walked, twenty-four would have strolled to the side of the pool.

Cathy headed toward Buck, and the other coaches tactfully left to see their prospects.

"I'm so glad you came over. We thought you might not be here, but I told all the Rattlerettes you would. They all want to meet you, they've heard me talk so much about you."

Buck knew Cathy was only teasing him, but he didn't mind. He was at the age where if a sweet young thing paid him some attention, he enjoyed it without questioning her motives. "I hope all the boys have been gentlemen this weekend and y'all didn't have any trouble."

"Nothing we couldn't handle," said Cathy with a coy smile.

As Buck reached to help her into her robe, his attention was diverted to the end of the pool where Hyspick was bouncing up and down on the high board like an Olympian. Behind him were Ignarski, Moore, Driscoll, and Barton, all in their swim shorts and T-shirts. Everybody had stopped talking and was staring at this crazy bunch of men.

"Hey, what's going on up there?" Buck yelled.

"It's sort of a challenge, Coach," answered Hyspick. "They all said if I'd do a flip off the high board, so would they. Watch the Big Cat operate." Hyspick bounced high off the board, spread his arms as if to take flight, and gracefully catapulted himself into the air. He lowered his head, tucked his legs, and did a perfect flip, entering the water without a splash. The crowd clapped and yelled, "Next! Next! Next!"

Buck and Cathy walked down to where Hyspick was climbing out at the pool. "Where'd y'all get bathing suits?" Buck asked.

"We wore 'em under our clothes so we could go swimming if we wanted to. I sort of encouraged it. I get tired of those old farts putting me down all the time. I just wanted to show 'em what I could do on the board. If they're dumb enough to try and compete with me, that's their problem."

Buck leaned over and whispered into Hyspick's ear. "I'll tell you whose problem it'll be if we don't get Eaarnel and all these other prospects. It will be *yours*." Buck clinched his teeth. The smile left Hyspick's face. "I don't want my coaches showing off in front of the women, and don't tell me you're doing it for the prospects. I've got the same equipment you've got, and I've shown off lots of times on the high board for cute little gals, and. . . ."

Before Buck could finish, he heard a loud scream. He looked up to see Ignarski in midair, flapping both arms like a chicken with its head cut off. He hit the water halfway through a flip, square on his back. It sounded like a fireworks explosion. Every prospect and Rattlerette ran to the side of the pool to see if Ignarski had survived. Seconds later, a crewcut bobbed up out of the water.

"Did anybody see what happened to the mattress that I landed on?

Felt so good I want to buy one just like it." Ignarski was grinning from ear to ear. The prospects loved it. They cheered, yelled, stomped their bare feet, and clapped their hands for more.

As if on cue, another body came flying through the air trying to do a flip. It was Moore, in somewhat the same, unenviable position as Ignarski had been in — upside down in midair. "Wham!" Kyle hit the water with a smack, and again the crowd ooohed and aaahed. Up popped Kyle with a big grin on his face. "Did anybody get the number of that truck, or was that Eaarnel I just tried to tackle?"

"Geronimo!" was the next scream from the high board. Driscoll and Barton were coming off the board together, hand in hand, feet kicking and arms flailing. As they approached the water, their feet began to rise above their heads. Two bodies hit the water at a forty-five-degree angle. Not quite as spectacular as Ignarski and Moore's, but still exciting as hell, Buck thought. The crowd clapped, whistled, and began chanting, "We want Buck! We want Buck!" The idea of seeing coaches almost kill themselves apparently was appealing to the prospects and the Rattlerettes.

Buck realized that Hyspick's grandstanding had turned into a great recruiting ploy. Instead of being a semi-dull barbecue to go home and forget, now the prospects would have something to talk about to their parents and friends.

Ignarski and Moore baited the crowd. "Let's hear it one more time. What do we want?"

"We want Buck! We want Buck! We want Buck!"

Without considering the consequences, Buck took off for the diving board, going up the steps like a shot. In seconds he was on the high board still wearing his sport coat, tie, lucky khaki pants, and Gucci loafers. He bounced up and down on the board while the crowd cheered. "Give us a back dive!" someone yelled. Buck looked down to find the voice, and his enthusiasm instantly waned. Although the board was only about thirty feet high, it looked like ninety. He was having second thoughts, but there was no way to back out now without embarrassment. He looked down again and spotted Cathy staring up at him. He imagined that he was nineteen again, wearing a tiny bathing suit at Lake Mulasnatchee, and that Cathy's beautiful eyes were glued to the bulge in his suit. His confidence soared. He walked out to the end of the board and turned around for the back flip. He placed his toes on the edge, raised his arms in front of his body, flexed his knees, and pushed off. Once again, he was going to show all those gorgeous gals at Lake Mulasnatchee the Buck Lee back flip. Halfway out, however, Buck realized he didn't remember how to do a back flip, and that he wasn't nineteen at Lake Mulasnatchee any more. "OOOOH SHEEITT," he screamed as he plummetted down parallel to the water. But neither the scream nor his kicking feet altered the laws of gravity: He hit flat on his back. Fortunately, his clothes absorbed most of the shock, so he survived the impact and came up laughing. The prospects, Cathy, and his assistants all were cheering and smiling as he climbed out of the pool. I'll do that dive twice a day if all the kids will sign, Buck thought.

Just then the Eastern Pep Band came marching through the door playing a jazzy version of the school fight song. The prospects and Rattlerettes turned their attention to the music and left Buck standing there dripping.

"You were great, Coach," said Kyle. "The prospects loved it. We didn't know you could trick dive, too. If we'd known, we would've let you in on the gag we were playing on Hyspick. He's so damned cocky."

"Yeah," said Buck, surprised and delighted to spot an honorable way out of an embarrassing situation. "I guess we showed Hyspick a thing or two, didn't we? Anybody can do a straight flip, but it takes guts to clown around from that height. Right?" The coaches nodded and slapped each other on the back. "Look, fellows, I've got to go change clothes. Y'all take care of Eaarnel until I get back."

Buck turned and started for the locker room but he felt a small hand on his arm.

"Coach Lee, maybe you need somebody to help you dry off," said Cathy.

"No, thanks, Cathy," he answered without thinking. "I've got to hurry and get back over here and go to work. Maybe another time." As he passed through the swinging doors and realized what he had just done, he disgustedly punched himself in the jaw. *You idiot! You idiot!* Eaarnel was turning out to be more expensive than he ever anticipated.

35

"COACH HILDEBRAND, THIS IS Mugsy Harmon. You remember me. I'm the one who's helping you with Tnassip."

Larry Hildebrand took the bottle of vodka from his desk drawer and poured himself and Noble Rockwell a double shot each. "Of course, I remember you, Mr. Harmon. What you got for me today? Are we closing in on this stud?"

"You bet we are," said Patrick "Mugsy" Flanagan. "He had a great game this week. Rushed for two hundred yards and scored four touchdowns. He's a great one, and he's really interested in our school. He can't wait to meet you. When are you going to come meet him?"

Hildebrand chugged his shooter and passed the bottle to Rockwell, who was waiting for a refill. "I've been real busy with my other prospects and just haven't had time. Now, as soon as I do get a free moment, I'll be out there. You can count on me."

"I know I can, Coach, so I'll be back in touch next week. Good hunting, Coach."

"Thanks a lot, Mr. Harmon, and I'll be expecting to hear from you next week." Hildebrand hung up the phone and looked up to see Rockwell taking all the stamps out of his desk drawer.

"Coach, do you have to take *all* my stamps? Can't you just take a few?"

Rockwell crammed the stamps into his pocket and, with a flick of his wrist, belted down his drink. "Coach Larry," he slurred, "when I had to retire from this job, I'd never bought a pair of socks or a jock strap, or licked or bought my own stamps. I don't intend to start now." Rockwell got up from the desk and started out the door. "Oh, by the way, what did that Tnassip boy do?"

"Two hundred yards and four touchdowns, Coach. He's a good 'un."

36

J. A. SYMINGTON WAS PUTTING the finishing touches on a pencil doodle of the Heisman Trophy when a breathy voice announced on his intercom, "Mr. Symington, Coach Moore is here to see you."

"Yes, well, send him in, Joyce."

Kyle Moore had been trying unsuccessfully for a week to get an audience with the athletic director to discuss the eligibility of his hottest prospect, Ivie Buchanan. But J. A. had been tied up. His ten-year-old daughter, Andrea, had been giving a series of piano recitals at school, and J. A. had spent five days auditioning candidates to turn her sheet music.

"Come on in, Coach Moore, have a seat. So, how's the recruiting coming along? You guys locate any gorillas to take us to the Sugar Bowl? The wife just loves New Orleans."

"As a matter of fact, J. A.," Kyle said, working on his flavorless chewing gum, "I've got one right here who could help put us *all* on Bourbon Street." J. A. raised an eyebrow as Kyle pulled out his scouting report with an eight-by-ten glossy attached. "His name is Ivie Buchanan and he's a killer. Plays linebacker, weighs 225, is 6′ 3″, and bench-presses 360. But his grades aren't so hot."

"Just how 'not so hot' are they?" asked J. A., preparing for the worst. Kyle shifted his gum and doubled his chewing cadence. He'd heard that J. A. Symington would bend a few rules now and then, but he didn't know how far he'd go. To let Ivie into school, he'd have to bend them and fold them over twice.

"Here you are, J. A." Kyle handed him the transcript. "But let me just say that Ivie has had to go to school and play ball under unusually difficult circumstances." J. A. put on his reading glasses and scanned the page with a look of horror. "See, J. A.," Kyle said, finally standing up, "Ivie's from Newark, New Jersey. He's a nice, good-hearted kid who's had to help raise his three younger brothers and his seven-year-old twin sisters. He's had to support himself by working nights in a cardboard-box factory, and on weekends he's a security guard at Three Mile Island. As you can see there, he has no father, and his mother is a hooker when she isn't in the hospital recovering from beatings by her pimp." Forgive me, Lord, for maligning that sweet, old woman, Kyle thought, but we need this ballbuster.

J. A. listened intently, folding his lower lip up over the top one, showing deep concentration and concern. "You'll also see there, J. A., that he's one hell of a physical specimen. It's like God created his body for one purpose — to knock the piss out of anybody carrying a football. He's a killer. He's 'agile, mobile, and hostile,' as Jack Gaithan used to say. Hell, by the second quarter, the Tennessee center will be calling him 'Sir' and paying him cash not to hit him anymore."

Kyle was now pacing the area in front of J. A.'s desk and shifting his gum from side to side with every stroke of his jaw. His voice had gone up an octave, and his tight little body was involuntarily flexing under his coaching shorts and purple short-sleeved sport shirt. J. A. made several fast pencil underlinings on the transcript, stood behind his desk, picked up his metal wastepaper basket, and walked around to Kyle. He held the basket under Kyle's chin.

"Spit it out, Coach."

"What?"

"Spit out the gum. Spit it into this can right now."

Kyle's jaw relaxed and the gum rolled off his tongue and into the can with a thunk.

"I have to do that with my ten-year-old daughter all the time. I won't allow gum-chewing in my presence. I'm sorry." J. A. returned the can to its place under the desk and sat down in his high-backed leather chair.

"Now let me get this straight. You want me to get somebody in school who has grades like this?" J. A. returned to the transcript and read the underlined sections aloud. "D in Wood Shop, D in First Aid, C in Decoupage, three Incompletes in Remedial English, and A in Physical Education. Coach, this man can't read or write."

"Well, he can sure read a play better than any high school linebacker I've ever seen," Kyle said. "And he has legs on him like a sumo wrestler. I tell ya, J. A., this boy has what it takes to be an all-American by his sophomore year. You know how long it's been since this school even *had* an all-American?"

"You better damn well believe I know how long it's been!" J. A. said with obvious irritation. "I'm your athletic director, and don't you ever forget that. I want to win just the same as everybody else in this program . . . hell, just like every kid in this school and every asshole in this town."

J. A. walked over to the window behind his desk and surveyed his athletic kingdom. He wanted Kyle Moore to know that he cared about the football program and cared about winning. He wanted him to know that he cared about a national championship as much as he cared about his daughter. But he didn't want him to see his tired old eyes water up like some senile old man who had never realized his childhood dreams. Kyle sat back down on the leather sofa and waited for the verdict. This was the first really terrible transcript he had brought in to J. A., and he didn't know quite what to expect.

"Coach Moore," J. A. began as he returned to his chair, "there's only one thing I hate worse than athletes who are poor students, and that's *poor* athletes who are poor students. I'll have to take this up with the committee. I'll let you know after we meet." Kyle stood up, thanked J. A., and started for the door. "Coach Moore."

"Yes, J. A.?"

"This Ivie Buchanan. He better be good."

Kyle nodded and smiled, then shut the door behind him. J. A. perused the transcript and scouting report one more time. Then he wrote, "Approved by the East Alabama Athletic Committee" across the page. He placed the papers in his OUT box and resumed his sketch of the Heisman Trophy.

* * *

"Buck, can I talk with you for a second?"

"Sure, Kyle, what's on your mind?"

"Well, I think we're gonna get Ivie. You did a great job on him, and he told me today that he wants to sign with us. I also just talked with J.

A. about Ivie's grades, and I'm sure he's gonna cooperate. The only problem is Ivie wants you to go home with him and sign him. I know you're tied up with Eaarnel, but this is some kind of stud horse. I mean, he won't stop until he hears glass. Eaarnel isn't gonna sign this week, anyway, so why don't you fly to New Jersey and sign Ivie? I'll help out with Eaarnel."

Buck pulled up his britches, scratched his jock itch, and wished he didn't have to go. "Kyle," he said, "they *all* want the head coach to be there when they sign. But, what the hell? Sure, I'll go sign him. I can sign anybody who really wants to sign."

Kyle reached out a hand and grabbed Buck's. "I'll have Peggy make your reservations. You'll have to leave real early in the morning, 'cause he's got to get back to school tomorrow. You know, when you're a math major like Ivie, you can't miss many days of school." Kyle winked and skipped out the door whistling. Buck leaned back and shook his head. He'd seen too many of them say *yes* and then change their minds when they got home.

37

COACH SHAVERS, THIS IS The Raven."

"Go ahead, Raven."

"I've got some very important news for you, Coach."

"Go ahead and tell me, then, goddammit. Don't keep me waiting."

"I won't."

"Raven, for the last time, what is it you have for me?" Shavers snarled. "And it had better be good. I'm right in the middle of dinner."

"Gee, that's great, Coach Shavers. Whatta you having?"

"Fried chicken, Raven. Now tell me what you have."

"The colored boy from the yankee town is going to sign with Buck Lee. I think his name is Ivory something."

"You *think,* you idiot, and you'll ruin the whole deal. So how's he going to sign him?" Shavers pounded his fist on the dinner table.

"He's gonna fly back with him and sign him. They have him all locked up."

"Raven, do you know the flight number and when they're leaving?" Shavers was looking at the appointment calendar he kept by the kitchen phone.

"They leave tomorrow morning at 6:45. It's Delta flight 456 to Newark . . . wherever that is."

"You done good, Raven. Now, go back and play checkers some more with Ethelyn. I'll send you a little side of ham for this."

"Thanks, Coach. This is The Raven, signing off. Good night."

38

COACH SHAVERS, THERE'S A police car following us, and it looks like he wants you to pull over. He's got his light on."

Shavers reached toward the glove compartment. "What color?" he said.

Kevin Morgan scratched his head. "Blue. Aren't they all?"

"No, goddammit, what color's the *officer*?" Shavers had the glove compartment open and was fumbling through a stack of cassette tapes.

Kevin turned around and looked. "He's black."

Shavers tossed aside a couple of tapes until he found the one he wanted. He crammed it into the tape player and turned the volume up. Kevin covered his ears as the booming voice of Dr. Martin Luther King, Jr., reverberated through the car. Shavers pulled over and waited for the New Jersey state trooper. He sat with a blissful look on his face. "*Free at last, free at last, thank God Almighty I'm free at last. . . .*" resounded from the car when Shavers opened the window and faced the young black trooper.

"Shhh, officer, I'll give you my license in just a minute, after I finish listening to this tape of Martin Luther King." Shavers was as reverent as a choir boy. "I just love to hear him speak." Dr. King's voice swelled and tailed off as he poured out his message.

Feeling a tap on his shoulder, Shavers turned the volume down to a quiet roar and looked forlornly at the trooper. "Sir," Shavers said, "I'm sorry I was speeding, but I got carried away listening to this. I would've stopped sooner, but I couldn't hear your siren for the tape." Shavers began to reach into his back pocket. "The Reverend King sounds better with the volume up."

"That's all right, sir, you don't have to show me your driver's license," the young officer said. "I'm a great admirer of the late

Martin Luther King, Jr., and I can understand someone listening to that speech and forgetting how fast they're going." He put his pad back into his coat pocket. "Just try and keep it under control a little bit better. You were doing almost eighty-five when I started clocking you."

Shavers reached out and shook the officer's hand. "I could tell by your eyes that you and I have the same feelings about Reverend King. God bless you."

Shavers removed the tape when the trooper left. "What if he'd been white?" Kevin asked. Shavers reached in the glove compartment, pulled out another tape, and jammed it into the tape player. The car was instantly filled with the beautiful music of a choir singing, "*I was lost in sin, but Jesus took me in . . .*" Then a voice said, "*Good evening, brothers and sisters, this is the Reverend Billy Graham. . . .*" The rented Lincoln sped off toward the Newark Airport as Billy Graham began praying for all the sinners.

* * *

Ivie and Buck strapped themselves into their seats in the first class section as Buck looked around for anybody who might recognize him. There was a school policy against flying first class, but old Noble Rockwell had shown the coaches many years ago how to beat the system. He had established the Rattler Slush Fund for situations like this. He arranged for tickets to the spring game to be sold by the Alumni Association. They would give Rockwell half the money for his slush fund, while the other half went for academic scholarships. It was a good deal for both parties.

The plane lifted off from Stanleyville and soared majestically upward. Buck, dressed in his lucky khakis, was always nervous flying, and this flight was no exception. But one look at Ivie made him feel more confident. The kid's teeth were clinched, his knuckles were white, and his armpits were soaked. Buck felt braver knowing that somebody was more afraid of flying than he was. As they leveled off and flew through plump white clouds, Buck loosened his seat belt and waited for Ivie to recover. He finally reached over and tapped him on the arm.

"You feeling OK, big fella?"

"I'm fine," said Ivie, still staring straight ahead.

The seat belt sign went off, but he still didn't budge. When the stewardess came by, Buck ordered a beer for himself and orange juice and a sweet roll for Ivie. Three glasses of orange juice and four sweet rolls later, Ivie was back among the living.

"Coach," he said as he washed down the last bite, "I need to ask some questions before we get back to New Jersey."

Buck reached out and opened the shade over the window. Sunlight streamed through, highlighting the sharp angles of Ivie Buchanan's face. The kid had a great one, and Buck wanted to see it. "Go ahead, Ivie. Ask me anything you like. I'll try to answer it."

"Well, Coach, is it true that drinking the water in Alabama will make your hair fall out? That's what a coach at Penn State told me last weekend, and while I was at Eastern, I noticed that all you coaches drink beer. Is that why?"

Buck ran his fingers through his hair to be sure it was still there. "Ivie, I'm gonna be honest with you. I have heard rumors about the water around West Alabama causing some thinning of the hair, but the water at Eastern is just as healthy as it can be."

"That's a relief. Now, I've got another question, but I don't know 'zactly how to ask it. I guess I'll just come right out with it: Is Coach Barton a queer?"

Buck almost gagged on a last swallow of beer, but managed not to spray it. "Ivie, what on earth makes you ask that?"

"Well, you know, he has that Afro hairdo, and they say only queers and blacks got hair like that." He laughed. "I can tell you one thing: He ain't black."

"Ivie," said Buck, "I can assure you that Coach Barton is not a homosexual. Why, he has a wife and three kids and belongs to the Baptist Church. No way anybody who belongs to the Baptist Church could ever be queer."

"I guess you're right. We belong to the Baptist church at home, and I *know* we ain't got no queers in *our* church." Ivie leaned back in his seat, obviously comforted. Then he straightened up again. "Coach Lee, I got one more."

"Go ahead, Ivie, we haven't started our descent yet. I won't get the cotton mouth until then, so we can still talk."

"Huh?"

"Forget it. Go ahead."

"Well, somebody told me," Ivie said, pausing, "I mean, well, somebody told me that if I go to school in the South, I'd be called *nigger* by the coaches. Is that true?"

Buck stared at him. "Ivie, that really irritates me. Now, to think that there are *no* Southerners who call blacks *nigger* is ridiculous, because we both know there are people like that. But remember, Ivie, people in other parts of this country talk the same way. The reason anybody uses racial slurs is because they feel better about themselves when they put others down. These are the same people who call others *shorty, ugly, fatty, skinny*, or anything they can think of to take the attention off their own inadequacies. You come to our school and I promise you no one will call you *nigger*. I'll fire their ass if they do."

The captain announced that the plane was starting its final approach to the Newark airport. The No Smoking sign went on, and Buck and Ivie tightened their seat belts. There was no more conversation. Both were too busy concentrating on the landing to talk. As the plane flared into the landing position, Buck leaned back and braced his feet against the floor. It was a necessary movement to help the pilot put on the brakes. The plane hit the ground, bounced, and came back down to earth. He breathed a sigh of relief and released the seat arms from his death grip. He turned to Ivie, who was just looking up from his prayer. "That's another one I owe the Lord," he said.

* * *

Kevin Morgan had worked for Buddy Shavers for six years, but he had never gotten used to his habit of constantly changing his underclothes. Nobody could sweat that much. And it didn't help Shavers, anyway; he still reeked of cigar smoke, which apparently had infiltrated his skin.

Kevin paced the airport lobby as he waited for Shavers to come out of the bathroom. He glanced at his watch and saw that it was only ten minutes before the plane with Ivie Buchanan and Buck Lee would arrive. What a weird business this is, he thought — standing in an airport lobby waiting to steal a prospect, or, in business terms, to prevent a sale. Kevin spotted Shavers strutting across the lobby, puffing on a long, black cigar. He had on a fresh shirt and his five o'clock shadow was covered with makeup.

"This'll be like old times," Shavers said. "We're gonna meet 'em when they get off the plane and challenge 'em. That asshole Lee thought he could slip by the master and sign that boy." He blew smoke into Kevin's face. "Well, he's wrong. I knew his schedule before he did. I'll guarantee you that kid won't sign that scholarship today."

"How'd you know which flight he was coming in on, Coach? I mean, the airlines won't tell you. I tried."

"I have my contacts. I know everything they're doing. They can't slip anything past me."

* * *

Buck was pissed but not surprised to see Buddy Shavers and his duck-footed assistant coach, Kevin Morgan, standing there when he and Ivie exited the plane. He knew Shavers too well to be surprised. Shavers and Morgan looked like the Bobbsey Twins in their gold britches, black blazers, and gold ties, with their arms folded and no smiles on their faces. They've scared the shit out of Ivie, Buck thought. Better watch him or he'll run home to mama. This was airport hardball — the confrontation that the fans don't get a chance to see.

With Ivie following behind him, Buck walked up to Shavers. There they were, eyeball to eyeball. "Why, Coach Shavers, what in the world are you doing in Newark?" he said. Shavers didn't answer but tried to stare Buck down while Morgan began talking to Ivie.

"Ivie, you know I've been recruiting you for the last six months, and you know how much I love you and your mama," Buck heard him say. "We've eaten together, talked about your future and what it means to you if you come to Western to play for the greatest coach in the country." Shavers wiped the sweat from his forehead, and reached into his pocket for another cigar without ever losing eye contact with Buck. Ivie was looking for a place to hide, but Kevin continued.

"Ivie, I've brought Coach Shavers all the way to Newark just to talk to you. This was the day he was supposed to be with his family, but he gave it up for you. Surely you can give us a few minutes."

"What should I do, Coach Lee?" said Ivie.

"Go ahead, Ivie," Buck answered. It was the *only* answer. "Coach Shavers has spent a great deal of money on you, so you owe him at least *ten minutes*."

Shavers smiled and started to walk away with Ivie, but Buck grabbed the prospect by the arm. "Ivie, just remember this. Shavers wants your body just like we do. All you should care about is who you want using it, and what they can do for you *while* they're using it." Buck knew he was taking a chance by being so direct, but that's what it came down to — you give your body to the person you like the most.

Shavers and Ivie disappeared around the corner. In an attempt to re-establish territorial rights, Buck yelled, "Ivie, I'll call your mama and tell her we'll be over there in about forty-five minutes. What do you want me to tell her to fix for lunch?" But it was too late. Kevin Morgan and Buck Lee were left standing there, natural enemies today, but possible allies a year from now. If Kevin got Ivie, Buck would try to hire him.

* * *

Shavers reached into his pocket and pulled out a $100 bill. He carefully placed the money in Ivie's hand, closed it, and guided it into his pocket. "Keep that for your mother. She can buy herself something nice." Ivie shoved the money deep in his pocket and never took his hand off it. The muscles rippled in his forearm as he squeezed the crisp bill. His shirt was drenched with sweat by now, and his pectorals stood out like a beautiful girl's in a wet T-shirt. It excited Shavers to look at this marvelous athlete. He'd made the first step and it looked good. Taking the money meant that Ivie wouldn't sign with Eastern for the moment. If you could stall a signing, it meant you had a chance.

"Ivie," Shavers said, "why would you sign with Eastern? They already have the best linebacker in the country, and they're gonna sign the son of their biggest booster as a linebacker. You know *he's* gonna play." Shavers was patting Ivie on the shoulder. "Where does that leave you? The way I see it, if you go to Eastern, you'll sit on the bench. If you come and play for me, you'll be an all-American the first year."

"Coach Shavers," Ivie said confidently, "I can play for *anybody*. Who they have and who they're signing don't bother me. I'll whip *anybody's* ass."

Shavers changed tactics quickly. Plan A was a bust. "How do you like that old car you're driving, Ivie?"

"Now we're getting down to business," he said.

"You don't sign with the Rattlers and we'll work something out. I'll take care of my boy." Shavers put his arm around Ivie. "Now, let's go back out front and tell Coach Lee you're not ready to sign with him. Tell him you need more time."

"Well, all right," said Ivie. "But first I need to ask you something about the water."

39

RICHARD CULPEPPER WAS SURPRISED to see Buck Lee's office lights on so late at night. He knew that Buck usually was home by nine o'clock, unless he was on a recruiting trip like the one he'd just returned from, but there he was, pacing around his office. This is really ideal, Richard thought. I'll just wait right here and give Buck the new information on Ivie Buchanan when he comes out. I know he was depressed about not signing him, so maybe this will cheer him up a little. Maybe this will be the breakthrough that forces him to hire me.

It shouldn't matter, Richard thought as he shivered in the cold night air, that I never played football. Lou Holtz doesn't look like he ever played. In fact, he thought, Holtz looks more like a character from the old "Dick Van Dyke Show" than a football coach. And how about Hank Stram? He probably was a floorwalker at Bloomingdale's before he became a coach.

The lights went off in Buck's office. The building now was completely dark. Richard stood outside the door waiting for him. As the door opened, he heard the squeak of rubber-soled shoes on the foyer floor.

The footsteps came closer. He waited. Taking a deep, silent breath, Richard hopped out onto the sidewalk and blurted, "How are you, Coach? Richard Culpepper here."

The skinny little man with big ears dropped everything he was carrying — the box of paper clips in his mouth, six legal pads and a book of stamps in his hands, the four erasers under his chin, the eight pairs of socks cradled under his armpits, and the football between his legs. He collapsed to the ground, rolled onto his back, and screamed, "Save me! I'm having a heart attack! But don't give me mouth-to-mouth resuscitation."

Richard looked down at the man clutching his heart. It wasn't Buck

Lee. It was Noble Rockwell.

"Coach *Rockwell.* I didn't mean to scare you like that. I thought you were Coach Lee. Are you all right, sir?"

Rockwell leaned up on one elbow and said, "You mean you weren't waiting for me?"

Richard didn't know whether he should try to help him up, call an ambulance, scream for Coach Lee, or just run. "No, sir, Coach Rockwell, I was waiting for Coach Lee. Can I help you, sir?"

Rockwell staggered to his feet, wiped himself off, and said, "Yeah, how about helping me pick up all this stuff?"

Richard scooped up the football and pitched it to Rockwell. As he handed the old coach the rest of the supplies, Rockwell again placed them in a carrying position. Without saying "thank you" or even acknowledging Richard's presence, Noble Rockwell waddled down the steps in front of the building and got into his 1968 Volkswagen.

As the tattered machine lurched down the street, Richard spotted the socks that Rockwell had left behind. He started to yell but realized that Rockwell was out of earshot. Richard stuck the socks into his pocket and headed home. He'd just have to catch the old coach and give him the socks some other time. Richard wondered if maybe Rockwell could help him get a job with Buck.

40

IT WAS EARLY ON a Tuesday morning, the first day that high school football players could legally sign a grant-in-aid with the college of their choice. A caravan of luxury cars snaked its way into the heart of the Newark ghetto. All were driven by white, middle class college football coaches. Like brazen commandos, with the mission of "get him or learn the insurance code," they had come to capture the not-so-secret weapon: Ivie Buchanan.

The only way Ivie could have avoided the fawning, persistent, three-year recruitment was to have played center on a team in the Eskimo league. Even then, some alum probably would have spotted him. He was not easy to overlook. If God were a football fan, Ivie would have been one of his special creations — 6′ 3″ of granite; 220 pounds of steel; hard upper body; long, sinewy legs; all-State since his sophomore year in high school; prep all-American for two years; could scald a forty-yard strip on a football field in 4.6 seconds, faster than most halfbacks and ends. Ivie Buchanan was a coach's dream: a ball-busting, head-hunting, mean-ass, son-of-a-bitching linebacker.

The cars inched along the narrow street as the drivers tried to find just the necessary space in which to park their big cars and their bigger fantasies.

* * *

Kyle Moore carefully positioned the brand-new, white, four-door, rented Cadillac against the curb. He got out and walked a few steps down the street until he could see the back of the Buchanan house. Perfect, he thought. I've got the car in just the right place. Now all I've got to do is find a way to get to Ivie ahead of the other guys. He walked hurriedly down the street and around the block.

* * *

Florida Buchanan stood on the small stone stoop and looked imperiously down on the group of men milling around on the sidewalk. A scowl rolled across her broad, flat face. It was her house, her turf, and, least anybody forgot, her boy, and she intended to run this show. She wore a tight, red and purple, floral printed dress and a pair of royal blue, terry cloth bedroom slippers. As she lumbered down the crumbling brick steps, her mammoth breasts shuddered.

"Shut up," she bellowed. "Y'all makin' a spectacle."

The twelve assistant coaches, from all the biggest football universities in the country, instantly and prudently heeded the big black woman's command. Kyle turned the corner just in time to hear Mrs. Buchanan giving orders.

"We're gonna have a system," Mrs. Buchanan shouted. "Everybody's takin' a number. The coach that draws number one gets to go in and talk to Ivie first."

Kyle broke into a jog. He *had* to get in to see Ivie first, but it wasn't going to be easy with this group of veteran recruiters lurking about.

"Somebody give me some paper," Mrs. Buchanan said. The coaches all grabbed for the nearest piece of paper, ripped it from whatever it was connected to, and thrust it at Mrs. Buchanan. She took one piece and began tearing it. She had divided the paper into quarters when Bob Jackson of Oklahoma, whose slip of paper she had chosen, yelled, "Wait a minute! Don't do that. That's my airline ticket."

"It's too late now, mister," Mrs. Buchanan said as she continued tearing the ticket into little pieces.

"But, but . . . goddammit," muttered Jackson.

Mrs. Buchanan jerked her head up and looked directly at the coaches. "Let's get one thing straight," she said, pointing her finger at Jackson but looking at them all. "Ain't none of you motherfuckers gonna be takin' the Lord's name in vain in my yard or in my house. You heah? Now, let's get on with this." She wrote a number on each slip of paper and then fanned them out in her hand. "OK, who's gonna pick first?"

As all the coaches stood rigidly still, not wanting to draw any attention to themselves, a small black kid walked up to Nolan Freeman of the University of Florida and said, "Hey, man, what y'all doing here?"

"Not now, kid, this is important," snapped Freeman.

The boy, small even for a ten-year-old, was dressed in blue jeans torn at the knees, black high-top sneakers, and a faded New York Giants football jersey. A Philadelphia Phillies baseball cap turned sideways engulfed his birdlike head.

"Say, sucker, I bet I can slip your ass in slap-five poker. You got ten bucks you want to lose?" said the boy.

"What?" Freeman said.

"Come on, who wants to pick first?" bellowed Mrs. Buchanan.

"You want to play some cards?" the boy said.

"Get the fuck out of here, kid," Freeman growled out of the corner of his mouth, trying to be inconspicuous.

The kid doubled his fists and held them up about waist high. He danced and jabbed several times in the direction of Freeman. The boy's flared nostrils, dark saucer eyes, and scarecrow limbs gave him an uncanny resemblance to a furious housefly of human dimensions. "Hey, mudderfucker, don't tell me to get the fuck out of my own neighborhood, man," shouted the boy. "I'll whip your ass, Jack." The kid shuffled, strutted, jived, danced, and pranced in a semicircle around an astonished group of coaches.

"Get out of here," boomed Mrs. Buchanan, who had spotted the disturbance. "You little jive-ass. Get outta here 'fore I beat your fanny." Then, with a move that would have brought pangs of envy to a middle linebacker, Mrs. Buchanan went after the kid. "Go on, *git!*" she yelled, swiping at his tiny head with her meathook hands. Like a chipmunk on the receiving end of a cat attack, the kid scurried away, screaming oaths of retribution.

"I ain't gonna wait no longer," Mrs. Buchanan said as she moved back to the porch. She was breathing deeply after her short chase. "Somebody's gonna pick a number or everybody's gonna go home."

"Wait a minute," Kyle said. He held up his hand like a kid asking to go to the bathroom. "Look, I'll volunteer to go in first."

"Huh?" Mrs. Buchanan grunted.

Jackie Sherman from the University of Texas yelled, "What are you trying to pull, Moore?"

"Come on now, guys, what could I possibly have to gain by going first," Kyle said, appealing to the group. "Think about it. The first one in will have his pitch torn to ribbons by all the others. But somebody has to get things started, and it might as well be me."

"Sounds fishy to me," said Hooks Cleveland from Indiana, but no one else responded.

"You," said Florida Buchanan, jabbing at Kyle, "get in there 'fore I change my mind."

"But wait a minute, I don't trust. . . ."

"Hush," said Mrs. Buchanan to P. W. Faldwell of Southern Mississippi. "I call the plays in this game."

Kyle had already bounded up the steps and into the house. Coach Lee was going to be so proud of him. As he walked down the hallway, his attention was drawn to a large, chipped table that stood beneath a gaudy, framed mirror.

On the table were hundreds of envelopes. Kyle walked over and curiously sifted through the large stack. Jesus, he thought, none of these has been opened. There must be letters here from every school in the country. He marveled as he thumbed through letters from the top head coaches in the country, as well as from some of the top business executives. There were letters from Coca-Cola, IBM, U.S. Steel, and Ford. If the heads of corporate America knew that their letters to a seventeen-year-old linebacker were not even opened, it would blow their minds.

Kyle turned to his right and walked into a room where the TV was blaring. "You is a *bad* puddy-tat," said a small bird on the screen. Ivie's grandfather was sitting directly in front of the television, no farther away than six inches, with a wool ski cap pulled down on his head. Directly behind him was Ivie's teen-age sister, leaning back in a peeling, plastic, rust-colored easy chair, breast-feeding a small baby. Kyle cleared his throat and asked the girl where Ivie was.

"Out back," she said without taking her eyes off the TV.

Kyle didn't bother to say thanks; nobody had looked at him since he came into the room, anyway. They probably think we're all crazy, he thought. He straightened his tie and walked to the dining room at the back of the house. Peering through a broken window, he spotted

Ivie playing basketball with three other boys on the school playground that was directly behind the house.

As Kyle approached the court, Ivie drove between two opponents, did a 360-degree turn, and slammed home a two-handed dunk. The force of the dunk sent shock waves through the rusty, netless rim down to the bottom of the skinny pole holding up the backboard. Even the concrete base into which the pole was sunk seemed to shake.

"Dr. J, slamming it on home," said Ivie's teammate.

"Shit, man, you ain't seen nothing yet," Ivie answered.

"Hey, Ivie, how you doing?" Kyle called from the perimeter of the court, trying to get his attention.

Ivie ignored him and blocked an attempted layup by a short youngster in a sleeveless sweatshirt.

"The chairman say NO!" Ivie yelled exuberantly, slapping a high-five with his teammate. Then he grabbed the basketball, dribbled back toward the other end of the court, leaped up with one hand holding the basketball, and slammed another crushing dunk down through the basket. "Dr. J lives!"

"Hey, Ivie, what's happening, man?" Kyle said. He was trying to remember all the black slang words he was supposed to use when operating in a black neighborhood. He wished he'd brought the book that Buck had passed out with all the catch words the kids used.

"Dr. Dunk!" yelled the tall skinny kid, who didn't look over fifteen, as he took a high pass from his heavyset teammate and jammed the basketball through the hoop.

"Shit, man, how'd that dude get free?" moaned Ivie.

"Hey, Ivie, what's happening, my main man?" said Kyle. He walked closer to the edge of the court.

Ivie stopped the game and stared at him with a faint look of recognition on his face. "Yeah, how you, man?"

"Looks like a great game you're having," Kyle said.

"Yeah, it's all right. You a coach, ain't you?"

"Yeah, man," Kyle said. He reached out and shook Ivie's hand with the soul-brother shake they all used in their recruiting. "I'm Coach Kyle Moore of the East Alabama Rattlers. You remember me. I brought you back to the campus twice. And remember a couple of weeks ago when Coach Buck Lee came back here to sign you and you changed your mind?"

"Yeah, I remember you, Coach. It's just that I've been so many places, I can't remember everybody's name. That's why I like football — you can just call everybody Coach. You don't have to remember their last name." Ivie looked longingly at the three other youngsters continuing with the game. It was now one-on-one with the other officiating.

"Hey, man, mind if I pop a few?" asked Kyle, trying desperately to get on Ivie's good side. "I used to be a pretty bad little guard. I played a lot of basketball in high school." Kyle reached down, picked up an imaginary ball, and shot a one-handed jumper.

"Sure, Coach, you go ahead, but be careful. Those dudes will take your head off." Ivie pointed to his friends, who had stopped and were looking with amazement at this thirty-eight-year-old white man in a coat and tie running onto the court. This is insane, Kyle thought, but what the hell? It might be fun and it sure won't hurt with Ivie. He took off his coat, loosened his tie, and prepared to play.

"You take it out, man," said the short, heavyset kid. "I'll guard you."

Kyle's teammate was a tough-looking, no-nonsense kid. He took the inbounds pass and dribbled back up the court, using behind-the-back moves to get free. When he reached the foul line, however, the tall "Dr. Dunk" kid with arms like a spider cut him off. Kyle raced down the concrete as fast as his penny loafers would carry him, and took a perfect bounce pass from his teammate. He could see the headlines, "White Man Dominates Black Basketball." He left his feet for the stuff, but something went wrong. About a foot short of the rim, he stopped going up. Suddenly a big hand reached over and slammed the basketball and Kyle to the concrete. It was the short, heavyset youngster who had blocked the shot and sent Kyle sprawling.

"Fast break, man, get it out of there," yelled the other side. They streaked down court, leaving Kyle on the ground with ripped pants, bloody elbows, and wounded pride.

He felt Ivie's strong hands picking him up off the concrete. "You OK, Coach? That's a rough bunch out there. Me, I never go up for a stuff with somebody close to me. Hell, they'll kill you."

"I'm all right, Ivie, just sorry I have to go so soon or I'd show 'em the moves I used back at Parker High."

As Kyle brushed himself off, he figured that now was the time to put his move on Ivie. If nothing else, maybe Ivie would feel sorry for him.

"Ivie, I know you're busy, but I've got to talk to you about signing with the Rattlers."

"Hey, I don't know, man, we're up by four." Ivie looked around at his buddies and wiped his hands on his green Notre Dame T-shirt. He wanted to avoid a decision for as long as possible.

Kyle went back to his recruiting lingo. "Hey, man, I got something to show you. I wouldn't jive you, Ivie. This will be worth your while."

"I don't know, man."

"What I want to show you, Ivie, is the Dr. J of its kind."

"Huh?"

"Come on, man we're gonna do some real jiving." Kyle took Ivie by the arm and led him away from the game. "It's on the street behind the alley."

* * *

Buck looked up from his disheveled desk to see Kyle Moore coming through the door. Even though he was limping, he had a smile six miles wide on his deeply tanned, unlined face.

"Well, here he is, the wonder-boy recruiter," Buck said. "We really didn't get a chance to talk on the phone last night. So tell me — how'd you sign Ivie? I thought we'd never get him after the trip I took."

"Oh, there was nothing to it," Kyle stated matter-of-factly. "I promised him I'd give him a car."

"You gave him a car!" Buck yelled, bolting out of his chair.

"No, no, Coach. I didn't give him a car, I just *promised* him I would give him a car. But enough of that. Let me tell you how I played basketball with three 6′ 4″ friends of Ivie's who play for the Knicks. I took the ball down court, see, and stuffed it, and then I. . . ."

41

DAVE BARTON STUCK HIS head into Buck's office and said, "Coach, could you join us in the meeting room for just a minute?"

"Yeah, Dave, I'll be right there."

When Buck walked in several minutes later, Larry Hildebrand was busy explaining how he had worked his butt off trying to get a commitment from Tnassip but hadn't been able to do so. His chief contact had been an alum named Mugsy Harmon, and between the two of them, they had tried everything on Tnassip.

"So what are we going to do about Tnassip, Larry?" asked Buck. "We've been recruiting him since the first meeting, and I still don't know anymore than I did at that time."

Before Hildebrand could offer an alibi, Barton stood up. "Maybe I can shed a little light on Tnassip," he said. "Although he's Larry's man, I've tried to keep up with him, too."

Barton walked over to the board and picked up a piece of chalk. Then he turned to Buck and said, "Do you know what Tnassip is when it's spelled backwards?" He wrote out the letters:

P-I-S-S-A-N-T

The whole room broke into loud laughter — except for Hildebrand, whose face turned a deep crimson color, and Buck, who appeared stone-faced. Hildebrand opened his mouth to try to defend himself, but nothing came out.

Buck pointed his finger at him and said, "You'd better get your ass in gear, or you'll be back milking cows at 4:30 in the morning. You understand?" Hildebrand's cheeks quivered; he was about to cry. "Now, all of you get out of here and go to work."

Everybody except Kyle and Dave left the room. Buck looked at them and burst out laughing. "That's the funniest thing I've ever heard of. Who was this Mugsy Harmon who kept feeding Hildebrand all the information on Tnassip?"

"Patrick Flanagan, who else?"

* * *

Buck walked back into his office, still laughing about Tnassip, and closed the door in hopes of getting some work done. As it swung around, he saw a blur of movement out of the corner of his eye. His reflexes took over, throwing him backwards and bringing his arm up to protect his face. Buck waited for the impact, but none came. He sheepishly look through his armpit and saw Richard Culpepper standing there grinning.

"Hi, Coach."

"Goddammit, Richard! How many times do I have to tell you — don't sneak up on me!" Buck's breathing was heavy and irregular.

"Gee, Coach, I didn't mean to sneak up on you, but Peggy wasn't out front so I just thought I'd wait for you in here."

Buck walked over to his chair and slumped down. "Well, what is it this time? A list of the best rugby players in Australia?"

"No, Coach, the information I have for you this time comes from a lot closer to home."

Richard told Buck about seeing his office light on late one night the week before, and about running into Noble Rockwell with all the supplies outside the door.

"I didn't think anything of it at the time, but later on I figured out that he had to be the one who was walking around in your office. So the next night, I waited outside until Coach Rockwell came back down about midnight, and I followed him in. He came straight to your office. He bumped around for awhile, opening and closing drawers, and then he made a phone call."

Buck couldn't believe what he was hearing. That pitiful old son of a bitch has been snooping around his office.

"I heard him say, 'Hello, Coach Shavers, this is The Raven.' And then he told him about Jake 'The Butcher' Block, the kid from Arkansas you're recruiting."

Buck's mind suddenly flashed back to the day he had left Shavers' office to take the job at Eastern. He'd heard Shavers put in a call for The Raven. So that was it. That was how the press knew Buck was going to be the new head coach the day before the press conference. And that was how Shavers happened to be at the Newark airport when he and Ivie arrived. That sorry old fart!

"Richard, this time you finally brought me something worthwhile. I appreciate your loyalty, and I won't forget it."

"Thanks, Coach. What are you going to do about Coach Rockwell — turn him over to Ignarski?"

"No, I don't think so. I think I'll just let The Raven stay in business, but from now on, he'll be passing only information that I want Shavers to have."

* * *

"Yeah?"

"Coach, Coach, this is Hildebrand."

"Uh-huh," Rockwell grunted into the phone as he wrapped tape around the handle of his tennis racquet.

"Coach, you won't believe what they did to me. I mean, I'm sixty years old. What do they expect?"

"Huh?" Rockwell grabbed a pair of scissors and cut the tape.

"Coach, I just don't see how they could do that to me, and me an old man." Hildebrand wiped the sweat from his forehead. "They can't expect a sixty-year-old man to do the work of a twenty-five-year-old. It's not fair."

"What the hell are you talking about?" growled Rockwell. His gnarled fingers straightened the racquet's strings.

"Coach," Hildebrand whined, "Tnassip, the prospect. It was a joke. The other coaches made up the name. *Tnassip* is *pissant* spelled backwards. Coach, please come over to the Elks Club and have a drink with me. Please?"

Hildebrand heard a click and then a dial tone. Noble Rockwell was dialing another number.

* * *

Shavers pounded his fist on the table and screamed. "What did you say, you dumb old fart? You'd better be kidding me, Raven, or the feathers are gonna fly."

"Coach Shavers, that's what my contact said. That if you spell *Tnassip* backwards, it spells *pissant*. He's not even a real person. I'm sorry about that."

"Sorry, hell! We've spent $5,000 just trying to find Tnassip. OK, Raven, I'm going to give you one more chance, but if you ever screw me again, I'll cut you off forever. You'll be on the bread line." He ground his cigar out on the coffee table. "Do you understand?"

"I won't let you down again, Coach Shavers, sir. Now, will you help me out a little this month? I'm a little short."

"No."

"Can I use your houseboat to go riding at the lake?"

"No."

"Well, give your wife my best. This is The Rav. . . ."

Shavers slammed down the phone, kicked the cat, and headed for the bathroom for another shower.

42

KIRK, IT'S TIME TO earn that big salary we pay you," Buck said facetiously as he reared back in his desk chair with the phone resting on his shoulder. "I need a big favor."

"You name it, you got it, Coach," said Kirk Battle.

"Tomorrow is the day that Eaarnel's supposed to make up his mind. They've invited the coaches of the final six teams to the house at nine o'clock tomorrow morning. What I want you to do is call Eaarnel and tell him you're Prune Juice. Find out, if you can, who the other five schools are. I want to know what we're up against."

"So, tomorrow's the big day. Great. Don't you worry, Coach, ol' Prune Juice is up for the game."

"And call me as soon as you've found out. I'll be at the house."

* * *

As Kirk waited for somebody to answer the phone at Eaarnel's, he shook each leg and spit on his hands like a return man before the opening kickoff. He'd done his imitation of P. J. lots of times, but this one had to be perfect. There could be no doubt in Eaarnel's mind that he was talking to the real P. J.

Someone picked up after the sixth ring but didn't say anything. "Hello?" Kirk figured it must be one of the small Simpson kids. He checked his list of Eaarnel's brothers and sisters, and started calling them off.

"Is this Lela?"

"No."

"Jeremiah?"

"No."

"Adora?"

"Yes."

"Hi, Adora. This is Prune Juice Butler. Can I speak with Eaarnel?"

"Mr. Prune Juice, he ain't here."

"Adora, will you go tell him that Prune Juice is on the phone? I'll give you a present next time I'm around."

"I've seen you play on TV lots of times. If you'll wave at me, I'll go get him."

"Next time we play, I'll wave. Now go ahead on. I'm practicing my wave right now."

Kirk doodled on the pad in front of him while he waited. He could hear voices in the background as they discussed who was on the phone.

"Hello?"

"Eaarnel, this is Prune Juice."

"Is this really P. J.? I been watching you play since I was a kid. You *really* P. J.?"

Kirk answered slowly like he'd heard P. J. do in his television interviews. "Eaar-nel, I want to talk with you about my alma mater, Eastern. You know how much I want you to wear my jersey number and play my old position. Are you gonna let me down?"

"Mr. Prune Juice, I don't want to let you down, but I still ain't been able to make a decision."

"Well, Eaar-nel, what schools are you considering?"

Eaarnel read from the list he kept by the phone: "Michigan, UCLA, Ohio State, USC, Western, and East Alabama. They're the ones who'll be here tomorrow."

"That's great Eaar-nel," Kirk said as he scribbled the names of the schools on his notepad. "Anyway, no matter what you do, I want to wish you luck. Now, if there's anything I can ever do for you, just let me know."

"I really appreciate it, Mr. Prune Juice. Bye."

"Goodbye, Eaar-nel," Kyle said. Then he dialed Buck and read off the names Eaarnel had given him.

"Great, Kirk, now here's your next assignment. Get in your car and drive down to Roanoke and send this wire to the head coaches at the schools you just gave me.

DEAR COACH. THE TIME OF THE MEETING HAS BEEN CHANGED TO TEN O'CLOCK. SIGNED, EAARNEL SIMPSON.

"Now, send that same wire to all the coaches who're gonna be there. It's important, though, that they be sent from Roanoke. You got it?"

"I'm on my way, Coach. Good luck tomorrow."

* * *

Buck checked the digital clock in the bedroom. It was only 5:30, an hour and a half before J. A. Symington was supposed to pick him up, but he was already nervous and couldn't sleep. How could he have done such a stupid thing as to schedule a flight to Roanoke in a helicopter? A helicopter doesn't even have any wings! But he had to do it. It was a critical part of the grand entrance he had planned to impress Eaarnel.

Buck's daydreaming was interrupted by the shrill sound of the alarm. He switched it off and turned toward Gail for some reassurance that helicopters seldom crash, but she didn't move. He leaned over and kissed her on the cheek. You'll be sorry if I don't make it, he thought. Bet you and the kid will miss me. She still didn't budge, so he rolled out of bed and headed for the shower.

An hour later, as he made coffee in the kitchen, Buck tuned in the local radio station. "Eaarnel Simpson is supposed to sign a scholarship this afternoon with a major university," the announcer read. "No one knows who will get the greatest back in the state, but it should be a test between our new coach, Buck Lee, and the old, established program at Western, under the leadership of Buddy Shavers."

Buck turned off the radio when he heard Shavers' name mentioned. He was still pissed off about losing Grant Johnson, and he hadn't felt very good about Eaarnel since Shavers had taken him off to Higgenbotham's plantation. No telling what they promised him down there. He could already be locked up, for that matter. That's why Buck was taking J. A. along today — he might need some leverage from the athletic director.

Buck saw the lights from J. A.'s Porsche through the kitchen window. He's about as much a Porsche man as Christie Brinkley is a tank commander, he thought, flicking the light on and off in the kitchen to let J. A. know he had seen him. J. A. returned the signal by flashing his lights. Buck tucked his shirt into his khaki pants, tightened his tie, put on his purple blazer, and headed off to war.

He squeezed into the Porsche and started to fasten his seat belt when J. A. slapped the car into first gear and hit the accelerator. Buck was thrown back against the seat and then forward as J. A. hit second gear. He had just enough time to buckle up before J. A. missed third and almost stripped the gear. The grinding noise was deafening.

"Sorry-ass car," said J. A., refusing to accept any blame. "Who do they think they are, selling me a car like this? I'm the A.D. in this town, and some heads are gonna roll." He finally managed to get the car into third, then fourth, and then fifth, all within a span of about ten seconds. Nobody ever told J. A. to use only three gears in town. He just loved to shift.

* * *

"Where in the hell are they?" Patrick Flanagan asked Perry Jackson as they stared out the window at the fog hanging over the airport.

"I don't know, but I hope they get here before the fog blankets the area and we can't get out. That'd be some kind of awful."

Patrick looked anxiously over at the two helicopter pilots to see if they looked nervous about the fog. The grizzled veterans of the skies couldn't have cared less, judging from the way they were laughing and carrying on. The lead pilot, wearing his sunglasses and Vietnam jacket with a lightning-bolt patch on the back, was chain-smoking Chesterfields. The other, who would be flying him and Coach Jackson, was decked out in a flying suit with a long, purple and white scarf hanging around his neck.

"Will we be able to get off the ground?" Patrick asked the one named Tiger.

"No sweat," Tiger said. He winked at the other pilot, Smiling Jack, and lit another cigarette.

"Does that mean we'll go?"

"It means everything is go. Just like 'Nam. We flew no matter what the weather was. And we intend to see this job completed."

His sentence was punctuated by the squealing of tires as J. A. slid the Porsche around the corner and came to a screeching halt beside the airstrip.

"Let's go, Coach," yelled Flanagan. "We got to get out of here before that fog sets in."

Buck and J. A. leaped from the car and sprinted toward one of the helicopters. Buck wondered why his pilot was wearing a big knife in one of his flying boots, but he didn't have time to ask. "Get in," the pilot said to Buck and J. A. "My name's Tiger Dawson." Without another word, they boarded the chopper and strapped in. The slapping of the helicopter blades was so loud that they couldn't have asked about the fog if they had wanted to. The helicopter suddenly lifted straight up, broke through the fog bank, and was on the way to Roanoke.

"Tiger," Buck shouted, "Eaarnel's house is on the east side of town, and it's located right next to a big vacant lot. That's where we want to land. They don't know we're coming in the copters, but they will when you turn on the Rattler fight song over the loudspeakers."

Tiger never turned his head. "No sweat, everything is go. The loudspeakers and the tape are set. All I gotta do is hit the switch."

"Roanoke is so small, you won't have any problem finding Eaarnel's house," Buck said. "There ought to be a lot of cars parked in front, because every newspaper, television, and radio station in the state will be there for the signing."

Buck leaned back and tried to relax. It would be a short trip to Roanoke by helicopter, but it would be a long one back if he didn't sign Eaarnel.

* * *

As the copters approached Roanoke, Buck nodded to Tiger, who threw a switch. Suddenly the town of Roanoke, at 8:45 A.M., was flooded by the sound of the Rattler fight song, blaring from loudspeakers hanging beneath the helicopter.

I'm a Rattler, a battler, yes I am;
I'm a damn Rattler, a battling Rattler man!

When they landed beside Eaarnel's house, forty to fifty neighborhood kids surrounded the helicopters. The blades wound down and the fight song ended, and Buck stepped out onto wobbly legs; he didn't know whether they were the result of the flight or what lay ahead. He thanked Tiger and Smiling Jack, and told them how long he thought the meeting would last. Then they started the walk across the lot to Eaarnel's house.

The front door opened, and Eaarnel and Mrs. Simpson stepped out on the porch to greet Buck and the others. "Coach Lee, you done scared me half to death with all that noise. Enough noise out there to wake the dead. I swear, I just don't know what you and all them other coaches are going to all this trouble for. Why, I ain't even seen this boy play football. I'm real proud of him, mind you, but it ain't because of all that running around he do on the football field. It's 'cause he's been a good boy. He's never given his mama a bit of trouble."

"We know that, Mrs. Simpson, and that's why we want him to come to Eastern." He looked at Eaarnel, hoping for a positive response, but the handsome face remained stoic. Buck steered the group into the house. There wasn't a lot of time before the other coaches arrived, but there was lots to do.

Mrs. Simpson had summoned support from Roanoke in the persons of the Reverend Griffin ("I want to thank you for enriching our offering that Sunday morning, Coach Lee. The new robes are quite lavish."); and Eaarnel's high school football coach, Cecil Upchurch, a hulking 6′ 8″ former pro defensive end who worried Buck by his brooding silence. And, of course, all of the Simpson children were on hand . . . and underfoot. Buck introduced Patrick Flanagan, who this day was posing as Dr. Ben Askew, Eaarnel's personal physician at Eastern. Nobody needed to introduce Perry, because he had been a permanent fixture in Roanoke. He'd followed Eaarnel to class, watched him practice basketball, and even eaten in the school cafeteria for six weeks trying to make Eaarnel like him more than the other ten assistant coaches who were doing the same things.

Eaarnel walked over to the window and looked out for a minute or two, while the others stood around looking for something to say. Buck knew what he was looking for: the coaches from UCLA, Michigan, USC, Ohio State, and West Alabama.

"Coach Lee," said Mrs. Simpson, "I wants to ask you something. What if my boy gets hurt and can't play? What'll y'all do? Will you let him go on and stay in school, or will y'all kick him out in the street?"

"Yeah, Coach Lee," chimed in Cecil Upchurch. "Now, what I think we need is for me to go with Eaarnel to the school of his choice just to make sure that he's taken care of. Me and Mrs. Simpson have talked it over, and we think that's the best solution. Ain't that right, Mrs. Simpson?" She nodded agreement.

Buck looked at J. A. They had expected this to happen at some point, and J. A. was prepared. "As athletic director at Eastern, I'd like to say that I can handle the request from Coach Upchurch about coming into our program. At the first sign of an opening, you can rest assured that we'll assign him a job as one becomes available. That's why we have the Fair Employment Act. We will put out the information that we're looking for a coach and if you, Coach Upchurch, will make application, we certainly will process your application through the federal government. Now, any questions?"

"Huh?" said Upchurch.

"Well, I'm sure J. A. answered that question," Buck said quickly. "I can assure you, Mrs. Simpson, that your son will always have a scholarship whether he's hurt or not." Eaarnel, bored with everything they were talking about, was immersed in *People* magazine.

Buck knew that the time left before the other coaches arrived would be better spent on emotional issues, rather than on rubbish like education, summer jobs, alumni, facilities, food, girls, dormitories, Merit scholars, weight room, professors, and who has the best turf to play on, so he moved into Phase Two of his plan.

"Eaarnel, Mrs. Simpson, Coach Upchurch — and certainly you, Reverend Griffin — I want ya'll to hear something." Buck reached into his briefcase and pulled out a tape recorder. He placed it on the coffee table, inserted a tape, and hit the *play* button.

"This is Newton Smith, the voice of the Rattlers. This has been an incredible football game between the Hawks and West Alabama and the fightin' Rattlers of East Alabama, led by their superstar Eaarnel

'The Cat Man' Simpson. The Rattlers trail the Hawks 24-28." Smith's well-known voice was gravelly and deep as he set the scene. "Seventy-five thousand fans are waiting to see what the Rattlers of Buck Lee will do. It's fourth-and-four, goal-to-go. The clock shows only twenty seconds. What will the Rattlers do?" The background noise was deafening as the simulated crowd roared. "The Rattlers break the huddle, line up in the I-formation with Simpson the deep man in the I. Simpson has already had the greatest day in the history of Rattler football." Newton Smith screamed to be heard over the crowd noise.

Eaarnel had thrown down the magazine and was cracking his knuckles. Mrs. Simpson looked to the ceiling for Divine help. Reverend Griffin was biting his fingernails and muttering, "Give it to Eaarnel."

"Eaarnel has had a greater day than even the legendary Prune Juice Butler," Smith screamed over the crowd noise.

Eaarnel said, "Give *me* the ball. I can do it."

"You can't hear yourself think," Newton Smith yelled in a voice getting hoarser by the minute. "The Rattler quarterback has asked for time out. The team can't hear the snap count. As Bledsoe steps away from the center, the Rattler crowd begins to chant. You hear them, folks. *Give 'em hell, give 'em Eaarnel! Give 'em hell, give 'em Eaarnel!*"

Now Eaarnel was standing up and holding a small pillow in his right arm, and feigning at imaginary tacklers with a left-handed stiff-arm.

"This is it, folks. The Rattlers are back at the line of scrimmage. Bledsoe puts Jones in motion from right to left. Out of the I-formation the ball is pitched to Eaarnel on a power sweep left. He's hit at the *five*." Smith stopped as the crowd noise swelled. "He spins free to the *three*. He's hit again, he goes to one hand, he spins out. He's running for the *corner*!"

Eaarnel smashed through the two chairs in the front room, stiff-armed Reverend Griffin, and leaped over the sofa as the tape continued to roll.

"There's only one man left between Eaarnel and the goal line, and that's Spike 'The Killer' Scott, the all-American safety for the

Hawks. Scott and Eaarnel collide at the one-yard line. Eaarnel is in the *end zone* holding the ball high above his head, and 'The Killer' is prone on the ground at the one. The Rattlers win! Unbelievable! The Rattlers win!" The band struck up the Rattlers' fight song. J. A. grabbed a jubilant Eaarnel, who was holding the pillow high above his head, and everybody was dancing.

Mrs. Simpson said, "I hope that Spike Scott ain't hurt. He's a nice boy — used to come over here all the time to play with Eaarnel."

"Wonder where all those other coaches are?" said Reverend Griffin, breaking Buck's spell.

Eaarnel put down the pillow and freed himself from a still-ebullient J. A. "Reverend, they were supposed to be here at nine. I don't know where they are. Why don't you call 'em up? And make it collect."

Buck knew time was short, so he figured he'd better get in all his gimmicks before the rest of the barracudas arrived. This was no time to ease off. "Before you call, Reverend, I want to show you a very important award we have for Eaarnel." Buck again reached into his briefcase and this time pulled out a beautiful, twelve-inch glazed ceramic trophy with a miniature football player on top that he had bought for $2.49. Buck massaged the trophy, looked at it with loving adoration, and then placed it on the coffee table in front of Eaarnel and his mother. "Eaarnel, you know how much Prune Juice wants you to sign with Eastern. He keeps asking me, 'When is Eaarnel going to be a Rattler?' I told P. J. that I thought you wanted to be a Rattler and wear his number 45, but that you were confused and just couldn't make up your mind. Isn't that right, Eaarnel?"

Eaarnel ducked his head and avoided Buck's eyes but still managed to look at the trophy on the coffee table. "I just don't know," he mumbled.

"Well, Eaarnel, P. J. said, 'I want to do something special for Eaarnel. What can I do?' he said to me."

The Reverend Griffin spoke up. "I love that P. J. Why, every Sunday, soon as church is over, I rush home and watch him play on television. He really loves his mama. Every time they interview him he says, 'Hi, Mom.'"

"Amen, Reverend," said Mrs. Simpson.

"So this is what P. J. decided to do, Eaarnel. He's established the

Prune Juice Scholarship Trophy. This is the first annual award, and P. J. has picked you as the winner. Cost him the price of a full scholarship, but he loves his university so much that he just had to do something for the school."

Mrs. Simpson reached down and touched the trophy as tears welled in her eyes. She reached over and gave Eaarnel a big bear hug and kissed him on the cheek. "I'm so proud of my baby boy, I just can't stand it."

Suddenly there was a loud knock at the door. Buck knew his time was up. One of Eaarnel's little sisters opened the door, and there, bigger than life, were Booster Skyflecter of Michigan, in his blue blazer with gold stripes; Dick Doonahay of UCLA, wearing a baby blue blazer with stripes on the sleeves; and Watson Hughes of Ohio State, in his conservative gray blazer with a big red buckeye on the pocket.

Reverend Griffin greeted them. "I thought you fellas were supposed to be here at nine o'clock. It's almost ten."

They all tried to speak at once. "We got telegrams to be here at ten," said Booster.

"Eaarnel hasn't signed yet, has he?" said Doonahay.

Watson Hughes of Ohio State snarled. "He better *not* have signed after a trip as long as this one. It's forever from here to Columbus. I thought I'd never. . . ." He quickly put his hand over his mouth when he realized he'd made a terrible faux pas. Mentioning how far away anything is to a mother is a cardinal sin. You're supposed to talk about how *close* your school is, not how far away.

Everyone's attention suddenly was diverted by the noise in the front yard. Jack Macabe, head coach at Southern Cal, had just ridden up on a huge white horse. He was wearing a helmet with a red plume and was waving a Roman sword. The horse neighed, and forty little kids and twenty reporters scattered. Jack finally calmed his steed and tied him to a hydrant. Then he marched through the front door and announced, "I'm Coach Jack Macabe of the University of Southern California football team, and I've come to sign Eaarnel Simpson." Macabe reached into his coat pocket, pulled out a net drawstring bag, and emptied ten of the biggest and gaudiest rings Buck had ever seen onto the coffee table. Trying to fake a Southern accent, Macabe said,

"Y'all don't have anybody else here with that many Rose Bowl rings, do you?"

Dick Doonahay reached into his coat pocket, pulled out a newspaper clipping, and spread it over the rings. "Let me read this to you, Eaarnel: 'Eight former UCLA players are now starring in the movies or television.' You know what that's worth?"

Booster Skyflecter pushed Doonahay aside. "At Michigan, Eaarnel, we don't believe in that Tinseltown stuff. Ask Doonahay here how many times we've knocked them on their ass in the Rose Bowl." He looked quickly to his left and said, "Excuse me, Reverend."

The bragging was interrupted by the sound of sirens approaching the house. Eaarnel, his little brothers and sisters, and all of the coaches ran over to the window to see what the ruckus was. A big black limo with two West Alabama school flags flying from the hood was being escorted down the street by two motorcycle policemen. The limo stopped in front of the house, and the chauffeur jumped out and opened the door. Shavers exited first, resplendent in his black blazer and gold tie with a big Hawk on it. His gold trousers matched his tie. Judson P. Higgenbotham was right behind Shavers. Wearing his white plantation suit with a straw hat, he looked like the ice cream man. But what everybody noticed about Higgenbotham was *not* how he was dressed, but that the briefcase he carried was secured to his left wrist by handcuffs. The two walked into the house followed by the uniformed officers. Without acknowledging the other coaches in the room, Shavers walked over to Eaarnel, put his arm around his shoulders, and said, "Hope we're not too late, but we had to make sure that we could get these two officers to come with us. Mr. Judson P. Higgenbotham has something valuable in his briefcase that he wants to protect."

Reverend Griffin stepped forward and assumed control of the meeting as if he were preaching at the church and telling everyone he needed more money. "Now, listen to me. We're glad you all could come to this auspicious occasion. Eaarnel here is gonna make a decision as to where he's gonna go to school. Now, right at this moment, he doesn't know where he's going, so what we're gonna do is go into the bedroom and pray over it. We're gonna ask for the

Lord's guidance." He paused and looked around the room. Nobody moved. "Now, Coach Upchurch and Mrs. Simpson, y'all come on in with us."

They went into the bedroom and closed the door. The six head coaches; Perry, Patrick, and J. A.; Eaarnel's twelve brothers and sisters; two policemen; and Judson P. Higgenbotham were left to fight for seats in a room that had only one sofa and two plastic-covered chairs. There was a mad scramble for the sofa. The six head coaches crammed into a space that was intended to hold four normal-size butts, not six middle-age spreads.

It was waiting time.

* * *

The Reverend Griffin clutched his well-worn King James Bible, stepped up on Eaarnel's saggy single bed, and rolled his tired eyes skyward. "Lord," he began in a volume that nearly rattled the window panes, "we come to you today, on a day that I know you probably don't want to be bothered, but we needs your help. We needs your powerful hand in the guidance of one of your greatest creations — the young Eaarnel Simpson. He needs you, and his lovin' mama needs you on this most important day."

Eaarnel's mother dropped to her knees while tugging at the hem of her best Sunday dress and said, "A-men to that, Brother Griffin. Help my little Eaarnel see the way."

Coach Upchurch pushed up the gathered elastic sleeves of his bright red windbreaker and fanned himself with a *Reader's Digest* he'd picked up in the living room. It was already heating up in the cluttered bedroom. Both windows were open, but the curtains hung limply.

Eaarnel placed the P. J. Scholarship Trophy Buck had given him on his dresser and knelt down beside his mother. He stared blankly at the new linoleum floor and watched the sweat fall from his chin and gradually run together in one big salty puddle. He thought about all those men in the front room who had been so nice to him over the past year and how he genuinely liked a couple of them. He closed his eyes and tried to open his mind to any sort of Divine message which might help him choose, but he was consumed by anguish. He felt like crying. He just wanted it to be over with. For two years he had looked forward to this day, but for most of that time he had dreaded it as well. No matter which school he finally chose, there would be people who would say that he made the wrong decision. He also knew that no matter where he decided to play football, five of the six men standing in the front room would be upset and would never speak to him again . . . except on Saturdays, from across the field, when they yelled for some linebacker to rip his head off.

The Reverend Griffin reached over to the dresser and picked up an eight-by-ten framed photo of Eaarnel streaking down some unidentified sideline. He held it up at arm's length, almost touching the ceiling, and continued his oration. "This gifted boy has got to make a decision today, Lord. He's got to decide where he want to play football for the glory of God. So far, neither he or his lovin' mama seems to know what to do. So, we are going to pray, Lord. We are going to pray and wait for a sign! Please give us a sign!"

Everybody bowed their heads, closed their eyes, and waited for some type of message. One minute passed. Two minutes passed. The Reverend Griffin opened one eye to check the room. Nothing. Eaarnel's puddle of sweat was now the size of a small pond, and his mother's knees were beginning to ache.

"I'm not getting anything, Reverend Griffin," Mrs. Simpson finally said.

"I'm not either," chimed in Eaarnel.

"How 'bout you, Coach?" asked The Reverend.

"Nothing," he said, stripping off his sweat-soaked windbreaker.

The Reverend let out a long sigh and stepped down from Eaarnel's bed. He began to pace the floor in the small area between the bed and the door. All eyes followed him back and forth, back and forth. Coach Upchurch took a deep breath and leaned against the dresser. As he did, the dresser tilted backwards and upset the trophy Buck had presented to Eaarnel. It toppled to the floor and smashed. The disembodied head went sliding and spinning across the floor.

"That's it! That's the sign!" shouted Coach Upchurch.

Eaarnel picked up the tiny ceramic head and said, "Yeah, but what does it mean? Who does it mean I should play ball for?"

Coach Upchurch rubbed his chin and stared at the floor. "Good question."

Eaarnel picked up the trophy base and placed it on the shelf beside all the other memories. This is never going to end, he thought. I'll spend the rest of my life in this room trying to decide where to play football. The important thing, he knew, was to play and to go to school. It really didn't matter where. Every day for the past six months, somebody had asked him where he was going to school. His friends, his coach, reporters, and even strangers in the street would stop him and say, "Well, Eaarnel, have you made up your mind yet where you're going to school?" And when he'd say that he hadn't, they'd look puzzled and say, "Aw, come on, Eaarnel, you can tell *me*." The past year was an endless series of phone calls, friendly visits, promises, boasts, pretty girls, and smiling white men who shook his hand and told him he was wonderful. He couldn't remember all the people he'd met and all the things they'd told him. He couldn't remember which campus was Ohio State and which was USC. But he couldn't put off the decision any longer. Only by making it would there be any peace.

Eaarnel walked over to Cecil Upchurch and said, "Coach, can I borrow your cap for a second?"

Upchurch handed over his red baseball cap and waited for an explanation. "Coach, Reverend, Mama," Eaarnel said to his bewildered audience, "I think the best thing to do is draw names. Tear up six pieces of paper and I'll write the school names on 'em and put 'em in this cap."

"Good idea, Eaarnel," said the Reverend Griffin. "That way the Lord can guide your hand to make the right choice." He tore his Bible bookmark into six pieces and handed them to Eaarnel, who spread the slips of paper out on the bed. With pen in hand, he looked up at Upchurch and said, "Now, what schools are out there, Coach?" Eaarnel scribbled down the names of all six schools as Upchurch called them out — Michigan, Ohio State, USC, UCLA, West Alabama, and East Alabama — and tossed them into the cap. The Reverend Griffin mixed them up to his satisfaction and said a silent prayer.

"OK," Upchurch said as he took the cap. "The first one you pull out will be fifth runner-up. The second one will be fourth, and so on. Now, the one name left in the cap will be the winner. Agreed?"

Eaarnel nodded and wiped his palms on his jeans. "How 'bout it, Mama, is this all right with you?"

"Mercy, yes," she answered. "Let's get this thing over with." Eaarnel kissed her on the cheek and plunged his hand into the cap of names.

When all the names had been drawn and the results recorded on another piece of paper, Upchurch said, "OK, Eaarnel, let's go tell 'em the news."

Eaarnel picked up a football that had been autographed by his entire team and began tossing it in the air. "Why don't you announce the winner, Coach?" he said as he tucked the ball under his right arm. "I'm tired."

* * *

"Well, Eaarnel, what's your decision?" Shavers asked in his most confident tone of voice as the foursome re-entered the living room. Buck's stomach crawled into his solar plexus, and the back of his neck began to tingle. He tried to make eye contact with Eaarnel and then with his mama, but they avoided looking at anyone. Buck could feel his jock itch flaring up. It felt like thousands of angry, little crabs with garden rakes. But the need to scratch was nothing compared to his need to know Eaarnel's answer. He could have stood there motionless for two days if he had had to.

Upchurch stepped forward and cleared his throat. "Gentlemen, after much deliberation and soul searching, Eaarnel has reached a decision." The room was dead silent. Upchurch held his paper up to the light and nervously cleared his throat again. "The fifth runner-up is . . . *Michigan*." Booster Skyflecter smiled lamely and hurried out the front door, where he was met by a dozen reporters. He shoved his way through them, got into his car, and ripped out the headliner in an uncontrollable, slobbering rage. Eaarnel, meanwhile, leaned against the wall and continued to spin the ball up in the air, then catch it and tuck it expertly under his right arm.

"The fourth runner-up is . . ." Upchurch paused for a beat. "*Ohio*

State." Watson Hughes's face turned burnt orange, but he maintained his poise and sense of good sportmanship. He shook hands with Eaarnel, walked outside, and politely made his way through the horde of cameras and buzzing reporters. He waved to the news media, climbed into his car, and punched the driver in the ear.

Upchurch was beginning to feel like Bert Parks, but he resisted a momentary urge to break into song and continued with his announcements. "The third runner-up is . . ." He paused longer this time, because deep down he wanted Eaarnel to go to this school, one noted for breeding tailbacks. He hesitated because he knew that if Eaarnel didn't play there, he certainly never would get to coach there. "*USC*," he finally said. Jack Macabe scooped his handful of rings off the table, tipped his hat to the other coaches, and said, "Good luck, Eaarnel. I hope you do well, son. I really do." Then he turned to Mrs. Simpson and said, "Could I use your phone to call a taxi? I'm not riding that goddamn horse another foot." Mrs. Simpson pointed to the phone in the hallway.

Buck's heartbeat shifted into high gear as Upchurch read the next loser. "The second runner-up is . . ." Upchurch again paused melodramatically. "*UCLA*."

Dick Donnahay spun on his heel and stiff-armed the screen door so hard that the top hinge snapped in two. The door hung pathetically from the bottom hinge as Donnahay stopped to talk to the press. "You wouldn't believe it!" he told the reporters, who were pushing and shoving each other for position. "It's like the Academy Awards in there. The winner is going to cry and thank the Academy and all the little people who made it possible."

Buck began to realize for the first time that his whole season, and ultimately his career, could ride on the next words out of Upchurch's mouth. Shavers looked Buck in the eye for the first time all day. A scowl covered his face. Eaarnel just spun the football in the air yet another time, apparently bored with the drama. All eyes turned to Upchurch. His next words would announce who came in second and who would have Eaarnel Simpson on the cover of their football program.

"The first runner-up is . . ."Upchurch gave the obligatory pause. Mrs. Simpson got up from her chair and said, "Excuse me. I'm gonna go in the kitchen and make a little iced tea." Shavers leaned forward at a forty-five-degree angle. Buck sat back but crossed his fingers on both hands. He knew that if Eaarnel went to East Alabama, it would almost guarantee his income for the next four years and knock Shavers right on his money-stuffed ass.

Upchurch cleared his throat for the last time and said, "I repeat. The first runner-up is . . . *West Alabama*!"

Shavers leaped three feet into the air and yelled, "AAALLL-RIIIGHT!" He spun around and beamed at Buck.

"Ah, Coach Shavers," Buck began, as if explaining something to a three-year-old. "Coach Upchurch said first *runner-up*. Get it? You came in second. You lost. *I won.*"

Shavers' look of joy turned to confusion and then to rage. "OK, smart-ass," he yelled at Buck. "I don't know what you did to get him, but I know it wasn't legal. From now on, you'd better watch your ass." Shavers wheeled 180 degrees and poked his finger into Eaarnel's rock-hard chest. "And you, big stud. You better strap it up tight, 'cause we're comin' after you. We're gonna eat your lunch!" He turned once more and said, "Come on, J. P. Let's get the hell outta here!"

Higgenbotham walked from the corner, where Perry, Patrick, and J. A. were hugging and slapping each other on the back, and stopped in front of Eaarnel. "You should've taken the money when you had the chance, boy." Then he and Shavers stormed out of the house.

Shavers greeted the wave of reporters with a diplomatic, "Go to hell, you little pissants!" He and Higgenbotham climbed into the limo and sped off into the noonday heat. The sirens were silent.

Buck's whole body felt like it was filling up with cool, refreshing spring water. An enormous, satisfied grin crossed his face, and his jock itch cleared up as if Oral Roberts had just laid hands on it. Eaarnel, however, appeared a bit shaken by Shavers' threat, and a tinge of regret glimmered in his brown eyes. Buck walked over to him, put his arm on his shoulder, and said, "That's OK, Eaarnel. He didn't love you anyway."

"*A-men*," said the Reverend Griffin.

"Who wants iced tea?" said Mrs. Simpson, returning to the room.

Eaarnel quickly signed the letter of intent, and Buck strutted out before the reporters who were waiting impatiently for a kind word from the winner.

43

EAARNEL SIMPSON WAS EVERYTHING that Buck had hoped for . . . and worth every dollar that appreciative alumni had slipped to him and his mama. In the first eight games of the Rattlers' season, Eaarnel scored twenty-three touchdowns, rushed for more than two hundred yards on six different Saturdays, and averaged 7.8 yards per carry. His performance had led Eastern Alabama to an unbeaten and untied record and had virtually assured Eaarnel of all-American status in his freshman season. Unfortunately, his season had ended early. He had broken his ankle in the ninth game — a narrow victory over LSU — and was out for the rest of the season. On the Sunday morning following Eaarnel's injury, Buck had received a funeral wreath with a note that read,

Eaarnel left, Eaarnel right,
That's all you call from morn till night.
But now that your boy is wearing plaster,
We'll see if Old Buck is really a master.
If I had to bet, I'd wager the roll,
That Old Buck Lee is just an asshole.

The note was unsigned, but Buck knew it came from Shavers. Who else would put black and gold ribbon on a funeral wreath?

The final game of the season, of course, would be against West Alabama — also unbeaten, untied, and winner of the last ten games against Eastern. Not since Prune Juice Butler had run ninety-six yards for a last-minute touchdown more than a decade earlier had the Rattlers defeated the Hawks. Buck, who was a young assistant at Western at the time, remembered it well. Shavers had refused to let any of the assistant coaches on the team bus after the game. He had told them to get home the best way they could, that they didn't deserve to ride. And on the training table the next morning, there was nothing except prunes and prune juice. Shavers was not a good loser.

But that was ancient history now, and Buck knew that without Eaarnel, his chances of sending Shavers home a loser again were slim and none. The slim chance the Rattlers had was to be better prepared for the game than the Hawks. That meant hard work, long hours, and cheating if at all possible. Buck needed to know exactly what the Hawks were planning, and he needed to confuse Shavers about what Eastern was planning.

The Raven had helped a lot. For two nights in a row, Buck had left bogus notes on his desk about trick plays, bizarre defenses, and different alignments. From the position of the papers the next morning, he knew that The Raven had been scratching around.

To find out what the Hawks were working on, Buck would have to bring in his mole — Kirk Battle.

"Can you do it, Kirk? Can you finagle your way into the Hawks' practice?"

"Coach, you know I can," Kirk answered confidently. "I'll bring back their game plan right off Shavers' desk if I have too."

* * *

Kirk strolled up to the potbellied guard at the gate. "How are you, sir?" he said, dusting imaginary lint off his suit. The grizzled old guard, who had been doing this for twenty years, knew everyone who was allowed in, but he didn't recognize this clean-cut young man.

"What can I do for you, young feller?" he asked, blocking the gate to the practice field.

"Sir, I'm Curt Whipple with the NCAA. Investigative Section. Here's my identification." Kirk handed the guard a phony ID card that he'd made up the night before. "We're all former FBI agents who're hired by the NCAA to investigate the recruiting practices of various colleges. What we do is go by the various practices unannounced to see if they're conducting any illegal tryouts. I'm here today as part of my swing through this section of the country. I was over at the Rattler camp a couple of days ago, and I've got to tell you, they're in big trouble."

The guard's eyes lit up like sparklers. "No kidding? You found 'em cheating, did you, uh, Mr., Mr. . . .?"

"Whipple. And what's your name, sir?"

"They call me Oleo, but my real name is Olaf Swenson."

"Well, Oleo, I'm not saying what we've got on the Rattlers, because that's confidential, but you can rest assured that Coach Shavers, who we know is an honest man, would love to hear about it. But I've still got to do my job and file a report on your activities, too, even though I'm sure I won't find anything wrong."

"Well, this is unusual, Mr. Whipple, but if it's a *covert* operation . . . I like that word *covert*. Sounds official. I've always wanted to be a spy myself." He cleared his throat and adjusted his mirrored, state patrol glasses. "Well, go ahead, but let me know when you come out if there's anything I ought to know."

"You bet I will, Oleo. I'll be in there for about an hour, and when I come out I'll tell you what I know." Kirk walked through the gate and into the stadium where the Hawks were practicing. Trying to look official, he immediately took out his notebook and started making notes about people he saw on the field. Kirk wrote that there were "no visible signs of prospects on field, but have to stay all through the practice to check . . . Coaches seem to be interested in job . . . Attitude of players and coaches terrific." About that time, as he expected, he felt a tap on his shoulder.

"Excuse me, sir, but what are you writing?" asked a grim little football manager, obviously sent over by Shavers.

"Son, I'm a special investigator for the NCAA," Kyle said. "My job is to see how you're running your practices and if you have any illegal prospects here. My job is to count 'em, too. Now, if your head coach would like to see my identification and what I've been writing, here they are."

The manager grabbed the papers Kirk handed him, along with the ID card, and raced over to the observation tower. Kirk was amazed as he watched Shavers' tower fold down like an accordian from a height of at least one hundred feet to about eye level.

"Let me see those papers, manager," Shavers said as he snatched them from his hand. He read all the great notes about his organization, how terrific everything looked, and he loved it. "What does that fellow do, manager?" he asked.

"He says he's a NCAA special investigator, Coach Shavers."

"Well, shit, boy, get him over here quick."

Kirk watched as the manager sprinted back across the field. "Sir, Coach Shavers said for you to come on over to his tower," he said breathlessly.

Kirk strutted over to Shavers, who greeted him with a smile and a handshake.

"I'm Coach Buddy Shavers. Welcome to Hawk Country."

"I'm Curt Whipple of the NCAA. I'm on a special investigatory assignment to check all the teams the week of their big game. I just got back from the Rattlers' practice."

Shavers' eyes lit up. "Well, Mr. Whipple, how'd the Rattlers' practice compare with ours?"

Kirk stuck a piece of gum in his mouth. "Oh, you're both doing a lot of the same stuff. There's one place, though, where you're completely different."

"Like what? Doesn't everybody do about the same thing at practice?"

"Well, not quite. I've noticed that you're practicing blocking punts," Kirk said. "All they're practicing is passing from punt formation."

"Oh, well, that's not so unusual," Shavers tried to say calmly. "We all practice that sometimes."

"Frankly, I'm glad to hear that, Coach. I certainly wouldn't want to divulge any secrets. Now, if you don't mind, I'm going to finish up with my report so I can catch the evening flight back to Kansas City. Nice to see you, Coach Shavers."

Kirk walked back to the sidelines and took notes for another fifteen minutes or so, occasionally smiling at Shavers, before he left the field. As he stood outside the gate chatting with Oleo, he heard Shavers yell, "Stop working on that punt block and watch out for the fake pass! You're gonna see it Saturday!"

* * *

"Hello, Coach? This is The Raven."

"Go ahead, Raven, what you got for me?" Shavers grabbed a pencil and notepad.

"I watched the team practice, and they're working hard."

"What kind of crap is that, Raven?" Shavers' pencil point broke as his hand tensed. "I know they're working hard, but what kind of plays are they running?"

"They're running the usual, some running plays and some passing plays."

"No shit, Dick Tracy. Working on running and passing, are they? What the hell do I send you all that money for — to tell me they're working out?"

"Well, there is one other thing, but I don't know if it's important or not. Says here they're going to run the wishbone in the second half."

"What!" Shavers screamed.

"I said, they're going to run. . . ."

"I heard you the first time, dumb-ass!"

"Thanks, coach. One more thing: Should I bet this week?"

"I'll tell you how *I'm* betting, Raven," Shavers growled, writing the figure 10,000 on his pad. "I'm betting ten big ones we'll kick their ass so hard they'll be tasting Kiwi for a week. We're gonna stick it to them. No prisoners!"

"Got it, Coach. I think I'll bet $10, too. This is The Raven, signing off."

44

SHAVERS CAREFULLY PUT ON his coat and straightened his black and gold tie. He inspected himself in the mirror to see if he were ready to go out on the field in front of sixty thousand people for this war with Eastern. He spotted a stray strand of silver hair and reached automatically for the can of spray, giving himself a couple of more shots to make sure it stayed in place. Then he dug into his tote bag and brought out the headset which he wore on the sideline during games. He carefully placed it on his head and looked at himself again in the mirror. Perfect. The headset covered up his bad ear and also made him look like he knew what he was doing. It made no difference that it was never plugged in. It just looked good, and that's what counted with the $1,000 contributors.

He checked his dressing stall one more time to be sure he still had two clean shirts — one for halftime after his shower and another for the post-game interview . . . after another shower, of course. Everything was in order.

* * *

The steamy ambience of the Rattlers' locker room came from the sweat of the pre-game workout. The pungent smell came from the analgesic balm used for rubbing down tight and sore muscles. The solemn atmosphere came from the pressure of a big game. Only a few precious moments of private thought remained before sixty thousand people enveloped them in a crescendo of sound. Final bits of tape were wrapped around knees, ankles, and wrists. Mouthpieces were hooked onto face masks. Chin straps were tightened. Thigh pads and knee pads were adjusted. Everything had to be right. The assault was about to begin.

Buck Lee stood on a bench and held up his hands for silence. "All right, men. Eaarnel isn't with us and there's nothing we can do about it. So the job today belongs to Norm Winkles." Winkles, leaning against the wall in the back of the room, looked like he would vomit. He had carried the ball only eighteen times all year, but now an undefeated season was resting largely on his shoulders.

The Rattlers, upon being reminded of Eaarnel's absence, acted as though they were paying respects to the dead — wall-to-wall drooping jaws. Buck knew he needed to loosen things up. "Norm's been with us for five years, and he's about the best sophomore we've got." Nothing doing. Not a single laugh.

"For five years he's run wind sprints and lifted weights and taken his licks. You know what that's called, don't you? It's called *guts*. And Norm's got an overdose. For five years he's put up with that shit, and for all of it he's played exactly thirty-one minutes of football. Everybody wants to run out on the field on Saturday and be a part of it — the crowd cheering, the band playing, the interviews and the write-ups after the game — but nobody wants to practice. Well, by God, I want y'all to understand something. Nobody in this room deserves to play in this game today more than Norm Winkles. Not even Eaarnel over there." Eaarnel, hanging his head as though he'd done something wrong, balanced himself on crutches in the rear of the room where he stood next to Winkles.

Buck jumped off the bench and raced over to Winkles. He grabbed him by his shoulder pads and looked him in the eyes.

"You're a winner, Norm."

"I'm scared to death, Coach."

"Of course you are, son. So'm I."

"I mean *real* scared."

"Good. Anybody who ain't scared don't understand the situation."

Buck let go of Winkles and mounted the bench again. "OK, men, football's not a one-man game, but I want Norm to lead us onto the field. If he plays like he's been practicing for five years, we're gonna blow the goddamn Hawks all the way back to Evergreen. No need to go over the game plan anymore. We've just gotta get mean."

That was the signal for Harry Ignarski to go crazy. He sounded like a bull as he charged across the room waving the sacred Rattler banner, the one traditionally presented to the game captain so he could lead the team onto the field. Ignarski stopped in front of Norm, held the banner aloft and screamed, "RAAATTTLLEERRRSS!"

"PRIDE!" answered the team in unison.

"Butt me!" Ignarski yelled to Norm, who by now was ready to lay down his life for the Rattlers. Norm lowered his head and charged before Ignarski could brace himself. The block knocked him flat on his ass. The players roared and beat their heads against the wall, and Ignarski jumped up and assumed a hitting position. He was livid that a second-string running back could knock a big, tough, defensive line coach on his rear. He looked at Norm and challenged him: "Don't ever turn your back on me." Winkles did an about-face and stood there, not saying a word. Buck loved it, and so did the team. Bedlam broke out as they prepared to leave the locker room.

"Hold it, hold it," yelled Hyspick. Buck knew what was coming when he saw who was with Hyspick. "Coach Lee, Coach Rockwell wants to lead the team in prayer."

"Go ahead, Coach Rockwell," Buck said. He stared at the old man with knobby legs in short pants and a whistle around his neck.

Rockwell began to speak in a shaky voice. "Men, when I coached, we always beat the Hawks. It wasn't necessarily my coaching, because we did have some good boys. But it was due to the teamwork between my team and the Lord. He always took care of my team, because I led them in prayer right before every game. He knew I was praying from the heart. So I'm going to ask the Lord to let you win today."

"Bow your heads, assholes, and don't forget to close your eyes," growled Hyspick.

"Oh, Dearest Father in Heaven, help these boys as you used to help me. Remember the time we were behind against SMU and you let my linebacker run eighty-two yards with a fumble to win the game? How about when we were going to lose to TCU? You had their back fumble at my one-yard line. Remember, Lord, how you made me Coach of the Year in 1947 against all odds?"

As Rockwell rambled, Buck looked at his watch and saw that it was only five minutes until kickoff. He punched Kyle in the side and whispered. "You gotta do something to get this pompous asshole off his soapbox. It was Bruiser Barnwell who made him Coach of the Year in '47, not the Lord."

Before Kyle could react, an official stuck his head inside and said, "Five minutes until kickoff, Coach Lee. We need your captain."

"All right, let's go, Norm," Buck yelled. Rockwell continued to pray.

"Let's get the bastards," screamed a voice from the back of the room. The frenzied Rattlers swarmed all around Coach Rockwell, who was giving thanks for the tenth special game the Lord had helped him win.

* * *

The Rattler band was in the middle of the field playing the fight song as the team charged into the stadium to do battle with the hated Hawks. Running across the field with his coat and tie on, Buck felt great but thought he looked a little silly — the coat and tie projected a successful image for the alumni, but how could you explain the football shoes, white socks, and britches rolled up above the ankles?

The Rattlers reached their side of the field and started to pound each other. Prospects, daddies, players, coaches, dentists, doctors — everybody went crazy on the sidelines. It was a way of relieving tension. Meanwhile, the band kept on playing the fight song over and over.

Buck started to get a little nervous when he saw the referee coming toward him with Buddy Shavers in tow.

"Coach Lee, I'm going to have to penalize your team fifteen yards for the Rattler band delaying the start of the game," said Bob Highpecker, the little referee who looked like a junior high principal.

"You gotta be kidding. I can't believe you'd let Shavers intimidate you like that."

"Sorry, but Coach Shavers pointed out that the home team has the responsibility for making sure that the game starts on time."

The Rattler band still hadn't missed a beat. They started the fight song one more time. Buck was nose-to-nose with Highpecker. "I'm not taking fifteen yards for the band. I'll take five. Maybe if they were the Southern Cal or Ohio State band, I'd even take twenty, but these pissants are worth only five."

"Nope," Highpecker said, "the rules say fifteen and that's what I have to do. As soon as they get off the field, I'll assess you fifteen yards on the kickoff." He and Shavers, like sidekicks, turned and walked away.

Buck turned to his squad, gathered around him for last minute instructions. "Men, we just lost fifteen yards for our band being on the field, so let's win this one for the band! Go get 'em for the tubas!"

* * *

High up in the press box, cordoned off to one side so they could be isolated from the rest of the sixty thousand fans at Rockwell Field, there was what the security cops referred to as "The Ass Box." This was where the Rattler coaches' wives sat during home games. Nowhere in the cavernous stadium was the tension greater or the palms sweatier or the invective spicier or the violence more flamboyant. These ladies meant business. They understood that if misfortune befell their husbands during the course of the afternoon, there was always the possibility that they soon would be saying bye-bye to their roomy homes and lawns and clubs and all the other "perks" in Stanleyville . . . left in the cold to start begging for a job at, say, North Dakota State.

They sat in The Ass Box brandishing their flasks, seated according to their husbands' rank — defensive coaches' wives on the right, offensive on the left, poor neutral Gail stuck in the middle as peacekeeper, wives of special-teams coaches and trainers and counselors cowering on the back row.

During the East Alabama-Florida game at midseason, ABC television cameras had memorialized them. It started when Harriet Ignarski, representing the defense, began jumping all over the Rattlers' offensive unit ("Bunch of peashooters!"). Delores Barton, representing the offense, took umbrage at this ("The fuckin' defense is playing like Jell-O!") and the riot was on. Delores reached across Gail and smeared the rattlesnake painted on Harriet's cheek. Harriet retaliated by throwing Delores' purple and white polka-dotted "game" wig to the crowd below. Then they were up, dousing each other with whiskey and pulling tits and punching bellies and tearing hair and screaming insults. It took five cops and a police dog to break it up.

After that nationally televised incident, Buck had assigned Larry Hildebrand to The Ass Box as a patrolman. Now, just before the kickoff against the Hawks, Hildebrand sat with much trepidation amid all of the Rattler wives. Jesus, he thought, these are the mothers of our children. Harriet, for this game, wore a hat featuring the fanged, open mouth of a purple rattlesnake. Delores was wearing a new wig — this one solid purple. The bronze-skinned Pamela Jackson, wife of the only black coach, was wearing a purple and white body suit in the pattern of leopard skin. And Janet Stone and Bobbie Sue Harris, who had caused Eastern to lose two top prospects when, in a friendly game of tennis doubles with their mothers, they called twenty-four faults in one set, wore their purple and white coordinated tennis togs.

As Larry Hildebrand squirmed in his seat, obviously uncomfortable with his role as peacekeeper in this den of feminine fury, Harriet Ignarski walked back and offered him a brownie, which she had made for today's game.

"Why, thank you, Harriet. That's a very nice thing to do." Maybe I have misjudged these women, he thought. Maybe they're just normal people trapped like me in a situation out of their control.

"You're welcome, Larry. I hope you enjoy it," Harriet said sweetly. Then, as she turned and headed back to her seat, she screamed, "All right, Rattlers, let's kill the motherfuckers!"

Coach Hildebrand gagged on his brownie.

* * *

The ball went tumbling end over end to Bubba Hancock, the deep man on the Rattlers' receiving team. He blew up the left sideline right toward the Rattler bench. Buck always called kickoff returns to his side of the field. He felt it took much more courage, or much less sense, for an official to throw a flag where there would be seventy-five outraged voices yelling at him than on the other side of the field where they would be cheering him. Hancock was finally driven out of bounds at the thirty-five yard line. There were no flags, despite a near-

clip back around the twenty.

Buck's offensive unit raced onto the field for the first play of the game. Quarterback Dave Bledsoe always liked to use a long count on the first snap to see if he could draw the other team offside. He got up under the center and started counting. "Hut-one, hut-*two*, hut-three, hut-*four*." He put more emphasis on the even numbers, hoping an overanxious lineman would jump. Finally, on the sixth "hut," Western's middle linebacker, Mad Dog Nelson, did just that. He flew across the line and hit Dave right in the mouth with an elbow. Buck saw Dave go down and blood spurt out of his mouth. Everybody on the offensive team gathered around and helped him up. The officials called an injury time-out, and Dave headed for the sidelines to let Doc Akers tend to his mouth.

"Dave, what happened out there?" Buck asked.

"Well, Coach, after he hit me, everybody on the team just stood there watching me bleed like a hog in November. They were all saying, 'Who did that to you? We'll kill 'em!' When I pointed to Mad Dog Nelson, they just looked at me and said, 'Fight your own damn battles.'" Buck stifled a laugh. "I'm ready now, Coach," said Bledsoe, racing back into the game. It was now on to the great battle of strategy and mass confusion.

As the game progressed, pandemonium engulfed the sideline. Coaches yelled obscenities at the officials, and players crashed into one another with all the strength their bodies could muster. Buck was so involved in the normal sideline-to-pressbox communications that he really didn't see as much as he needed to. Once, when Western buried Bledsoe under an avalanche of beef, Jack Stone handed Buck the headset. "Billy Tom wants to talk with you, Coach. He's got some information for you." Buck took the headset.

"Billy Tom, what you got?"

"Coach, we've gotta protect the passer!" he screamed.

"No shit, Billy Tom! They just maimed our quarterback and you tell me we've got to protect the passer. Maybe next time you can tell me *how*!"

The game continued with neither side doing much until late in the first quarter, when Western's big fullback, Sugar Bear Henson, ran right up the middle for forty yards and a touchdown. "Coach Lee,

Ignarski wants to talk with you." Stone handed him the headset again.

"Coach," Ignarski was yelling, "they're trapping us up the middle."

"Really, Harry? You don't say. More inside poop from the pressbox."

Buck called Bledsoe to the sideline. "All right, Dave, when we get the ball, I want you to give it to Winkles. He's tough and we need to make some first downs."

* * *

"Winkles, off right tackle, snap on two," Dave called in the huddle. Winkles heard the snap count, heard the clashing of twenty-two bodies, and heard voices yelling, "Butt him!" "Knock his cock off!" "Kill Him!" He slashed off tackle for four. As he went down under a stack of bodies, he felt teeth biting into his right leg. "Get off me, you fucking vampire!" he screamed.

Same play again. Four more yards. Dave called the play a third time, except he varied it by going left and snapping the ball on three. Norm started for the hole, but it closed quickly, so he spun outside for the three yards he needed for a first down. Just as he turned the corner, he was met by Mad Dog Nelson, who put his headgear right under Norm's chin, lifted him off his feet, and drove him into the ground. Norm's head snapped back and hit the ground with a thud. Mad Dog jumped up and beat his chest like Tarzan. As Norm struggled to his feet he said, "You look like Tarzan, but you hit like Jane." Mad Dog promised, in no uncertain terms, to continue the discussion as soon as possible.

Big Ernie Jackowitz, the Rattlers' right guard, looked at Dave and said, "Give the ball to Norm again. We'll make some yards if you run behind me." Norm followed Ernie through the hole, and again he was met by Mad Dog after a short gain.

"Second and six, guys," Dave said in the huddle. "I'm gonna give it to Norm once more."

Norm looked at Dave and then at the others. "Dave, I think they have a clue as to when I'm gonna carry the ball. I turn white as a sheet, while the other two backs are black and they're smiling. Norm don't want the ball no more." He staggered off the field, waving for a substitute. Practice was never like this.

* * *

Charlie Brown, senior manager for the Hawks, looked at his watch to see how much time remained before the second-half kickoff. Seven minutes. Time to go get Coach Shavers out of the shower. Brownie, as the players liked to call him, never understood why Coach Shavers took so many showers. The previous manager had told him that the coach had a Howard Hughes-type cleanliness fetish. Maybe that explained why Brownie always had to carry a cup of alcohol over for the coach to sterilize his whistle each time he blew it. Before Brownie could call to Shavers, the burly coach walked out of the shower wearing only his headset. The plug at the end of the long cord bounced against the floor as Shavers walked back into the team dressing room. He stepped up on the table in the middle of the room and began his halftime pep talk. The players were wide-eyed. They couldn't believe this fifty-five-year-old man was standing in front of them butt-naked — stretch marks, shriveled pecker, and all.

"Hawks, you all know how much I want to win this game," Shavers began, dripping onto the table. "We've beaten these pricks for the last ten years, and I want to make it eleven straight. So, before you go out there for the second half, there's just one thing I want to say: Claw 'em, de-ball 'em, eat their nuts! We're the Hawks, we'll kick their butts!" The team let out the perfunctory cheer, but they were still mesmerized by Shavers' exhibitionism.

"Hold it, team," Shavers continued. "You all know how I feel about saying a prayer at halftime. To me, it's the most important thing we do in this locker room. It's much more important than any diagrams we put up on the board. It's the meat-and-potatoes of our program." He strutted up and down the table, dragging the cord behind him. "Bartlett, why don't you lead us in a little prayer before we go back out on the field."

Assistant Coach Hawg Curley turned pale. He had forgotten to tell Skip Bartlett that he would be called on for the halftime prayer, and

Bartlett certainly wasn't smart enough to ad-lib. Most of the players, in fact, brought cheat-sheets into the lockerroom when they knew they had the assignment to pray. Hawg Curley spotted Bartlett across the room. Sweat was popping on his forehead, and his eyes appeared to be rolling back into his head. Suddenly a smile spread across his face, and he asked everyone to bow their heads.

"Now I lay me down to sleep. . . ."

* * *

Even though the Rattlers were behind 7-0, Buck felt good. His kids had played a solid first half and seemed to be holding their own against the Hawks, even without Eaarnel. As the assistant coaches yelled at their players and trainers patched up the wounded to get them back out for the second half, Buck went to his phone in the back of the locker room and called a prospect. This game was important, but signing a blue-chipper could make a difference in *forty* future games.

"Hello, Whizzer, this is Coach Buck Lee. I'm calling you from the locker room at halftime to see how you're doing."

"Great, Coach Lee, and it sure is nice of you to call. I'm sorry I couldn't get up for the game. How's it going?"

"We're behind 7-0 right now, but if we had you playing for us, we'd be winning this game." Buck sucked on a Coke.

"Coach, Mom says to say hello."

"Shit. I can't find my goddamned jersey," screamed a voice from the dressing room.

"That's nice, Whizzer, and how's your little sister, Totie?" Buck asked, checking his file card on the family.

"Totie's fine, Coach. She's standing beside me and wants to say hello, too."

"Hi, Coach Lee. This is Totie," said the six-year-old.

"How are you, Totie, and how is your little dog, Smoak?"

"Smoak's fine, Coach Lee. I'll see if he'll bark for you." Buck waited on the phone for the dog to bark. Finally, Totie came back on the phone and said, "Smoak won't talk."

"Let's go kill those assholes!" came another scream.

"Rattlers!"

"Pride!"

"Hawks!"

"Suck!"

Buck had to end this sales pitch soon. "Totie, tell your mother and daddy goodbye for me, and let me talk with Whizzer."

"Goodbye, Coach Lee. Here's Whizzer." Totie dropped the phone.

Finally, Whizzer came back. "Whizzer, I've got to go, but have a nice weekend. And remember, we *really* care about you here at Eastern."

"Thanks, Coach, and give me a call after the game to let us know how you did. I'll see you. Goodbye."

"Goodbye, Whizzer," Buck said. What a grown man won't do for a seventeen-year-old piece of ass, Buck thought as he returned to the battle.

* * *

The second half had produced some crazy bounces, and with four minutes to go, the Hawks had the ball and a 16-7 lead. Buck's Rattlers had played their hearts out, but they were about to lose to a stronger football team.

This was the moment Shavers had been waiting for. With the crowd on its feet, yelling for the WAS Hawks to put away the upstart Rattlers, it was time for him to go into his act. Danny Lanier, the Hawks' senior quarterback, was coming over to the sidelines to confer with the offensive coordinator, Wayne Casey. Shavers started walking toward Casey so he'd be standing beside him when the quarterback arrived. Danny reached the sideline, took off his headgear, and listened to Casey, who was calling the plays. While they were in deep conversation about the next series of downs, Shavers began to open and close his mouth as if he were talking to Danny and Casey. He even shook his head up and down like a puppy gnawing on a bone. As he went through the pantomime he'd done hundreds of times, he knew what the big contributors in the stands were thinking: Ol' Shavers is really giving Casey and Lanier hell. When the official signaled time was up and Lanier started back onto field, Shavers turned his back, walked down to the middle of the sidelines, faced the field, folded his arms across his chest, and assumed the position of a leader of men. He was now going to watch his gladiators go back into battle.

* * *

A big groan went up from the Eastern fans as Tommy Rogers limped off the field bent over at the waist. As usual, he had been kicking ass from his middle linebacker position, and the Rattlers certainly didn't need to lose him.

"Bludworth, get in there for Rogers," yelled Buck. Putting Buddy Bludworth in the game was a mistake, he knew, but he hadn't planned on having to make that decision quite so fast.

"What's the matter, Tommy?" asked Buck as he put his arm around the shoulder pad of the gutsy linebacker.

"Coach, I think I broke my dick," Tommy moaned.

"You *can't* break your dick," said a trainer standing next to Tommy.

"Don't tell *me* I can't break it," said Tommy, rubbing his crotch.

Buck turned his attention to the field just in time to see Bludworth get a fifteen-yard penalty for piling on.

"Son of a bitch!" said Buck. "That pisses me off."

"Hell, Coach, I didn't mean to break it," said Tommy.

"No, I mean the idiot who just cost us fifteen yards. Take him in the locker room and see if it's broken," Buck said to the trainer.

The crowd rose to give Tommy Rogers, number 55, a standing ovation as he left the field. At the same time, Bludworth, his shirttail flapping, hit late again. Fifteen more yards. "Get that madman out of there before we get penalized into the end zone and they get a safety," Buck screamed. Stone, who coached the linebackers, sent a calmer substitute into the game. Bludworth left the defensive huddle and sprinted across the field to where Buck was standing on the sideline.

"My fault, Coach. My fault, Coach," he blubbered with big tears rolling down his face.

"It wasn't your fault, Buddy. It was my fault for having you in there," Buck said.

"Gee, that's great, Coach. I thought you'd be mad at me."

Just then Tommy and the medical team came running out of the locker room. Tommy didn't hesitate; he ran straight back onto the field. The crowd went wild. They didn't know or care what had been wrong. They were just glad to see their warrior return to the arena.

"Was his dick broke, Doc?" asked Buck.

"Hell, no," said Doc. "I told him it got crushed a little, but it wasn't any worse than a rough hand-job. He's OK." Buck turned his attention back to the field where the sound of pad meeting pad, body meeting body, was like the sound of music. He loved it.

* * *

After a time-out, the Hawks lined up and ran an off-tackle play. As the tailback reached the line of scrimmage, there was a mad scramble and up jumped a purple jersey waving the football. "Our ball! Our ball!" screamed thousands of voices from the purple-colored side of the field.

The offensive unit went into the game. On the next play, Bledsoe rolled out and hit Jim Scott, the wingback, for a fifty-eight-yard touchdown pass. The extra point was good, making it 16-14. A field goal could win the game. Buck looked at the clock and saw about two minutes left. Then he looked across the field and saw Shavers kicking the kid who fumbled in the seat of the pants.

"Ettinger," Buck said to his kickoff man, "I want you to try an onside kick. Can you do it?" Buck knew that if it failed, the game was over.

"I can do it, Coach. I've practiced it for hours."

Buck sent him in, squatted down on the sideline, closed his eyes, and waited for the roar of the crowd to tell him whether it was successful. When the purple side roared, he knew the Rattlers had recovered the kick.

Without waiting for instructions, the offensive team sprinted back on the field. Bledsoe dropped back to pass. Incomplete. He went back to pass again and was thrown for a twelve-yard loss. Now it was third and twenty-two. Bledsoe called time out and came over to the sidelines where Buck was waiting to give him the play that hopefully would win the game.

"Dave, you remember the first quarter when we called 200-X-Post-H and you threw to Jack Eskew, the split receiver?"

"Yeah. They intercepted it."

"Well, Dave, I want you to throw the same pass. Except this time, I want you to hit Norm Winkles down the sideline. You understand?"

"Yes, sir," he replied, running back onto the field.

Buck knew it was an intelligent call, but he held his breath. You just never knew. The ball was snapped, Bledsoe went back to pass, Norm Winkles sprinted down the sideline, and Buck waited for Bledsoe to hit him. Instead, Bledsoe threw right down the middle of the field to Eskew for a touchdown. Kyle, who had been standing next to Buck when he called the play, leaned close to him and yelled above the noise that was rocking the stadium, "I won't tell if you won't, Coach."

Buck looked at Kyle and smiled. "It just goes to show that even a lousy coach can't mess up a good player."

Ettinger kicked off, and on the Hawks' first play, the Rattlers intercepted a desperation pass. Buck could taste the victory. 21-16. Only forty-five seconds left to play. All Bledsoe had to do was fall on the ball, and they would take the big game right away from Shavers. As the Rattlers' offensive team rushed into the game, Bledsoe stopped in front of Buck. "What do you want me to do, Coach, try a triple reverse?"

"Real funny, Dave," Buck said. "Just run the old fetus play. It's the best one in the book, unless the other coach is using it."

"Right, Coach, you got it," he said. Dave went back into the game, jumping up and down, running across the field to join his teammates. He broke the huddle and took them to the line. Buck could hear the count: "Hut-one, hut-two," and then the ball was snapped. Dave fell on it, and twenty-one bodies piled on top of him — ten to protect him and eleven to get the ball. When the officials unstacked the bodies, Dave was out cold. He didn't move a muscle. Somebody had gotten to him. A hush fell over the stadium as the doctor and trainer ran onto the field. They couldn't revive him immediately, and Buck knew he had to put in Sylvester Crow, the second-string quarterback, for the last play of the game. He spotted Sylvester hiding at the end of the bench.

"Coach Stone," Buck yelled as he tried to figure out what to do.

Sylvester hadn't played a down all year, and he wouldn't even have been on the team if his daddy hadn't given a million dollars to the school.

"Yeah, Coach," said Stone as he rushed up from the other end of the bench."

"Coach, you recruited that wimp, and you're responsible for him. I want you to talk to Sylvester and tell him how important it is that he not fumble and how much his teammates are depending on him. You got it?"

"I'll talk to him, Coach. I'll use some psychology I learned while I was coaching in high school."

Moments later, as Buck held his breath on the sideline, Sylvester broke the huddle, gave the count, took a perfect snap, and fell on the ball. Buck went crazy. "Great job, Jack! Damn, what'd you tell him?"

"Simple, Coach. I put my hands around his throat and said, 'Fumble that ball and I'll kill you.' It's elementary psychology."

As the crowd counted the seconds off the clock, Hyspick tapped Buck on the shoulder and said, "Coach, I'm going to tell the players to carry you off the field, so you get ready." Buck could see Hyspick out of the corner of his eye talking to the players on the bench. He could just imagine him saying, "Let's carry Coach Lee off the field. Give him a victory ride over to Shavers."

"Ten, Nine, Eight, Seven . . ." The players on the field were shaking hands as the crowd continued to count. "Six, Five, Four . . ." Buck bent down and got into his coach-carrying position — butt stuck out, knees bent, and arms out in front so they could grab him under the armpits and pick him up for the great ride. "Three, Two, One, *Boom*!" The game was over. They'd won. Players rushed from the sideline toward the field. Buck could feel bodies rushing past him, but he was left in the squatting position, like a man taking a dump in the woods. Nobody picked him up. Embarrassed, Buck stood up and started to walk out to midfield, but before he could take two steps, he felt big strong hands grabbing him and throwing him up on shoulders.

"You didn't think we'd let you be shorter than Coach Shavers, did you Coach, when y'all shake hands?" asked Bulldog Campbell, the giant defensive tackle.

Hog Helms, another mammoth lineman, was under the other side. "That was Coach Moore's idea, Coach Lee, to make you think we weren't going to carry you."

"Hog, I really couldn't care less, except that I *do* want to look down on Shavers when we shake hands," he said. They looked for Shavers across the field but couldn't find him. "Sportsmanship never has been one of his strong suits," Buck said. "You guys let me down and go find your families and girlfriends." As Buck left the field amid well-wishers, he spotted Shavers beside the locker room shaking his finger at the bus driver. A couple of assistant coaches were asking around for rides.

45

EVERYONE NODDED AND SMILED or spoke to Buck as he walked through the lobby of the Hilton Hotel. Being a nominee for Coach of the Year had made him a star at the annual coaches' convention, but winning the honor would make him more than that — it would make him rich: television and radio appearances, commercials, endorsements of sporting goods, probably a renegotiated contract, and honorariums when he spoke, which certainly would render the rubber-chicken circuit more palatable.

Buck was justifiably proud of his success, but as he looked around the lobby at the small groups of coaches, he remembered days gone by when his stock wasn't so high. One year he had made the "all-lobby team" at the coaches' convention by standing around for twenty-three hours straight, always *lobbying* for a better job. Now others apparently had taken his place. The lobby was full of young, middle-aged, and old coaches talking football or about the honey they *almost* picked up last night. They never talked about recruiting. That would be like talking about making love — everybody thought they did it better than the other fellow, but nobody wanted to tell how. So they usually just hung around until it got dark. Then they roamed the streets and bars trying to make out. The majority ended up shit-faced from the free booze supplied by the pro teams and sporting goods salesmen in their hospitality suites. They were the ones who wound up trying to demonstrate how to block a punt with their face at three in the morning in the hotel lobby.

Buck spotted lovable old Dawg Gumbel, former coach at Iowa State, on the other side of the room. He was holding court, standing in the middle of a horseshoe-shaped table that was used by tour directors. Dawg was telling anybody who would listen how he defensed the wishbone. He was the stereotype of a coach — big, loud, tough, sincere, likeable, and with forearms like a gorilla's. He was all of those things, and he was also unemployed. Dawg had had a couple of great teams earlier, but then bad times settled in. His players began to get into all kinds of trouble. Dawg tried everything: athletic dormitories, no dormitories, apartments, no apartments. You name it, he had tried it. But every year at least one of his players got picked up for rape. The bad press hurt, but what really did him in was opposing coaches who went around telling prospects that Dawg had "the best fucking team in America." Dawg's contract was not renewed.

That's the problem with this business, thought Buck. One day it's fourth and long, and then the next day it's fourth and gone.

As Buck turned to avoid Dawg's glance, he literally ran into Cecil Hopkins, head coach at Virginia State. "Hop, you old son of a gun, I thought you'd be in jail by now."

"Nope, Buck, they haven't caught up with me yet."

Cecil, the Errol Flynn of the coaching profession, had been caught sleeping with the chancellor's wife. It didn't take that very long to get around the country, the way coaches like to gossip, so Cecil was on the hot spot with all the "good people." Before long there were bumper stickers out that said, *Cecil's got it in for the chancellor*. In self-defense, Cecil did what any good, red-blooded coach or politician born in the South would do — he got religion. He joined the Fellowship of Christian Athletes, went to church every Sunday, and walked around on the campus holding his wife's hand. Soon all was forgiven and Cecil kept his job.

Buck grinned at Cecil, punched him gently on the shoulder, and said, "I don't know if I should be seen with you. No wine, women, or song. Isn't that the new Hopkins? You could be bad for my reputation."

"Hell, Buck, I finally figured it out," Cecil said. "They didn't care who I fucked as long as I also fucked Tennessee, Alabama, Nebraska, and everybody else on my schedule."

"I know what you mean, brother. I know what you mean."

* * *

Buck pushed the watery mashed potatoes around on his plate and tried to look calm. He'd been anticipating this moment for weeks.

"And the winner of the Coach of the Year award is . . ." The emcee hesitated, waiting for the suspense to build. "Buck Lee of the East Alabama Rattlers!"

Buck stood up to a wave of applause and slaps on the back. There was no greater compliment than to be honored by those he had competed against, and yet he felt strangely hollow as he walked toward the podium to make his acceptance speech. I guess it's like sex, he thought — the expectation is usually better than the prize.

"I'm very honored to be selected Coach of the Year, especially by such an august body," he began, "but this award really should be called Recruiter of the Year. As we all know, that's what separates the winners from the unemployed." A smattering of laughter came from the media tables, but no coaches even smiled. "That's why the people I have to thank for this award are my assistant coaches. I know what they went through this year, because I was an assistant coach for a long time before I had the chance to be a head coach," Buck said, smiling toward Shavers' table.

"Assistant coaches drive all night across the country to see some kid play a game and to meet his little brothers and sisters. They fly in all kinds of weather, endure storms and bad roads and hostile state troopers and egotistical daddies and protective mamas. Then, after spending months of their lives pandering to a seventeen-year-old, they discover that the little creep has already signed with somebody else while he's still telling them that he hasn't made up his mind yet. But, what they hell? I guess the bottom line is that we're nothing more than men playing like boys. Or boys playing like men. I'm not sure I know the difference. Anyway, I thank you very much for this honor, and I'll see you on the hustings."

The applause was weak at first as Buck left the podium with his trophy; the seriousness of his message was slowly settling in. But by the time he reached the floor, his colleagues were giving him a standing ovation. Through the crowd of well-wishers he saw Hyspick and Ignarski, tears running unabashedly down their cheeks, coming toward him. The two giants hoisted Buck up on their shoulders and paraded him around the room. Just men playing like boys.

Epilogue

IT HAD BEEN DRIZZLING sporadically since Buck and his new recruiting coordinator had left Albany, Georgia, late that morning. The drab chilly weather seemed to be a fitting end to a particularly unproductive week in the Albany area. In fact, the three months since Christmas had produced little more for Buck than a bad cold, two dog bites, and a handful of remarkably average recruits.

"OK, Richard," Buck said as the muddy Ford wheeled into the pine straw-covered driveway of the Lee residence in Stanleyville. "I'll see you back here in an hour and a half. I'm not sure what unpronounceable food Gail has planned for dinner, but I'm sure we'll have plenty of cold beer and pretzels. Dave will get here with his phenom at about the same time. So just hang out and observe. I just want you to see how we operate on the superstars."

"Right, Coach."

"And if Flanagan can make it, we might even have a little surprise. So just play it cool and don't say anything."

"Right, Coach. See you then." Richard Culpepper put the car in reverse and backed out of the driveway.

Buck shuffled up the door. He rang the doorbell while fishing for his keys, but there was no answer. He unlocked the door, entered, and wearily dropped his luggage onto the bench in the foyer.

"Gail, it's me. The tennis pro. Is your husband home?"

There was no answer. She probably had made a last-minute run to the grocery store. Buck walked back to his office to collect his messages. The only light on in the house was a fluorescent lamp on his desk. It was tilted toward his Coach of the Year trophy, which strangely was sitting in the middle of the desk. He sat down and spotted an envelope under the heavy marble base of the trophy. He withdrew the letter from the unsealed envelope and began reading. He was halfway through the first paragraph before he realized it was from Gail.

Dear Coach,

You will notice that you now have the entire closet in which to hang your Rattler slacks, Rattler sport shirts, and Rattler windbreakers. Your Rattler wife and son have decided to leave you.

I sat here at your desk for almost an hour before I started. I couldn't help but remember your first office at Stanford. Remember the one with bare, cinder-block walls and no windows? The only pictures on the wall were of you and me. There was an old black and white of you in a three-point stance and a very flattering, beautifully framed, eight-by-ten of me leaning on a redwood tree. I miss those trees, Buck, and I miss being the only other person on your wall. Look around you. The only pictures on the wall now are of you and me hugging some 6′ 5″ teen-aged gorilla.

Bucky and I have been alone in this house with these pictures and trophies for three months. The only conversations I've had are with people I don't like, and all they want to know is the scoop on this year's recruiting. It's insane.

I've thought about this for a long, long time. Even though I'm going to miss you and I love you, please understand that I love myself, too. I refuse to remain the smiling little waspy cheerleader in your life. I will not continue to be someone that I'm not. I guess I was never meant to be a head coach's wife.

If you should ever decide to make your living like a grown-up, let me know. You can do anything you want to, Buck. Otherwise, please don't try and contact me. At least not for a while.

Love,
Gail

P.S. There is plenty of Pabst in the refrigerator. I'll always love you. Please remember that.

Buck stared at the letter for a long time. He read it over and over. After the third time, its meaning began to sink in. He walked briskly to the bedroom and turned on the light in the cedar closet. Only *his* clothes remained. She had pushed them to the end of the rack; they hung in one small forlorn bunch in the corner of the closet. She had taken everything but her half-dozen tennis racquets. They remained on the floor against the wall.

Buck walked back into his office. He felt the anger welling up. He wanted to scream. He wanted to punch something, to smash something. He picked up the heavy, gleaming Coach of the Year trophy and threw it against the far wall. It smashed into a picture of Eaarnel, broke another trophy, and sent a couple of autographed footballs rolling across the carpet.

* * *

The doorbell rang at eight o'clock. Buck slammed down the phone after another unsuccessful attempt to reach Gail's sister in Big Sur. He hadn't showered or shaved since returning home, and he had forgotten all about the dinner with Dave Barton and the prospect he was bringing by.

"Nice fucking timing, Gail!" he said to no one as he headed for the door. "If we lose this kid, it'll be all your fault."

"Hi, Coach," said Barton as Buck opened the door. "I'd like you to meet Mat Seabeck."

"Hello, Mat. Y'all come on in." Buck shook hands with the towering Nordic prospect. Even in his despair, Buck couldn't help noticing that the kid had the great face. "Here, have a seat in the living room. I've got to talk with Coach Barton for just a second." Mat sat down uncomfortably as Buck dragged Dave back to his office.

"What the hell's going on, Coach?" Dave was puzzled by Buck's grubby appearance and strange behavior toward a quarterback who had broken every passing record in the state of Georgia. Mat Seabeck had an arm like a rifle and was big enough to play tight end.

"Read this," Buck said, handing Barton the note. He fidgeted while Dave read down the page mouthing the words and frowning.

"Have you talked to her?"

"No, but I know she's gone to California. I've been trying to reach her at her sister's house in California for the past hour."

"Just give her time, Buck. She'll feel different about it after awhile. The main thing is to keep moving. Give her some time and keep busy."

Buck nodded and took a deep breath. He liked Dave and had always felt closer to him than to any of the other coaches. Dave was the only person he would have shared this sort of problem with, and what he said always made sense. It was really what he wanted to hear, anyway. He did *not* want to hear what he really suspected: that he ultimately would have to make a choice between football and Gail. Football was the only thing he knew how to do. It was the only thing he ever *wanted* to do. It was the way he defined himself as a person. He'd always been a football player or a football coach. He hadn't always been married. Dave motioned for them to leave the office.

"Come on, let's snow this kid."

"What the hell are we gonna do with him?" Buck whispered. "There's nothing to eat."

"I don't know. Let's wing it."

They walked into the living room where Mat was crouched over a *Sports Illustrated*.

"Sorry, Mat," Dave said, "but Coach Lee had to show me a new offense he's been working on."

"Right," Buck said. "It's a pro set to utilize a gifted quarterback. Lots of deep routes and even has the flexibility to run the option out of it. But we need a big, strong quarterback with a great arm to do that."

"Yeah, and right now we don't have him," Dave said. Mat smiled and looked like he'd rather be somewhere else.

"By the way, Mat," Buck said. "I know we promised you a big home-cooked dinner, but my wife . . . well, she had to fly to California. Emergency. Her mother's sick. You know how that is."

"You'd probably rather have pizza, anyway, would't you?" Dave said.

"Sure, Coach. That'd be great." Mat rose and towered over them. "I hope she's OK."

"Who's OK?" Buck said.

"Your wife's mother," Barton said.

"Oh, yeah. She'll be OK. It was her knee. She tore some cartilage playing shuffleboard."

Buck pulled three cold ones out of the refrigerator and passed them around. It was usually at this point that Gail had the prospect laughing and feeling like he was Tom Selleck walking into a women's aerobics class. He glanced around the kitchen and wondered what he was going to do. The house felt empty. He felt empty. He took a big swallow from the Pabst. Barton was on the phone to a pizza joint. Buck had to figure out something to do with Seabeck.

"Do you play ping-pong, Mat?" he asked.

"Yes, sir. We have a table in our basement. I used to play my little brother all the time."

"How old's your brother? Dave didn't tell me you had a brother."

"He's almost sixteen. Gonna be bigger than me, probably. He's already up to 190 and can run like a danged deer."

"Is that so?" said Buck as he led Mat down to the game room.

Mat was smooth, confident, and had a nice touch with the paddle. He rolled up his sleeves, and Buck marveled at the size of his forearms. Probably has huge calves too, Buck thought.

After hitting for awhile, they decided to play a game. Buck jumped out to a 12-8 lead, but then Mat backed away from the table and began returning everything Buck sent his way. Soon both men were perspiring. Mat made a quick comeback, and halfway through their second beer, the kid led 19-18. Buck was intense, as though he had transferred his frustration about Gail to this game of ping-pong. He was diving and lunging for shots. Mat led 21-20 when the doorbell rang and Barton went to answer it. Buck was scowling and breathing loudly through his nose. By the time Richard Culpepper joined the party, Buck had tied the score at 21-all. Mat smashed a cross-table return that sent Buck diving across the indoor-outdoor carpet. He missed, and Mat led 22-21.

"Fuck you, Lee!" Buck screamed at himself. "You can do better than that!"

"What the hell is he doing?" Culpepper whispered to Barton.

"He's trying to *win*," Dave said.

Mat served a hard one to the forehand, and Buck slammed it back into the top of the green net. The ball hung for a moment before it fell to Mat's side, tying up the score again. Mat groaned and looked around the room. Buck's enthusiasm was infectious.

"Come on, Mat, you can get him," Dave said.

Buck hit a perfect serve that glanced off the tip of Mat's paddle. The ball fell silently to the floor, and Buck led by one. Buck's second serve was returned crisply to his forehand, but he swatted it back with a violent, upward motion. The topspin of the ball caused it to drop suddenly. It hit the edge of the table and careened out of Mat's reach for the winning point.

Everybody seemed relieved that Buck had pulled it out, although Mat was a little surprised by Buck's intensity. They all tried to make Mat feel like a winner by patting him on the back and telling him how good he was.

As Dave and Richard began to play, Buck pulled Mat over to the side. "I understand you want to study marine biology, Mat."

"That's right, Coach. I've always loved the ocean. My family went to The Keys last year, and I got a chance to do a lot of scuba diving. I loved it."

"You know, we have one of the best marine biology departments in the country at Eastern. In fact, I took the liberty of inviting Dr. Patterson, the head of the marine biology department, over for dinner. He should have been here by now. Hey, Coach Barton, what happened to Dr. Patterson?"

"Oh, he's coming. I just spoke with him. He's stopping by the restaurant to pick up the pizza for us."

As if on cue, the doorbell rang. In seconds Patrick Flanagan appeared holding two large pizza boxes and looking like he'd just had a beer with Lloyd Bridges. His hair was blond and wet, and his face was tanned. He wore jeans, a bright yellow T-shirt that said *Cayman Islands* across the front, and on his left wrist was a big black Cromsport diving watch.

Buck introduced Flanagan to Mat as Dr. Patterson, head of the marine biology department.

"Good to meet you, son. I've heard wonderful things about you. Hey, do you like oysters?" Flanagan said.

"Yeah, I love 'em," Mat answered.

"Great. I've got some fresh ones out in the cooler. Just brought 'em in today from the Bahamas. Be right back."

"You know, Mat," Buck said, "Dr. Patterson runs diving trips to The Keys a couple of times a year. He usually takes a few of his interested players and their girlfriends down right after spring practice. You might want to talk to him about that."

"Yeah, I'll mention it to him for sure." Mat was wide-eyed. "That sounds fantastic!"

They all tore into the hot pizza and raw oysters, and by the end of the evening, Flanagan was telling Mat fascinating war stories about diving on old German U-boats in the North Sea and finding treasure off the coast of Aruba. Of course, when Mat reported for two-a-day practices that summer, he would be told that Dr. Patterson had resigned and now worked aboard the *Calypso* with Jacques Cousteau.

Dave Barton, Richard Culpepper, Patrick Flanagan, and Mat Seabeck left around midnight after a beery evening of food, ping-pong, rock music, and talk of everything from football to Bo Derek's tits. Buck caught the tail end of ABC's "Nightline," where Ted Koppel was doing a special on the NCAA's new guidelines for "student-athlete" classroom eligibility, but he didn't have the spirit to pay close attention. The drizzle continued outside. The night light cast a pale blossom on the framed color portrait of Gail on the night table. Just before dawn, bolting awake from a nightmare about a scuba-diving Doberman pinscher, Buck reached across the bed and found nothing.